The Temple Within

The Temple Within provides a structured approach to Masonic education, emphasizing reflection, study, and dialogue.

By

Raymond E. Foster

Copyright

Dedication

To my grandchildren:

Jaden, Matthew, Kayleigh, Liam, and Sean—

May your lives be guided by light, your hearts anchored in truth, and your actions always measured with compassion and integrity.

This book is offered in the hope that, one day, its words may speak to the temple you each are building within yourselves.

Love,
Grandpa

Table of Contents

Introduction

The journey of Freemasonry is one of self-discovery, moral growth, and connection to timeless wisdom. This book, *The Temple Within*, seeks to illuminate the principles and practices of the Craft; exploring the rituals, symbols, and teachings that have guided Freemasons for centuries. Drawing from personal experiences, historical contexts, and philosophical reflections, this volume serves as both a guide and an invitation to delve deeper into the mysteries of Freemasonry.

My own journey to understand the rituals, symbols, customs, and etiquette of the lodge began with awe and curiosity. Like many Masons, I was drawn to the Craft by its promise of deeper knowledge and personal growth. However, I quickly realized that understanding Freemasonry required more than memorizing ritual or attending meetings; it demanded thoughtful reflection, diligent study, and perseverance.

Freemasonry, a centuries-old fraternity, offers a pathway to personal transformation. For those who enter its sacred spaces, it provides lessons on leadership, ethics, and the pursuit of knowledge - delivered through its unique blend of ritual and symbolism. However, the lessons of the Craft are not confined to the lodge room. They resonate in our daily lives, encouraging us to embody the values of Brotherly Love, Relief, and Truth

When I first attempted to introduce education into my lodge, my efforts met little success. My initial focus on the deeper meanings of Freemasonry - exploring ancient Greek philosophy and referencing obscure cultural traditions - was fascinating to me but not to my audience. The brethren nodded politely, but their lack of engagement was evident. Determined to improve, I reassessed my approach.

I noticed that nearly all the men in my lodge shared a limited foundational knowledge of the Bible, primarily from a Christian perspective. This common language became my starting point. Instead of abstract philosophical references, I began rooting my presentations in biblical stories and passages. For instance, when the ritual mentioned the Book of Ruth, I studied Ruth in depth, seeking the Masonic lesson hidden within the reference. I began breaking down words and phrases, exploring both their overt and hidden meanings. This redirection of efforts would also lead me through some of the debates among Masonic scholars on the influence of Christianity in our Craft, further deepening my understanding of its historical and cultural dimensions.

Over time, I built a library of Masonic scholars and gained a deeper understanding of the history of Freemasonry - including its gaps and ambiguities. Slowly but surely, the atmosphere in the lodge changed. At the end of meetings, when I delivered eight-to-ten-minute lessons, the brethren were listening attentively. Visiting brothers began asking me to present at their lodges. Encouraged, I continued researching, refining my presentations, and keeping meticulous notes in a large notebook filled with outlines and ideas.

A pivotal moment came when a nearby lodge invited me to lead a once-a-month, two-hour Masonic education program for a year. I adopted a graduate seminar-style format, beginning each session with a prepared lesson followed by a facilitated discussion exploring the implications of the material. These outlines eventually evolved into essays, and the essays became this book.

This book strives to strike a balance between maintaining the secrecy of our rituals and fostering honest intellectual discourse. Only tools, phrases, and symbols commonly divulged in other Masonic writings are used, ensuring that the integrity of the Craft's obligations is upheld. However, this approach may sometimes leave a non-Masonic reader or a Mason with limited knowledge feeling a little lost. For instance, references to the Book of Ruth or the Book of Judges stem from phrases in our ritual, which this book does not divulge. Moreover, there are times when Biblical passages, people, events and even tools seem out of place to the non-Mason. The lessons are still valuable, but a full disclosure is for those who have been initiated, past and raised. Simply, these explorations aim to illuminate the profound lessons of Freemasonry while respecting its sacred boundaries.

Throughout this journey, I often reflected on the insights of Manly P. Hall, one of Freemasonry's most profound interpreters. In works like "The Lost Keys of Freemasonry", Hall emphasized a symbolic, philosophical, and spiritual approach to the Craft. His teachings on self-improvement and spiritual growth resonated deeply with my own experiences. Hall viewed Freemasonry as a journey of inner transformation, symbolized by the transition from a "rough ashlar" to a "perfect ashlar." This metaphor of refinement captures the essence of the Masonic journey: a constant striving toward moral and spiritual excellence.

The Temple Within begins outside the lodge, acknowledging that a man's journey in Freemasonry often starts long before he is obligated, even if unknowingly. Exploring the journey before the degrees felt like a sensible starting point. Much of the information on the degrees is widely available or discussed in other Masonic literature. I have worked diligently to remain within the bounds of our obligations of secrecy, focusing on the universal principles that transcend regional rituals.

Freemasonry, a centuries-old fraternity, offers a pathway to personal transformation. For those who enter its sacred spaces, it provides lessons on leadership, ethics, and the pursuit of knowledge—all delivered through its unique blend of ritual and symbolism. However, the lessons of the Craft are not confined to the lodge room. They resonate in our daily lives, encouraging us to embody the values of Brotherly Love, Relief, and Truth.

This book is organized to reflect the three degrees of Freemasonry: Entered Apprentice, Fellow craft, and Master Mason. Each section begins with foundational lessons and builds toward deeper philosophical inquiries, culminating in essays that connect Masonic teachings to contemporary challenges. Throughout, the emphasis is on reflection and application, ensuring that the timeless wisdom of the Craft remains relevant in today's world.

The purpose of this book is to serve as a companion on your Masonic journey. Whether you are new to the Craft or a seasoned Mason, the essays and reflections within aim to deepen your understanding and inspire you to share the light of Freemasonry with others. By blending historical insights, philosophical musings, and practical applications, this book invites you to engage with the rich tapestry of Masonic tradition.

Above all, Freemasonry is a journey inward. The rituals and symbols are guides, pointing toward the middle chamber within ourselves. As you read this book, may you find inspiration to continue your personal transformation and to build a temple worthy of the Great Architect of the Universe.

Before the Gate: The Path to Masonic Initiation

The Secret within the Light: Understanding Masonic Secrecy and Its Foundations

Explore the enduring legacy of Masonic secrecy and its essential role in safeguarding principles, knowledge, and growth.

Freemasonry, a centuries-old fraternity, has long been shrouded in secrecy, a feature that has intrigued and sometimes confounded both members and outsiders. Yet, this secrecy is not merely a relic of tradition but a vital mechanism designed to protect, preserve, and impart knowledge in a way that ensures its integrity and ethical application. This essay delves into the historical and philosophical foundations of Masonic secrecy, exploring its roots in an era of persecution, the destruction of knowledge, and the inherent dangers of untrained minds misinterpreting esoteric truths.

Historical Context

Religious and Political Persecution

The founding of the Grand Lodge of England in 1717 came at the heels of an era rife with religious and political turmoil. Freemasonry emerged as a sanctuary for individuals seeking a neutral space for intellectual and spiritual discourse. However, this required the protection of its principles through secrecy, as open affiliation could be perilous. For example:

- **The English Civil Wars and the Execution of King Charles I (1649):** England's 17th century was marked by fierce conflicts between monarchy and parliament. Allegiances shifted rapidly, and the trial and execution of King Charles I illustrated the brutal consequences of political dissent. In this climate, open discussion of governance and reform within Freemasonry could have led to dire consequences;

- **The Glorious Revolution (1688)**: This event deposed the Catholic King James II in favor of Protestant rulers William and Mary. The suppression of Catholic rights that followed revealed the dangers of publicly aligning with unpopular ideologies. Freemasonry, welcoming members of various beliefs, had to guard its inclusive ethos;

- **The Salem Witch Trials (1692–1693):** Across the Atlantic, paranoia over differing religious practices reached a fever pitch, with dozens accused and executed for supposed witchcraft. Freemasonry's philosophical discussions, misunderstood or exposed, could have easily attracted similar suspicion; and,

- **The Edict of Fontainebleau (1685):** In France, Louis XIV's revocation of the Edict of Nantes led to widespread persecution of Protestants. This period demonstrated the precariousness of openly practicing or espousing beliefs that contradicted state-sanctioned doctrine.

Preservation of Knowledge

Another critical aspect of Masonic secrecy lies in its historical awareness of how easily knowledge can be erased through the destruction of books and libraries. Freemasonry's founders understood that passing knowledge directly from person to person could safeguard it against obliteration. For example:

- **The Library of Alexandria (circa 48 BCE):** Often romanticized as the ancient world's most comprehensive repository of knowledge, its destruction symbolizes the irretrievable loss of intellectual heritage;

- **The Qin Dynasty's Burning of Books (213 BCE):** In an effort to suppress dissent, Emperor Qin Shi Huang ordered the burning of Confucian texts and the execution of scholars. The systematic destruction of knowledge stifled intellectual progress for generations;

- **The Spanish Conquistadors' Destruction of Mayan Codices (16th Century):** In the name of religious conversion, conquistadors burned countless Mayan manuscripts, erasing invaluable records of a sophisticated civilization;

- **The Fourth Crusade and the Sack of Constantinople (1204):** This event saw the looting of Byzantine libraries, furthering the loss of ancient Greek and Roman manuscripts that chronicled centuries of human thought; and,

- **Nazi Germany's Book Burnings (1933):** In a chilling display of state-sponsored censorship, the Nazi regime orchestrated public book burnings across Germany to eradicate ideas deemed "un-German." Works by Jewish, socialist, and liberal authors, as well as scientific and philosophical texts, were targeted. These bonfires not only silenced dissenting voices but also symbolized a deliberate attempt to reshape culture and erase intellectual diversity. The destruction of books under the Third Reich serves as a stark reminder of how censorship and ideological control can decimate the free exchange of ideas.

Freemasonry's oral traditions ensured that its teachings remained intact despite the fragility of written records in turbulent times.

Safeguarding Knowledge

The Philosophy of Gradual Learning

Freemasonry emphasizes the responsible transmission of its knowledge. The degree system—an incremental process where initiates progress through ranks—ensures that members gain understanding and ethical grounding before accessing more profound teachings. This process mitigates the risk of misinterpretation or misuse.

Without the proper preparation, a person could misconstrue Masonic principles, potentially applying them in ways that harm themselves or others. This gradual approach aligns with the adage, "A little knowledge is a dangerous thing."

Ethical and Practical Considerations

The dangers of exposing esoteric knowledge to untrained minds extend beyond personal misinterpretation. For instance, symbolic tools like the Square and Compasses are meant to guide moral behavior and personal discipline. However, divorced from their ethical context, they might be wielded as instruments of manipulation or self-interest.

Contemporary Relevance

In today's age of transparency, the concept of secrecy might appear outdated or even suspect. Yet, Masonic secrecy underscores an important lesson: not all knowledge is best served by unfettered access. In an era when misinformation spreads rapidly, the deliberate and measured dissemination of information remains crucial. Moreover, the fraternity's ability to balance tradition with modernity continues to inspire reflection on how timeless principles can adapt to evolving societal norms.

The secrecy that defines Freemasonry is far from a barrier; it is a protective veil, safeguarding its principles, members, and the timeless truths it seeks to impart. It fosters a space for growth, understanding, and ethical application. As society grapples with questions of openness and confidentiality, Freemasonry offers a model of deliberate and meaningful guardianship of knowledge.

Reflections on the Craft: Questions for Deeper Understanding

- **Protecting Knowledge:**
  - How does the concept of secrecy, as employed by the Freemasons, encourage a greater respect for the preservation and ethical use of knowledge in today's world?
- **Understanding Context:**
  - How does awareness of historical persecution shape our understanding of Freemasonry's emphasis on protecting its teachings?
- **Knowledge Through Experience:**
  - What lessons can we draw from the degree system about the importance of experiential learning in personal and ethical development?

The Call to the Craft: Recognizing the Signs of Readiness for Freemasonry

Embarking on a Journey of Self-Discovery, Brotherhood, and Enlightenment

Freemasonry, one of the world's oldest and most enduring fraternal organizations, is rooted in principles of moral integrity, personal growth, and communal service. Its rituals and teachings are not merely symbolic; they guide individuals on a transformative journey of self-discovery and ethical living. But what prompts a man to knock on the West Gate? What signs indicate that he is ready to embark on this profound journey? This essay explores the qualities and internal readiness that signal a prospective Mason's readiness for the Craft.

The Inner Call: A Desire for Growth

Freemasonry appeals to individuals seeking to improve themselves and contribute positively to their communities. Readiness for Freemasonry often begins with an internal yearning—a desire to align one's life with higher principles. Prospective Masons are drawn to the Craft's teachings on morality, self-discipline, and the pursuit of truth. This inner call is not superficial; it stems from deep introspection and a genuine desire to live a life of purpose and virtue.

Alignment with Masonic Values

Freemasonry espouses virtues such as Brotherly Love, Relief, and Truth, which align with timeless principles of ethical living. A man ready to join the Craft often exhibits:

- Brotherly Love: The capacity to respect and support others, regardless of differences.

- Relief: A willingness to aid those in need, embodying charity and compassion.
- Truth: A commitment to honesty and the pursuit of wisdom.

These virtues are not mere ideals. They are practices that prospective Masons often demonstrate in their personal and professional lives before entering the Lodge.

Openness to Ritual and Symbolism

Freemasonry communicates its teachings through allegory, ritual, and symbolism. Prospective members must be open to learning through these methods, recognizing that symbols like the Square and Compass, the Ashlar, and the Trestleboard represent profound life lessons. Readiness for Freemasonry includes an appreciation for the symbolic language of the Craft and a willingness to uncover deeper meanings through study and reflection.

A Commitment to Brotherhood

Freemasonry thrives on a strong sense of fraternity. Prospective Masons must be prepared to engage with others in a spirit of equality, humility, and mutual respect. Readiness is marked by a man's ability to contribute to the collective growth of the Lodge while receiving the support and wisdom of his brothers.

Seeking Light: The Path of Inquiry

The phrase "seeking light" symbolizes a Mason's quest for knowledge, wisdom, and self-improvement. A prospective Mason's readiness is evident when he:

- Asks meaningful questions about life, morality, and existence;
- Seeks knowledge beyond material pursuits; and,
- Demonstrates a willingness to learn from others and to teach in return.

Practical Readiness

Readiness for Freemasonry also involves practical considerations. A prospective Mason must:

- Be of lawful age and good repute;
- Demonstrate a stable life situation, allowing him to devote time and effort to Masonic duties; and,
- Express an understanding of the commitment involved in joining the Fraternity.

The Journey Begins

The decision to join Freemasonry is not taken lightly. It requires a harmonious blend of moral integrity, intellectual curiosity, and practical preparedness. Those who feel the inner call to the Craft must reflect deeply on their readiness, ensuring they are prepared to embrace the transformative journey ahead.

Freemasonry does not seek perfect men; it seeks men willing to perfect themselves. The signs of readiness for Freemasonry are not external accolades or achievements but internal alignments with the values, teachings, and aspirations of the Craft. By recognizing these signs, prospective Masons can approach the West Gate with confidence, knowing they are prepared to embark on a lifelong journey of enlightenment, brotherhood, and service.

Reflections on the Craft: Questions for Deeper Understanding

- **The Inner Call to Growth**:
    - What experiences or reflections have led you to consider Freemasonry, and how do they align with your aspirations for personal and moral development?
- **Symbolism and Understanding:**
    - How can Freemasonry's use of symbols and allegories enhance your understanding of life's deeper meanings and guide your actions?
- **Brotherhood and Contribution:**
    - In what ways are you prepared to contribute to the Masonic community, and how do you envision the Fraternity aiding your personal growth?

Identifying Masonic Potential: The Power of Freedom, Fervency, and Zeal

Seeking those who live by the virtues of freedom, fervency, and zeal, and recognizing them as the true candidates for the Brotherhood

In Freemasonry, the virtues of freedom, fervency, and zeal are fundamental principles that define both the Craft and the ideal qualities of its members. These principles are the hallmarks of moral readiness and dedication to the values that Freemasonry holds dear. Freemasonry is more than a social organization; it is a journey of moral and spiritual growth, and these three qualities serve as markers for those seeking to join the Fraternity. They are not merely ideals they are characteristics that can be observed in those whose actions reflect the essence of what it means to be a Mason.

Freedom: The Desire to Choose a Path of Virtue

At the heart of Freemasonry lies the concept of freedom— the freedom to choose a virtuous path despite external pressures. This internal freedom allows the individual to align their life with moral values, rather than pursuing self-interest or personal gain. For Masons, true freedom is the ability to think independently and make ethical decisions that align with their principles.

Benjamin Franklin, one of the Founding Fathers of the United States and a prominent Freemason, often wrote about the role of freedom in personal development. In his Autobiography, Franklin emphasized the importance of moral freedom: "The great object of my life has been to develop my own mind and to improve the society I am a part of." (Franklin, 1791). His words reflect the Masonic ideal that the pursuit of knowledge and moral integrity is an essential aspect of true freedom, where one can shape their destiny through virtuous choices.

Fervency: The Glow of Masonic Virtues

Fervency, derived from the Latin fervere, meaning "to boil" or "to glow," represents the intensity and passion with which Masons should live their virtues. A fervent Mason is one who embodies the Masonic ideals of temperance, fortitude, and justice in their daily actions. Fervency is not just a belief in these virtues but a passionate commitment to living them out in all aspects of life.

Johann Wolfgang von Goethe, a well-known philosopher, poet, and Freemason, believed fervency to be a core principle in achieving greatness. He once stated, "The best way to predict the future is to create it." (Goethe, 1825). Although not directly speaking of Freemasonry, Goethe's sentiment echoes the fervency of action required of a Mason—creating the future by actively living out one's principles. This proactive approach, driven by fervency, helps a Mason contribute to the betterment of society, reflecting the Masonic values of brotherhood and service.

Zeal: The Drive to Improve and Serve

Zeal is the energetic commitment to the pursuit of knowledge, self-improvement, and the betterment of society. It is the passion to continually strive for excellence, both in personal conduct and in service to others. Zeal is what drives Masons to contribute to their communities, improve themselves, and pursue knowledge that can be applied for the good of all.

As American Revolutionary leader and Freemason John Hancock expressed, "In the pursuit of freedom and justice, zeal is the engine that powers our success." (Hancock, 1776). His words serve as a reminder that zeal is not merely enthusiasm but a focused and purposeful energy directed towards noble goals. Just as Hancock played a key role in the American Revolution, Masons are encouraged to use their zeal to act for the benefit of society and to live out the ideals of Freemasonry in their everyday lives.

The Role of Freedom, Fervency, and Zeal in Potential Masons

These three qualities—freedom, fervency, and zeal—serve as guiding principles when considering potential Masons. They are the virtues that set apart individuals who are ready to embrace the journey of self-improvement, brotherhood, and service. As we search for new members, we look for those who demonstrate these traits in their daily lives—those who choose a life of virtue, who glow with moral passion, and who are zealous in their pursuit of knowledge and service to others.

Potential Masons who embody these qualities, whether they are already members or not, reflect the essence of what it means to be a Mason: a man who lives by principles of virtue, who serves others, and who strives for self-improvement. These qualities make them ideal candidates for the Masonic journey of personal growth, moral enlightenment, and service to humanity.

Reflections on the Craft: Questions for Deeper Understanding

- **Freedom and Ethical Choices**
  - o Benjamin Franklin described moral freedom as the ability to align one's life with virtuous principles. How do you practice this form of freedom in your daily life, and how does it align with your Masonic journey?
- **Living with Fervency**
  - o Johann Wolfgang von Goethe highlighted the importance of fervency in creating the future. How do you demonstrate fervency in living out Masonic virtues, and how does this passion inspire those around you?
- **Zeal and Service to Others**
  - o John Hancock described zeal as the engine driving the pursuit of justice and freedom. How does your zeal guide you toward self-improvement and service to your community, and how can it be further cultivated within the Lodge?

The Role of the Recommender: Guiding a Candidate to the Threshold

Serving as the guardian of the West Gate, the recommender ensures the integrity and future of the Craft

In the world of Freemasonry, few roles carry as much significance as that of the recommender. Tasked with the responsibility of introducing new candidates to the Craft, the recommender's role is far more than procedural; it is an act of mentorship, guidance, and moral evaluation. The journey to the threshold of initiation is not one to be taken lightly, and it is the recommender who ensures that the candidate is both ready and worthy to take the first step.

The Recommender's Responsibilities

At its core, the recommender's duty is to identify individuals who embody the virtues that Freemasonry upholds: integrity, moral uprightness, a genuine pursuit of knowledge, and a commitment to the betterment of self and society. The recommender serves as a gatekeeper, ensuring that only those who can honor and uphold the principles of the Craft are allowed to proceed. This responsibility requires discernment, patience, and a deep understanding of Masonic values.

Identifying Potential Candidates

The journey begins with observation. The recommender must identify individuals who demonstrate qualities such as honesty, kindness, and a willingness to grow. A candidate's actions in daily life are often the best indicators of their suitability. The recommender looks for men who exhibit a natural curiosity about moral and philosophical matters, who respect tradition and community, and who have a reputation for fairness and integrity.

Providing Guidance

Once a potential candidate is identified, the recommender's role transitions to mentorship. This involves explaining the purpose and expectations of Freemasonry, addressing any misconceptions, and preparing the candidate for the commitment they are about to undertake. The recommender helps the candidate understand the seriousness of the journey, emphasizing that Freemasonry is not merely a social organization but a lifelong path of personal and moral development.

Conducting Moral Evaluation

The recommender must also assess the candidate's moral readiness. This includes an honest evaluation of their character, motivations, and ability to contribute positively to the fraternity. The recommender's role is not to judge but to ensure that the candidate's values align with those of the Craft. Questions such as "Does this individual seek to improve themselves?" and "Will they uphold the integrity of the Lodge?" guide this evaluation.

The Significance of the West Gate

The West Gate serves as a symbolic checkpoint in Freemasonry, representing the threshold a candidate must cross to enter the Craft. The recommender plays a pivotal role in this process, acting as both a guide and a guardian. By vouching for a candidate, the recommender affirms their readiness and suitability, ensuring that the sanctity of the Lodge is preserved.

The implications of guarding the West Gate extend beyond procedural duties. The recommender's actions safeguard the integrity of the Lodge and its members. This role demands an unwavering commitment to the principles of truth and justice, as the recommender's choices shape not only the immediate composition of the Lodge but also its long-term legacy. As a sentinel of the Craft, the recommender ensures that the values of Freemasonry remain untainted, fostering an environment of mutual respect and moral growth.

The act of recommending someone is also a personal commitment. The recommender's reputation within the Lodge is tied to the candidate they present. This underscores the importance of diligence and sincerity in the recommendation process. The West Gate is not merely a passage but a moment of transformation, and the recommender's role is to prepare the candidate for this profound experience.

Mentorship beyond the Threshold

The recommender's responsibilities do not end once the candidate is initiated. On the contrary, the recommender becomes a mentor, guiding the new Mason through the early stages of their journey. This includes helping them navigate the rituals, understand the symbols, and integrate into the Lodge's community. The recommender serves as a source of support, ensuring that the new Mason feels welcomed and empowered to contribute meaningfully to the Craft.

Reflections on the Recommender's Role

The role of the recommender is both a privilege and a responsibility. It is an opportunity to shape the future of the fraternity by selecting and mentoring individuals who will carry its principles forward. The recommender's work is a testament to the values of Freemasonry: dedication, integrity, and the pursuit of enlightenment.

By fulfilling this role with care and commitment, the recommender not only upholds the traditions of the Craft but also enriches their own journey. Guiding a candidate to the threshold is an act of brotherly love and service, reflecting the true spirit of Freemasonry.

Reflections on the Craft: Questions for Deeper Understanding

- **Guarding the West Gate:**
    - How do you balance the responsibilities of ensuring the integrity of the Craft with the openness necessary for its growth and inclusivity?
- **Mentorship and Moral Evaluation:**
    - In what ways can the recommender's guidance shape a candidate's journey beyond their initiation?
- **Legacy and Accountability:**
    - How does the recommender's role influence the long-term values and direction of the Lodge?

The West Gate: Entering the Craft with a Sense of Humor and Self-Reflection

Reflect, laugh, and seek truth: Embracing the Masonic journey with Mark Twain's wit and wisdom

Mark Twain, the iconic humorist and author, was not just a sharp wit and observer of human nature; he was also a Freemason. Initiated as an Entered Apprentice at Polar Star Lodge in
St. Louis on February 18th, 1861, Twain had a personal connection to Freemasonry that would have shaped his thoughts on the Masonic journey. Known for his humor, his insightful critiques of society, and his deep reflections on morality, Twain's perspective on Freemasonry might have been both profound and entertaining. Imagine, then, if he were speaking to a prospective Mason standing at the West Gate, poised to begin his journey into the Craft.

Note: The conversation and quotes presented in this essay are fictional and creatively imagined based on the character and wit of Mark Twain, as well as the themes explored in his writings. While Twain was indeed a Freemason and his humor and reflections on life undoubtedly align with many of the values emphasized in Freemasonry, the dialogue here is a work of imagination designed to bring his unique perspective to the Masonic journey.

The West Gate: A Threshold of Reflection

Before entering the lodge, a candidate stands at the symbolic threshold—the West Gate. This is a moment of decision, where the individual reflects on the step he is about to take into Freemasonry, a journey that promises moral growth, brotherhood, and self-discovery. Twain, as a Mason, would have been keenly aware of the significance of this moment.

With his characteristic wit, he might say to the candidate, "Well, my friend, you're standing at the West Gate, and you're about to walk into a world where the real work begins. This isn't just about wearing aprons and attending meetings—it's about looking into the mirror and asking, 'How can I be a better man?' And believe me, the answers are not always easy."

Twain's humor would help the candidate realize that Freemasonry is not merely about external rituals but internal transformation. The candidate is not only committing to be part of an organization but to embark on a lifelong journey of self-improvement and moral reflection. Twain would have reminded the candidate that, as in life, the Masonic journey is filled with both joy and challenges. "You're about to learn more about yourself than you ever thought possible," Twain might say, "and not just by listening to speeches, but by taking a good, hard look at your own character and choices."

The Importance of Self-Examination

Freemasonry places a strong emphasis on self-examination, an aspect that Twain often championed in his writings. He understood the value of looking inward and questioning one's own beliefs, attitudes, and actions. To the prospective Mason, Twain might have said, "You'll soon learn that Freemasonry expects you to be your own harshest critic. It's easy to blame the world for its problems, but it takes a real man to ask, 'What part of the problem am I?' You're about to enter a society that asks you to leave behind pride and face the truth of who you really are."

Twain would likely have warned the candidate that the Masonic journey was not one for those seeking an easy path or instant results. "Just like life," he would say with a grin, "this journey is about facing uncomfortable truths, learning from mistakes, and striving to do better. No one ever said the road to self-improvement was smooth—but it sure is worth it in the end." His point would be clear: Freemasonry offers no shortcuts to becoming a better man; instead, it offers tools, teachings, and support for a long and challenging journey of growth.

The Role of Humor in Freemasonry

Although Freemasonry is often seen as a serious and solemn institution, Twain would likely remind the candidate of the importance of humor in navigating life's challenges. "In Freemasonry," Twain might say, "we learn to take life seriously, but not too seriously. You'll find that you can be a good Mason, a moral man, and still find plenty of reasons to laugh—especially at yourself. In fact, if you can't laugh at yourself, you might be in the wrong place!"

Humor, for Twain, was an essential part of dealing with life's absurdities. Freemasonry, while teaching profound lessons of morality and self-discipline, also encourages a sense of camaraderie and joy among its members. Twain's wit would serve as a reminder that, while the Masonic journey is serious, it should also be filled with laughter, friendship, and a shared sense of lightheartedness. Through humor, members are reminded not to take themselves too seriously but to enjoy the fellowship and wisdom of their brothers.

The Pursuit of Truth

Above all, Twain valued truth, not only as a moral principle but as a guide to navigating the complexities of life. As a Mason, Twain would likely have reminded the prospective candidate, "You're here to seek truth, my friend—truth about the world, truth about your fellow man, and most importantly, truth about yourself. But remember, truth is a tricky thing. It's often hidden in plain sight, and you'll spend a lot of time digging for it."

For Twain, truth was never a simple, straightforward concept. It was something that required constant seeking, questioning, and challenging. He would likely have encouraged the candidate to approach the Masonic journey with the same curiosity and skepticism that he brought to his own life. "Don't expect Freemasonry to give you all the answers," Twain might say. "Instead, it's here to teach you how to find your own answers—and to keep searching, even when the answers don't come easily."

The Masonic Journey Begins

As the candidate stands before the West Gate, ready to step into the Lodge, Twain's final advice would encapsulate the essence of the Masonic journey: "Remember, this is just the beginning. You're about to embark on a lifelong adventure. You'll face challenges, you'll learn a lot about yourself, and, with any luck, you'll become a better man for it. But above all, you'll do it with brothers who will support you, laugh with you, and help you when you stumble."

Mark Twain's perspective on Freemasonry, rooted in his experience as a member of Polar Star Lodge, would offer the candidate both a realistic view of the journey ahead and a reminder to approach it with an open mind and a sense of humor. Freemasonry, Twain would suggest, is a lifelong school of moral development, a place where one can grow, reflect, and serve with joy—and always, always, with a healthy dose of self-deprecating humor.

Reflections on the Craft: Questions for Deeper Understanding

- **The Role of Self-Examination**
  - o Mark Twain suggested that true growth comes from asking, "What part of the problem am I?" How often do you critically examine your own actions and beliefs, and how can Freemasonry help you deepen this practice of self-reflection?
- **Humor and the Masonic Journey**
  - o Twain emphasized the importance of humor in navigating life's challenges. How can maintaining a sense of humor and lightheartedness enhance your journey as a Mason, even when faced with serious challenges?
- **Truth and the Masonic Path**
  - o Twain observed that truth is often hidden in plain sight and requires effort to uncover. How do you approach the pursuit of truth in your Masonic journey, and how has it influenced your understanding of yourself and the world?

The First and Last: The Initiation Declarations and the Charge

Exploring the Foundations of Freemasonry: Commitment, Integrity, and the Lifelong Journey of Self-Improvement

In Freemasonry, the journey of a candidate is framed by two significant moments that shape their path: the Initiation Declarations and the Charge. These two stages play a vital role in guiding the candidate from entry into the Fraternity to the responsibilities they take on as a full-fledged Mason. While the Initiation Declarations ensure that the candidate is genuinely prepared to join, the Charge delivered after initiation serves as a reminder of the long-term duties and the moral principles that will guide the candidate in their new life as a Mason.

The Initiation Declarations: A Commitment to Begin the Journey

The Initiation Declarations are a key part of the candidate's journey before initiation, acting as a safeguard to ensure that they are truly ready and committed to the Masonic journey. The candidate must affirm that their decision to join Freemasonry is not influenced by external pressures but rather by a genuine desire for knowledge and a wish to serve others. The Declarations also emphasize the candidate's readiness to adhere to the ancient customs and practices of the Fraternity, marking the beginning of their commitment to the values of Freemasonry (Duncan, 1866).

These declarations confirm that the candidate is prepared to enter the Craft with a pure heart, free from mercenary motives, and with a sincere wish to learn and grow in the Masonic teachings. This stage highlights the importance of self-awareness and authenticity, ensuring that the candidate is genuinely prepared to embark on a journey of moral and spiritual development (Surrey Freemasons, n.d.).

The Charge: A Guide for the Masonic Journey

Once initiated, the candidate is presented with the Charge, a powerful message outlining the duties and responsibilities they are now expected to uphold. The Charge serves as a reminder of the Fraternity's ancient and honorable nature, describing Freemasonry as an institution dedicated to promoting moral and intellectual excellence. It emphasizes the importance of the Volume of the Sacred Law as the ultimate source of truth and justice, guiding the Mason's actions in accordance with divine precepts (The Square Magazine, 2021).

The Charge instructs the new Mason in their duties to God, their neighbor, and themselves, encouraging a life marked by reverence, justice, and self-discipline. It also stresses the importance of civic responsibility, urging Masons to be exemplary citizens who contribute to the peace and order of society. Furthermore, the Charge highlights Masonic virtues such as temperance, fortitude, prudence, and justice, encouraging the new member to live by the principles of Brotherly Love, Relief, and Truth (Durham Freemasons, n.d.).

The Balance Between the Declarations and the Charge

Although both the Initiation Declarations and the Charge emphasize honor and integrity, they serve different purposes. The Declarations focus on ensuring that the candidate's motivations for joining are sincere and that they are truly ready to begin their journey as a Mason. In contrast, the Charge shifts the focus to the long-term responsibilities that come with being a Mason. It calls on the new member to live up to the moral ideals of Freemasonry, to continuously seek knowledge, and to contribute to the betterment of society and the Fraternity (The Square Magazine, 2022).

Together, these two moments form the foundation of the Masonic journey. The Declarations ensure that the candidate is entering with the right intentions, while the Charge provides the moral and ethical framework to guide their actions as they progress through the Craft.

A Lifelong Journey of Self-Improvement

The Initiation Declarations and the Charge serve as bookends to the Masonic journey, with the Declarations marking the beginning and the Charge pointing to the lifelong responsibilities that lie ahead. Freemasonry is not merely a set of rituals or traditions; it is a living philosophy that challenges its members to reflect on their values, improve their character, and contribute to the greater good.

The Masonic journey is one of constant learning, self-reflection, and growth. The Declarations and the Charge together emphasize that the path of Freemasonry is not about reaching a destination but about embracing the ongoing process of becoming a better man. Through these two foundational moments, Masons are reminded of their commitment to live with integrity, serve others, and continually strive for moral and spiritual excellence.

The Initiation Declarations and the Charge are integral to the Masonic experience. They establish the framework for a life dedicated to self-improvement, moral integrity, and service to others. By beginning their journey with sincere intent and embracing the lifelong responsibilities outlined in the Charge, Masons uphold the values that define the Fraternity. These moments serve not only as milestones but as enduring reminders of the purpose and principles of Freemasonry, guiding members on their path toward personal growth and meaningful contribution to society.

Reflections on the Craft: Questions for Deeper Understanding

- **Authenticity in Commitment**
    - The Initiation Declarations emphasize entering Freemasonry with a pure heart and sincere intentions. How do you ensure that your motivations for joining or continuing your Masonic journey remain aligned with the principles of integrity and self-improvement?
- **Living the Charge**
    - The Charge highlights a Mason's duties to God, their neighbor, and themselves. In what ways do you strive to balance these responsibilities in your daily life, and how do the Masonic virtues of Brotherly Love, Relief, and Truth guide your actions?
- **The Path of Lifelong Learning**
    - The essay describes Freemasonry as a living philosophy that encourages constant growth and reflection. How have the teachings of the Declarations and the Charge shaped your understanding of personal growth, and how do you apply these lessons to your journey?

Guided by the Saints: The Balance of Zeal and Knowledge in Freemasonry

Embrace the balance of zeal and wisdom, as the Two Saints John guide your Masonic journey toward moral and spiritual enlightenment.

As a candidate prepares to enter the world of Freemasonry, reflecting on the symbolism of the Two Saints John—John the Baptist and John the Evangelist—is integral to understanding the principles of the Craft. These figures embody the dual qualities of zeal and wisdom, providing a framework for the balanced development of moral and spiritual character.

The Dual Symbolism of the Two Saints John

John the Baptist, recognized for his fervent zeal and commitment to righteousness, represents action and dedication. His association with the summer solstice, a time of light and growth, reflects the importance of external engagement and proactive efforts to live a virtuous life. As Stevenson (2012) explains, Freemasonry incorporates such figures to teach "the necessity of balancing active moral discipline with reflective spiritual insight" (p. 158).

In contrast, John the Evangelist symbolizes introspective wisdom and understanding. Associated with the winter solstice, a period of reflection and renewal, he represents the inner work necessary for personal and spiritual enlightenment. The balance between these qualities—zeal and wisdom—is at the heart of Masonic teachings, urging members to harmonize external action with internal reflection (Hamill, 2010).

Masonic Teachings on Balance

Freemasonry emphasizes the importance of balance in personal and communal life, a lesson exemplified by the Two Saints John. The juxtaposition of their feast days—June 24th and December 27th—reminds Masons of the cyclical nature of growth and reflection. This concept aligns with Pythagorean principles, which heavily influenced Masonic thought, suggesting that harmony and equilibrium are foundational to moral and spiritual development (Stevenson, 2012).

The Square and Compasses, a central symbol in Freemasonry, further emphasize the need for balance. As Mackey (1921) notes, the Compasses teach members to "circumscribe their desires and keep them within due bounds," while the Square represents uprightness and justice in dealings with others (p. 234). Together, these symbols encapsulate the balance between personal discipline and ethical engagement with the world.

The Role of Solstices in Masonic Symbolism

The summer and winter solstices, associated with the Two Saints John, carry profound meaning in Masonic rituals. These celestial events symbolize the ebb and flow of enlightenment and introspection, mirroring the journey of a Mason. As Pike (1871) observed, "The solstices remind us of the cyclical nature of existence, urging us to seek light in times of darkness and to reflect during times of abundance" (p. 321).

By aligning the feast days of the Saints John with these astronomical events, Freemasonry underscores the interconnectedness of the natural world and moral development. This connection encourages Masons to recognize the rhythm of their own growth, embracing both active pursuit and contemplative understanding.

Personal Reflection Through Masonic Symbolism

Incorporating the lessons of the Two Saints John into daily life encourages Masons to pursue a holistic approach to personal development. Balancing the zeal of John the Baptist with the wisdom of John the Evangelist allows members to align their actions with the ethical and spiritual principles of Freemasonry. This journey is not linear but cyclical, requiring continual reflection, adjustment, and growth.

As Mackey (1921) emphasizes, "Freemasonry does not offer a path of ease but one of challenge, where the virtues of zeal and wisdom must be cultivated equally to achieve the balance necessary for enlightenment" (p. 245).

Conclusion

The Two Saints John—John the Baptist and John the Evangelist—serve as guiding figures in Freemasonry, representing the balance of zeal and wisdom that is essential for moral and spiritual growth. By embodying their virtues, Masons harmonize action with reflection, pursuing both moral integrity and enlightenment. This balance forms the foundation of the Masonic journey, inspiring members to strive for continual growth and meaningful service to others.

Reflections on the Craft: Questions for Deeper Understanding

- **Balancing Zeal and Wisdom**:
    - o How can you integrate the qualities of zeal and wisdom, as exemplified by the Two

Saints John, into your personal and Masonic endeavors?

- **Cycles of Growth and Reflection:**
  - o The solstices symbolize times of light and reflection. How do you embrace these cycles in your own life to maintain a balance between action and introspection?
- **Symbolism in Daily Life:**
  - o How do Masonic symbols like the Square and Compasses help you navigate the balance between personal discipline and ethical engagement with others?

Guarding the West Gate: Fidelity to Principles and Masonic Integrity

Exploring the timeless responsibility of guarding Freemasonry's West Gate to uphold integrity and preserve the Craft's noble traditions.

The duty of guarding the West Gate is a fundamental responsibility within Freemasonry, emphasizing integrity, morality, and adherence to principles. The concept of the West Gate symbolizes the entry point into the Craft, representing not only a physical threshold but also a metaphorical space where potential members are assessed for their suitability and alignment with Masonic values. This symbolic duty ensures that the integrity of Craft is preserved by allowing only those who embody its core tenets to enter (Stevenson, 1988; Hamill & Gilbert, 2010).

Fidelity to Principles in Freemasonry

Fidelity, derived from the Latin "fidelitas", signifying faithfulness or devotion, is central to Masonic teachings. It is a cornerstone of the Craft, demanding that members adhere to the organization's Constitutions and preserve the Ancient Landmarks. The Masonic commitment to fidelity extends beyond private practice, requiring members to live these principles in all facets of life, thereby reflecting the high ethical standards expected within the Fraternity (Ridley, 2011). This adherence ensures the honor and dignity of Freemasonry, which has been preserved through centuries of tradition and ethical expectations (Hamill, 2007).

The process of guarding the West Gate can be seen as an extension of this fidelity, emphasizing the evaluation of candidates not just for their intent but for their alignment with the Craft's moral and ethical ideals. Prospective members must demonstrate a commitment to integrity, truth, and moral excellence—qualities integral to Masonic tradition and philosophy (Stevenson, 1988). The West Gate serves as a symbolic checkpoint to maintain the purity of the Fraternity, ensuring that only those who embody these virtues are initiated into its ranks.

Leadership and Masonic Ideals

Leadership within Freemasonry is deeply connected to its foundational values of integrity, character, and accountability. Historical figures associated with Freemasonry, such as
Theodore Roosevelt, exemplified these ideals through their commitment to ethical leadership and the upholding of principles even in challenging circumstances (Levine, 1995). Roosevelt's emphasis on accountability and moral courage aligns closely with the responsibilities entrusted to Masons, especially those guarding the West Gate (Morris, 2010).

Similarly, Franklin D. Roosevelt's belief in the importance of character and resolve resonates with the Masonic duty to safeguard the integrity of the Lodge. His speeches, while addressing broader societal challenges, reflect themes of perseverance and ethical fortitude that are integral to Masonic philosophy (Rosenman, 1941). These examples illustrate how leadership, both within and outside the Lodge, is enhanced by the application of Masonic principles.

Ensuring the Integrity of the Craft

The task of guarding the West Gate requires unwavering commitment to Freemasonry's principles. This responsibility falls on every Mason, particularly those in leadership roles, to scrutinize the character of candidates seeking admission. The Masonic tradition, built on a foundation of moral and ethical standards, endures through the diligent efforts of its members to uphold these values (Hamill, 2007).

By maintaining fidelity to principles, exercising sound judgment, and fostering a commitment to justice and service, Freemasons ensure that the Craft remains a beacon of moral integrity. This responsibility not only safeguards the Fraternity's traditions but also contributes to the moral development of its members and their communities. The sacred duty of guarding the West Gate symbolizes this ongoing commitment, reflecting the timeless and honorable foundations of Freemasonry (Stevenson, 1988; Ridley, 2011).

The Consequences of Failing to Guard the West Gate

Failure to guard the West Gate can have profound and far-reaching consequences for the Craft. If unworthy candidates who lack the commitment to Masonic principles are admitted, the integrity and reputation of the Fraternity may be compromised. These individuals may undermine the moral and ethical standards that are central to Freemasonry, leading to discord and a weakening of the bonds of brotherhood within Lodges. Over time, this erosion of values could result in a loss of trust and respect for the organization, both internally among members and externally within society.

Unvetted candidates may also introduce personal agendas that conflict with the collective mission of Freemasonry, shifting the focus from the shared pursuit of enlightenment and service to individual interests. This could dilute the strength of Masonic teachings, causing a drift away from the principles that have sustained the Craft for centuries.

Furthermore, allowing those who are not aligned with Masonic values to join could create rifts within Lodges, leading to division and disunity.

The consequences extend beyond internal dynamics. Freemasonry's reputation as a moral and ethical organization could be tarnished, diminishing its ability to attract and inspire individuals of high character. This could hinder the Craft's ability to fulfill its purpose of fostering personal and societal betterment. Therefore, the duty of guarding the West Gate is not only about protecting the present integrity of the Fraternity but also ensuring its legacy and future relevance. Vigilance, discernment, and a steadfast commitment to Masonic principles are essential to preserving the sanctity and honor of the Craft.

Reflections on the Craft: Questions for Deeper Understanding

- **Fidelity in Action:**
  - o How can you embody fidelity to Masonic principles in both the evaluation of prospective candidates and your own actions, ensuring the Craft's integrity is upheld in all areas of life?
- **Guarding the West Gate:**
  - o In fulfilling the symbolic duty of guarding the West Gate, how do you balance the responsibility of upholding the Craft's ethical standards with the inclusivity and openness necessary for Masonic growth?
- **Leadership and Legacy:**
  - o How can the examples of historical figures like Theodore and Franklin Roosevelt inspire your approach to leadership within the Lodge and your broader community?

Operative vs. Speculative Masonry:

A Journey from Craftsmanship to Philosophy

Discover the transformative journey of Masonry from stonecutting guilds to a brotherhood of moral and philosophical enlightenment.

The evolution of Freemasonry from operative to speculative forms is a tale of transformation, symbolizing humanity's shift from physical craftsmanship to intellectual and spiritual growth. This journey encapsulates how an ancient trade guild of stoneworkers gradually became an influential global fraternity that emphasizes moral teachings and self-improvement.

The Roots of Operative Masonry

Operative Masonry originates from the medieval guilds of stonemasons who constructed Europe's great cathedrals, castles, and other architectural wonders. These guilds were structured organizations that protected the interests of their members, ensured high craftsmanship standards, and provided a social network for workers. They met in lodges adjacent to construction sites, where masons honed their craft and shared tools and techniques.

Historian John Hamill notes, "Operative Masonry was defined by its emphasis on practical skills and the tangible results seen in architectural achievements" (Hamill, 1994). The tools of their trade—the square, compasses, and plumb line—were essential for precision and became enduring symbols of the Masonic tradition.

Transition to Speculative Masonry

The late medieval and early modern periods witnessed the decline of cathedral building and a corresponding reduction in the demand for skilled stonemasons. This economic and societal shift led to a transformation within Masonic lodges. Non-operative members, or "gentlemen Masons," began joining lodges, bringing with them interests in philosophy, science, and morality.

The formation of the Grand Lodge of England in 1717 marked a significant milestone in this evolution. "By incorporating speculative elements, Freemasonry expanded its scope beyond the operative craft to address broader philosophical and ethical questions," writes Andrew Prescott (Prescott, 2004).

Speculative Masonry: Philosophy and Practices

Speculative Masonry reframes the tools and techniques of the operative masons as symbols for moral and spiritual development. For example, the square symbolizes fairness and virtue, while the compasses represent self-restraint and the ability to circumscribe one's desires. These symbols are integrated into rituals designed to teach moral lessons and encourage introspection.

Enlightenment thought heavily influenced speculative Masonry, aligning it with ideals of reason, progress, and universal fraternity. "Freemasonry's speculative dimension reflects the Enlightenment's emphasis on individual improvement and collective harmony," asserts Margaret C. Jacob (Jacob, 2007).

Comparative Analysis: Operative and Speculative Masonry

Purpose and Focus

Operative Masonry focused on practical craftsmanship and the physical construction of edifices. In contrast, speculative Masonry shifted its focus to intellectual and moral pursuits, emphasizing the building of character rather than structures.

Membership

Operative lodges were exclusive to skilled stonemasons, while speculative Masonry opened its doors to individuals from diverse professions, fostering inclusivity and intellectual exchange.

Rituals and Symbolism

Operative rituals addressed the practicalities of the craft, such as project management and skill certification. Speculative rituals, on the other hand, employ allegory and symbolism to impart moral and philosophical lessons.

Legacy

Operative Masonry's legacy is evident in the architectural masterpieces of medieval Europe. Speculative Masonry's impact lies in its promotion of ethics, personal development, and global fraternity.

Impact on Modern Freemasonry

Today, Freemasonry honors its operative roots through the symbolic use of tools and continued emphasis on craftsmanship—both literal and metaphorical. Modern lodges serve as spaces for members to reflect on ethical principles, engage in charitable activities, and build lasting connections.

Freemasonry's dual legacy inspires a holistic approach to life, balancing the tangible and intangible, the practical and philosophical. As Hamill observes, "Freemasonry bridges the gap between the medieval and the modern, combining respect for tradition with a forward-looking ethos" (Hamill, 1994).

Reflections on the Craft: Questions for Deeper Understanding

- **Preserving Operative Traditions:**
  - How do Masonic rituals today honor the legacy of operative Masonry?
- **Symbolic Interpretation:**
  - What personal insights have you gained from the speculative interpretation of operative tools?
- **Masonry's Dual Legacy:**
  - How can the practical achievements of operative Masonry inspire the philosophical pursuits of speculative Masonry?

The Presidents' Gathering: A Story of Brotherhood, Leadership, and Freemasonry

A reflective tale of how Freemasonry shaped the leadership and lives of five U.S. presidents.

Note: This essay is a fictional account inspired by the Masonic affiliation and lives of notable men, designed to explore themes of brotherhood, leadership, and service. Let us imagine six men, all former United States Presidents, meeting in the Celestial Lodge and discussing Freemasonry.

It was a quiet evening in a room that exuded history and reflection. The ambiance was humble yet dignified, with oak-paneled walls and a warm glow emanating from a nearby fireplace. In this space, six former U.S. presidents, each a proud member of the Masonic Fraternity, had gathered for an informal conversation. The air was thick with respect, camaraderie, and a shared sense of purpose. They were all men who had guided the nation through trials and triumphs, but this evening, they spoke not as leaders of the country, but as brothers of the Craft.

At the head of the gathering sat George Washington, the first president of the United States, his dignified presence lending an air of wisdom to the room. To his right, Andrew Jackson, the fiery, no-nonsense seventh president, leaned forward, eager to share his thoughts. Theodore Roosevelt, always the energetic and determined voice in the room, sat across from him with a smile, his trademark enthusiasm palpable even in the company of such great men. Beside him, Franklin D. Roosevelt sat thoughtfully, his calm and reflective demeanor a reminder of the quiet strength he had displayed throughout his presidency. Harry S. Truman, the straight-talking president who had faced some of the most difficult decisions in history, sat with a gentle smile, his sharp mind still ever-present. Lastly, Gerald Ford, the last in the line of US Presidents who were also Freemasons stood nearby.

The conversation began when Washington, looking over the group, spoke with the depth and deliberation of a man who had lived through both the birth of a nation and the challenges of leading it.

"Brothers," he said, his voice steady, "we are united not only by our shared history as presidents but by a deeper bond—a bond forged in the ideals of Freemasonry. I have often reflected on why we, each of us, came to the Craft. What drew us to this noble institution, and what lessons has it provided us as men, as leaders?"

Jackson, his eyes intense with purpose, was the first to respond. "For me, Freemasonry was always about honor and duty," he said. "I came from humble beginnings, and Freemasonry helped me refine my character. As a soldier, I learned the importance of integrity, respect for others, and personal accountability. These values, embodied in the Craft, were central to my leadership and my sense of purpose."

Roosevelt, ever the passionate advocate for action, leaned forward and added, "I joined Freemasonry because it represented the values I held dear—service, action, and the belief that we are all bound to help one another. Freemasonry doesn't just teach us ideals; it demands that we live them. Throughout my time in public office, it became a constant reminder that leadership isn't about power but service, about duty to our fellow men and women."

Franklin D. Roosevelt, sitting back in his chair, spoke with a calm, reflective tone. "For me, the Craft came at a time when I was grappling with personal adversity. Polio changed my life, but Freemasonry reminded me that adversity does not define us; our response to it does. The values of the Craft gave me strength to lead during one of the most challenging periods in American history. It was the sense of unity and the understanding that we can always do more, together, that carried me through."

Truman, who had navigated the nation through the aftermath of World War II, looked around the room thoughtfully. "For me, Freemasonry was a constant source of moral grounding. In times of crisis, when faced with some of the hardest decisions of my life, the principles of the Craft were a reminder to act with integrity and honor. It kept me focused on what was right, not what was easiest."

The five men sat in a reflective silence, each of them contemplating their individual journeys in the Craft. Washington broke the silence, his voice calm but resolute. "It seems clear to me that each of us found something in Freemasonry that resonated deeply with our personal values and our leadership. But it was more than that. It was a tool that shaped us—both as men and as leaders. The lessons we learned in the Lodge stayed with us, guiding us through our public and private lives."

Jackson nodded, his gaze unwavering. "Exactly," he said. "The Lodge provided a way to sharpen our moral compass, to remind us of the values we must always strive for. It helped me maintain my focus and my integrity, even in the face of adversity."

Roosevelt, ever the optimist, smiled. "The true beauty of Freemasonry is that it not only teaches us what it means to be a good leader—it teaches us what it means to be a good man. The lessons we learned were not just about governance or strategy; they were about service, about caring for others, and about leading with compassion."

Franklin D. Roosevelt looked toward Truman, the two men sharing a moment of quiet understanding. "We were fortunate, gentlemen," he said softly, "to have been given the tools to serve, to lead, and to better ourselves through the principles of Freemasonry. These principles are timeless, guiding us to be the best versions of ourselves, no matter the circumstances."

Truman smiled, his face reflecting a deep sense of satisfaction. "Freemasonry gave us the foundation to do what was necessary when the times were toughest. It gave us the strength to make hard choices, knowing that we were guided by principles that transcended any one individual."

Ford, who had been silently observing, finally spoke. "It's incredible to think about how Freemasonry not only shaped our actions but also our legacy. We were able to pass those principles on to future generations, and those lessons continue to resonate today."

Washington, with a final, thoughtful glance at his fellow leaders, raised his glass. "To Freemasonry," he said, "to brotherhood, and to service. May we always be guided by its teachings, and may we continue to uphold the virtues it imparts."

The five men raised their glasses, united not just by their shared history, but by the lasting impact that Freemasonry had on their lives and leadership. It was a bond forged in the Lodge, where the values of integrity, service, and brotherhood had helped shape their path—not just as presidents, but as men dedicated to the betterment of themselves and the world around them.

Reflections on the Craft: Questions for Deeper Understanding

- **Brotherhood and Leadership:**
  - How has the principle of brotherhood influenced your leadership style and your interactions within the Lodge?
- **Adversity and Growth:**
  - What lessons from Freemasonry have helped you navigate personal challenges, and how have they shaped your character?
- **Legacy and Service:**
  - How can the principles of Freemasonry be passed on to future generations to ensure the Craft's enduring impact on society?

The Candidate's Dilemma: Overcoming Doubts and Uncertainty before the Journey

Navigating the uncertainties and embracing the transformative path to Freemasonry.

Every significant journey begins with a moment of hesitation. For a candidate on the brink of joining the Masonic Craft, these moments of uncertainty can be both profound and paralyzing. The Masonic journey promises personal growth, moral enlightenment, and an enduring brotherhood, yet the path to initiation is often fraught with doubts. Understanding and addressing these doubts is essential for candidates to embrace the transformative experience awaiting them within Freemasonry.

The Nature of Doubt and Uncertainty

Doubt is a natural response to the unknown. For Masonic candidates, this can manifest as questions about personal worthiness, alignment with the values of the Craft, or the demands of commitment. These doubts are not signs of weakness but indications of a reflective and thoughtful individual—qualities Freemasonry values deeply. As William Shakespeare aptly observed, "Our doubts are traitors, and make us lose the good we oft might win by fearing to attempt."

Worthiness and Self-Assessment

Candidates often question their readiness or moral worthiness to join the Craft. Freemasonry, however, does not seek perfection but a commitment to self-improvement. The Fraternity welcomes individuals willing to confront their imperfections and strive toward ethical and spiritual growth. The rough ashlar, symbolizing the imperfect stone, represents this process of self-refinement, where each member works to shape their character into a perfect ashlar through perseverance and dedication.

Misconceptions About Freemasonry

Public misconceptions about Freemasonry can also breed uncertainty. Some candidates may be apprehensive due to myths or misinformation surrounding the Craft. Addressing these concerns requires transparency and dialogue. Potential members are encouraged to engage with current Masons, ask questions, and explore credible resources to understand Freemasonry's true purpose: fostering moral, intellectual, and spiritual growth.

Commitment and Expectations

The fear of overcommitment or the unknown expectations of membership can deter candidates. Freemasonry, while requiring dedication, is designed to complement a balanced life. Candidates are encouraged to view their involvement as an opportunity for growth rather than a burden, aligning their participation with personal and professional responsibilities.

Guidance for the Hesitant Candidate

Embrace Reflection

Doubt can serve as a powerful tool for self-exploration. Candidates should reflect on their motivations for joining, their personal values, and the alignment of these with the principles of Freemasonry. Writing down questions, seeking clarity, and meditating on the transformative potential of the Craft can help solidify their resolve.

Seek Mentorship

Engaging with experienced Freemasons can provide reassurance and insight. Masonic mentors can share their personal journeys, demystify the process of initiation, and highlight the benefits of membership. This connection fosters a sense of belonging and eases the transition from uncertainty to commitment.

Focus on the Bigger Picture

Freemasonry is a lifelong journey, not a one-time decision. Candidates should view the process of joining as the first step toward greater self-awareness, moral refinement, and service to humanity. Keeping the broader perspective in mind can diminish the weight of initial doubts.

Overcoming the Threshold

Freemasonry's initiation process is rich with symbolism, designed to guide candidates through the darkness of uncertainty into the light of understanding. The rituals emphasize the value of humility, the pursuit of knowledge, and the strength found in brotherhood. By stepping forward despite doubts, candidates embody the courage required to embrace transformation.

The candidate's dilemma is not a barrier but a vital part of the journey. Doubts and uncertainties, when confronted with honesty and courage, prepare the individual for the profound experiences and lessons of Freemasonry. By addressing concerns, seeking guidance, and embracing reflection, candidates can move confidently toward initiation, ready to embark on a path of growth, enlightenment, and fellowship. Freemasonry does not demand perfection; it invites those willing to strive for it—one step, one lesson, and one degree at a time.

Reflections on the Craft: Questions for Deeper Understanding

- **Personal Motivations:**
    - o What values or aspirations draw you to Freemasonry, and how do they align with the principles of the Craft?
- **Overcoming Doubts:**
    - o How can reflection and dialogue help you address any uncertainties or misconceptions you may have about joining Freemasonry?
- **Lifelong Commitment:**
    - o How do you envision balancing the responsibilities of Freemasonry with your personal and professional life, and what benefits do you foresee from this commitment?

Entering the Craft: The Journey of the Entered Apprentice

Ask, Seek, Knock: The Masonic Path to Enlightenment and Achievement

Step into the Masonic journey of personal growth and enlightenment—where asking, seeking, and knocking guide us toward wisdom, virtue, and service.

Before entering the Lodge, a candidate for Freemasonry is already introduced to the profound process embodied in the biblical verse from Matthew 7:7: "Ask, and it will be given to you; seek, and you will find; knock, and the door will be opened to you." This verse encapsulates the journey that every Mason embarks on, a journey that begins before the first steps are even taken into the Lodge. The candidate asks for a recommendation, seeking approval from those already in the Craft. He then seeks admission into the Lodge, contemplating the meaning and the responsibility of what it means to be a part of Freemasonry. Finally, the candidate knocks on the door, symbolizing his request to enter and take his place in the Fraternity. This foundational lesson is not only learned before the obligation is taken, but it is actively demonstrated and reinforced throughout all three degrees of Masonry.

In Freemasonry, this process of asking, seeking, and knocking becomes a guiding principle that the candidate will return to at each stage of his journey. The initiation into the Craft begins with asking for admission, a symbolic gesture that mirrors the verse's first step. The candidate must seek the recommendation and approval of existing members, thereby beginning the path toward enlightenment. Once this step is taken, he moves on to the next phase—seeking— where the candidate, in his heart and mind, contemplates what he is about to undertake. It is a time for reflection on the significance of Freemasonry and the personal growth he hopes to achieve through it. Finally, the candidate knocks, a literal and symbolic action signifying his willingness to take the next step, to enter the Brotherhood, and to undergo the teachings that await him inside.

This lesson of asking, seeking, and knocking is not a one-time event; rather, it is a recurring theme throughout the three degrees of Freemasonry. Each degree can be seen as a further elaboration of this initial request for knowledge, understanding, and self-improvement. When the candidate knocks on the door, he is not just entering the Lodge for the first time; he is stepping forward to a lifelong journey of self-discovery and growth. Each stage of the Masonic journey, from the Entered Apprentice to the Fellow craft and finally to the Master Mason, involves asking deeper questions, seeking further enlightenment, and knocking on the doors of higher understanding and action.

As Winston Churchill once said, "To each, there comes in their lifetime a special moment when they are figuratively tapped on the shoulder and offered the chance to do a very special thing, unique to them and fit for their talents. What a tragedy if that moment finds them unprepared or unqualified for that which could have been their finest hour." (Churchill, 1941). In the Masonic journey, this moment comes repeatedly: as Masons, we are offered countless opportunities to apply the lessons we have learned and act upon the insights we have gained. Asking, seeking, and knocking, as a continuous process, ensures that we are ready for the moments of growth that come with each new stage in our journey.

The process mirrors the way in which each Mason is continually guided by these principles of asking, seeking, and knocking throughout his life, both in and outside of the Lodge. This cyclical process shapes a Mason's ability to grow intellectually, spiritually, and morally. Asking leads the

Mason to inquire more deeply into his own nature, seeking helps him understand the greater truths of the Craft and the world, and knocking compels him to take action toward applying these insights in a practical and meaningful way. Each action reinforces the next, creating a cycle of growth and development that pushes the Mason toward his ultimate goal—living a life of virtue and service.

The Subconscious Power of Ask, Seek, Knock

Beyond the ritual and symbolism, the process of asking, seeking, and knocking also plays a critical role in shaping the Mason's subconscious mind. Each step serves as a catalyst for deeper reflection and personal growth. The act of asking is not merely a verbal request but an intentional invocation of the subconscious mind. By verbally stating our questions, we give shape to our desires, placing our intentions clearly before our inner selves. The act of seeking then directs the subconscious to actively pursue the answers, focusing attention on uncovering the hidden truths that lie ahead. This phase of deep contemplation, aided by study and reflection, prepares the individual to knock—to take meaningful action toward achieving those truths and goals.

The act of knocking, which symbolizes physical action, then reinforces the other steps. By taking action, whether it is through participation in the Lodge, performing duties, or engaging in life's challenges with purpose and clarity, the Mason brings his intentions into the material world. Action and contemplation go hand in hand, creating a feedback loop where each step of the process leads to further insight and deeper growth. Through this cycle, Masons continue to refine their understanding of the Craft, their personal virtues, and their place in the world, all while contributing to the greater good of their communities and their Brothers.

The Power of Ask, Seek, Knock in the Masonic Journey

The principles embodied in asking, seeking, and knocking provide a timeless framework for personal development and spiritual growth, and they are deeply woven into the fabric of Freemasonry. These three steps are more than just rituals or metaphors; they are a guiding principle that shapes the Mason's life and his journey through the Craft. Through asking, we begin the search for knowledge; through seeking, we deepen our understanding; and through knocking, we take action to bring our insights into the world. These actions create a continuous cycle of growth and discovery, reinforcing the Mason's journey toward enlightenment, both within the Lodge and beyond. As Freemasons, we are called to ask, seek, and knock in all aspects of our lives, using these actions to guide us toward wisdom, understanding, and service.

Reflections on the Craft: Questions for Deeper Understanding

- **The Power of Request:**
  - How does the act of asking for guidance or admission in your Masonic journey reflect your willingness to learn and grow personally?

- **Deepening the Search:**
  - In what ways can seeking deeper truths within the teachings of Freemasonry enhance your understanding of yourself and the world around you?
- **Taking the Next Step:**
  - When you knock on the door to new opportunities, how do you ensure you are

prepared to embrace the responsibilities and wisdom they bring?

The Beauty of Holiness: Exploring the Intersection of Plato's Philosophy and Masonic Virtue

Pursuit of Beauty Through Moral Excellence: Plato's Vision and Freemasonry's Journey

In the heart of Freemasonry, the phrase "beauties of holiness" is often invoked during rituals, such as the prayer that seeks divine wisdom for the candidate about to enter the Fraternity. This concept is deeply connected with Freemasonry's core values and the Masonic journey toward self-improvement. It speaks to the transformative process of becoming a better person and developing virtues such as brotherly love, relief, and truth. But what does this concept really mean, and how does it relate to the philosophical traditions that have shaped human thought, including the teachings of Plato? Moreover, how does it tie into the essence of Freemasonry, where beauty, holiness, and virtue are ever-present?

The phrase "beauties of holiness" can be traced to Psalm 110:3, where "holy garments" are referred to as the "beauties of holiness." In a religious context, this speaks to the purity and divine sanctity that comes with dedicating oneself to a life of righteousness and devotion. Similarly, in Masonic ritual, the idea of "holiness" extends beyond religious practice to the moral integrity and virtuous conduct expected of every Freemason. The commitment to living a life dedicated to truth and justice is central to the Masonic journey. But this idea of "beauty" in holiness is not just about ritualistic purity. It also extends to the concept of beauty in the sense Plato described — beauty as something that transcends the material world and connects us to something higher and more eternal.

Plato's Definition of Beauty: Beyond the Physical Realm

For Plato, beauty was not confined to physical appearance or superficial aesthetics. In his "Symposium" he described beauty as an ideal form — one that is inherently tied to the eternal and the divine. Plato argued that beauty is a manifestation of the Good, an essential and immutable principle that transcends the changing material world. To appreciate beauty, one must move beyond the physical and begin to contemplate the higher, more abstract forms of beauty — such as the beauty of virtue, the beauty of the soul, and the beauty found in the pursuit of knowledge and truth. In this framework, beauty becomes something far more significant than simple attraction; it is a reflection of the divine order and a path toward moral and intellectual enlightenment.

The Connection between Plato's Philosophy and Freemasonry

In many ways, Freemasonry mirrors Plato's view of beauty. Masonic teachings encourage brothers to seek enlightenment and understanding through a process of self-improvement and the pursuit of moral excellence. The concept of "holiness" within Freemasonry, as it pertains to personal development and virtue, aligns closely with Plato's philosophy of beauty. Just as Plato urged his followers to move beyond the material world to discover the eternal and perfect forms of beauty, Freemasonry encourages its members to rise above base desires and behaviors and aim for higher moral ground. The "beauties of holiness" that are referenced in Masonic ritual can be seen as the pursuit of this higher beauty — one that is grounded in the ethical and virtuous life that every Mason is called to lead.

The Role of Beauty and Holiness in Masonic Practice

In Freemasonry, the journey toward personal development is a key part of the initiation process. The concept of beauty, as reflected in the rituals of the Craft, is not merely an aesthetic ideal; it is a guiding principle that shapes the way Masons approach life. It encompasses more than just outward actions — it is an inner transformation that involves the cultivation of virtues such as temperance, fortitude, prudence, and justice. These virtues, which are central to Masonic teachings, correspond to the kinds of beauty Plato admired. They are not just moral duties but also ideals that elevate the soul, reflecting the divine order in human form.

This emphasis on inner transformation aligns with Oscar Wilde's famous statement, "Be yourself; everyone else is already taken" (Wilde, 1891/2024). A Freemason and an advocate for personal authenticity, Wilde's words remind us that the journey of self-improvement is uniquely individual and rooted in an honest expression of self. His affiliation with Freemasonry underscores the alignment between his philosophy and the Craft's emphasis on personal growth and moral excellence.

Holiness in the Masonic Journey: The Beauty of Transformation

The Masonic journey is a journey of transformation — a journey that begins with a request for admission and continues through rituals that focus on personal growth, virtue, and service to others. The concept of "holiness," as it is practiced within Freemasonry, is not merely about outward observance but about the inner commitment to moral principles that will elevate the soul. As the candidate progresses through the degrees, he is expected to embody the beauty of holiness, just as Plato suggested that the most beautiful forms are those that reflect the truth of the divine and the good.

In this sense, the Masonic journey is deeply philosophical. The pursuit of truth, justice, and brotherly love is not just a commitment to perform certain deeds but a path toward understanding the divine, an effort to embody the divine order in one's own life. This is where Freemasonry's "beauties of holiness" intersect with the philosophical teachings of Plato. Both paths encourage individuals to rise above the mundane and connect with something greater, something more permanent — be it through the pursuit of virtue, wisdom, or understanding the ultimate truth of the universe.

A Path to Divine Beauty

Just as Plato's philosophy taught that beauty leads us toward the divine, so does the Masonic journey. Through the practice of brotherly love, relief, and truth, Masons strive to embody the beauty of holiness in their lives. They are encouraged not only to reflect on the spiritual and moral aspects of beauty but to actively live them out in their communities. In Freemasonry, beauty is not simply an ideal to be admired; it is a transformative force that shapes the soul, guiding Masons toward enlightenment and divine wisdom.

Thus, the "beauties of holiness" in Freemasonry serve as a powerful reminder of the Craft's true purpose: to guide each individual toward moral excellence, to seek truth, and to live a life filled with virtue — a life that reflects the divine beauty found in both Plato's philosophy and the deeper teachings of Freemasonry.

Reflections on the Craft: Questions for Deeper Understanding

- **Beauty as Transformation:**

- How does your understanding of the "beauties of holiness" influence your personal journey toward self-improvement and moral excellence?
- **Plato and the Craft:**
  - Plato described beauty as a reflection of the divine and a path to the Good. In what ways can you align your Masonic practices with this philosophical pursuit of higher truth and virtue?
- **Living the Ideal:**
  - How can you embody the Masonic virtues of brotherly love, relief, and truth to reflect the beauty and holiness central to both Plato's teachings and Masonic principles in you
  - r daily life?

Circumambulation vs. Perambulation: A Masonic Perspective

Discover the symbolic movements of circumambulation and perambulation, and their profound roles in guiding Masonic candidates on their journey to enlightenment and moral integrity

In the Masonic Lodge, two terms related to movement and observation—circumambulation and perambulation—carry significant symbolic meaning. While these terms both imply a form of walking or traveling through space, their use and application within the context of Freemasonry differ in their ceremonial significance and purpose. By understanding the definitions of these terms and their usage, particularly during the initiation and ritual processes, we can appreciate their roles in shaping the Masonic experience.

Circumambulation: The Journey of the Candidate

Circumambulation, derived from the Latin circumambulatio ("to walk around"), refers to the act of walking around in a circular motion. In Masonic rituals, circumambulation is a key part of the candidate's journey through the degrees. This ritual movement is not merely physical; it is symbolic of the candidate's spiritual journey and progression toward enlightenment. As the candidate moves around the Lodge, he is figuratively circumnavigating the path to wisdom, knowledge, and self-improvement.

The significance of circumambulation in Masonic rituals can be seen in the movement around the Lodge in a specific direction, typically clockwise, which is said to represent the course of the sun, a powerful symbol of light, wisdom, and knowledge. The candidate is led around the Lodge room by the officers, symbolizing the journey of a man seeking the "light" of Masonic teachings. It is at this point that the candidate is inspected by the Worshipful Master and the officers, who stand at their designated stations—South, West, and East. Their stations are significant not only for their symbolic alignment with the sun's movement across the sky but also for the roles they play in guiding the candidate and ensuring the proper flow of the ritual. The candidate's movements, and the Master's inspection, serve to ensure that he is ready for further progression in the Craft, while simultaneously teaching him humility and self-awareness.

Perambulation: Surveying the Sacred Ground

Perambulation, in contrast, is a term that refers to walking around or traveling across a specific area, often for purposes of inspection or surveying boundaries. In a Masonic context, perambulation can be understood as the act of inspection by the Master and the officers, particularly when they evaluate the candidate's readiness and sincerity. The perambulation of the Master and officers, as they move around the candidate and the Lodge, serves to reinforce the spiritual and moral inspection of the candidate's character and commitment to the Fraternity. This term could also extend to the concept of ensuring that the candidate fully understands the significance of the symbols and stations within the Lodge.

Whereas circumambulation is generally the candidate's action—reflecting his journey toward enlightenment—perambulation is often associated with the officers' responsibility to examine and evaluate. Just as a surveyor might walk the boundaries of a land parcel to define its limits, the officers "perambulate" the space to ensure that the ritual's spiritual boundaries are being upheld and that the teachings are being properly conveyed. In this context, the Master, moving through the South, West, and East, represents the overseeing figure who ensures the sanctity and correctness of the ritual, providing guidance to the candidate.

Stations of the Lodge: South, West, and East

The distinction between circumambulation and perambulation can also be observed in the significance of the stations within the Lodge—South, West, and East—each representing a particular role and responsibility in the Masonic experience. The South is the station of the Junior Warden, who oversees the candidates and the moral and physical conduct of the Lodge. The West, where the Senior Warden stands, represents the setting sun and the completion of a day, symbolizing the progression of life toward wisdom. The East, where the Worshipful Master presides, represents the rising sun and enlightenment, symbolizing the beginning of a new day and the pursuit of knowledge and truth.

During the circumambulation, the candidate passes these stations in a structured pattern, learning from each officer's position and understanding their symbolic significance. The Worshipful Master, positioned in the East, is the ultimate source of guidance, overseeing the entire ritual and ensuring that it proceeds in accordance with Masonic teachings. The Senior Warden in the West offers support and direction as the candidate moves toward completion, while the Junior Warden in the South maintains the balance of virtue and propriety within the Lodge.

Albert Mackey, a noted Masonic historian and scholar, described Freemasonry as "a science of symbols, in which, by their proper study, a search is instituted after truth" (Mackey, 1869/2024). This perspective aligns seamlessly with the symbolic journeys of circumambulation and perambulation, as they guide candidates to deeper understanding and personal enlightenment. Mackey's contributions to Masonic literature and his affiliation with the Grand Lodge of South Carolina highlight his profound influence on the Craft's teachings and traditions.

Symbolic Meaning of Movement and Inspection

Both circumambulation and perambulation play vital roles in Masonic rituals, yet they serve distinct purposes. Circumambulation reflects the candidate's spiritual and moral journey, symbolizing the pursuit of wisdom and knowledge as he circles the Lodge in search of enlightenment. Perambulation, however, relates more to the inspection and supervision of the candidate's progression by the officers, ensuring that he is spiritually prepared for the next step.

The roles of the Master and officers at their stations, combined with the symbolic meanings of these movements, emphasize the importance of discipline, self-reflection, and moral guidance in the Masonic journey. The perambulation and circumambulation of the candidate are essential parts of the ritual, reflecting the balance between individual progression and collective oversight, both of which are key to Freemasonry's transformative power. Through these practices, Freemasonry continues to promote the values of wisdom, integrity, and self-improvement, ensuring that each candidate's journey is both personal and guided by the light of the Craft.

Reflections on the Craft: Questions for Deeper Understanding

- **Walking the Path:**
    - How does the act of circumambulation during Masonic rituals reflect your own journey toward enlightenment and self-

improvement, both within and outside the Lodge?

- **Inspection and Reflection:**
  - o Perambulation involves the inspection of readiness and sincerity. How do you ensure that you are spiritually and morally prepared for the challenges and lessons of the Masonic journey?
- **Stations of Wisdom:**
  - o As you pass through the symbolic stations of the South, West, and East, what lessons or insights have you gained about balance, completion, and new beginnings in your personal and Masonic life?

The Darkness of the North: The Lodge as a Solar Day and Its Symbolism

Unveil the profound symbolism of the Masonic lodge as a solar day, where the interplay of light and darkness reveals the path to enlightenment and self-discovery.

In Freemasonry, the symbolism of the lodge, particularly the concept of the "north as dark," is rich in meaning and reflection. The idea that the north represents darkness is not merely a geographic or architectural consideration, but rather a deeply ingrained metaphysical and philosophical symbol that reflects the duality of light and darkness in both our physical and spiritual worlds. It is within this context that the lodge itself can be understood as a metaphor for a solar day, with each of its stations reflecting different times of the day, each contributing to the overall journey of enlightenment.

The Masonic lodge, much like the celestial sphere, operates as a symbolic "solar day." The Master, stationed in the East, is associated with the dawn—the time when light first breaks the darkness, signaling the beginning of a new day. This is a powerful symbol of enlightenment and the start of the Masonic journey, where the initiate begins to move from ignorance into knowledge. The Master, as the source of light and wisdom, represents the potential for personal transformation and the illumination of the soul, guiding the candidate toward a higher understanding of life and virtue.

As noted by Manly P. Hall, a renowned Freemason and esoteric scholar, "The Masonic journey begins in darkness and ends in light" (Hall, 1928). This profound statement encapsulates the transformative nature of the Masonic experience, where enlightenment emerges from confronting and understanding the darkness. Hall's contributions to

Masonic literature emphasize the spiritual and intellectual growth central to Freemasonry.

Moving through the lodge, the Senior Warden, positioned in the West, corresponds with the time of sunset. As the sun sets, the light fades and darkness gradually overtakes the day. In the lodge, the Senior Warden represents this transition from light to darkness, mirroring the closing of the day, when reflections on the lessons learned throughout the day come to a close, and the mind is prepared for rest or further contemplation. The Junior Warden, located in the South, represents noon, the height of the sun's power and the fullness of light. This is the peak of the day, where the sun is at its highest and most intense, much like the moment in the lodge where the teachings of the Craft are most vibrant and evident, shining brightly for all to witness.

The North, by contrast, is referred to as a place of darkness. This absence of light in the north quadrant of the lodge reflects the absence of a physical light source in the northern part of King Solomon's Temple, which was situated so far north of the ecliptic that neither the sun nor the moon could shine upon it at noon. Symbolically, the north is considered a place where light does not reach, representing both the unknown and the unilluminated aspects of the human experience. This is not merely a spatial designation but an acknowledgment of the spiritual and intellectual journey that every Mason undertakes.

The north's darkness symbolizes the areas of our lives where knowledge is still lacking, where we may encounter confusion, ignorance, or even adversity. It is here, in this absence of light, that Masons are encouraged to seek understanding, to illuminate the darkness with the teachings and principles of the Craft. In a more profound sense, the north represents the potential for growth, as it is through confronting the darkness that one moves closer to enlightenment.

In addition to this, Masonic teachings often draw parallels between the lodge's layout and the movement of celestial bodies. The positions of the Master, Senior Warden, and Junior Warden reflect not only the hours of the day but also the movement of the sun across the sky. This symbolism is enhanced when considering the houses of the zodiac and the influence of the planets. The signs of the zodiac, which circle the ecliptic, can also be seen as symbolic representations of the journey a Mason takes through life. As each sign governs specific traits and lessons, they parallel the challenges and growth opportunities that a Mason encounters on his path toward moral enlightenment.

The planets, too, have their symbolic meanings in the context of Masonic teachings. For example, Jupiter, the planet of wisdom, could be associated with the Master in the East, bringing enlightenment and expansion of knowledge. Saturn, the planet of discipline and structure, could be aligned with the Senior Warden in the West, guiding Masons through the process of reflection and understanding. The Moon, representing intuition and the subconscious, might be linked with the Junior Warden in the South, a symbol of the balance between light and darkness, and the harmony between thought and action.

As Masons continue their journey of self-improvement, the lodge serves as a symbolic mirror of the cosmic order, reminding us that life is a balance between light and dark, known and unknown, certainty and doubt. The darkness of the North, like the shadow that always follows the light, teaches us that there is much to learn from the parts of ourselves and our world that are still shrouded in mystery. It is through our pursuit of wisdom and our willingness to confront the darkness, guided by the principles of Freemasonry, that we move closer to understanding the mysteries of life, just as the light of the sun moves across the sky, illuminating the world and guiding us along our journey.

Reflections on the Craft: Questions for Deeper Understanding

- **Cycles of Light and Darkness:**
  - How does the symbolism of the lodge as a solar day help you reflect on the importance of balancing periods of light and growth with times of introspection and darkness in your life?
- **The Enlightening Journey:**
  - Considering the lodge's stations as representations of the sun's movement, what lessons can be drawn from each stage— dawn, noon, and sunset—about your own path toward enlightenment and understanding?
- **Illuminating the North:**
  - In what ways can the concept of the "darkness of the North" inspire you to explore and confront the unilluminated or unknown areas of your own experience or understanding?

The Masonic Floor: Symbolism of Life's Boundaries and Choices

Step onto the Masonic floor and explore the profound symbolism of life's duality, where every choice shapes the journey toward balance, wisdom, and enlightenment

In Freemasonry, the floor of the Lodge is much more than just a place where Masons gather—it is a powerful symbol of life's journey, encompassing both physical and spiritual elements. Central to this symbolism is the black-and-white tiled pattern, which not only represents the duality of good and evil but also serves as a reminder of the boundaries and rules that govern our lives. These boundaries cannot be transgressed beyond a certain point, illustrating that, much like the structured rituals of Freemasonry, there are moral lines that we must respect as we walk through life.

Life's Dualities

The black-and-white tiles on the Masonic floor are rich with multifaceted significance. On one level, they represent the ancient battle between good and evil—light and darkness. The black tile, often associated with darkness, can symbolize ignorance, evil, or the confusion that arises when we stray from a righteous path. In contrast, the white tile is connected to light, knowledge, purity, and goodness. These opposing forces remind Masons that life is full of choices, and it is only through the pursuit of knowledge and wisdom that we can make the right decisions. The pattern of black and white offers a visual guide to living a balanced life, where we acknowledge the existence of both good and evil, but strive to align ourselves with the light of virtue and truth.

This symbolic division of the floor also reflects the profound principle of personal choice—each man has the free will to choose his path. In Masonic teaching, the floor encourages us to live in a state of balance, acknowledging that while we will face moments of darkness and confusion, we must always strive to keep one foot firmly planted in the white square—the symbol of virtue, goodness, and knowledge. In doing so, we can navigate the darker moments of life, represented by the black squares, with clarity and moral direction. This is not just about maintaining balance, but about understanding that our choices shape our journey. As we continue along our path, by focusing on the white square, on light, knowledge, and moral clarity, we are better equipped to face the trials represented by the black tile without losing our way.

Furthermore, the symbolism of the Masonic floor is echoed in the works of two prominent Freemasons—John Locke and Voltaire—both of whom were instrumental in shaping Enlightenment thought. Locke, known for his emphasis on personal liberty and the power of reason, stated, "To love truth for truth's sake is the principal part of human perfection in this world, and the seed-plot of all other virtues" (Locke, 1706/2024). This perspective aligns perfectly with the symbolism of the white tile as representing reason, goodness, and the pursuit of virtue. For Locke, the black tile would signify ignorance or misguided passions—the obstacles to achieving moral clarity.

Similarly, Voltaire, a fierce advocate for reason and enlightenment, emphasized the importance of rational thought over superstition, stating, "Superstition is to religion what astrology is to astronomy, the mad daughter of a wise mother" (Voltaire, 1764/2024). His interpretation of the Masonic floor would reflect the struggle between knowledge and ignorance, with the white tiles representing the triumph of reason and enlightenment over the darkness of superstition.

Grounding in Virtue

In addition to the physical representation of good and evil, the Masonic floor also serves as a guide for the spiritual journey. The white tile symbolizes divine wisdom, purity, and truth, offering spiritual guidance and clarity. The black tile, on the other hand, can be seen as the testing ground of life's trials, representing the times when we must confront evil, chaos, and uncertainty. For Masons, this symbolism teaches us that our spiritual journey is a constant process of learning, growth, and self-discipline. It reminds us that the path to enlightenment is not always straightforward, and that we must confront and overcome the challenges that life presents us. As long as we stay grounded in the virtues of wisdom, knowledge, and moral integrity—represented by the white tile—we can navigate the darkness with confidence, knowing that the light of truth will always lead us toward righteousness.

The Masonic floor, therefore, is not merely a physical space—it is a metaphor for the journey of life itself. The boundaries set by the black and white tiles remind Masons that life offers both light and darkness, and that our role is to strive for balance, to make moral choices, and to grow in wisdom. Just as the Lodge is constructed with these symbolic elements, so too is our personal journey built upon the choices we make. As long as we remain grounded in the virtues symbolized by the white square, we can face the challenges of the darker moments represented by the black square with the knowledge that the guidance of truth and light will always lead us toward the right path.

In essence, the Masonic floor is a space of balance—where lessons are learned, the soul is shaped, and the journey toward moral, intellectual, and spiritual enlightenment unfolds. By keeping one foot grounded in the white square, we embrace the lessons of the Craft and work to create a life filled with wisdom, virtue, and truth, guided by the eternal principles of light.

Reflections on the Craft: Questions for Deeper Understanding

- **Navigating Life's Duality:**
  - How does the interplay of black and white tiles on the Masonic floor inspire you to reflect on the duality of life and the choices that define your journey toward balance and enlightenment?
- **Grounding in Virtue:**
  - In moments of uncertainty or moral conflict, how can you ensure that your actions remain grounded in the values symbolized by the white tile—truth, wisdom, and purity?
- **The Impact of Choice:**
  - Recognizing that each step on the Masonic floor symbolizes a choice, how do you align your daily decisions with the principles of light and virtue, while learning from the challenges symbolized by the darker tiles?

Psalm 133: The Beauty of Unity, the Blessings of Mount Hermon, and Masonic Reflections

Unite in harmony and explore the profound connections between Psalm 133's timeless message and the illuminating principles of Freemasonry

Psalm 133, nestled within the Book of Psalms, is a timeless and profound song of unity and brotherhood. With only three verses, this poetic hymn resonates across faiths and backgrounds, conveying a powerful message of harmony and blessings that arise when people come together in unity. In this essay, we explore the essence and timeless relevance of Psalm 133, emphasizing its significance in fostering interconnectedness and shared purpose among humanity, its link to the blessings of Mount Hermon, and how its themes resonate deeply within the Masonic tradition.

Verse 1: The Pleasure of Unity

The psalmist opens with a captivating image: "Behold, how good and pleasant it is when brothers dwell in unity!" This declaration sets the tone for the entire psalm, emphasizing the immense pleasure and joy that arise when people coexist in harmony. Unity is likened to a bountiful garden, where love and respect are nurtured, and where individual differences blend harmoniously to create a beautiful tapestry of collective strength.

For Freemasons, this verse aligns with the central tenet of the Craft: the Brotherhood of Man under the Fatherhood of God. It mirrors the principles espoused in Masonic lodges, where members of diverse backgrounds come together as equals, united by shared values of morality, charity, and truth. The Lodge itself becomes a microcosm of the psalmist's vision—a sacred space where unity fosters enlightenment and personal growth.

Verse 2: The Anointing of Unity

The second verse portrays unity's blessings, comparing it to the precious anointing oil used to consecrate priests and kings. Just as the oil was considered sacred and symbolized divine favor, so too is unity seen as a divine blessing that enriches and empowers the community. When individuals unite, barriers crumble, and a sense of divine grace envelops them, fostering prosperity, joy, and spiritual abundance.

The anointing oil can be understood in Masonic terms as a symbol of enlightenment and consecration. In Masonic rituals, oil represents purification, dedication, and the elevation of the soul. Similarly, unity among brothers in the Lodge is seen as a consecration of their collective purpose, empowering them to work for the betterment of society. The oil flowing down from Aaron's beard signifies the trickle-down effect of unity and wisdom, spreading light and harmony to the world beyond the Lodge.

Verse 3: The Symbolism of Unity and Mount Hermon

The concluding verse beautifully reinforces the image of unity's abundance, comparing it to the dew of Mount Hermon descending upon the hills of Zion. Mount Hermon, with its majestic snow-capped peaks, is the highest point in the region, symbolizing the divine source of blessings. The dew from Mount Hermon flows down to nourish the hills of Zion, representing the far-reaching impact of unity's blessings on all levels of society.
Masonic Interpretation:

Mount Hermon's dew, sustaining life in Zion, can be seen as a metaphor for the flow of Masonic wisdom and virtue. Just as the dew nourishes the land, the teachings of Freemasonry nourish the hearts and minds of its members, encouraging them to act as moral guides in their communities. Mount Hermon also represents the high ideals and aspirations of the Craft, with Zion serving as the manifestation of these principles in the world. The interconnectedness of the two symbolizes how spiritual growth in the Lodge inspires positive action in the larger society.

While Psalm 133 holds deep significance in the context of ancient Israel, its message remains universally applicable and timeless. The psalm's themes align closely with Masonic values, offering lessons for individuals, communities, and nations.

- **Community Cohesion**: Psalm 133 reminds us that unity is the foundation of strong communities. Embracing diversity and fostering inclusivity can help overcome conflicts and create environments where peace, understanding, and cooperation flourish. Masonic Lodges serve as exemplars of this principle, welcoming individuals from varied walks of life to work toward common goals.

- **Global Harmony:** In our interconnected world, Psalm 133 underscores the necessity of international unity. By uniting in purpose, humanity can address global challenges such as poverty, climate change, and humanitarian crises more effectively. Masonry, as a global fraternity, emphasizes the importance of universal brotherhood and encourages its members to be agents of positive change.

- **Interfaith Dialogue:** The psalm's theme of brotherhood speaks to the significance of interfaith dialogue and cooperation. Encouraging understanding and respect between diverse religious traditions fosters mutual appreciation and harmonious coexistence. Freemasonry, with its principle of respecting all faiths, provides a platform for fostering interfaith harmony and upholding the ideals of brotherly love.

The Timeless Relevance

Psalm 133 stands as a timeless testament to the beauty and power of unity and brotherhood. Its poetic verses offer guidance and inspiration to individuals, communities, and nations seeking to build bridges, overcome differences, and embrace the richness of collective strength. Within the Masonic tradition, the psalm resonates as a call to live by the principles of the Craft, to act as beacons of light in a divided world, and to cultivate harmony in all our undertakings.

As we contemplate the words of this ancient psalm, let us strive to nurture unity, love, and respect in our lives, fostering a world where the blessings of Psalm 133, flowing like the dew from Mount Hermon, become a reality for all—a world illuminated by the eternal light of Masonic virtue.

Reflections on the Craft: Questions for Deeper Understanding

- **Unity and Brotherhood:**
  - How can the principles of unity in Psalm 133 inspire deeper connections within your Masonic Lodge and in your broader community?
- **Symbolism of Blessings:**

- The anointing oil and Mount Hermon's dew symbolize the spread of blessings. How can Masonic teachings guide you to become a source of harmony and enrichment in your personal and professional life?
- **Applying Timeless Values:**
  - Psalm 133 speaks of dwelling together in unity. How can you apply its lessons to foster understanding and cooperation in today's diverse and interconnected world?

The Three Great Lights of Freemasonry: The Holy Bible, Square, and Compass

Illuminate your journey with the timeless wisdom of the Bible, the precision of the Square, and the focused discipline of the Compass—the Three Great Lights of Freemasonry.

In Freemasonry, the Three Great Lights—the Holy Bible, the Square, and the Compass—are profound symbols that guide members on a journey of moral and spiritual growth. Each Light holds deep significance: the Bible represents spiritual wisdom, the Square symbolizes moral rectitude, and the Compass illustrates the boundaries of ethical living and focused discipline. Together, these tools serve as metaphors for the infinite, connecting Masons to divine principles and inspiring them to construct lives of integrity and purpose.

The Holy Bible: Spiritual Wisdom and Moral Guidance

The Bible, the most foundational of the Three Great Lights, serves as the cornerstone of Freemasonry. It represents divine law, eternal truth, and moral clarity, offering guidance for a life of justice, compassion, and integrity. Albert Pike emphasized its importance, stating, "The Bible is an indispensable part of the furniture of a Masonic lodge, as it is the great light by which the Mason must walk and work" (Morals and Dogma, 1871, p. 745).

Beyond its religious significance, the Bible symbolizes universal truths that inspire Masons to align their lives with enduring principles. Johann Wolfgang von Goethe, a philosopher, poet and Freemason eloquently reflected on its transformative power, noting, "The Bible grows more beautiful as we grow in our understanding of it" (Goethe,

1806/2024). These insights emphasize the Bible's role as a source of moral inspiration and spiritual growth.

The Square: Measuring Our Actions According to Virtue

The Square, a central symbol in Freemasonry, represents morality, virtue, and the necessity of living a life of integrity. Functioning as a practical tool to ensure the accuracy of angles, it also serves as a guide for evaluating one's actions against principles of fairness and righteousness. Albert Pike explained, "The Square teaches us to regulate our conduct and actions according to the principles of morality and virtue" (Morals and Dogma, 1871, p. 1).

Symbolically, the Square measures all squares, representing its capacity to assess the infinite angles of life. It reminds Masons to act with equity and justice, fostering trust and harmony in their relationships. By embracing the Square's teachings, Masons construct lives rooted in stability, morality, and ethical excellence.

The Compass: Restraint, Focus, and Spiritual Growth

The Compass, another essential tool in Freemasonry, symbolizes self-discipline, restraint, and the boundaries that guide ethical behavior. Practically, it is used to draw circles, but its symbolic significance extends far beyond geometry. As A. E. Waite described, "The Compass instructs us to circumscribe our desires and keep them within due bounds with all mankind" (The Secret Tradition in Freemasonry, 1922, p. 164).

The Compass's ability to create smaller and smaller circles symbolizes the refinement of goals and the focus required for personal growth. This narrowing process teaches Masons to channel their energies effectively, directing their passions toward meaningful and disciplined pursuits. By doing so, the Compass represents infinite potential and divine guidance, reminding Masons of their capacity for continuous self-improvement.

The Square and Compass: Metaphors for the Infinite

Together, the Square and Compass illustrate the balance between structure and exploration, discipline and creativity. The Square, which measures all squares, symbolizes the principles of stability, morality, and justice that underpin life. The Compass, capable of creating all circles, represents the infinite nature of human potential and the divine. These tools remind Masons that their journey is both grounded in ethical responsibility and open to boundless spiritual growth.

Conclusion

The Three Great Lights of Freemasonry—the Bible, the Square, and the Compass—are not merely symbolic artifacts but dynamic tools for personal and spiritual transformation. The Bible provides a moral and spiritual foundation; the Square ensures actions are measured against the highest standards of virtue; and the Compass inspires focused discipline and the pursuit of infinite potential. Together, they guide Masons on a journey toward integrity, enlightenment, and purpose.

By embracing these symbols, Freemasons navigate life's complexities with clarity, balance, and a commitment to the principles of the Craft. Through this journey, they construct lives of virtue and meaning, building a legacy that reflects the highest ideals of Freemasonry.

Reflections on the Craft: Questions for Deeper Understanding

- **Inspiration from the Infinite:**
  - How do the metaphors of the Square and Compass as representations of the divine inspire your personal growth and spiritual journey?
- **Refining Goals and Intentions:**
  - How can the Compass's ability to create smaller circles guide you in refining your goals and focusing your energies on meaningful pursuits?
- **Building Stability and Trust:**
  - In what ways does the Square help you ensure your actions promote balance, equity, and trust in your relationships and endeavors?

The Twenty-Four Inch Gauge: A Masonic Metaphor for Time, Service, and Purpose

Discover how the Twenty-Four Inch Gauge inspires balance, purpose, and service in the timeless teachings of Freemasonry.

In Freemasonry, the Twenty-Four Inch Gauge is an ancient tool traditionally used by operative Masons to measure and prepare their work, specifically stones for construction. However, as Free and Accepted Masons, we are taught to use this instrument metaphorically, for a nobler and more significant purpose – to divide our time. The twenty-four parts of the gauge, representing the twenty-four hours of the day, remind us to balance our responsibilities and duties in life. The guidance we receive from this emblem is profound, suggesting that we divide our daily time into three parts: one part for the service of God and assisting a distressed worthy brother, another for our usual vocations, and the final portion for refreshment and repose.

The Service of God and the Distressed Worthy Brother

The phrase "service of God and a distressed worthy brother" evokes a powerful Masonic commitment to charity and brotherly love. The "distressed worthy brother" refers not only to those who are in physical or financial distress but also to those who may need emotional or spiritual support. A distressed worthy brother is anyone who, within the Fraternity, requires aid, be it material or moral, and is deserving of it due to his integrity and commitment to Masonic principles. Helping a brother in distress, whether through monetary assistance or simply providing comfort during difficult times, is one of the core teachings of Freemasonry, reminding us to put the needs of others before our own at times.

"The practice of charity, which extends beyond mere almsgiving, is a distinguishing virtue of Freemasonry and involves moral support and fraternal kindness" (Mackey, n.d.). This principle encourages us to think beyond material contributions and engage deeply with our fellow brethren, fostering a true sense of unity and support.

Vocation: Work as a Calling

The second part of the Twenty-Four Inch Gauge calls us to devote time to our usual vocations. The word "vocation" comes from the Latin "vocatio," meaning "a calling" or "summoning." This root word highlights the notion that work is not merely a means of earning a living but also a calling—a way of serving society and contributing to the greater good. In Freemasonry, we are encouraged to approach our vocations not just as a job but as a means of applying our talents for the betterment of ourselves and our community. This perspective turns everyday work into a sacred duty and reminds Masons that their vocations serve a higher purpose, aligned with the values of Freemasonry.

"Labor is worship, and a Mason is taught to view his vocation as an expression of the nobility of work, contributing to the greater good" (Claudy, 1931). This sentiment inspires Masons to approach their vocations with a sense of duty and purpose, ensuring that their efforts benefit society.

Refreshment and Repose: The Need for Balance

The final part of the day is reserved for "refreshment and repose." This is a crucial part of the Masonic teaching, underscoring the importance of balance in life. The roots of the word "repose" come from the Latin "repositus," meaning "to put back" or "to rest." This serves as a reminder that after hard work and service, rest is necessary for rejuvenation and renewal. Refreshment refers to the renewal of both mind and body—whether through physical rest, leisure activities, or mental relaxation. The pursuit of knowledge, self-improvement, and service must be balanced with times of repose to ensure that a Mason remains well-rounded, healthy, and prepared for the duties of the following day.

"By teaching the value of refreshment and repose, Freemasonry underscores that rest is essential to prepare the mind and body for further labor and service" (Oliver, 1823). In recognizing this need, Freemasons embrace a holistic approach to life, ensuring that no aspect of personal well-being is neglected.

General Henry "Hap" Arnold: A Model of Service and Duty

General Henry "Hap" Arnold, a Medal of Honor recipient and one of the most influential figures in the development of the U.S. Air Force, exemplifies the ideals reflected in the Twenty-Four Inch Gauge. As a Freemason and a military leader, Arnold demonstrated the balance between duty, vocation, and service to others. His commitment to the principles of service, both to his country and to his fellow citizens, mirrors the Masonic charge to dedicate time to our vocations and assist those in need.

"Freemasonry taught me discipline in balancing the demands of leadership, devotion to fraternity, and service to the nation" (Arnold, 1949). Arnold's Masonic service was as distinguished as his military career. He was known for his dedication to his Brethren and upheld the values of Freemasonry in every aspect of his life. His role as a leader during World War II required him to manage the tremendous responsibility of organizing and overseeing the U.S. Army Air Force. His ability to balance the demands of his military duties with his devotion to his Masonic obligations serves as a powerful example of how the Twenty-Four Inch Gauge can guide us in our personal and professional lives.

Through his actions, Arnold taught that service—whether to our country, to our fellow Masons, or to humanity—requires dedication and selflessness, qualities reflected in the teachings of the Gauge. As a Masonic leader and a Medal of Honor recipient, Arnold demonstrated that time, when divided with purpose, can be used for the highest good.

The Twenty-Four Inch Gauge is not merely a symbol; it is a practical teaching tool for Masons, guiding us to balance our time between service, work, and rest. By dividing our time into these three essential parts, we fulfill our duties as Masons and strive to become better men, better citizens, and better Brothers. The teachings of the Gauge are exemplified by figures like General Henry "Hap" Arnold, who managed to balance military service, Masonic duty, and personal well-being. His life serves as a modern reflection of the ancient principles Freemasonry upholds, reminding us of the importance of time management and the nobility of service. In doing so, we can all seek to live our lives more fully, with purpose and balance, in line with the teachings of the Craft.

The Twenty-Four Inch Gauge: A Masonic Metaphor for Time, Service, and Purpose

The timeless teachings of the Twenty-Four Inch Gauge offer practical guidance for navigating the complexities of daily life. Whether responding to the needs of a distressed brother, balancing professional demands with personal growth, or recognizing the importance of rest and renewal, these scenarios highlight the Gauge's wisdom in fostering harmony and purpose. By examining these real-life applications, Masons are invited to reflect on how they can embody the values of charity, balance, and self-care in their lives and within the Craft.

Reflections on the Craft: Questions for Deeper Understanding

- **Balancing Zeal and Wisdom:**
  - How can you integrate the qualities of zeal and wisdom, as exemplified by the Twenty-Four Inch Gauge, into your personal and Masonic endeavors?
- **Cycles of Growth and Reflection:**
  - The division of the day into parts for service, vocation, and rest symbolizes balance. How do you embrace these cycles in your life to maintain equilibrium between action and introspection?
- **Symbolism in Daily Life:**
  - How does the Twenty-Four Inch Gauge, as a Masonic symbol, inspire you to manage your time effectively and harmoniously in service to others, your vocation, and personal well-being?

The Common Gavel: A Symbol of Self-Refinement in Freemasonry

Discover the profound lessons of the Common Gavel and its call to self-refinement and moral excellence in the Masonic journey

The Common Gavel, an essential tool for operative Masons, serves a functional purpose in shaping stones to fit the precise specifications required for construction. This tool, used to break off the rough and superfluous parts of stones, is symbolic in its deeper application within Freemasonry. While its literal purpose is to prepare physical material for the building of structures, we, as Free and Accepted Masons, are taught to apply this tool symbolically—to refine our hearts and consciences by divesting them of the vices and superfluities that hinder our moral and spiritual growth.

The Latin root of the word "gavel" comes from the Old French "gavelle" or "gavel," which itself is derived from "gafol" meaning "a toll or payment." This connection evokes the idea that the gavel is not only a tool of labor but also a method of measurement and assessment, much like the toll we must pay to progress on our Masonic journey. In a more symbolic sense, it can be seen as a representation of the price we must pay in discipline and self-improvement as we work on our moral character. Just as the operative mason uses the gavel to remove imperfections from a stone, we too use it to chip away the rough and unworthy elements of ourselves that prevent us from fully realizing our potential.

In Freemasonry, the purpose of using the gavel extends far beyond physical labor. The gavel is employed as a tool of spiritual refinement. We are encouraged to remove from ourselves all that is impure and unrefined, allowing us to become living stones fit for the spiritual building of the

Temple not made with hands, eternal in the heavens. This process parallels the transformation of the rough ashlar into the perfect ashlar. The rough ashlar symbolizes a man in his raw state, full of vices and imperfections, while the perfect ashlar represents the goal—a well-formed man, morally refined and prepared for the higher purposes of life and Freemasonry.

The lessons of the Common Gavel resonate with the teachings of Freemasons like
Benjamin Franklin and Ralph Waldo Emerson. Benjamin Franklin emphasized the importance of continuous growth and self-improvement when he said, "Without continual growth and progress, such words as improvement, achievement, and success have no meaning" (Franklin, as cited in Grand Lodge of Pennsylvania, 2024). His perspective aligns perfectly with the symbolic use of the gavel, urging us to consistently refine our character.

Similarly, Ralph Waldo Emerson, also a Freemason, encapsulated the essence of self-determination and personal transformation with his words, "The only person you are destined to become is the person you decide to be" (Emerson, as cited in Grand Lodge of Massachusetts, 2024). This underscores the active and intentional effort required in the Masonic journey to remove imperfections and shape oneself into a better man and Mason.

The Common Gavel, therefore, is not just a symbol of physical labor but a profound emblem of the Masonic journey toward self-improvement. Through its metaphorical application, we are reminded to constantly strive for moral and spiritual refinement. The act of using the gavel to chip away the vices that cling to our hearts mirrors the work of a Mason chipping away at his own flaws, striving to become more virtuous, more aligned with the principles of Brotherly Love, Relief, and Truth.

George Washington reflected on the importance of personal transformation and moral refinement in his address at the Constitutional Convention when he declared, "Let us raise a standard to which the wise and the honest can repair; the rest is in the hands of God" (Washington, 1787). His words echo the Masonic call for self-improvement and the continuous effort to refine one's character, as symbolized by the Common Gavel. This tool reminds Masons that the journey of personal transformation—removing the rough and superfluous parts of our nature—is essential to achieving moral excellence and contributing to the construction of a harmonious world.

In conclusion, the Common Gavel is a powerful symbol of the work Masons are called to perform on themselves. By using the gavel to chip away the rough edges of our character, we fit ourselves as living stones for the eternal spiritual building. As we labor to improve our minds and hearts, we are reminded that this is the true and noble purpose of our Masonic journey. Through the symbolism of the gavel, Freemasons are encouraged to commit themselves to a life of discipline, personal growth, and the continual pursuit of moral perfection.

Reflections on the Craft: Questions for Deeper Understanding

- **The Symbolism of the Common Gavel:**
    - How does the symbolic use of the Common Gavel in removing moral imperfections inspire you to engage in self-refinement?
- **Cycles of Growth and Reflection:**

- Benjamin Franklin emphasized continual growth, while Ralph Waldo Emerson highlighted self-determination. How do these teachings inspire you to embrace cycles of self-reflection and personal transformation?
- **Applying Masonic Lessons:**
  - How do the lessons of the Common Gavel encourage you to actively pursue the principles of Brotherly Love, Relief, and Truth in your daily life?

Masonic Virtues: Temperance, Fortitude, Prudence, and Justice

Explore the timeless virtues of temperance, fortitude, prudence, and justice through the lens of Masonic teachings and ancient philosophy

In Freemasonry, the four Cardinal Virtues of temperance, fortitude, prudence, and justice form the foundation of the moral and ethical framework that guides a Mason's personal development. These virtues, deeply rooted in ancient philosophy and emphasized in the teachings of Plato and Aristotle, are integral to the Masonic journey toward self-improvement and societal contribution. By understanding and embodying these virtues, Masons strive for moral excellence and intellectual growth in their daily lives.

Defining the Cardinal Virtues

The four cardinal virtues—temperance, fortitude, prudence, and justice—are timeless principles first systematically outlined by Plato in The Republic. Plato described these virtues as the pillars of a just society and essential traits for individual character development:

- **Temperance**: Plato defined temperance as self-control and moderation, the ability to regulate one's desires and impulses to ensure that reason governs action. Temperance ensures that passions do not dominate one's life (Plato, trans. 2007).

- **Fortitude**: Fortitude, or courage, is the strength to face challenges and adversity without fear. Plato viewed it as the capacity to endure hardship while maintaining adherence to wisdom and justice (Plato, trans. 2007).

- **Prudence**: Prudence, or wisdom, allows individuals to make sound judgments and decisions. For Plato, prudence guided actions in accordance with reason, steering away from impulsivity (Plato, trans. 2007).

- **Justice**: Justice, the most important virtue according to Plato, ensures harmony within society and the individual. It balances the soul by enabling each part to fulfill its proper role, fostering unity and equity (Plato, trans. 2007).

These virtues are interconnected, each playing a vital role in achieving personal and societal harmony.

Aristotle and the "Golden Mean"

Aristotle expanded on Plato's teachings by introducing the concept of the "Golden Mean," which emphasizes balance between extremes as the essence of virtue. In Nicomachean Ethics, Aristotle argued that virtue lies in finding moderation between deficiency and excess. For example, courage (fortitude) exists between cowardice and recklessness, while temperance balances indulgence and self-denial (Aristotle, trans. 2009).

This philosophy of balance aligns with Masonic teachings, which encourage members to seek moderation and avoid extremes in all aspects of life. Masons apply the "Golden Mean" by cultivating habits that foster balance, ensuring their personal development aligns with the principles of Freemasonry.

Integrating Virtues into Masonic Teachings

Freemasonry incorporates these virtues into its moral teachings, emphasizing their practical application:

- **Temperance**: Benjamin Franklinchampion of self-discipline, encapsulated the importance of temperance: "Temperance puts wood on the fire, meal in the barrel, flour in the tub, money in the purse, credit in the country, content in the house, clothes on the back, and vigor in the body" (Franklin, 1750). In Masonic teachings, temperance extends beyond physical restraint to include emotional and moral self-control.

- **Fortitude**: General Douglas MacArthur, a military leader and Freemason, highlighted the significance of fortitude: "The soldier, above all other men, is required to practice the greatest act of religious training—sacrifice" (MacArthur, 1945). Fortitude in Freemasonry represents the moral courage to uphold principles despite adversity.

- **Prudence**: Johann Wolfgang von Goethe, a Freemason and literary giant, reflected on the challenge of prudence: "To think is easy. To act is difficult. To act as one thinks is the most difficult" (Goethe, 1806/2024). Prudence in Masonic practice emphasizes thoughtful decision-making guided by wisdom and ethics.

- **Justice**: Harry S. Truman, a Freemason and U.S. President, declared: "Justice remains the greatest power on earth. To that tremendous power alone will we submit" (Truman, 1948). Justice in Freemasonry signifies fairness, integrity, and the unwavering commitment to doing what is right.

Practical Application in Freemasonry

Masonic teachings encourage the daily practice of these virtues to foster personal and societal growth. By embracing temperance, fortitude, prudence, and justice, Masons strive to balance their responsibilities, maintain moral integrity, and contribute positively to their communities. These virtues are not abstract ideals but practical tools for living a virtuous life, grounded in the principles of balance and moderation.

The cardinal virtues—temperance, fortitude, prudence, and justice—serve as guiding principles for Freemasons, shaping their journey toward self-improvement and societal harmony. Drawing from the wisdom of Plato and Aristotle, as well as Masonic teachings, these virtues inspire Masons to live balanced, ethical, and meaningful lives. By integrating these virtues into their daily practice, Masons not only honor the traditions of the Craft but also contribute to building a better world for all.

Reflections on the Craft: Questions for Deeper Understanding

- **Harmony of Self-Control and Balance:**
  - How can the practice of temperance help you achieve a balance between your desires and your duties within your Masonic journey and personal life?
- **Endurance in Adversity:**
  - Reflect on a time when fortitude guided you through a challenge. How might this virtue empower you further to uphold the principles of the Craft in the face of difficulty?
- **Judicious Living and Ethical Actions:**

- How do prudence and justice guide your decision-making in both your Masonic duties and your broader interactions with society?

Brotherly Love, Relief, and Truth: The Three Principal Tenets of Freemasonry

Freemasonry: Building a better world through love, charity, and truth.

In Freemasonry, the principles of Brotherly Love, Relief, and Truth form the foundation of the Masonic journey. These tenets guide the actions of every Freemason and shape their character as they move through life, emphasizing moral virtue, mutual assistance, and the pursuit of truth. Although these values are central to Masonic philosophy, their meanings extend beyond the lodge room, reaching into the deeper traditions of humanity's ethical systems. These tenets, ancient in their origins, resonate across cultures, philosophies, and religious teachings, offering universal guidance for a virtuous life.

Brotherly Love: A Universal Concept of Unity

The tenet of Brotherly Love emphasizes the unity of humanity and mutual respect among individuals. As Psalm 133:1 declares: "Behold, how good and how pleasant it is for brethren to dwell together in unity" (KJV). This sentiment aligns seamlessly with the Masonic ideal of fostering harmony and fraternal affection. The verse underscores the beauty and divine approval of unity, making it a cornerstone of relationships both within and beyond the lodge.

Joseph Fort Newton, a distinguished Masonic scholar, theologian, and author of The Builders: A Story and Study of Freemasonry, reflects this principle: "Masonry was not made to divide men, but to unite them, leaving each man free to think his own thoughts and fashion his own system of ultimate truth. All its emphasis rests upon two extremely simple and profound principles, love of God and love of man" (Newton, 1922).

Definitions of Brotherly Love

Brotherly love encompasses philosophical, theological, and ethical dimensions, each contributing to its profound meaning. Philosophically, it is often described as *philia*, a Greek term signifying deep friendship and camaraderie, characterized by mutual goodwill and an enduring bond between equals. Theologically, brotherly love, referred to as philadelphia in Christian tradition, reflects God's love extended through individuals, as highlighted in John 13:34: "Love one another; as I have loved you." Ethically, brotherly love represents a commitment to treat others with compassion and dignity, recognizing the inherent worth of every individual. Together, these perspectives provide a comprehensive understanding of brotherly love as a foundational principle for personal and communal relationships.

Reconciling these definitions with Masonry reveals their shared essence: fostering mutual respect, compassion, and a commitment to community. In Masonry, Brotherly Love transcends individual differences, uniting members in the shared pursuit of virtue and truth.

Relief: More Than Just Monetary or Physical Aid

Relief in Freemasonry represents a holistic approach to alleviating suffering, encompassing financial, emotional, and spiritual support. Albert Pike, a lawyer, Confederate general, and Sovereign Grand Commander of the Scottish Rite Southern Jurisdiction, eloquently emphasized the enduring impact of selflessness: "What we have done for ourselves alone dies with us; what we have done for others and the world remains and is immortal" (Pike, 1899).

Eudaimonia: Human Flourishing and Relief

The Greek concept of eudaimonia—often translated as human flourishing—provides a profound philosophical foundation for Relief. Aristotle viewed eudaimonia as the highest human good, achieved through living virtuously and fostering the well-being of others. This perspective aligns with both Christian and Masonic philosophies, which emphasize the moral imperative to serve others.

In Christian teachings, eudaimonia resonates with the call to "love thy neighbor as thyself" (Matthew 22:39, KJV), advocating for a life of service, compassion, and charity. Similarly, Freemasonry promotes acts of Relief as essential to moral and spiritual development, urging members to offer aid in times of distress and to work toward the collective betterment of humanity.

Relief in Freemasonry, therefore, is not confined to material charity; it is a comprehensive ethic of care that seeks to address the physical, emotional, and spiritual needs of others.

Truth: The Foundation of Every Virtue

In Freemasonry, Truth is regarded as the foundation of all virtues, for without truth, the edifice of moral integrity collapses. This reverence for Truth aligns closely with Plato's concept of "forms," which he described as ideal and eternal archetypes existing beyond the physical world. Plato likely considered Truth to be one of these Forms—an unchanging, transcendent ideal that serves as the foundation for enlightenment. In his allegory of the cave, Plato portrays

Truth as the ultimate illumination, attainable only through reason and philosophical inquiry. Within this framework, the material world is seen as a shadow or imperfect reflection of higher realities, such as beauty, justice, and goodness, which, like Truth, transcend sensory perception and represent the immutable principles guiding human understanding and moral development.

Etymology of Truth

The word truth originates from the Old English trēowth, meaning "faithfulness" or "constancy," and is closely linked to the notion of trustworthiness. The Greek aletheia, meaning "unconcealment," reflects the idea of Truth as revealing the underlying reality of existence. In Latin, veritas underscores the alignment with facts and reality.

Truth as a Masonic Principle

Goethe poetically captured the challenge of Truth: "Truth is a torch but a tremendous one. That is why we hurry past it, shielding our eyes, indeed, in fear of getting burned." Truth, in Freemasonry, is both a spiritual and intellectual pursuit. It is the relentless quest to uncover deeper meanings, understand moral responsibilities, and align oneself with the eternal principles that govern existence.

By embracing Truth, Freemasons aim to cultivate virtues such as honesty, integrity, and wisdom, which serve as the foundation for personal growth and societal harmony.

Masonic Values in Action

The principles of Brotherly Love, Relief, and Truth offer a roadmap for Freemasons to navigate life with purpose and moral clarity. Brotherly Love teaches us to support one another; Relief encourages us to alleviate suffering in all its forms; and Truth inspires us to seek a higher understanding. Together, these tenets empower Freemasons to embody the ideals of ancient philosophy and modern ethical thought, contributing to the betterment of themselves and their communities.

Reflections on the Craft: Questions for Deeper Understanding

- **Brotherly Love in Action**
  - o How do you embody the principles of unity and mutual respect as expressed in Brotherly Love within your Masonic and personal relationships?
- **Holistic Relief**
  - o Albert Pike emphasized selflessness as immortal. How can you incorporate this holistic perspective on Relief—beyond material charity—into your daily interactions with others?
- **Truth as a Cornerstone**
  - o Plato described Truth as ultimate enlightenment. How does the pursuit of Truth inspire you to cultivate integrity, wisdom, and alignment with the universal principles of existence?

Fides: The Goddess of Oaths and Her Reflection of Masonic Values

Fides and Freemasonry: Bridging ancient traditions with modern values of trust and fidelity

In ancient Roman mythology, Fides was the goddess of trust, loyalty, and oaths. Revered as the protector of promises, Fides embodied the moral and social bonds that upheld Roman civilization. Her role was central to fostering trustworthiness and integrity in both private and public life. Fides was often depicted holding sacred symbols like a staff or sacrificial bowl, emphasizing her function as a guardian of covenants and contracts. She was closely associated with the right hand, a universal symbol of fidelity, strength, and the solemn act of swearing oaths. The Romans believed that invoking Fides during agreements would ensure that the commitments made were honored, reinforcing a culture of reliability and accountability.

The values embodied by Fides—trust, integrity, and loyalty—resonate deeply with the principles of Freemasonry. In Masonic rituals, the right hand holds a special significance, mirroring its association with oaths in Roman tradition. Freemasons swear solemn commitments, pledging their fidelity to the Craft, their brothers, and society. This connection to Fides provides a historical and moral foundation for understanding Masonic practices and their emphasis on trust and honor.

In the Latin language, the words fides and fideles offer a window into the nuanced world of trust and loyalty. At its core, fides represents an abstract concept—faith, trust, or belief. This singular noun captures the essence of trustworthiness and reliability, often invoked in the context of sacred duties, personal honor, or divine faith. The Romans saw fides as foundational to relationships, whether between individuals or between mortals and gods. For instance, the phrase Fides tua te servabit ("Your faith will save you") underscores the power of belief to provide strength and guidance, while Fides publica ("Public trust") highlights its role as a cornerstone of societal integrity. Grammatically, fides belongs to the fifth declension and stands as a feminine noun, embodying the timeless nature of trust as an ideal.

On the other hand, fideles brings the abstract into the tangible, referring to those who embody faithfulness. As the plural form of the adjective fidelis—"faithful" or "loyal"— fideles can function as a substantive noun to describe individuals or groups known for their steadfast devotion. Whether speaking of Fideles servi ("Faithful servants") or Sancti et fideles ("Saints and the faithful"), this word captures the living essence of loyalty in action. In Christian traditions, fideles has a special significance, often used to refer to believers or members of the church who remain unwavering in their faith. Grammatically versatile, fideles modifies nouns of any gender, reminding us that the spirit of loyalty transcends boundaries.

Together, these terms—fides as the principle of faith and fideles as those who live it—paint a rich picture of trust and loyalty as both an ideal and a lived experience. This connection is vividly echoed in the United States Marine Corps motto, Semper Fidelis ("Always Faithful"), which encapsulates an unwavering commitment to duty, brotherhood, and integrity. Just as the Romans revered fides as the foundation of trust, the Marines embody fideles as faithful individuals who uphold their values in action. In this way, the Marine Corps motto serves as a modern expression of ancient principles, bridging the timeless power of loyalty with the enduring dedication of those who live by it.

Samuel Nicholas: A Mason and a Marine

Samuel Nicholas, born in 1744 in Philadelphia, was a man whose life exemplified the virtues celebrated by Fides and upheld in Freemasonry. As the first commissioned officer of the Continental Marines—the precursor to the U.S. Marine Corps—Nicholas laid the groundwork for one of the most respected military institutions in the world. His leadership during the American Revolutionary War, particularly in the Battle of Nassau in 1776, demonstrated courage, strategic brilliance, and unwavering fidelity to his oath of service.

Nicholas was also a Freemason, and his Masonic principles undoubtedly influenced his actions both on and off the battlefield. His dual roles as a Mason and a Marine exemplified the interconnected values of loyalty, trust, and integrity. While Nicholas's contributions to the Marine Corps remain his most visible legacy, they are deeply rooted in the Masonic virtues he upheld throughout his life[1].

Fides and the Symbolism of the Right Hand

The goddess Fides was a symbol of the sacred trust formed by oaths, and her association with the right hand highlights its significance as a tool for swearing allegiance and affirming one's word. In Roman culture, the act of extending the right hand was not merely a gesture of greeting but a powerful symbol of fidelity. This tradition is mirrored in Freemasonry, where the right hand is central to Masonic rituals.

---

[1] The U.S. Marine Corps motto, "Semper Fidelis," meaning "Always Faithful," was officially adopted in 1883 during the commandancy of Colonel Charles McCawley. The motto encapsulates the enduring commitment and loyalty expected of all Marines, a value deeply aligned with Masonic principles of fidelity and honor (Marines.com).

When a Freemason swears an oath, it is done with the right hand raised or placed on a sacred text. This act signifies more than a promise; it represents a moral and ethical commitment to live by the values of integrity, trustworthiness, and honor. Fides, as the divine witness to oaths in Roman tradition, is reflected in the Masonic emphasis on keeping one's word and demonstrating reliability in all actions.

Fides and Masonic Values

Fides represents the moral ideals that are central to Freemasonry. In ancient Rome, her presence in legal and public ceremonies reinforced the sanctity of promises, ensuring that individuals honored their commitments. Similarly, Freemasons are bound by their oaths to uphold the principles of the Craft, act with integrity, and support their brothers and communities.

Freemasonry teaches that fidelity is essential to maintaining the bonds of trust within the Fraternity and society. A Mason's word is considered inviolable, a sacred bond that echoes the teachings of Fides. Just as the Romans invoked Fides to protect their agreements, Freemasons use the symbolism of the right hand and sacred oaths to affirm their loyalty to the principles of charity, brotherhood, and moral rectitude.

The Right Hand: A Symbol of Strength and Fidelity

The right hand has long been associated with trust, strength, and loyalty. In Freemasonry, it represents the physical and moral act of committing oneself to the values of the Craft. This gesture of fidelity ties directly to the Roman tradition of invoking Fides. The act of swearing an oath with the right hand is more than a ritual; it is a declaration of one's dedication to living a life of honor and responsibility.

Nicholas's life as a Marine and a Mason exemplifies these principles. His leadership in the Continental Marines, marked by unwavering loyalty to his men and his mission, reflects the values of Fides in action. His ability to inspire trust and maintain fidelity to his oath of service demonstrates how the virtues of Fides and Freemasonry converge in practice.

The Role of Fides in the Masonic Journey

The influence of Fides extends beyond the individual. In Freemasonry, fidelity is the cornerstone of the Fraternity's strength and unity. Masons are taught to honor their commitments, whether to their brothers, their families, or society. The shared covenant formed during Masonic rituals mirrors the sacred bonds protected by Fides in Roman culture.

This emphasis on trustworthiness and loyalty fosters a sense of collective responsibility among Freemasons. Just as Fides safeguarded the integrity of Roman society, Masonic principles aim to build a better, more reliable world. By embodying the virtues of Fides, Masons contribute to a culture of honor and mutual respect that transcends their individual lives.

Fides, the Roman goddess of trust and oaths, serves as a powerful symbol of the values upheld in Freemasonry. Her association with the right hand and the sanctity of promises reflects the Masonic commitment to fidelity, integrity, and loyalty. Samuel Nicholas, as a Marine and a Mason, demonstrated these principles through his life of service and leadership, embodying the ideals of Fides in action.

Freemasonry's rituals, symbols, and teachings echo the ancient reverence for Fides, reminding Masons of their responsibility to uphold truth and trust in all aspects of life. By honoring the virtues of Fides, Freemasons strengthen the bonds of their Fraternity and contribute to the creation of a more trustworthy and virtuous society.

Reflections on the Craft: Questions for Deeper Understanding

- **The Role of Fidelity in Personal Growth:**
  - How can the values of Fides—trust, integrity, and loyalty—be mirrored in your Masonic commitments to enhance personal and fraternal relationships?
- **Symbolism and the Right Hand:**
  - Considering the shared symbolism of the right hand in Roman and Masonic traditions, how does this physical gesture deepen the ethical commitments you make within the Craft?
- **Historical Influences and Modern Practice:**
  - How does understanding the historical significance of Fides inspire you to uphold the ideals of reliability and accountability in both your Masonic journey and daily life?

Obligation in Freemasonry: Its Meaning, Roots, and the Arts, Parts, and Points of Masonic Ritual

Freemasonry: Binding words and actions through the timeless power of obligation.

In Freemasonry, the concept of "obligation" holds a deep and sacred significance. It refers to the solemn vow or promise that a candidate makes during the initiation ceremonies, as well as the ongoing commitments each Mason undertakes throughout his journey in the Craft. Understanding the word "obligation" itself, and its Latin roots, can provide a deeper insight into its profound meaning and importance in Freemasonry.

The Word Obligation: Meaning and Latin Roots

The term "obligation" is derived from the Latin word "obligatio," which means "to bind" or "to tie." The root word, "obligare," is composed of two parts: "ob," meaning "to" or "toward," and "ligare," meaning "to bind" or "to tie." This gives the word a powerful connotation—one who is obligated is bound to something, often by a promise or a solemn vow. As noted by the Alberta Masonic Library, "The term 'obligation' encompasses a binding promise, connecting the candidate with the moral and ethical framework of the Craft" (Alberta Masonic Library, n.d.).

In the Masonic context, an obligation is not just a verbal promise but a binding commitment to act with integrity, uphold the principles of the Craft, and live according to its moral teachings. The very act of taking an obligation in Freemasonry symbolizes a powerful, personal decision to be bound by the laws, traditions, and values of the Fraternity. It is, as Freemasonry researcher Brent Morris explains, "a transformative act that binds a man's words, actions, and spirit to the principles of brotherhood and virtue" (Morris, 2015).

This binding commitment is not only a personal promise to uphold Masonic principles but also a contract with the fraternity and the larger moral order that Freemasonry seeks to create. It is an agreement to live by a code of ethics and contribute positively to the welfare of society. As the Grand Lodge of Alberta suggests, the Masonic obligation "transcends individual promises and becomes a shared covenant of moral and spiritual unity" (Grand Lodge of Alberta, 2020).

The Arts, Parts, and Points in Masonic Ritual

Masonic ritual is rich with symbolism and profound lessons, which are conveyed through what are called the Arts, Parts, and Points of each degree. These elements help to create a well-rounded understanding of the obligations and responsibilities that Masons undertake.

The Arts: What the Candidate is Taught

In Freemasonry, the Arts represent the physical and verbal methods of recognition, along with the teachings associated with each degree. They are the practical aspects of ritual that the candidate learns during his initiation. "The Arts teach candidates the importance of self-discipline and the power of symbolic actions in moral development" (Mackey, 1921). These include physical gestures, verbal responses, and modes of address that are integral to Masonic tradition.

Each degree of Freemasonry involves specific instructions on how to carry oneself, step in the Lodge, and address the Master and other officers. These customs are deeply symbolic and represent the candidate's journey of moral and spiritual growth.

The Parts: The Ritual and Symbolism

The Parts of a degree refer to the specific elements of the ritual, including the ceremonial actions, the symbolic teachings, and the ritual's moral lessons. These Parts involve physical acts, such as taking an oath or performing symbolic gestures, designed to instill profound moral and ethical understanding.

"The Parts of a Masonic degree serve as a roadmap for the candidate, guiding them through lessons of morality, charity, and self-improvement," explains Stevenson (2012). Tools like the square and compass are employed as symbols of moral rectitude and personal growth.

The Points: The Contractual Obligations of the Obligation

Finally, the Points refer to the contractual aspects of the obligation itself. These are the binding elements—the promises made by the candidate that form the core of the Masonic commitment. The Points emphasize personal integrity, mutual aid, and the upholding of the Fraternity's moral and ethical teachings.

"Through the Points, the candidate pledges his fidelity to the Craft and his brothers, reaffirming the collective responsibility inherent in Freemasonry," states Morris (2015). This contractual nature reinforces the sacred bond formed during initiation.

The concept of obligation in Freemasonry is deeply rooted in the history and symbolic structure of the Craft. The Latin roots of the word obligation underscore its significance as a binding commitment to the principles of Freemasonry. Through the Arts, Parts, and Points of Masonic ritual, the candidate is taught not only how to act but also the deeper moral and ethical lessons that will guide them on their journey. These elements combine to form the foundation of the Masonic experience—one of personal development, moral commitment, and a lasting bond with the Brotherhood. The obligation is a powerful act, an expression of trust, and a pledge to live by the highest standards of integrity, reflecting the profound responsibility of every Mason to uphold the values and ideals of the Craft.

The Power of Obligation in Masonic Ritual:

- **Moral Commitment and Brotherhood:**
    - o How does the concept of obligation as a binding moral and ethical promise inspire you to deepen your commitment to the values and traditions of Freemasonry?
- **Symbolic Significance of the Arts, Parts, and Points:**
    - o In what ways do the Arts, Parts, and Points of Masonic ritual provide a framework for understanding your responsibilities and fostering personal growth within the Craft?
- **Living the Masonic Covenant Daily:**
    - o How can the lessons of obligation, particularly its shared and transformative nature, guide your interactions and responsibilities within your lodge and the broader community?

The Story of Ruth: A Tale of Commitment, Legacy, and Masonic Values

Ruth and Boaz: A biblical tale of commitment and redemption, echoed in Masonic values.

The story of Ruth in the Bible is a powerful narrative about loyalty, commitment, and the enduring strength of familial ties. It unfolds in the Book of Ruth, set during the period of the Judges, a time of turmoil and uncertainty in Israel's history. Ruth, a Moabite woman, is widowed and left to care for her mother-in-law, Naomi. In a moment of profound personal sacrifice, Ruth decides to leave her homeland and return with Naomi to Bethlehem, vowing to remain by her side no matter the cost. Her famous declaration, "Where you go I will go, and where you stay I will stay" (Ruth 1:16, New International Version), embodies the essence of commitment (Hubbard, 1988).

A pivotal moment in the story occurs when Ruth seeks to marry Boaz, a relative of Naomi, to secure her family's legacy. According to Jewish tradition, a kinsman-redeemer could marry a widow to continue the deceased husband's family line. Boaz, being a man of virtue and integrity, agrees to marry Ruth, but only after a legal matter is settled. The closer relative (who had the first right of redemption) refuses to marry Ruth. Boaz then officially takes on the role of redeemer, sealing the agreement in front of witnesses by a symbolic gesture: he removes his sandal and gives it to the elders (Ruth 4:7–10, NIV; Younger, 2002).

The Significance of the Shoe Removal

The act of removing a shoe as a symbol of commitment is deeply significant. In ancient Israel, the removal of the shoe was a legal gesture, signifying the transfer of a right or ownership. When Boaz removes his shoe, it is a public demonstration of his willingness to redeem Ruth and marry her, ensuring the continuation of her husband's family line (Hubbard, 1988). This act reflects both personal and communal responsibility, reinforcing the importance of fulfilling one's obligations for the greater good.

This symbolic act aligns closely with Masonic values, where commitment to duty, moral integrity, and the importance of upholding one's word are fundamental principles. Freemasonry teaches the importance of fulfilling one's obligations, whether to the Fraternity, family, or society (Hamill, 2010). The symbolic removal of the shoe as a mark of commitment resonates with the Masonic teachings of duty, loyalty, and responsibility—virtues that Masons strive to embody in their personal and communal lives.

Boaz: The Great Grandfather of Solomon

Boaz is more than just a redeemer in the story of Ruth; he plays a pivotal role in the lineage that leads to King David and ultimately to Solomon, the builder of the First Temple in Jerusalem. The Book of Ruth concludes with a genealogy that traces the lineage of David back to Boaz and Ruth, positioning Boaz as a foundational figure in Israel's royal lineage (Hubbard, 1988; Younger, 2002). This connection between Boaz and Solomon is significant not only for its historical context but also for its symbolic importance in Masonic tradition.

The Pillar of Boaz in Solomon's Temple

The connection between Boaz and the construction of Solomon's Temple is particularly notable in Freemasonry. In the building of the Temple, two great pillars were erected at the entrance: one named Jachin and the other named Boaz.

These pillars symbolize strength, stability, and support. The pillar of Boaz represents the strength and stability of the royal lineage that comes through the House of David, as well as the enduring moral virtues upheld by those in the lineage (Hamill, 2010; Morris, 2006).

For Masons, the pillar of Boaz serves as a reminder of the importance of maintaining one's commitment to the ideals of the Craft, just as Boaz demonstrated his commitment to redeeming Ruth and ensuring the continuation of her family line. The Masonic connection to Boaz extends beyond the symbolism of the pillars to the virtues of dedication, integrity, and duty, all of which are foundational to Freemasonry (Hamill, 2010).

How the Story of Ruth Demonstrates Masonic Values

The story of Ruth and Boaz aligns with key Masonic values. At its core, the story emphasizes the importance of commitment to one's obligations, whether to family, community, or the greater good. Boaz's decision to redeem Ruth is a model of integrity and responsibility, qualities that Freemasons seek to embody in their lives (Morris, 2006). Moreover, the story illustrates virtues such as kindness, charity, and loyalty—values integral to Freemasonry. Ruth's loyalty to Naomi, Boaz's generosity and sense of justice, and the eventual reward of their actions in the form of their descendant, King David, underscore the significance of living virtuously and honoring one's promises (Hubbard, 1988).

Freemasons are called upon to contribute to the betterment of society and uphold moral and ethical standards that transcend generations. Just as Boaz's actions had a lasting impact on the lineage of Israel, the actions of Freemasons, driven by virtue, integrity, and commitment to service, continue to strengthen communities (Hamill, 2010). The story of Ruth, with its themes of loyalty, redemption, and moral duty, serves as a timeless reminder of the importance of living by one's principles, fulfilling one's responsibilities, and honoring commitments that shape the course of history.

The story of Ruth and Boaz is a beautiful narrative of love, duty, and redemption, and a powerful allegory for the values that Freemasonry upholds. The act of removing the shoe symbolizes a commitment that is both personal and public, paralleling the Masonic ideals of loyalty, duty, and responsibility. Boaz, as the great-grandfather of Solomon, serves as a bridge between the past and the future, a symbol of strength and integrity. His legacy, reflected in the royal line of David, is honored through the symbolism of the pillars in Solomon's Temple, making it a poignant reminder of the Masonic virtues that continue to guide Masons in their personal and communal lives.

Reflections on the Craft: Questions for Deeper Understanding

- **Commitment in Personal Growth:**
  - Ruth's unwavering commitment to Naomi and Boaz's adherence to the principle of kinsman-redeemer reflect profound personal and communal responsibility. How can you, as a Mason, deepen your commitment to supporting others within your lodge and community?
- **Symbolism in Actions:**
  - The act of Boaz removing his sandal represents a public and legal commitment. In what ways can symbolic acts in your Masonic journey remind you to uphold integrity and responsibility in daily life?

- **Legacy and Lineage:**
  - The legacy of Ruth and Boaz ultimately leads to King Solomon and the construction of the Temple. How does this connection inspire you to consider the long-term impact of your Masonic contributions and personal actions on future generations?

The Roman Eagle: Symbol of Power and Sovereignty

Freemasonry: Connecting ancient symbols with the timeless pursuit of wisdom and virtue.

The Roman Eagle, or Aquila, was the emblem of the Roman Empire, symbolizing strength, authority, and imperial power. In Roman times, the eagle was associated with Jupiter, the king of the gods, and was used as a symbol of divine authority and unity. The eagle appeared on military standards, coins, and official emblems, representing the emperor's sovereignty and the cohesion of the Roman people (Roberts, 2008).

In Freemasonry, the Roman Eagle serves as a reminder of the qualities Masons should embody: strength, wisdom, and the pursuit of excellence. Its association with soaring above earthly concerns aligns with the Masonic aspiration to rise above materialism and gain insight into both material and spiritual realms. According to Mackey (1921), "The eagle's flight symbolizes the intellectual elevation that Masons strive to achieve through the practice of their craft." This symbolism connects to the Masonic apron, which serves as a constant reminder of the moral and intellectual elevation Masons are encouraged to pursue.

The Golden Fleece: A Symbol of Adventure and Virtue

The Golden Fleece, central to the myth of Jason and the Argonauts, is one of the oldest and most revered symbols in European tradition, representing heroism, perseverance, and the pursuit of an ideal. According to Greek mythology, the Fleece originated from a divine, golden-haired ram sent by the gods to rescue Phrixus and Helle from their cruel stepmother. After safely delivering Phrixus to Colchis, the ram was sacrificed to Zeus, and its fleece was hung in a sacred grove, guarded by a fearsome dragon. Jason's quest for the Golden Fleece was not merely a mission of adventure but a test of unwavering resolve, courage, and virtue, as the treasure could only be claimed by those possessing these qualities (Stevenson, 2012).

Accompanied by the Argonauts, Jason faced countless trials, including clashing rocks, hostile warriors, and other supernatural challenges. His success hinged on the aid of Medea, the daughter of King Aeëtes of Colchis, who used her magic to help Jason complete impossible tasks and ultimately subdue the dragon guarding the Fleece. Beyond its mythological significance, the Golden Fleece has been interpreted as a symbol of power, kingship, and prosperity, embodying the divine right to rule and the pursuit of moral and spiritual excellence.

Historically, some scholars suggest the legend may have been inspired by real practices in the Caucasus region, where fleece was used to trap gold particles from river water. In Freemasonry, the Golden Fleece holds a place of honor as a symbol of purity, nobility, and the relentless pursuit of higher ideals. Jason's legendary quest continues to resonate as a timeless allegory for courage, self-discovery, and the transformative power of overcoming great challenges.

In Freemasonry, the Golden Fleece represents high moral standards and the pursuit of virtue. As Mackey (1921) explains, "The Golden Fleece is emblematic of the Mason's quest for moral and spiritual perfection." This symbolism resonates with the Masonic apron, which represents the commitment to living a life of honor and responsibility. Just as Jason had to prove his worth to obtain the Fleece, so too must Masons demonstrate their moral integrity through their actions while wearing the apron.

The Order of the Star and Garter: Symbolizing Chivalric Virtues

The Order of the Star and Garter, established in 1348 by King Edward III, is one of the most prestigious orders of knighthood. It symbolizes the highest virtues of chivalry, including loyalty, honor, and duty. The star and garter represent light and service, reflecting the ideals of purity and dedication expected of those who belong to the order (Hamill, 2010).

For Freemasons, the Order of the Star and Garter mirrors Masonic values of brotherhood, virtue, and charity. As Hamill (2010) notes, "The Order's commitment to service and honor parallels the Mason's dedication to upholding the ethical standards of the Craft." Similarly, the Masonic apron is a symbol of a Mason's dedication to a virtuous life. The apron's role as a marker of integrity and moral commitment is akin to the star and garter's representation of the highest chivalric ideals.

The Masonic Apron: A Symbol of Virtue, Service, and Legacy

The Masonic apron is one of the most significant symbols in Freemasonry, representing the moral and spiritual progress that Masons strive to achieve. It serves as a reminder of the commitment to live a life of virtue and honor, drawing parallels with the Roman Eagle, the Golden Fleece, and the Order of the Star and Garter. The apron represents the journey toward enlightenment and moral excellence (Morris, 2006).

The Roman Eagle's connection to wisdom, the Golden Fleece's association with virtue, and the Order of the Star and Garter's emphasis on service and integrity are all reflected in the Masonic apron. As Mackey (1921) describes, "The apron symbolizes the Mason's ongoing commitment to moral discipline, intellectual growth, and service to humanity." Just as the Golden Fleece was the reward for Jason's heroic journey, the Masonic apron represents the reward of a life dedicated to truth, service, and brotherly love.

The Roman Eagle, the Golden Fleece, and the Order of the Star and Garter carry significant historical and philosophical meanings that align with the values and teachings of Freemasonry. These symbols, combined with the Masonic apron, remind us of the virtues and commitments that Freemasonry seeks to instill in its members. Through these ancient and noble symbols, Masons are reminded to strive for wisdom, virtue, service, and integrity, both within the Lodge and in their everyday lives. The Masonic apron, as a symbol of these values, becomes a constant reminder of the high ideals and moral path that Freemasons are called to walk.

Reflections on the Craft: Questions for Deeper Understanding

- **Soaring to Wisdom:**
    - The Roman Eagle represents strength, wisdom, and the pursuit of excellence. How can the symbol of the Eagle inspire Masons to rise above life's challenges and focus on intellectual and spiritual growth?
- **Ancient Power, Modern Meaning:**
    - The Roman Eagle once unified the Roman people under its emblem of sovereignty and authority. How can Masons apply the Eagle's

lesson of unity and strength to foster harmony within their lodges and communities?

- **Masonic Symbols in Practice:**
  - o Mackey emphasized the Eagle's flight as a metaphor for intellectual elevation. How do symbols like the Roman Eagle and the Masonic apron serve as tools to remind us of our commitments to continuous moral and intellectual self-improvement?

The Rough Ashlar, Perfect Ashlar, and Trestle board: The Path of Transformation in Freemasonry

Freemasonry: Transforming lives, one stone at a time.

In Freemasonry, symbols play a pivotal role in conveying profound lessons and guiding the personal growth of each Brother. Three symbols central to this journey are the Rough Ashlar, the Perfect Ashlar, and the Trestleboard. These symbols represent stages in a Mason's moral and personal development and encapsulate the transformative process that every Freemason undergoes. To truly understand their significance, it is essential to explore their meanings, historical roots, and roles within the Masonic framework of self-improvement.

The Latin Roots: Rough Ashlar and Perfect Ashlar

The word "Ashlar" derives from the Latin term axilla, meaning "a smooth, square stone." In Freemasonry, the Rough Ashlar represents an unshaped stone, symbolizing the unrefined character of a man before engaging in self-improvement. Conversely, the Perfect Ashlar is a polished stone, representing the ideal state of moral and spiritual refinement that Masons strive to achieve (Mackey, 1921).

The transformation from Rough Ashlar to Perfect Ashlar is not about attaining flawlessness but about personal progress. As Stevenson (2012) explains, "The Rough Ashlar represents potential and possibility, while the Perfect Ashlar embodies the fulfillment of that potential through deliberate and disciplined action." This journey mirrors the personal development of Masons, who seek to refine their character and align their actions with Masonic principles.

The Rough Ashlar and Guarding the West Gate

In operative Masonry, the selection of stones from the quarry was a critical task. Masons chose stones based on their potential to be shaped and fitted for a specific purpose in the building. Stones that were cracked, flawed, or unsuitable for refinement were left behind, as no amount of labor could make them fit for the Master Builder's plan. This practice provides a profound commentary on the Masonic principle of "guarding the West Gate."

Freemasonry selects good men—men with potential—from the "quarry of life" to be shaped into better men. This principle emphasizes that the Fraternity does not attempt to reform those who are inherently unsuitable for the moral and ethical ideals of the Craft. As Mackey (1921) observes, "The Rough Ashlar is not just any stone but one chosen for its potential to be shaped and polished into a Perfect Ashlar." This selection process underscores the importance of admitting men of sound character and integrity into the Brotherhood.

Guarding the West Gate ensures that only those with the capacity for self-improvement, dedication to the Craft, and commitment to its principles are allowed to join. This practice reflects the operative Mason's wisdom in selecting only those stones that could contribute to the structure's strength and beauty. Similarly, speculative Freemasonry seeks to build a moral and virtuous edifice by admitting men who embody the potential to uphold its values.

The Trestleboard: The Blueprint for Transformation

The Trestleboard serves as a metaphorical blueprint for the Mason's moral and spiritual development. Traditionally, the Trestleboard was the surface upon which a Master Builder would draft architectural designs. In Freemasonry, it symbolizes the plans and goals that guide a Mason's transformation from Rough Ashlar to Perfect Ashlar (Hamill, 2010).

Without the Trestleboard, the process of refinement lacks direction. It provides the framework within which the Mason works to align his actions with the virtues of wisdom, strength, and beauty. As Mackey (1921) notes, "The Trestleboard is the roadmap for a Mason's journey, offering clarity and purpose to the labor of self-improvement." Furthermore, the Trestleboard evolves as the Mason gains experience and wisdom, reflecting his ongoing journey toward moral excellence.

The Symbolic Relationship: From Rough to Perfect

The Rough Ashlar, Perfect Ashlar, and Trestleboard form a triad of symbols that guide a Mason's journey of self-improvement. The Rough Ashlar represents the beginning of the journey, full of potential but requiring refinement. The Perfect Ashlar symbolizes the ultimate goal: a man who embodies virtue, wisdom, and moral discipline. The Trestleboard acts as the guiding plan, ensuring that progress is intentional and aligned with Masonic principles (Hubbard, 1988).

These symbols are considered movable jewels in Freemasonry because they travel with the individual Mason as he progresses. Unlike the immovable jewels of the lodge, these symbols are personal, reflecting the unique journey of each Brother. As Morris (2006) explains, "The transformation from Rough Ashlar to Perfect Ashlar is not fixed or uniform but is shaped by each Mason's experiences and efforts."

The Journey of Transformation: A Lifetime of Work

The progression from Rough Ashlar to Perfect Ashlar is a lifelong journey. Just as a stone is shaped gradually, so too is a Mason's character developed over time. The Trestleboard serves as a guide, helping the Mason establish goals and track his progress. However, it is the Mason's responsibility to take the necessary actions to achieve those goals.

Freemasonry emphasizes the process of striving rather than immediate perfection. Benjamin Franklin, a prominent Freemason, observed, "Human felicity is produced not so much by great pieces of good fortune that seldom happen, as by little advantages that occur every day" (Franklin, 1771). This sentiment reflects the Masonic belief in gradual improvement, where each small step contributes to the Mason's ultimate transformation.

The Continuous Transformation

The symbols of the Rough Ashlar, Perfect Ashlar, and Trestleboard encapsulate the essence of the Masonic journey. They represent the stages of growth and transformation that every Mason undergoes as he strives to refine his character and align himself with the divine plan. The Rough Ashlar is a symbol of potential, the Perfect Ashlar represents the desired state of moral and spiritual excellence, and the Trestleboard provides the roadmap for achieving these goals.

The Rough Ashlar also serves as a reminder of the importance of guarding the West Gate. Freemasonry, like ancient stone masonry, selects only those with the potential for refinement and excellence, ensuring the integrity of the Craft. By adhering to these principles, Freemasonry continues to encourage men to pursue their highest potential, following the timeless blueprint provided by the teachings of the Craft.

Reflections on the Craft: Questions for Deeper Understanding

- **Personal Transformation Through Symbolism:**
  - o How does the metaphorical journey from the Rough Ashlar to the Perfect Ashlar inspire you to refine your character and align your actions with the principles of Freemasonry in daily life?
- **Planning and Progress with the Trestleboard**:
  - o In what ways can the Trestleboard serve as a guiding framework for your moral and spiritual growth, ensuring that each step you take is purposeful and reflective of your aspirations as a Mason?
- **Guarding the West Gate with Integrity:**
  - o How do the principles of selection and potential, as symbolized by the Rough Ashlar and the practice of guarding the West Gate, influence your understanding of admitting worthy individuals into the Brotherhood?

The Point within a Circle: A Masonic Symbol of Self-Discipline, Moral Conduct, and Spiritual Guidance

The Point Within a Circle: A Masonic guide to balance, morality, and the cyclical journey of enlightenment.

In the rich tradition of Freemasonry, few symbols are as significant or as widely recognized as the "Point Within a Circle." This emblem, displayed prominently in Masonic lodges and teachings, represents not only the individual Brother but also the moral and spiritual boundaries that guide his actions. The Point Within a Circle serves as a reminder that, while each Mason is an individual, he is part of a larger whole, constantly bound by the ethical framework of Freemasonry.

The Symbol of the Point Within a Circle

At its core, the Point Within a Circle consists of a central point surrounded by a circle, often flanked by two parallel perpendicular lines. The point represents the individual Mason, while the circle defines the moral boundaries within which his actions and conduct must remain. This symbol emphasizes self-regulation and ethical behavior, as noted by Mackey (1921): "The Point Within a Circle teaches a Brother to circumscribe his passions and keep them within due bounds" (p. 123).

The two perpendicular lines are traditionally associated with the patron saints of Freemasonry, Saint John the Baptist and Saint John the Evangelist. These lines, along with the circle, signify balance and support, guiding the Mason through both zeal and wisdom. The association with these two Saints aligns Freemasonry with the cyclical nature of time and enlightenment, as their feast days coincide with the summer and winter solstices, marking turning points in the natural and spiritual year (Hamill, 2010).

A Point, Circle, and Line: The Basis of All Creation

The geometrical simplicity of a point, circle, and line forms the foundation of many symbolic and practical systems, including Freemasonry. According to Pythagorean philosophy, the point represents the origin of matter and unity, while the circle symbolizes infinity and completeness. In Freemasonry, this aligns with the idea that all creation stems from a single point, reflecting interconnectedness and moral unity (Stevenson, 2012).

The inclusion of the point, circle, and line in Masonic teachings reinforces the idea that the Mason's journey begins with personal accountability (the point) and expands to universal understanding (the circle), all guided by moral principles (the line). As Roberts (2008) explains, "The Point Within a Circle is not merely a diagram but a representation of the balance between individuality and universal moral truth" (p. 78).

The Moral Boundaries of the Circle

The circle, as a boundary, represents the moral limits within which a Mason must operate. It serves as a safeguard, ensuring that his passions and actions remain aligned with the core principles of Freemasonry: Brotherly Love, Relief, and Truth. As Pike (1871) eloquently stated, "To circumscribe and keep passions within due bounds is to live in harmony with the divine law, which is the ultimate purpose of the Craft" (p. 85).

This moral boundary is not restrictive but protective, encouraging Masons to act with integrity while pursuing self-improvement. The Point Within a Circle is a constant reminder of this balance, emphasizing that freedom must be tempered with responsibility and ethical conduct.

The Circle in Esoteric Traditions

The circle is a profound symbol in various esoteric traditions, representing concepts such as eternity, unity, and the cyclical nature of existence. Its unbroken, continuous form signifies infinity and the interconnectedness of all things, embodying the idea of life without beginning or end. In many spiritual practices, the circle delineates sacred space, serving as a boundary between the physical and spiritual realms during rituals. This usage underscores its role in symbolizing wholeness and protection (Mastermind Content, n.d.).

Beyond its representation of infinity and sacred space, the circle also embodies the concept of cyclical time, reflecting the natural cycles of birth, life, death, and rebirth. This symbolism is prevalent in various cultural and spiritual contexts, where the circle is used to illustrate the perpetual cycles inherent in the universe. Additionally, in sacred geometry, the circle is considered the most fundamental shape, symbolizing the unity and interconnectedness of all creation (Thoth Adan, n.d.). These multifaceted interpretations highlight the circle's enduring significance as a symbol of profound esoteric concepts across diverse traditions.

The Influence of the Solstices: Symbolism of Life's Highs and Lows

The association of the Point Within a Circle with the summer and winter solstices adds depth to its symbolism. The summer solstice, marked by the feast day of Saint John the Baptist, represents growth and enlightenment, while the winter solstice, associated with Saint John the Evangelist, symbolizes reflection and renewal. These solstices mirror the cycles of life and learning, emphasizing that a Mason's journey is one of continual transformation (Hamill, 2010).

By integrating the solstices into its symbolism, Freemasonry teaches that life involves periods of light and darkness, progress and introspection. The Point Within a Circle reminds Masons to remain steadfast during these cycles, adhering to the moral framework provided by the Craft.

A Spiritual and Philosophical Journey: The Point Within the Circle

The Point Within a Circle is more than just a symbol; it represents a Mason's spiritual and philosophical journey. The central point reflects the individual Mason, who must remain true to the moral boundaries defined by the circle. The perpendicular lines provide support, symbolizing the balance between zeal and wisdom, action and reflection. Together, these elements encourage Masons to seek balance, maintain integrity, and strive for continuous self-improvement.

This journey aligns with Freemasonry's broader teachings on self-discipline and moral conduct. As Mackey (1921) noted, "The Point Within a Circle encapsulates the balance between individuality and collective responsibility, guiding the Mason to harmonize his personal actions with the greater good" (p. 126).

The Path of Light

The Point Within a Circle encapsulates the moral and spiritual boundaries that define a Mason's journey toward self-improvement and enlightenment. By adhering to the principles represented by this symbol, Masons are reminded to balance zeal and wisdom, stay within the moral boundaries of the Craft, and embrace the cyclical nature of growth and reflection. The Point Within a Circle is not just a symbol—it is a guide, ensuring that each Mason remains true to the teachings of Freemasonry and continues on the path toward becoming a better man.

Reflections on the Craft: Questions for Deeper Understanding

- **Personal Boundaries and Moral Conduct**
    - How does the concept of the Point Within a Circle inspire you to examine the boundaries you set in your own life to ensure your actions align with Masonic principles of Brotherly Love, Relief, and Truth?

- **Balance Between Zeal and Wisdom**
    - The two perpendicular lines in the symbol represent Saint John the Baptist (zeal) and Saint John the Evangelist (wisdom). How do you strive to balance passionate action with thoughtful reflection in your Masonic journey?

- **Symbolism and the Solstices**
    - The association of the Point Within a Circle with the solstices emphasizes cycles of growth and renewal. How have periods of light (growth) and darkness (reflection) shaped your personal and Masonic development?

The Blazing Star in Freemasonry: Its Shape, Location, Meaning, and Cultural Connections

Illuminating Truth and Harmony: The Blazing Star in Freemasonry as a Symbol of Divine Wisdom and Universal Enlightenment.

The Blazing Star is one of the most prominent and revered symbols in Freemasonry. Often depicted as a radiant star or pentagram, it represents divine light, enlightenment, and the pursuit of moral and spiritual truth. This essay delves into the geometric and symbolic intricacies of the Blazing Star, its location and significance within the Lodge, and its cross-cultural connections, particularly with Sirius, the Dog Star.

The Shape and Geometric Representation

In Freemasonry, the Blazing Star is most commonly depicted as a pentagram or a star with radiant beams emanating from its center. The pentagram holds deep symbolic meaning, representing balance, harmony, and perfection. Each point of the star aligns with one of the core Masonic virtues: Wisdom, Strength, Beauty, Justice, and Mercy. These virtues guide the Mason's moral and spiritual journey, reflecting the harmony between human conduct and higher principles (Stewart, 2011).

The geometry of the star is rooted in ancient traditions. The pentagram, revered by the Pythagoreans, symbolized the unity of the five elements—earth, air, fire, water, and spirit—which together formed the foundation of existence. This geometric precision and philosophical depth align seamlessly with Freemasonry's emphasis on moral balance and enlightenment (Jones, 2005).

The Location and Meaning within the Lodge

In the Masonic Lodge, the Blazing Star is positioned prominently in the East, symbolizing the rising sun and the light of divine wisdom. It is often associated with the Master of the Lodge, who serves as the source of guidance and enlightenment for the brethren. The star's rays, extending outward, symbolize the dissemination of knowledge and moral clarity, serving as a constant reminder of the Mason's duty to seek truth and share it with the world (Hamill & Gilbert, 1994).

The Blazing Star also signifies the omnipresence of the divine, emphasizing that Masons operate under the watchful eye of a higher power. Its central position in the Lodge underscores its importance as a guiding symbol for moral and spiritual advancement.

Cross-Cultural Representations of the Blazing Star

The significance of the Blazing Star extends beyond Freemasonry, finding parallels in various cultures. In ancient Egyptian mythology, Sirius, also known as the Dog Star, held immense importance. Sirius was associated with the goddess Isis and marked the annual flooding of the Nile, a life-sustaining event for the civilization. This connection to fertility, renewal, and guidance mirrors the Masonic interpretation of the Blazing Star as a symbol of enlightenment and spiritual growth (Clark, 2007).

In Greek and Roman traditions, Sirius was considered the brightest star in the night sky and was believed to bring both blessings and challenges. The term "Dog Days of Summer" originates from its heliacal rising[2], which marked the hottest part of the year. The star's brilliance and influence on human life further echo its symbolic resonance in Freemasonry (Allen, 1899).

The Star's Universal Symbolism

The Blazing Star's symbolism is universal, transcending cultures and epochs. In Freemasonry, it represents the divine light guiding individuals toward moral and spiritual excellence. In other cultures, such as the ancient Near East and indigenous traditions, the star often symbolized guidance, hope, and the omnipresence of the divine. These shared meanings underscore the star's enduring significance as a beacon of enlightenment and renewal (Baigent & Leigh, 1989).

The Blazing Star in Freemasonry is a profound symbol of divine guidance, moral virtues, and the quest for truth. Its geometric perfection and prominent location within the Lodge emphasize its role as a source of enlightenment for Masons. Beyond Freemasonry, the star's associations with Sirius and other cultural interpretations highlight its universal appeal as a symbol of renewal and illumination. By understanding the multifaceted meanings of the Blazing

---

[2]The heliacal rising of a star occurs when it first becomes visible above the eastern horizon at dawn, shortly before sunrise, after having been hidden from view by the Sun's glare. This astronomical phenomenon was significant in many ancient cultures, as it often marked the beginning of seasons or agricultural cycles. For example, the heliacal rising of Sirius, the brightest star in the sky, was crucial to ancient Egyptians, signaling the annual flooding of the Nile and the start of their New Year. This event is dependent on the observer's latitude and the star's declination, making its timing vary by location.

Star, Masons and non-Masons alike can appreciate its timeless significance.

Reflections on the Craft: Questions for Deeper Understanding

- **Harmonizing Virtues Through Geometry:**
    - How does the geometric representation of the Blazing Star, particularly as a pentagram, inspire you to balance the five Masonic virtues—Wisdom, Strength, Beauty, Justice, and Mercy—in your life?
- **Cultural Parallels and Personal Growth:**
    - The Blazing Star has parallels with Sirius in ancient Egyptian and Greco-Roman traditions. How can understanding these cross-cultural connections deepen your appreciation of its Masonic symbolism?
- **Guidance and Leadership:**
    - Positioned in the East within the Lodge, the Blazing Star represents divine wisdom and the role of the Master. How can you embody these principles of enlightenment and guidance in your personal or professional leadership roles?

Ethical Leadership Through Lens of the Entered Apprentice Degree

Applying timeless Masonic teachings to lead with integrity and purpose in the modern age

The Entered Apprentice Degree, the foundational step in Freemasonry, offers timeless principles that can shape ethical leadership in the complexities of the modern world. This degree introduces essential symbols, teachings, and virtues that encourage personal growth, moral discipline, and a commitment to justice—qualities essential for effective and ethical leadership. By applying the lessons of the Entered Apprentice, individuals can cultivate integrity, inspire trust, and lead with a vision rooted in moral excellence.

The Foundation of Ethical Leadership: Self-Improvement and Reflection

The Entered Apprentice Degree begins with a call to self-reflection and self-improvement. The Common Gavel, one of the working tools introduced, symbolizes the effort required to remove the rough edges of one's character. This metaphor urges leaders to refine their actions and intentions, ensuring that their decisions align with ethical principles. Ethical leadership begins with an unyielding commitment to personal integrity, and the Common Gavel reminds leaders to continually assess and improve their moral compass.

The ritualistic emphasis on the Entered Apprentice's journey also highlights the importance of humility. Before assuming positions of power or influence, ethical leaders must recognize their limitations and commit to learning and growth. This foundation ensures that their leadership is not self-serving but focused on uplifting others and achieving collective goals.

Balancing Zeal and Wisdom in Leadership

The Entered Apprentice Degree teaches the necessity of balancing zeal with wisdom. Zeal, represented by fervent commitment and enthusiasm, must be tempered by thoughtful reflection and measured actions. Ethical leaders draw upon this balance to inspire their teams without losing sight of the bigger picture or the long-term consequences of their decisions.

In a modern context, this balance is critical for navigating complex ethical dilemmas. Leaders must exhibit passion and drive to achieve their objectives, but they must also demonstrate restraint and prudence, ensuring that their actions uphold fairness, justice, and the well-being of all stakeholders.

Guiding Actions with the Three Great Lights

Central to the Entered Apprentice Degree are the Three Great Lights—the Holy Bible, the Square, and the Compass. These symbols serve as guiding principles for ethical decision-making:

The Holy Bible: Represents spiritual wisdom and moral guidance, urging leaders to ground their actions in universal principles of justice and compassion. In a modern context, this means ensuring that every decision is made with fairness and empathy, considering the impact on individuals and communities. Ethical leaders can draw on spiritual or philosophical texts to reinforce their commitment to integrity and service. For instance, incorporating principles of kindness and accountability into corporate policies or community initiatives demonstrates the practical application of this guidance.

The Square: Symbolizes fairness and virtue, reminding leaders to act justly and equitably in all interactions. In today's world, leaders can use the Square as a metaphorical tool to evaluate the fairness of their policies, decisions, and practices. Whether in the workplace, community, or public service, aligning actions with the principles of equity and justice fosters trust and collaboration. Leaders can also create systems that ensure transparency and accountability, such as regular reviews of their conduct and the implementation of ethical standards within their organizations.

The Compass: Represents self-discipline and the boundaries of ethical behavior, encouraging leaders to circumscribe their actions within the bounds of integrity. Modern leaders can apply this by setting clear boundaries for themselves and their teams, ensuring that goals are pursued with honesty and respect. The Compass also serves as a reminder to prioritize personal and professional growth while maintaining ethical consistency. Leaders might consider regular reflection on their motives and decisions, using the Compass as a guide to align their actions with their values and commitments.

Together, these tools provide a framework for ethical leadership, guiding leaders to make decisions that are not only effective but also morally sound.

Unity and Inclusivity: Lessons from Brotherly Love

Brotherly Love, a principal tenet of Freemasonry, emphasizes the value of unity, mutual respect, and inclusivity. Ethical leadership in the modern world requires a commitment to these values, fostering an environment where diverse perspectives are valued and collaboration thrives. The Entered Apprentice learns that strength lies in harmony, and this principle can be applied by leaders to build cohesive teams and equitable communities.

In today's interconnected world, inclusivity is more than a moral ideal; it is a practical necessity for fostering innovation, trust, and cooperation. Leaders can translate Brotherly Love into inclusivity by creating spaces where diverse voices are not only heard but actively valued. This requires intentional practices such as diverse hiring, equitable decision-making, and fostering open dialogue. Inclusivity also means addressing unconscious biases and ensuring that policies and practices do not exclude or disadvantage any group. By embodying Brotherly Love, leaders demonstrate a commitment to shared humanity, encouraging collaboration and unity across cultural, social, and ideological boundaries.

When inclusivity is prioritized, teams thrive, and individuals feel empowered to contribute their unique strengths. Ethical leaders who practice inclusivity build stronger, more resilient organizations and communities, paving the way for lasting harmony and success.

Service and Responsibility: The Twenty-Four Inch Gauge

The Twenty-Four Inch Gauge, another working tool of the Entered Apprentice, teaches the importance of time management and the division of one's day into periods for service, vocation, and refreshment. Ethical leaders must balance their professional responsibilities with their commitments to others and their own well-being. This balance ensures that leaders remain effective, grounded, and capable of making sound decisions.

Leadership is inherently a service-oriented role, and the Twenty-Four Inch Gauge reminds leaders of their duty to prioritize the needs of their communities and organizations. By dedicating time to service and self-care, leaders can sustain their ability to inspire and guide others.

The Pursuit of Truth and Justice

The Entered Apprentice Degree underscores the importance of truth and justice as foundational elements of ethical leadership. Leaders must be unwavering in their pursuit of truth, ensuring transparency and honesty in their actions. They must also uphold justice, making decisions that are fair and equitable, even in the face of adversity.

The emphasis on truth and justice equips leaders to navigate challenges with integrity, fostering trust and respect among their teams and stakeholders. These values serve as the bedrock of ethical leadership, guiding leaders to act with courage and conviction in the face of moral dilemmas.

Building Ethical Leadership Through Masonic Principles

The lessons of the Entered Apprentice Degree provide a timeless blueprint for ethical leadership in the modern world. By committing to self-improvement, balancing zeal with wisdom, embracing the guidance of the Three Great Lights, fostering unity through Brotherly Love, managing time effectively, and pursuing truth and justice, leaders can inspire trust, drive meaningful change, and uphold the highest standards of integrity.

In a world often marked by complexity and uncertainty, the teachings of the Entered Apprentice offer clarity and purpose. By embodying these principles, leaders can not only achieve personal success but also contribute to the betterment of society, leaving a legacy of ethical leadership that reflects the enduring values of Freemasonry.

Reflections on the Craft: Questions for Deeper Understanding

- **Balancing Faith and Empathy:**
  - How can the guidance of the Holy Bible inspire you to integrate fairness and compassion into your leadership decisions?
- **Measuring Fairness:**
  - In what ways can you use the Square to ensure that your actions and policies promote equity and trust within your organization or community?
- **Discipline in Leadership:**
  - How does the Compass's focus on ethical boundaries and self-discipline guide you to align your leadership actions with your core values?

The Journey of the Fellow craft: Growth, Wisdom, and Mastery

The Supremacy of Love: Insights from 1 Corinthians 13 and Freemasonry

Exploring how love (agape) serves as the foundation for spiritual and Masonic life.

The thirteenth chapter of 1 Corinthians, often referred to as the "Love Chapter," is one of the most profound explorations of love (*agape*[3]) in Christian scripture. Written by the Apostle Paul, this passage is nestled within a discussion of spiritual gifts, highlighting the supreme importance of love as the cornerstone of ethical and spiritual behavior. Similarly, Freemasonry holds love, particularly in the form of charity, as a guiding principle for individual growth and fraternity. By examining the roots of key terms and their implications, this essay seeks to uncover the shared ethos of love between these two traditions: Christianity and Freemasonry.

The Necessity of Love: A Foundation for Action

---

[3] The term agape (Greek: ἀγάπη) refers to a profound, unconditional love that transcends personal or romantic attachment, often described as selfless and altruistic. In classical Greek, agape denoted a general sense of affection or goodwill, but in Christian theology, it took on a deeper spiritual meaning. Agape became associated with divine love, the love God has for humanity, and the love individuals are called to show to one another as part of a moral and spiritual ideal.

This concept is famously explored in the New Testament, such as in 1 Corinthians 13, where agape is described as patient, kind, and enduring beyond all things. Unlike eros (romantic love) or philia (brotherly love), agape is unconditional and universal, encompassing love for all beings regardless of merit. It serves as a central ethical and spiritual principle in many faith traditions and philosophies, encouraging selflessness, compassion, and forgiveness.

Paul begins by emphasizing the futility of gifts like prophecy, tongues, and knowledge without love. The term agape—translated as love—stems from Greek roots indicating unconditional, selfless affection and a commitment to the well-being of others. Paul writes, "If I speak in the tongues of men or of angels, but do not have love, I am only a resounding gong or a clanging cymbal" (1 Corinthians 13:1, NIV). In Freemasonry, love similarly acts as the "cement of the fraternity," binding members together in mutual respect and service. As historian Albert Mackey noted, "Charity, in the Masonic sense, is not mere almsgiving but that virtue that leads to a sincere and disinterested love for all mankind" (Mackey, 1865).

The absence of love renders any spiritual or fraternal action hollow, no matter how impressive. Both Paul's and Masonic teachings warn against the perils of vanity, stressing that actions must be rooted in genuine care for others.

The Characteristics of Love: A Code for Life

Paul's description of love includes patience, kindness, humility, and forgiveness, qualities essential for maintaining harmony. He writes that love "is not self-seeking, it is not easily angered, it keeps no record of wrongs" (1 Corinthians 13:5, NIV). These virtues resonate deeply with Freemasonry, where symbols like the Square and Compasses remind members to act justly and temper personal desires for the benefit of others.

The Greek root of *makrothymia* (patience) suggests endurance and long-suffering, reflecting a deliberate choice to remain steadfast in adversity. In his analysis of Masonic rituals,

Arturo de Hoyos (2010) highlights how patience and forbearance are indispensable for building a harmonious lodge, complementing Paul's ideals.

The Supremacy of Love: An Eternal Virtue

Paul concludes the chapter by proclaiming the eternal nature of love, contrasting it with the temporary nature of spiritual gifts. He states, "And now these three remain: faith, hope, and love. But the greatest of these is love" (1 Corinthians 13:13, NIV). This triad forms the cornerstone of Masonic teachings, as charity (agape) is considered the "greatest of the three, for it extends beyond the grave" (Mackey, 1865).

Freemasonry's emphasis on charity underscores its eternal relevance. Through acts of service and kindness, members embody this enduring virtue, reinforcing its timeless significance in both spiritual and communal contexts.

Love in Action: Reflections for Today

Both Paul's message and Masonic teachings challenge us to move beyond superficial displays of virtue. As Paul admonishes the Corinthians, love must be practiced in deeds, not merely words. Freemasonry echoes this call, urging members to "walk uprightly in their several stations" (Anderson, 1723). The transformative power of love lies in its ability to unify, inspire, and guide individuals toward higher ideals.

Reflections on the Craft: Questions for Deeper Understanding

- **Love as the Ultimate Virtue:**

- o How can you integrate Paul's vision of selfless love into your daily life and Masonic practice?
- **Symbolism and Ethics:**
  - o How do Masonic symbols like the Square and Compasses help you embody the characteristics of love, such as patience and humility?
- **Eternal Legacy:**
  - o In what ways can your actions today reflect the enduring nature of love as described by Paul and celebrated in Masonic teachings?

Understanding Key Concepts in Communication and Symbolism

Unlock the deeper meanings of Freemasonry by mastering the tools of moral science: signify, inculcate, allegory, symbol, and emblem.

Freemasonry is a rich and intricate system of moral science, teaching profound lessons through symbolism, allegory, and ritual. Understanding the precise definitions of terms like signify, inculcate, allegory, symbol, and emblem is essential for unlocking the deeper meanings embedded in Masonic teachings. These concepts are the building blocks of Masonic philosophy, providing the framework through which members explore moral and ethical principles.

Signify: Conveying Meaning in Moral Teachings

The term signify originates from the Latin *significare*, meaning "to make known" or "to indicate." In Freemasonry, to signify is to convey meaning through actions, words, and symbols. This act of indication is central to the rituals and tools of the Craft, which are designed to signify greater truths. For example, the act of wearing the Masonic Apron signifies purity of conduct and the labor required to achieve moral excellence.

Understanding what is signified in Masonic symbols and rituals allows members to grasp the moral lessons they teach. The concept of signifying ties the physical and symbolic together, ensuring that outward acts reflect inner virtues.

Inculcate: Instilling Masonic Principles

Derived from the Latin inculcare, meaning "to tread on" or "impress upon," inculcate refers to the persistent and deliberate teaching of values and ideas. Freemasonry inculcates virtues like brotherly love, relief, and truth through repetition and ritual, ensuring these principles are deeply embedded in the hearts of its members. For example, the repetition of oaths and charges during Masonic ceremonies serves to inculcate the ideals of fidelity, charity, and morality.

Inculcation in Freemasonry goes beyond simple instruction. It involves creating habits of thought and action that align with the teachings of the Craft, fostering continuous moral growth.

Allegory: Unveiling Deeper Truths

An allegory is a narrative or representation that conveys hidden meanings, often related to moral, philosophical, or spiritual themes. Freemasonry is rich in allegories, which simplify complex ideas into relatable stories. For example, the allegory of the building of King Solomon's Temple teaches lessons about the construction of one's moral and spiritual character.

In Freemasonry, allegories are not mere stories; they are instructional tools that reveal layers of meaning upon reflection. Recognizing and interpreting these allegories requires an understanding of their structure and purpose, enabling Masons to uncover profound truths.

Symbol: Universal Keys to Understanding

A symbol is not merely a sign or representation; it is a living entity that bridges the conscious and unconscious mind, inviting the individual to explore its depths. In Freemasonry, symbols act as vessels of profound meaning, distilling intricate truths into potent archetypes that resonate on both personal and collective levels. They are not confined to rational explanation but instead stimulate the psyche to engage with the mystery of their significance.

Take, for instance, the Square and Compass. These symbols, while outwardly simple, embody the archetypal principles of morality and self-discipline, urging members to align their actions with higher ethical ideals. Such symbols are universal in their essence, drawing upon the shared unconscious of humanity, yet their interpretation is profoundly personal. Each Mason's engagement with these images becomes a transformative dialogue, connecting the individual to the timeless principles of Freemasonry while simultaneously fostering personal growth and deeper self-awareness.

Emblem: Fixed Representations of Masonic Identity

An emblem is a crystallized expression of meaning, a fixed representation that embodies the conscious values and ideals of an institution or tradition. Unlike the fluid, transformative nature of a symbol, an emblem stands as a defined marker of identity and purpose. In Freemasonry, emblems serve as outward manifestations of inner principles, anchoring the collective consciousness of the Craft in tangible forms.

The Masonic Apron, for instance, is an emblem of purity and moral integrity, a visible testament to the ethical commitments each Mason undertakes. While its meaning is consciously understood and universally agreed upon within the fraternity, its power lies in its ability to evoke a deeper sense of duty and connection. Through engaging with these emblems, the Mason reaffirms not only their dedication to the Craft but also their alignment with the shared ideals that transcend the individual, grounding the journey of self-improvement within a collective framework

The Role of Definitions in the Moral Science of Freemasonry

Freemasonry, often described as a "moral science," relies on precision and clarity in understanding its teachings. Central to this discipline is the accurate comprehension of terms such as signify, inculcate, allegory, symbol, and emblem. These definitions are not merely academic; they are essential to the deeper engagement and practice of Masonic principles.

Clear definitions provide a foundation for interpreting the layers of meaning inherent in Freemasonry's teachings. Without this precision, rituals and symbols could be misunderstood, leading to diluted or incorrect interpretations. Furthermore, these definitions create a framework for deeper engagement with Masonic philosophy. They allow members to go beyond the surface, extracting profound insights that enrich their understanding of the Craft.

This clarity also has a practical dimension, enabling Masons to translate the symbolic teachings of Freemasonry into ethical actions in their daily lives. By understanding the terms that underpin their lessons, members can more effectively embody the principles they are sworn to uphold. Definitions also serve as a bridge to Freemasonry's historical and philosophical roots, connecting individual members to the traditions of the Craft and fostering a sense of continuity and belonging.

Moreover, precise knowledge elevates the experience of Masonic rituals, imbuing them with greater significance and impact. When members fully grasp the meanings behind the words and symbols, the rituals become more than formalities—they transform into profound, shared experiences that reinforce the moral and spiritual aims of Freemasonry. In this way, definitions play an indispensable role in ensuring that Freemasonry remains a disciplined and meaningful journey for all who seek its light.

Conclusion

In Freemasonry, understanding key concepts such as signify, inculcate, allegory, symbol, and emblem is not merely an academic exercise but a transformative process that deepens a Mason's engagement with the Craft. These terms provide the foundation for interpreting the moral, philosophical, and spiritual lessons embedded in Masonic teachings, guiding members in their journey toward self-improvement. By mastering these concepts, Masons unlock the ability to move beyond surface interpretations, extracting richer insights and applying them to their lives with purpose and clarity. This comprehension also bridges the individual to the collective, connecting each Mason to the historical and philosophical roots of Freemasonry while fostering a sense of unity and shared mission.

Ultimately, Freemasonry's reliance on precise definitions underscores its nature as a "moral science." It enables Masons to interpret rituals with greater significance, translating symbolic teachings into ethical actions that honor the timeless principles of Brotherly Love, Relief, and Truth. Whether through the fluidity of symbols or the fixed identity of emblems, these tools enrich the spiritual and intellectual journey of every Mason, ensuring that the Craft remains not only relevant but profoundly impactful for generations to come. Through this understanding, Freemasonry continues to inspire personal growth, moral reflection, and a deeper connection to the universal truths it represents.

Reflections on the Craft: Questions for Deeper Understanding

- **Conveying Meaning Through Action:**
  - How can understanding the concept of "signify" enhance the depth and authenticity of your Mas.onic practices and daily interactions?
- **Embedding Principles Through Repetition:**
  - In what ways do rituals and the inculcation of values through repetition influence your moral growth within and beyond the Lodge?
- **Engaging with Allegory and Symbolism:**
  - How do the Masonic use of allegory, symbols, and emblems deepen your understanding of ethical principles, and how might you apply these teachings to navigate challenges in your personal life?

Guardians of the Craft: The Masonic Lexicon and its Symbolic Lessons

Explore the meanings behind cowans, eavesdroppers, cable tow, and hoodwinked, and discover the timeless lessons they offer to Freemasons and the world alike.

Freemasonry, one of the world's oldest and most enduring fraternal organizations, is rich with symbolic language that conveys profound ethical and philosophical teachings. Among the many terms used within Masonic rituals and teachings are "cowans," "eavesdroppers," "cable tow," and "hoodwinked." Each carries historical significance and deep symbolism, encapsulating values central to the Masonic tradition.

Cowans and Eavesdroppers: Guarding the Secrets of the Craft

Historically, a cowan referred to an unskilled worker or one who attempted to practice masonry without proper qualifications. Within Freemasonry, the term symbolizes those unprepared or unauthorized to access the Craft's teachings. "The cowan represents the outsider, someone who has not undergone the requisite moral and intellectual preparation" (Steinmetz, 2007). This term serves as a reminder to members to value knowledge, integrity, and the discipline required to truly belong to the fraternity.

Similarly, eavesdroppers are individuals who attempt to gain unauthorized access to Masonic secrets. This term derives from the literal act of listening under the eaves of buildings. In Masonic lore, the eavesdropper warns of the necessity to guard the Craft's teachings from those who seek knowledge without proper understanding or initiation.

The Cable Tow: A Symbol of Commitment

The cable tow is a rope symbolically used during Masonic initiation ceremonies. It physically represents the obligations and responsibilities a Mason undertakes. "In the ritual, the cable tow binds the initiate to the fraternity, signifying his commitment to its principles and his readiness to serve" (Jones, 2013). Beyond its ceremonial use, the cable tow symbolizes the ties that bind a Mason to his duties, both within the fraternity and to his community. It underscores the value of accountability and the importance of upholding one's word.

Hoodwinked: From Darkness to Light

To be hoodwinked in Masonic initiation involves the use of a blindfold. This act symbolizes ignorance, emphasizing the aspirant's journey from darkness (a lack of knowledge) to light (enlightenment and understanding). "The hoodwink represents trust in the process of learning and the necessity of humility in seeking knowledge" (Harrison, 2016). For the initiate, the hoodwink is not just a physical covering but a metaphor for the moral and intellectual awakening that comes through Masonic teachings.

Synthesis of Teachings

Together, these terms encapsulate the essence of Freemasonry: vigilance against unwarranted access (cowans and eavesdroppers), steadfast commitment (cable tow), and the transformative journey of personal growth (hoodwinked). They remind Masons of the values of integrity, dedication, and the pursuit of enlightenment—lessons that resonate far beyond the Lodge.

Reflections on the Craft: Questions for Deeper Understanding

- **The Value of Preparedness:**
    - How do the lessons of cowans and eavesdroppers encourage you to guard your personal values and ensure readiness before undertaking significant commitments?
- **Commitment in Action:**
    - The cable tow represents ties of duty and responsibility. In what ways can you strengthen your commitments to both personal and communal obligations?
- **The Path to Enlightenment:**
    - The hoodwink emphasizes the transformative power of learning. How can you embrace humility and trust in your own journey from ignorance to understanding?

The Plumb: A Tool of Precision and Integrity

Explore the profound significance of the plumb in operative masonry, scripture, literature, and Freemasonry's moral philosophy.

The plumb, a simple yet indispensable tool, has served as a cornerstone of both practical and moral alignment throughout history. While its physical purpose in ensuring verticality in construction is well-known, its metaphorical applications extend far beyond the operative trade. From scriptural symbolism to Masonic teachings, the plumb remains a powerful emblem of justice, integrity, and upright living.

The Plumb in Operative Masonry

Historically, operative masons have relied on the plumb to ensure structures stand true. This tool, consisting of a weighted bob and a string, creates a perfect vertical line, vital for the stability of edifices such as cathedrals and pyramids. "The plumb line's utility," as noted by architectural historian Curl (2006), "was paramount in the construction of towering Gothic cathedrals, ensuring their spires reached heavenward without deviation" (p. 124). Its precision made it an essential instrument for builders across civilizations.

Operative masons utilized the plumb alongside other tools like the square and level, ensuring percesion and balance in their work. The consistent application of these tools underscored the masons' commitment to craftsmanship and precision, qualities that transcend their physical labor.

Biblical References to the Plumb

The plumb's symbolism is deeply rooted in biblical scripture. In Amos 7:7-8 (New International Version), God declares, "I am setting a plumb line among my people Israel; I will spare them no longer." This passage uses the plumb line as a metaphor for divine justice and moral rectitude. Similarly, Isaiah 28:17 states, "I will make justice the measuring line and righteousness the plumb line."

Biblical scholars like Wright (2001) emphasize that the plumb line represents God's unwavering standards of righteousness: "The imagery of the plumb line underscores an expectation of ethical alignment and moral uprightness" (p. 98). These references resonate with Masonic values, which emphasize living in alignment with universal truths and ethical principles.

Religious and Philosophical Significance

The plumb's symbolic resonance extends to religious and philosophical teachings. In Christian theology, it represents the need for spiritual integrity—a life lived in alignment with God's will. The tool's emphasis on uprightness parallels the moral obligations espoused by many religious traditions.

Philosophically, the plumb embodies principles of balance and rectitude, serving as a guide for upright moral and ethical conduct. Aristotle's doctrine of the "golden mean" aligns conceptually with the plumb, advocating a life of balance between extremes (Lear, 1988). For example, courage lies between the extremes of recklessness and cowardice, just as the plumb ensures a structure remains upright by keeping it centered between opposing forces. This symbolism finds practical expression in rituals and teachings across cultures, offering a tangible reminder of the importance of integrity and the pursuit of harmony in both personal actions and societal responsibilities. The plumb, therefore, is not merely a tool but a profound metaphor for maintaining equilibrium in thought and behavior

The Plumb in Popular Literature

In literature, the plumb frequently symbolizes truth and fairness. In Nathaniel Hawthorne's The House of the Seven Gables, the concept of moral uprightness is likened to structural soundness, a theme reinforced by metaphors of construction. "The plumb line," as Hawthorne suggests, "is a guide not only for walls but for human conscience" (Hawthorne, 1851, p. 62).

Modern literature continues to use the plumb as a metaphor for navigating life's challenges with honesty and precision. Its enduring relevance underscores its role as a universal symbol of ethical and practical alignment.

The Plumb as a Masonic Metaphor

For Freemasons, the plumb is more than a tool; it is a moral compass. It teaches members to walk uprightly in their dealings with others and to maintain integrity in all aspects of life. As illustrated in Masonic rituals, the plumb serves as a constant reminder of the importance of living in alignment with moral and ethical truths.

Masonic teachings integrate the plumb with other working tools, such as the square and compasses, to form a cohesive moral philosophy. The tools collectively guide Masons in their pursuit of self-improvement and their commitment to upholding justice, charity, and fraternity.

Reflections on the Craft: Questions for Deeper Understanding

- **Alignment in Life and Work:**
  - How can the concept of a plumb line help you assess and realign your own life's priorities?
- **Moral Uprightness:**
  - In what ways do Masonic teachings on the plumb inspire you to uphold justice and integrity?
- **Symbolism and Practice:**
  - How does the integration of symbolic tools like the plumb enrich your understanding of Masonic philosophy?

The Square: Symbolism, Practice, and Influence in Freemasonry

A cornerstone of ethical alignment, the square embodies operative skill and moral rectitude in equal measure

The square is one of the most ubiquitous and vital symbols in Freemasonry, embodying a profound connection between the operative and speculative dimensions of the Craft. Historically, biblically, and symbolically, the square bridges technical expertise, ethical alignment, and philosophical inquiry, serving as a cornerstone for Masonic thought and action. This essay examines the square through multiple lenses, including its use in operative masonry, biblical references, religious significance, literary appearances, and its metaphorical application in Freemasonry. Additionally, it explores how the square's two sides symbolize the dual responsibility to align actions with at least two of the four cardinal virtues: prudence, temperance, fortitude, and justice.

Operative Masonry and the Square

In operative masonry, the square was a fundamental tool for ensuring precision and integrity in construction. It served to measure and guide the layout of stones, ensuring right angles essential for building stability and aesthetics. A vivid historical example is the construction of medieval cathedrals, where stonemasons used squares to align the stones of grand structures like Notre Dame and Canterbury Cathedral. Without this tool, the symmetry and durability of these edifices would be unattainable.

Moreover, operative masons saw the square as a marker of their craftsmanship. It ensured that their work conformed to the geometric principles that underpinned their trade, symbolizing their commitment to quality and excellence. The square's association with moral rectitude likely stems from this practical utility—a well-aligned square was both a literal and metaphorical measure of a mason's skill and character.

Biblical References to the Square

The square's presence in biblical texts reinforces its symbolic resonance. While not always mentioned explicitly, the concept of squaring aligns closely with themes of justice, fairness, and integrity. In the construction of Solomon's Temple, as described in 1 Kings 6:7, the precision required—stones perfectly prepared before being brought to the site—echoes the square's role in ensuring perfect alignment and balance[4]. The temple itself, often considered the archetype for Masonic symbolism, was constructed with tools and methods that adhered to principles represented by the square.

Another reference lies in Isaiah 28:17: "I will make justice the measuring line, and righteousness the plumb line." While the plumb line is more prominent here, the interplay of measuring instruments implies the square's presence in the pursuit of ethical foundations.

In Ezekiel 40–47, the prophet's vision of the new temple emphasizes symmetry and alignment, further underscoring the moral and architectural significance of precision, often symbolized by the square[5].

---

[4] 1 Kings 6:7 "And the house, when it was in building, was built of stone made ready before it was brought thither: so that there was neither hammer nor axe nor any tool of iron heard in the house, while it was in building."

[5] Ezekiel 40–47 refers to a significant section of the prophetic book of Ezekiel in the Bible, detailing a vision of the restored Temple, its measurements, rituals, and the renewed land of Israel. This vision

Religious and Ethical Significance of the Square

The square has profound religious significance, often symbolizing righteousness, justice, and moral alignment. In Christian theology, it reflects the adherence to divine principles—a life lived "in square" with God's will. This symbolism extends into Masonic thought, where the square becomes a moral guide.

For Freemasons, the square is not merely a tool but a standard for conduct. It teaches members to "square" their actions by the precepts of morality and virtue, aligning their lives with the Masonic principles of brotherly love, relief, and truth. It represents the golden rule: treating others fairly and maintaining honesty in one's dealings.

By considering the square's two sides, a Mason may also analyze whether his actions align with at least two of the four cardinal virtues. For example:

- Does an action display both fortitude and prudence?

- Is an action just as well as temperate?

- Can the action be squared with the principles of both courage and fairness?

This dual analysis encourages Masons to uphold multiple ethical dimensions simultaneously.

The Square in Literature

---

is often called the "Vision of the New Temple" or "Ezekiel's Temple Vision" and spans chapters 40–48, but chapters 40–47 focus on the Temple itself and its immediate surroundings.

The square's metaphorical significance has also penetrated popular literature, often symbolizing fairness, stability, and moral rectitude. For instance, in Shakespeare's plays, the square frequently appears as a metaphor for justice and equity. In Measure for Measure, the Duke's reference to aligning "lives by a square" underscores its association with fairness and order.

The square also appears in allegorical works, such as John Bunyan's The Pilgrim's Progress, where it embodies ethical steadfastness and alignment with divine principles.

The Square as a Metaphor in Freemasonry

Within Freemasonry, the square transcends its operative origins to become a central moral and philosophical metaphor. The phrase "to act on the square" signifies living honestly and maintaining fairness in all dealings. It is a reminder to Freemasons that their actions should align with the Craft's values.

The square is also an emblem of equality and fraternity. By representing a shared standard, it unites Masons across the world, fostering a sense of brotherhood grounded in mutual respect and shared principles. In the ritual, the square is often paired with the compasses, symbolizing the balance between earthly and divine pursuits.

Reflections on the Craft: Questions for Deeper Understanding

- **Balancing Craftsmanship and Morality:**
  - How can the operative utility of the square inspire speculative Masons to integrate craftsmanship and ethical living in their daily lives?

- **Biblical Foundations of the Square:**
    - How do the biblical references to alignment and justice enhance your understanding of the square's moral and spiritual significance?
- **Symbolism in Modern Practice:**
    - In what ways can Freemasons apply the metaphor of the square to foster harmony and fairness within their Lodges and communities?

The Symbol of the Level: Unity and Equality in Operative and Speculative Masonry

Exploring the Level's journey from operative craftsmanship to its profound moral lessons in Freemasonry.

The level is one of the most iconic symbols in Freemasonry, encapsulating values of equality, fairness, and humility. Used as both a practical tool by operative masons and a moral emblem in speculative Freemasonry, it signifies the profound philosophy of leveling distinctions among individuals in pursuit of universal brotherhood.

The Level in Operative Masonry

In the construction of grand cathedrals, castles, and temples, operative masons relied on the level as an essential tool. It ensured horizontal surfaces were truly even, contributing to structural integrity. For example, in the construction of Gothic cathedrals such as Notre-Dame de Paris, masons used levels to align stone courses accurately. This precision was vital for the stability of towering walls and arches.

The traditional carpenter's level, often a wooden instrument filled with liquid and an air bubble, allowed artisans to achieve exactitude. When erecting sacred spaces like Solomon's Temple—a cornerstone of Masonic lore—tools like the level symbolized the balance and order essential in both construction and moral undertakings.

The Level in Biblical References

The level's significance is interwoven with biblical texts that emphasize fairness, justice, and moral balance. For instance:

- Isaiah 40:4 (NIV): "Every valley shall be raised up, every mountain and hill made low; the rough ground shall become level, the rugged places a plain." This passage metaphorically highlights the leveling of disparities, a core value in Masonic teachings.

- Proverbs 4:26 (NIV): "Give careful thought to the paths for your feet and be steadfast in all your ways." The level, as a tool, embodies the virtue of steadfastness, urging individuals to live a balanced and upright life.

- Amos 7:7-8: In this passage, the Lord uses a plumb line—a complementary tool to the level—to signify divine justice. Together, these instruments metaphorically emphasize spiritual and moral alignment[6].

These references underscore the level's role in symbolizing moral equilibrium and divine fairness, resonating deeply within Masonic principles.

The Level in Popular Literature

Throughout literature, the level often symbolizes balance and impartiality. In William Shakespeare's Hamlet (Act III, Scene 3), the character Claudius laments: "Oh, my offense is rank, it smells to heaven." Though not explicitly about the level, this reflection on moral imbalance resonates with the level's metaphorical significance. Similarly, 19th-century

---

[6] Amos 7:7-8 "Thus he shewed me: and, behold, the Lord stood upon a wall made by a plumbline, with a plumbline in his hand. And the Lord said unto me, Amos, what seest thou? And I said, A plumbline. Then said the Lord, Behold, I will set a plumbline in the midst of my people Israel: I will not again pass by them any more."

American writers like Emerson invoked the imagery of leveling societal distinctions to advocate for equality and justice. Charles Dickens explores a comparable theme in A Tale of Two Cities, where the French Revolution's cry for equality and the "leveling" of class distinctions underscores the human pursuit of justice amidst chaos. In George Orwell's Animal Farm, the leveling principle is ironically subverted as the pigs proclaim, "All animals are equal, but some animals are more equal than others," revealing the challenges of maintaining true equity in practice. More recently, in Harper Lee's To Kill a Mockingbird, Atticus Finch serves as a moral level, advocating for fairness and justice in a deeply divided society. These literary works collectively underscore the enduring metaphorical power of the level, reflecting humanity's ongoing struggles with morality, equality, and justice.

The Level in Masonic Philosophy

In Freemasonry, the level stands as a profound metaphor. The phrase "on the level" embodies the Masonic belief in equality within the fraternity, regardless of external rank or wealth. Within the lodge, all Masons meet as equals—as brethren united by shared values of integrity, respect, and mutual aid. As stated in Masonic teachings, "on the level" signifies that all men are considered equal in moral worth and fraternity. While recognizing differences in talent and societal roles outside the lodge, Freemasonry emphasizes that every member deserves equal respect and dignity.

The level also serves as a reminder to practice humility and impartiality. The Master of a lodge, during rituals, uses the level to teach that leadership should be guided by fairness, ensuring that no one is elevated above others unjustly. Operatively, the level is used by the workman to measure his work, ensuring that it is straight and true. Symbolically, it reminds the Mason that his life, like the work of the operative craftsman, has an exact measurement—a fixed duration known only by the Great Architect of the Universe. This reflection underscores the preciousness of mortality, reminding us to live our lives with purpose and integrity. As Shakespeare poignantly wrote in Hamlet (Act III, Scene 1), life's unknown conclusion lies in the "undiscovered country from whose bourn no traveler returns," encouraging reflection on the finite nature of human existence.

From its operative roots to its symbolic prominence in speculative Freemasonry, the level remains a timeless emblem of equality and justice. It challenges all Masons to live uprightly, to recognize the intrinsic worth of others, and to work harmoniously toward a balanced and just society.

Reflections on the Craft: Questions for Deeper Understanding

- **Equality in Action:**
  - How does the principle of equality, symbolized by the level, guide your interactions within and beyond the lodge?
- **Balancing Fairness and Leadership:**
  - In what ways can the Masonic use of the level inspire leaders to govern with fairness and humility?
- **Applying Symbolism in Life:**
  - How can the lessons of the level help you navigate life's challenges with integrity and balance?

Jachin and Boaz: Pillars of History, Mystery, and Meaning

From Solomon's Temple to modern symbolism, the pillars of Jachin and Boaz bridge ancient wisdom and Masonic philosophy

The pillars Jachin and Boaz, prominently placed at the entrance of Solomon's Temple, have captivated the imaginations of scholars, theologians, and Freemasons alike. Mentioned in the Bible and steeped in historical, architectural, and esoteric symbolism, these pillars have been the subject of both scholarly debate and metaphorical interpretation. This essay explores their etymology, biblical significance, potential use as family names, their role in King Solomon's Temple, and their profound Masonic and esoteric meanings.

Etymology and Biblical Significance

The names "Jachin" and "Boaz" are derived from Hebrew. Jachin (יָכִין) is often translated as "He establishes," and Boaz (בֹּעַז) as "In Him is strength." They are first mentioned in 1 Kings 7:21: "And he set up the pillars in the porch of the temple: and he set up the right pillar, and called the name thereof Jachin: and he set up the left pillar, and called the name thereof Boaz."

Biblical genealogies and records occasionally use similar names, hinting at familial or tribal affiliations. For instance, "Boaz" is also the name of Ruth's husband in the Book of Ruth, connecting the name to the lineage of King David.

Historical and Architectural Context

Scholars debate the purpose of Jachin and Boaz in Solomon's Temple. Some argue that the pillars were purely ornamental, while others suggest they had a functional or symbolic role, such as representing cosmic duality or the covenant between God and Israel. The pillars were made of bronze, described as hollow, and adorned with intricate capitals featuring pomegranate motifs and chains, possibly symbolizing fertility and unity (2 Chronicles 3:15-17).

Use as Family Names

While direct biblical evidence does not explicitly associate these pillars with family names, their symbolic prominence suggests they may have influenced naming practices in ancient Israelite tribes. Families or clans with connections to the priestly or temple functions might have adopted names invoking strength (Boaz) or establishment (Jachin), resonating with their religious or societal roles.

Masonic Significance

In Freemasonry, Jachin and Boaz are central to the ritual and symbolism of the Craft. Representing the pillars of wisdom and strength, they are often seen as metaphors for stability and balance in life. Masonic teachings emphasize their spiritual significance, highlighting virtues such as steadfastness (Jachin) and moral fortitude (Boaz).

Albert Mackey, in his Encyclopedia of Freemasonry, notes, "The symbolic use of these pillars is to inspire the candidate with the essential need for strength and stability in both moral and physical endeavors" (Mackey, 1924, p. 174).

Esoteric Interpretations

Esoterically, the pillars may represent dualities such as light and darkness, masculine and feminine, or mercy and severity, akin to the Kabbalistic Tree of Life. They serve as a reminder of the spiritual journey: to achieve enlightenment, one must balance opposing forces and walk the middle path.

Manly P. Hall writes in The Secret Teachings of All Ages, "Jachin and Boaz were not only architectural marvels but also glyphs of the great pillars of creation, standing as sentinels at the gateway to the mysteries" (Hall, 1928, p. 543).

Jachin and Boaz stand as enduring symbols of strength, stability, and spiritual duality. From their biblical origins to their Masonic reinterpretation, these pillars remind us of the balance required to navigate life's challenges and seek higher truths.

Reflections on the Craft: Questions for Deeper Understanding

- **Balancing Strength and Stability:**
  - How can the dual symbolism of Jachin and Boaz inspire you to balance strength and stability in your daily life and Masonic journey?
- **Exploring Dualities:**
  - What dualities in your life could benefit from a more harmonious balance, as represented by the two pillars?
- **Symbolism and Purpose**:
  - How do the architectural and symbolic roles of Jachin and Boaz reflect broader Masonic teachings about moral and spiritual fortitude?

The First Three Steps of the Winding Staircase: Reflections in the Fellow Craft Degree

Journey through the Winding Staircase: Exploring timeless Masonic wisdom on self-improvement, reflection, and the art of renewal

The Winding Staircase in the Fellow Craft degree is a metaphorical journey into self-improvement and enlightenment. In the narrative of King Solomon's Temple, it leads to the Middle Chamber, a space symbolizing inner wisdom and spiritual achievement. Among its many lessons, the first three steps of the staircase embody profound symbolic meanings that relate to the three ages of man, the Three Principal Officers of a Lodge, the three degrees of Masonry, and the foundational pillars of wisdom, strength, and beauty. This essay explores these dimensions while connecting them to personal growth, daily reflection, and the cellular renewal that occurs within our bodies.

Metaphors in the Middle Chamber

The Middle Chamber[7] of King Solomon's Temple represents a sanctified place of reflection, labor, and reward. It parallels the Fellow Craft's journey into intellectual and spiritual maturity. As Albert G. Mackey (1912) noted, "The

---

[7] 1 Kings 6:8 (KJV): "The door for the middle chamber was in the right side of the house: and they went up with winding stairs into the middle chamber, and out of the middle into the third."

This verse describes the architectural details of Solomon's Temple, specifically the access to the middle chamber through a staircase. In Masonic traditions, the middle chamber holds significant symbolic meaning, often representing the pursuit of knowledge, enlightenment, and spiritual growth as one progresses through the degrees of Freemasonry. The "winding stairs" also serve as a metaphor for the gradual ascent to wisdom and understanding.

Middle Chamber represents the division between earthly toil and spiritual illumination, where the Fellow Craft contemplates the lessons of morality and virtue" (*The Symbolism of Freemasonry*, p. 219). Each step signifies incremental progress—an essential lesson for Masons and non-Masons alike: the path to mastery is neither immediate nor effortless.

The Three Steps: Yesterday, Today, and Tomorrow

The three steps can metaphorically represent time— yesterday, today, and tomorrow. Standing on the first step, one reflects on past actions, contemplating whether they improved compared to the previous day. The second step, representing today, is a call to action, a reminder to strive for excellence in the present moment. As Wilmshurst (1922) observed, "Each degree of the Craft demands the aspirant to labor within the present, using the tools of the mind and heart to shape the future" (*The Meaning of Masonry*, p. 63). The third step, symbolizing tomorrow, invites the aspirant to invest in growth and prepare for future challenges. This progression embodies the essential Masonic principle of continual self-improvement.

Lessons from the Three Ages of Man

The steps also reflect the three ages of man: youth, adulthood, and old age. Each stage emphasizes unique lessons—the energy of youth, the productivity and responsibility of adulthood, and the wisdom and reflection of later years. "The Mason is taught to regard the entire span of human life as a series of opportunities for learning, service, and contemplation," writes Bernard E. Jones (1950, *Freemasons' Guide and Compendium*, p. 91). Together, they encapsulate the Masonic journey of lifelong learning and contribution to humanity.

Guidance from the Three Principal Officers and Three Degrees

In the Lodge, the Worshipful Master, Senior Warden, and Junior Warden—the Three Principal Officers—guide members in wisdom, strength, and harmony. Similarly, the three degrees of Masonry—Entered Apprentice, Fellow Craft, and Master Mason—structure a framework for intellectual and moral growth, fostering reflection at every stage of life. Mackey (1912) elaborates, "The officers and degrees serve as allegories, demonstrating the aspirant's progress through stages of enlightenment and self-awareness" (*The Symbolism of Freemasonry*, p. 178).

Cellular Renewal: A Scientific Parallel

At the cellular level, humans undergo continuous renewal. Our stomach lining is replaced approximately every 24 hours, and nearly all cells in the body regenerate within seven years. "The process of renewal reminds us that transformation is a natural and essential part of existence," states Wallace (2017), "just as Masonry encourages us to renew our commitment to moral and intellectual growth" (*Biology and Metaphor in Freemasonry*, *Freemasonry Today*, p. 37). Just as cells adapt and renew to maintain vitality, Masons are encouraged to refine their character and wisdom over time.

Setting Goals on the Winding Staircase

The three steps remind us to set goals and strive for consistent growth. Yesterday's step challenges us to learn from mistakes. Today's step demands effort and presence. Tomorrow's step encourages preparation and vision. As Wilmshurst (1922) explains, "Through the progression of steps, the Mason learns the art of balancing reflection, action, and foresight, which are vital for personal and communal success" (*The Meaning of Masonry*, p. 72). Together, these steps teach the value of balancing reflection, action, and forward planning—key elements for personal and Masonic growth.

Reflections on the Craft: Questions for Deeper Understanding

- **Growth in Time**
  - How can the metaphor of yesterday, today, and tomorrow help you reflect on your progress and set meaningful goals?
- **Renewal and Resilience:**
  - How does understanding the body's natural renewal process inspire you to embrace change and strive for continuous improvement?
- **Symbolism in Action:**
  - How do the symbolic lessons of the Winding Staircase influence your approach to balancing reflection, present action, and future aspirations?

The Five Orders of Architecture: A Metaphor for Personal Development

Building a Life of Balance and Beauty: Lessons from the Five Orders of Architecture

Just as architecture shapes the physical world, personal development shapes the essence of who we are and who we become. The Five Orders of Architecture—Doric, Ionic, Corinthian, Tuscan, and Composite—are not merely structural designs but reflections of values, principles, and phases of growth. These classical orders offer a framework to explore the metaphorical and practical aspects of personal development, as inspired by the seminal work of Vitruvius.

Vitruvius and the Foundations of Architectural Philosophy

Marcus Vitruvius Pollio, an ancient Roman architect and engineer, authored De Architectura (The Ten Books on Architecture), where he documented the principles and significance of the Five Orders. Vitruvius emphasized the interplay of *firmitas* (strength), *utilitas* (utility), and *venustas* (beauty), asserting that "architecture depends on order, arrangement, proportion, symmetry, and economy" (Vitruvius, 1914, p. 13). These principles resonate deeply with personal development, as they mirror the necessity of balance in building a robust and meaningful life.

The first three orders—Doric, Ionic, and Corinthian—were developed by the ancient Greeks and are considered originals, representing the pinnacle of classical design and thought. The Tuscan and Composite orders, introduced by the Romans, build upon Greek traditions but do not constitute entirely new creations. Instead, they synthesize and extend the original concepts. In Freemasonry, the Five

Orders, particularly the first three, metaphorically reflect our dependence on Greek philosophical thought and its enduring influence on our intellectual and moral frameworks.

Doric Order - Strength and Foundation

The Doric Order, renowned for its sturdy design and simplicity, represents strength and resilience. Its lack of ornate details and firm, unadorned structure reflect the foundational aspects of personal growth. As Vitruvius stated, the Doric is "designed for strength and stability," making it an apt metaphor for the foundational elements of self-awareness and determination (Vitruvius, 1914, p. 27).

Metaphorically, the Doric Order reminds us to cultivate inner fortitude. Practically, it teaches us the value of foundational habits such as discipline and consistency, which are essential for achieving long-term success (Curl, 2013).

Ionic Order - Grace and Elegance

The Ionic Order, with its scroll-like volutes and slender columns, symbolizes grace and poise. Its design is both balanced and visually engaging, representing the cultivation of emotional intelligence and self-confidence. The base of the Ionic column signifies the necessity of standing on a firm footing of inner security and awareness (Fleming & Honour, 2005).

Grace and elegance in personal growth involve navigating life's complexities with finesse and dignity. As Rykwert (1981) noted, "The Ionic column's proportions suggest balance and harmony, qualities vital to interpersonal relationships" (p. 88).

Corinthian Order - Beauty and Ornamentation

The Corinthian Order, distinguished by its ornate capitals adorned with acanthus leaves, signifies the pursuit of beauty and refinement. This most elaborate of the classical orders encourages us to focus on the aesthetic and compassionate aspects of life. "The Corinthian Order is a celebration of artistic achievement and human creativity" (Winter, 1993, p. 42).

On a metaphorical level, the Corinthian Order reflects the importance of kindness, empathy, and creativity in enhancing our character. Practically, it reminds us to seek harmony and adorn our lives with meaningful acts that bring joy to ourselves and others. The intricate design encourages a deeper appreciation for life's nuances and complexities.

Tuscan Order - Simplicity and Stability

The Tuscan Order, characterized by its straightforward and robust structure, epitomizes simplicity and stability. This unembellished order demonstrates the strength found in clarity and minimalism. "Simplicity in design is not the absence of complexity but the mastery of essentials," according to Vitruvius (1914, p. 63).

Metaphorically, the Tuscan Order advocates removing the unnecessary clutter from our lives to focus on what truly matters. Practically, it emphasizes stability and consistency, helping us establish an unwavering sense of purpose and balance in an ever-changing world.

Composite Order - Synthesis and Integration

The Composite Order blends the elegance of the Ionic Order with the ornamentation of the Corinthian Order, symbolizing synthesis and integration. This hybrid design showcases the harmonious unification of diverse elements, encouraging a multifaceted approach to growth (Curl, 2013).

In personal development, the Composite Order reflects the journey of integrating different aspects of our identity—strengths, passions, and values—into a cohesive whole. Practically, it invites us to embrace complexity, adapt to change, and create a unified and authentic self.

The Architect of Personal Growth

The Five Orders of Architecture offer profound metaphors for personal development. By drawing inspiration from Vitruvius and these timeless principles, we can design a life that embodies resilience, grace, refinement, stability, and authenticity. Just as architects blend strength, utility, and beauty, we too can craft a fulfilling and harmonious existence.

Reflections on the Craft: Questions for Deeper Understanding

- **Balancing Structure and Creativity:**
    - o How can you integrate the strength of the Doric Order and the beauty of the Corinthian Order into your personal and professional life?
- **Simplicity in Complexity:**
    - o The Tuscan and Composite Orders represent stability and synthesis. How can you simplify your approach to challenges while embracing complexity?
- **Architectural Inspiration for Growth:**
    - o Vitruvius emphasized the harmony of strength, utility, and beauty. How do these

principles guide your personal development journey?

The Trivium, Quadrivium, and Liberal Arts and Sciences

Explore the timeless wisdom of the trivium and quadrivium, uncovering their role in shaping the Fellow Craft's journey to enlightenment and Masonic virtue

In the Fellow Craft degree of Freemasonry, the liberal arts and sciences are presented as essential tools for intellectual and moral improvement. These disciplines, rooted in the medieval education system and classical antiquity, are traditionally divided into the "trivium" and the "quadrivium." Their inclusion in Masonic teachings underscores the Fraternity's commitment to self-improvement and enlightenment. By examining the Latin origins, medieval meanings, and their relevance to Freemasonry, we gain a deeper appreciation of how these disciplines shape the Fellow Craft's journey (Blum et al., 2018; Matthews, 2020).

The Trivium: The Arts of Language and Reason

The word "trivium" is derived from the Latin terms *"tri"* (three) and *"via"* (way or road), signifying the intersection of three paths. In medieval education, the trivium consisted of grammar, rhetoric, and logic, disciplines that formed the foundation for critical thinking and effective communication.

- **Grammar**: The study of language structure, grammar focuses on the rules that govern speech and writing. It enables the Fellow Craft to understand and articulate ideas clearly, an essential skill for engaging with others in meaningful dialogue (Taylor, 2016).

- **Rhetoric**: The art of persuasion, rhetoric teaches how to present arguments compellingly and eloquently. In the Masonic context, rhetoric fosters the ability to inspire and lead within the Lodge and the broader community (Matthews, 2020).

- **Logic**: As the science of reasoning, logic trains the mind to discern truth from falsehood. It cultivates a disciplined approach to problem-solving and decision-making, qualities that are invaluable in both Masonic work and personal life (Blum et al., 2018).

The trivium is often considered preparatory, equipping the student with the intellectual tools necessary for higher learning. In Freemasonry, it reflects the Fellow Craft's initial steps toward understanding and applying knowledge (Hillman, 2021).

The Quadrivium: The Arts of Number and Harmony

The term "quadrivium" combines the Latin words *"quadri"* (four) and *"via"* (way), referring to the four advanced disciplines of medieval education: arithmetic, geometry, music, and astronomy. These subjects extend the intellectual framework established by the trivium, guiding the student toward a deeper comprehension of the universe.

- **Arithmetic**: The study of numbers and their properties, arithmetic emphasizes precision and abstraction. Numbers exist in their purest form in arithmetic, symbolizing clarity and universality. For the Fellow Craft, it underscores the importance of accuracy and intellectual rigor (Blum et al., 2018).

- **Geometry**: As numbers in space, geometry explores relationships between shapes, spaces, and dimensions. It serves as a metaphor for understanding the structure and order of the universe and reflects the Fellow Craft's role in building both literally and metaphorically (Matthews, 2020).

- **Music**: Representing numbers in time, music reveals the harmony and proportion inherent in creation. Its inclusion reminds the Fellow Craft of the importance of rhythm, balance, and unity in life and the cosmos (Taylor, 2016).

- **Astronomy**: The study of celestial bodies, astronomy is numbers in time and space. It invites contemplation of the vastness and order of the cosmos, inspiring a sense of wonder and humility while connecting the Fellow Craft to the Great Architect of the Universe (Hillman, 2021).

Together, arithmetic, geometry, music, and astronomy form a harmonious progression, each discipline building upon the previous one to deepen the Fellow Craft's understanding of the universe and their place within it. Arithmetic establishes the foundation, presenting numbers in their purest form as symbols of precision and universality. Geometry expands this foundation by situating numbers within space, revealing the structural and spatial relationships that govern both natural and man-made creations. From there, music introduces the dimension of time, illustrating how numerical relationships create rhythm and harmony, uniting the spatial with the temporal. Finally, astronomy synthesizes these elements, exploring the interplay of numbers in both space and time on a cosmic scale. By contemplating the celestial order, the Fellow Craft is reminded of their connection to the Great Architect of the Universe and the intricate, interwoven principles that govern all creation. This layered progression, from abstraction to spatial and temporal integration, not only enriches intellectual understanding but also inspires a sense of unity, balance, and awe in the Fellow Craft's journey.

The quadrivium disciplines cultivate an appreciation for the interconnectedness of knowledge and the natural world. They teach the Fellow Craft to perceive the unity underlying seemingly disparate elements of existence (Blum et al., 2018).

The Liberal Arts and Sciences in the Fellow Craft Degree

In medieval times, the trivium and quadrivium formed the foundation of the seven liberal arts, a curriculum designed to prepare individuals for a life of virtue and civic engagement. The term "liberal" derives from the Latin *"liberalis,"* meaning "worthy of a free person," signifying education that fosters intellectual and moral freedom (Taylor, 2016).

In the Fellow Craft degree, the liberal arts and sciences symbolize the tools necessary for the Mason's self-improvement and service to society. By studying these disciplines, the Fellow Craft is encouraged to:

- **Cultivate Wisdom**: Through grammar, rhetoric, and logic, the Fellow Craft learns to think critically, communicate effectively, and discern truth.

- **Embrace Harmony:** Arithmetic, geometry, music, and astronomy reveal the order and beauty of creation, inspiring the Fellow Craft to align their actions with these principles.

- **Seek Enlightenment**: The liberal arts and sciences provide a framework for lifelong learning, a hallmark of the Masonic journey (Hillman, 2021).

This emphasis on education aligns with Booker T. Washington's statement: "Education is the key to unlock the golden door of freedom" (Washington, 1901/2024). A distinguished Freemason and advocate for education, Washington's words remind us that knowledge empowers individuals to achieve personal and societal liberation, resonating with the Fellow Craft's pursuit of enlightenment.

Symbolism and Practical Application

The inclusion of the liberal arts and sciences in the Fellow Craft degree serves both symbolic and practical purposes. Symbolically, they represent the steps toward intellectual and spiritual enlightenment. Practically, they equip the Mason with the skills to contribute meaningfully to society (Taylor, 2016).

Freemasonry's emphasis on education reflects its belief in the transformative power of knowledge. Just as the trivium and quadrivium prepared medieval scholars to navigate the complexities of the world, they prepare the Fellow Craft to fulfill their duties as a Mason and a citizen (Blum et al., 2018).

The Pursuit of Light

The trivium, quadrivium, and liberal arts and sciences form a cornerstone of the Fellow Craft's instruction, highlighting the Masonic commitment to intellectual and moral growth. By engaging with these disciplines, the Fellow Craft embarks on a journey of self-discovery and enlightenment, equipped to build a life of virtue and service. In this pursuit, the Mason reflects the timeless ideals of Freemasonry: the quest for truth, the cultivation of wisdom, and the aspiration to live in harmony with the divine order of the universe (Hillman, 2021).

Reflections on the Craft: Questions for Deeper Understanding

- **The Journey of Knowledge**:
  - How do the trivium and quadrivium align with your personal path of intellectual and moral improvement as a Mason?
- **Harmony in Practice:**
  - In what ways can the study of arithmetic, geometry, music, and astronomy help you build harmony and balance in your daily life?\

- **Symbolism and Application**:
  - How can you translate the symbolic teachings of the liberal arts and sciences into practical contributions to your Lodge and society?

The Winding Staircase: Comprehensive Analysis and Symbolism in the Fellow Craft Degree

Unlock the mysteries of the Winding Staircase: a journey through architecture, arts, and timeless Masonic wisdom

The Winding Staircase in the Fellow Craft degree serves as a profound allegory for intellectual, spiritual, and moral development. It consists of three, five, and seven steps, each layer imbued with symbolic meanings derived from Masonic ritual, ancient traditions, and educational ideals. While recent explorations have highlighted the staircase's metaphorical role in personal growth and renewal, this analysis will integrate missing components such as the Five Orders of Architecture, the Seven Liberal Arts and Sciences, and their essential connections to the traditional Staircase Lecture. By drawing upon verifiable academic sources, this essay aims to provide a holistic understanding of the Winding Staircase as both a symbolic and practical Masonic teaching tool.

The Winding Staircase, like the journey it represents, is not a linear path but one that ascends and descends, winds and turns, inviting reflection at every step. It can be examined level by level, where each segment—three, five, and seven steps—offers distinct lessons tied to specific Masonic principles and teachings. Alternatively, it can be understood as a whole, a unified journey that weaves together intellectual, moral, and spiritual growth. The staircase's winding nature emphasizes the non-linear progression of knowledge and the importance of both ascent and descent: moments of discovery and advancement balanced by periods of introspection and grounding. The purpose of this essay is to help the Fellow Craft see the stairway from multiple perspectives, encouraging them to approach their Masonic journey with a deeper awareness of its complexities. By exploring both the individual components and the staircase's broader symbolism, the Fellow Craft can better appreciate its profound lessons and integrate them into their personal and Masonic development.

The Three Steps: Foundational Lessons in Progress

The first three steps of the staircase represent foundational lessons tied to the ages of man (youth, adulthood, and old age), the Three Principal Officers of a Lodge (Worshipful Master, Senior Warden, and Junior Warden), and the pillars of wisdom, strength, and beauty. Albert Mackey (1912) explains, "These steps are not merely an ascent but signify stages of understanding through which a Mason evolves morally and intellectually" (The Symbolism of Freemasonry, p. 178).

Each step also symbolizes time: yesterday, today, and tomorrow. As Wilmshurst (1922) notes, "The Mason learns the value of living in the present while drawing lessons from the past and striving for improvement in the future" (The Meaning of Masonry, p. 72).

The Five Steps: The Orders of Architecture

The five steps correspond to the Five Orders of Architecture—Doric, Ionic, Corinthian, Tuscan, and Composite. These architectural forms, rooted in Vitruvian principles, represent stages of human development and values such as strength, elegance, and synthesis. Vitruvius (1914) emphasizes their philosophical significance: "The orders are a reflection of proportion, harmony, and balance, attributes essential to both construction and character" (De Architectura, p. 27).

- **Doric Order**: Represents strength and resilience, serving as a metaphor for establishing a strong foundation in character and discipline.
- **Ionic Order**: Signifies grace and balance, aligning with emotional intelligence and ethical behavior.
- **Corinthian Order**: Reflects beauty and creativity, encouraging the cultivation of aesthetics and empathy.
- **Tuscan Order**: Highlights simplicity and stability, reminding Masons to focus on essentials.
- **Composite Order**: A synthesis of qualities, symbolizing the integration of diverse strengths.

Curl (2013) elaborates that the Orders guide Masons in constructing a balanced life that harmonizes physical, intellectual, and moral elements.

The Seven Steps: The Liberal Arts and Sciences

The seven steps culminate in the liberal arts and sciences, which are divided into the trivium (grammar, rhetoric, and logic) and the quadrivium (arithmetic, geometry, music, and astronomy). These disciplines are not merely academic pursuits but tools for shaping a Mason's intellect and morality.

- **Grammar**: The structure of language, enabling clear communication and comprehension.
- **Rhetoric**: The art of persuasion, fostering the ability to inspire and lead.
- **Logic**: Critical reasoning, essential for discernment and decision-making.
- **Arithmetic**: Numerical precision, reflecting clarity and order.
- **Geometry**: Spatial understanding, symbolizing the interconnectedness of the universe.

- **Music**: Harmony and rhythm, representing balance in life.
- **Astronomy**: Contemplation of the cosmos, inspiring awe and humility.

Blum et al. (2018) argue that these arts "cultivate a universal perspective, connecting the Mason's intellectual pursuits with the divine order of creation" (The Liberal Arts Tradition, p. 47).

Practical and Ritual Integration

The Winding Staircase is more than a symbolic journey; it is a framework for practical application. Within Lodge practices, the steps encourage members to reflect on their progress, align their actions with Masonic virtues, and contribute to the betterment of society. Bernard E. Jones (1950) highlights the importance of ritual in reinforcing these lessons: "Each degree's symbols are designed to remind Masons of their obligations to themselves, their Lodge, and humanity" (Freemasons' Guide and Compendium, p. 91).

The Winding Staircase in the Fellow Craft degree encapsulates the essence of Masonic teachings—progress, balance, and enlightenment. By integrating the three steps' foundational lessons, the architectural significance of the five steps, and the intellectual framework of the seven steps, Masons are equipped to navigate both their inner and outer worlds. This analysis underscores the staircase as a comprehensive guide to personal and communal growth, bridging traditional Masonic teachings with modern interpretations.

Reflections on the Craft: Questions for Deeper Understanding

- **Foundations of Growth:**
  - How do the first three steps of the Winding Staircase inspire you to reflect on your past, act meaningfully in the present, and prepare for the future?
- **Balance in Design and Life:**
  - The Five Orders of Architecture symbolize strength, elegance, and harmony. How can these principles guide you in building a balanced and resilient character?
- **Pursuit of Enlightenment:**
  - The Seven Liberal Arts and Sciences represent tools for intellectual and moral improvement. How can you apply these disciplines to achieve personal growth and contribute meaningfully to your Lodge and community?

The Doric Order: Evolution and Masonic Significance of a Timeless Style

Where timeless architecture meets the enduring strength of Masonic virtue

The Doric Order, one of the three principal classical architectural styles, stands as a symbol of strength, resilience, simplicity, and proportion. Emerging in ancient Greece, this style encapsulates ideals that resonate deeply within Freemasonry. Its enduring appeal lies not only in its aesthetic simplicity but also in its symbolic representation of strength—one of the foundational virtues of the Craft. This essay explores the development of the Doric Order from its origins in Dorian Greece, its architectural evolution, and its Masonic significance.

Origins of the Doric Order

The Doric Order is intrinsically tied to Dorian Greece, a region marked by its emphasis on discipline and order. The Dorians, one of the major Hellenic tribes, migrated into the Greek mainland around 1100 BCE, bringing with them cultural and architectural innovations that would later crystallize in the Doric style. Early Dorian temples, such as the Temple of Apollo at Thermon, reflected their practical and unadorned ethos. These structures utilized timber for construction, a feature later translated into stone as techniques advanced.

The simplicity of the Doric Order symbolized the disciplined and austere Dorian worldview, which emphasized structure, balance, and ethical living. Its fluted columns without bases mirrored the rugged, grounded lifestyle of its creators, while its straightforward design rejected excessive ornamentation in favor of proportion and strength. The Dorian worldview, rooted in a commitment to order and collective welfare, deeply influenced not only their architecture but also their societal values, particularly those exemplified in Spartan austerity and moral rigor. According to Pollitt (1972), "the Dorian emphasis on functionality and durability found its ultimate expression in the Doric style, making it a perfect architectural counterpart to their cultural identity." This ethos of simplicity and strength would later align seamlessly with Masonic values, emphasizing moral fortitude, harmony, and the enduring beauty of well-balanced simplicity.

Defining Characteristics

The Doric Order is defined by its robust and straightforward design. The columns are characterized by fluted shafts without bases, topped by simple capitals that support an entablature composed of three distinct sections. The architrave, plain and unadorned, serves as the foundational support above the columns. The frieze alternates between triglyphs—rectangular blocks with vertical grooves—and metopes, which may be plain or adorned with sculptural reliefs, creating a rhythmic balance that reflects the disciplined and orderly ethos of the Dorians. Above this, the cornice projects outward, incorporating mutules with guttae, reinforcing the sense of geometric precision and structural harmony. This emphasis on proportion and balance reflects a deep understanding of geometry, principles highly regarded in Freemasonry.

In Masonic symbolism, the Doric column represents strength, one of the three supporting pillars of the Lodge. Its unadorned form and sturdy structure embody the purity of intent and resilience required of a Mason, aligning with the disciplined worldview of the Dorians. The entablature's layered design mirrors the layered moral and spiritual lessons taught within the Craft, urging Masons to build their lives with the same attention to integrity and balance. As emphasized by Rykwert (1981), "The Doric Order's structure serves not merely as architectural elegance but as a moral lesson in balance and support." Its evolution and refinement over centuries have not diminished its symbolic power; rather, it continues to inspire both architectural and moral aspirations.

- **Archaic Period**: The earliest Doric temples, such as the Temple of Hera at Olympia, exhibit a raw simplicity. These structures laid the groundwork for the refinement seen in later periods.

- **Classical Period**: During the Classical era, the Doric Order reached its zenith with the construction of the Parthenon in Athens. The meticulous proportions of its columns and the harmony of its design exemplify the Greek pursuit of perfection.

- **Hellenistic Adaptations:** The Hellenistic period saw a fusion of the Doric Order with other architectural styles, incorporating more decorative elements while maintaining its core principles of strength and order.

The Doric Order in Freemasonry

Freemasonry draws heavily on the symbolic aspects of the Doric Order, specifically aligning it with Strength, one of the three principal pillars of the Craft. The Doric column, with its robust and unadorned design, represents not only physical strength but also moral fortitude—the steadfastness required to uphold the values of Freemasonry. Its simplicity and durability symbolize the resilience and reliability that support the Lodge and its principles. The Doric column serves as a visual and symbolic reminder of the Strength necessary to sustain the moral and ethical framework of the Craft, complementing the virtues of Wisdom and Beauty.

In Masonic architecture, the influence of the Doric Order is evident in designs that prioritize simplicity, durability, and functionality, echoing the timeless values of balance and integrity. These principles mirror the enduring truths of Freemasonry, grounding the symbolic teachings in both physical form and moral ideals. As Curl (2002) observes, "Freemasonry's integration of classical architecture, particularly the Doric Order, reflects its commitment to enduring truths and moral rectitude." By associating the Doric column with Strength, Freemasonry reinforces its focus on stability, fortitude, and the enduring support required for personal and collective growth.

Influence Beyond Greece

The adoption of the Doric Order in Roman and Renaissance architecture allowed its principles to influence global design. During the Enlightenment, the resurgence of classical architecture brought the Doric style into Masonic temples, public buildings, and monuments. This era witnessed the alignment of architectural beauty with democratic and ethical ideals.

The Doric Order Today

In modern times, the Doric Order continues to inspire architectural designs in both public and Masonic contexts. Its principles of strength, order, and simplicity serve as a timeless reminder of the values it embodies.

Reflections on the Craft: Questions for Deeper Understanding

- **Strength in Simplicity**
  - o How does the simplicity of the Doric Order inspire you to cultivate strength and humility in your personal and Masonic life?
- **Symbolism in Architecture**
  - o In what ways can the Doric column's representation of strength help you navigate challenges in your journey as a Mason?
- **Timeless Values**
  - o How does the enduring appeal of the Doric Order encourage you to reflect on the permanence of Masonic virtues in a changing world?

The Ionian Order and Its Relationship to Freemasonry

Exploring the intertwining of architectural elegance and Masonic symbolism.

The Ionian Order, one of the three classical orders of Greek architecture, holds a special place in the history of design and philosophy. Its blend of balance and beauty resonates profoundly within the traditions of Freemasonry, a fraternity deeply invested in symbolism and the pursuit of enlightenment.

Historical Context of the Ionian Order

The Ionian Order emerged during the 6th century BCE in the region of Ionia, modern-day Turkey. This architectural style is characterized by its elegant volutes, slender columns, and elaborate base structures. The Ionic column's proportions were designed to embody grace and harmony, distinguishing it from the robustness of the Doric Order and the intricate details of the Corinthian Order.

In classical Greece, the Ionian Order often adorned temples dedicated to female deities, such as the Temple of Artemis at Ephesus. Its design symbolized balance and refinement, integral qualities that aligned with Greek ideals of civilization. As architectural traditions evolved, the Ionian Order's influence extended into the Roman period, where it became a cornerstone of classical architecture. "The Ionian style represents a blend of structural ingenuity and aesthetic grace that remains unparalleled," notes Vitruvius in The Ten Books on Architecture (1960).

The Significance of the Doric Influence on Ionian

The Ionian Order's development did not occur in isolation; it was heavily influenced by its predecessor, the Doric Order. Originating in Dorian Greece during the 7th century BCE, the Doric Order is marked by its simplicity, strength, and functional design. Doric architecture often represented the ethos of Dorian city-states, such as Sparta, emphasizing order, discipline, and communal harmony.

While the Doric Order was reserved and austere, its principles laid the foundation for the refinement seen in the Ionian Order. As Masonic scholar Albert Mackey noted, "The Doric provided the framework upon which the Ionic built its elegant expressions of beauty and balance" (Mackey, 1912). This interplay of strength and elegance mirrors the Masonic ideals of combining wisdom with action to achieve enlightenment.

Symbolism in Freemasonry

The Ionian Order finds its symbolic representation within the Masonic tradition. The Ionic column is one of the three pillars in Freemasonry, symbolizing Beauty—a complement to Wisdom (associated with the Doric column) and Strength (represented by the Corinthian column). Together, these pillars form the triadic foundation upon which the Craft builds its teachings.

In the ritualistic setting of Masonic lodges, Ionic columns are often depicted as integral structural elements, symbolizing balance and ethical decorum. "Just as the Ionic Order bridges the strength of the Doric and the intricacy of the Corinthian, so does Beauty bridge the practical and the aspirational in Freemasonry," writes historian John Hamill (Hamill, 1994).

The Influence on Masonic Architects

Prominent Masonic architects have drawn inspiration from the Ionian Order, incorporating its design principles into their works. Scottish architect Robert Adam, for example, utilized Ionic elements extensively in his neoclassical projects, demonstrating his mastery of proportion, harmony, and classical aesthetics. Adam's designs, such as Kedleston Hall in Derbyshire, Osterley Park in London, and The Adelphi development, reflect the elegance of Ionic columns and their slender, fluted shafts with volute capitals. These projects exemplify his ability to blend classical principles with innovative architectural practices, emphasizing balance and grace. Similarly, his work on The Register House in Edinburgh showcased Ionic detailing in public architecture, underscoring the alignment between architectural beauty and Masonic ideals of order, unity, and harmony. As Watkin (1986) notes, "Adam's integration of Ionic design reflects the enduring influence of classical principles within Freemasonry's moral and symbolic framework."

Contemporary Applications

Today, the Ionian Order remains a significant aspect of Masonic architecture and symbolism. Modern lodges continue to integrate Ionic motifs, reflecting the timeless relevance of its ideals. Additionally, Masons uphold the philosophical essence of the Ionian Order by pursuing balance, wisdom, and ethical beauty in their personal and communal lives.

Reflections on the Craft: Questions for Deeper Understanding

- **Harmonizing Strength and Beauty:**
    - o How does the combination of Doric strength and Ionian beauty inspire your approach to personal growth and community building?

- **The Evolution of Tradition:**
  - o In what ways can Masons draw lessons from the evolution of the Ionian Order, particularly its roots in Dorian Greece, to enhance their understanding of Masonic principles?
- **Architectural Symbolism in Daily Life:**
  - o How do the Ionic Order's symbols guide you in achieving harmony and balance in your daily endeavors?

The Corinthian Column: Elegance, Innovation, and Masonic Symbolism

Explore the profound connections between ancient architecture and the timeless principles of Freemasonry

The story of the Corinthian column, originating in ancient Corinth, illustrates how art, nature, and spirituality intertwine to inspire both architectural masterpieces and enduring Masonic principles. This narrative, attributed to the Greek architect Callimachus, reflects themes of balance, remembrance, and beauty—concepts central to Masonic teachings.

Corinth: A Hub of Creativity and Cultural Exchange

Ancient Corinth, located on the narrow isthmus connecting mainland Greece to the Peloponnese, was a thriving center of commerce and culture. Known for its architectural innovations, Corinth refined earlier styles, such as the Doric and Ionic, and laid the foundation for the Corinthian order. Its wealth and openness to cultural exchange fostered an environment where artistic and intellectual pursuits flourished.

Callimachus and the Acanthus Inspiration

Callimachus, a sculptor and architect renowned for his intricate designs, was pivotal in creating the Corinthian order. As Vitruvius recounts in De Architectura, Callimachus came upon a poignant scene: the grave of a young maiden in Corinth adorned with a basket of her belongings, covered by a tile, and surrounded by flourishing acanthus leaves. The leaves' elegant curves inspired Callimachus to replicate the design in stone, crafting the first Corinthian capital (Vitruvius, 1914).

This column, with its ornate acanthus decoration, symbolized the harmonious blend of nature and human ingenuity. As art historian J.J. Pollitt notes, "The Corinthian capital achieves a perfect synthesis of natural beauty and structural functionality" (Pollitt, 1990, p. 76).

Masonic Themes in the Corinthian Column

The Corinthian column resonates deeply within Masonic symbolism, embodying ideals central to the Craft:

- **Beauty and Harmony:** Freemasonry emphasizes the pursuit of beauty in moral and ethical life, akin to the Corinthian column's elegance. The column symbolizes the Pillar of Beauty, one of the three principal Masonic pillars, alongside Wisdom and Strength.

- **Resilience and Growth**: The acanthus leaves, growing from the base of the grave, represent resilience and spiritual renewal. These themes align with the Masonic journey of self-improvement and perseverance through life's challenges.

- **Tribute and Remembrance**: The column's origin story, tied to a grave, echoes the Masonic emphasis on honoring the past and learning from the lives of those who came before. Just as Callimachus immortalized the maiden's memory through his design, Masons preserve and venerate ancient wisdom.

- **Architectural Mastery**: Callimachus, like the legendary Hiram Abiff of Masonic tradition, exemplifies the archetype of the inspired architect.

Both figures teach that dedication and creativity can transform raw materials into timeless monuments.

Legacy of the Corinthian Column

The Corinthian column remains a symbol of sophistication in both classical and modern architecture. In Freemasonry, it is not only a physical motif but a spiritual reminder of the values of harmony, refinement, and reverence for life's beauty. As Vitruvius aptly observed, the column "speaks of grace and precision, elevating the spirit" (1914, p. 232).

Reflections on the Craft: Questions for Deeper Understanding

- **Resilience in Growth:**
    - How can the symbolism of the acanthus leaves inspire you to persevere and grow, even in challenging circumstances?
- **Beauty in Masonic Practice:**
    - How does the concept of the Pillar of Beauty guide your actions in daily life and within the Craft?
- **Architectural and Personal Legacy:**
    - Like Callimachus, how can your contributions leave a lasting legacy of harmony and inspiration?

Corn, Wine, and Oil: A Trifecta of Symbolism in Masonry and Beyond

Exploring the cultural, philosophical, and Masonic dimensions of these enduring symbols

Corn, wine, and oil hold profound significance in Freemasonry, serving as symbols that encapsulate essential aspects of life and spirituality. These elements transcend their physical forms, offering a rich tapestry of meanings that intertwine with cultural traditions, philosophical insights, and Masonic rituals. This essay delves into their multifaceted symbolism, drawing from historical and contemporary perspectives to illuminate their enduring relevance.

Cultural and Historical Significance

Throughout history, corn, wine, and oil have been staples of human civilization, revered not only for their practical uses but also for their spiritual connotations. Corn, or grain, is synonymous with abundance and sustenance. As Durant (2010) observes, "The cultivation of grain marked the beginning of organized human society, representing not only survival but also the potential for growth and prosperity" (p. 55).

Wine, on the other hand, has been celebrated as a symbol of joy and communion. Its role in religious and cultural ceremonies underscores its connection to life's pleasures and shared experiences. According to Smith (2012), "Wine has been a vehicle for expressing sacredness and conviviality, a bridge between the mundane and the divine" (p. 89).

Oil, particularly olive oil, carries a rich history as a symbol of anointing and enlightenment. Its use in consecration and healing rituals highlights its sanctifying properties. As noted by Carter (2009), "Oil's role in ancient rites reflects its function as a medium of divine favor and spiritual illumination" (p. 74).

Philosophical Dimensions

The philosophical underpinnings of corn, wine, and oil speak to universal human values. Corn represents productivity and the fruits of labor. As a sustainer of life, it invites reflection on the virtues of hard work and the necessity of providing for others.

Wine embodies joy and fellowship. It is a metaphor for the sweetness of life and the bonds formed through shared experiences. Its symbolic resonance is captured in Freemasonry as a reminder of harmony within the Craft.

Oil signifies purity, peace, and enlightenment. Its association with anointing rituals in various cultures underlines the importance of spiritual dedication and the aspiration for moral excellence. In this triad, oil's role completes the balance of physical, emotional, and spiritual sustenance.

Masonic Symbolism and Rituals

In Freemasonry, corn, wine, and oil play a prominent role in cornerstone-laying ceremonies, reflecting gratitude, fellowship, and consecration. These symbols are "emblems of nourishment, joy, and sanctity, reminding Masons of their duty to labor for the common good while striving for personal and spiritual growth" (Henderson, 2015, p. 23).

Corn is offered as a token of gratitude for life's abundance and as a call to share these blessings. Wine, poured as a libation, symbolizes unity and the celebratory spirit of

Masonic fellowship. Oil, used to sanctify, invokes peace and divine favor, reinforcing the sacred nature of the work at hand.

Together, these elements form a holistic representation of what it means to live a balanced and meaningful life. They call Masons to reflect on their obligations to themselves, their communities, and the divine, urging them to embody these virtues in all aspects of their existence.

Reflections on the Craft: Questions for Deeper Understanding

- **Balancing Sustenance and Spirit:**
  - How do corn, wine, and oil inspire you to balance your physical, emotional, and spiritual needs in daily life?
- **Community and Contribution:**
  - In what ways can the symbolism of corn encourage you to contribute to the prosperity and well-being of your community?
- **Sacred Dedication:**
  - How does the sanctifying role of oil challenge you to approach your Masonic endeavors with greater commitment and moral clarity?

The Evolution of Architecture: A Journey Through History and Meaning

Exploring the timeless interplay of form, function, and philosophy in the built environment.

Architecture, as an art and science, has evolved alongside humanity, reflecting cultural values, technological advancements, and philosophical ideals. The history of architecture is not merely a chronology of styles and structures but a testament to humanity's quest for meaning, harmony, and expression. From the monumental pyramids of ancient Egypt to the refined symmetry of neoclassical design, architecture has consistently served as a mirror of the human spirit. Within this vast narrative, the principles of balance, proportion, and symbolism—central to Freemasonry—stand out as enduring themes that continue to inspire and guide architectural thought (Curl, 2002; Watkin, 1986).

Ancient Beginnings: The Foundations of Civilization

The earliest architectural achievements emerged from humanity's need for shelter, safety, and community. In ancient Egypt, monumental structures such as the pyramids of Giza were not only feats of engineering but also profound spiritual symbols. These colossal works, aligning with celestial bodies, demonstrated the Egyptians' mastery of geometry and their belief in the afterlife (Curl, 2002). Similarly, in Mesopotamia, ziggurats served as architectural representations of sacred mountains, bridging the earthly and divine realms.

Greek architecture, particularly the Doric, Ionic, and Corinthian orders, introduced a refined understanding of proportion and harmony. The Parthenon, a Doric masterpiece, exemplifies the balance and simplicity that resonate with Masonic ideals of strength and integrity. The Ionic Order, with its elegant volutes and slender columns, speaks to beauty and grace, principles that Masonic architects, such as Robert Adam, would later adapt in their neoclassical works. The Greeks' use of mathematical precision and their exploration of the "golden mean" laid the groundwork for architecture as a discipline of both art and science (Watkin, 1986).

Roman Innovation: The Power of Engineering

Building upon Greek foundations, Roman architecture expanded the scale and scope of design through innovations such as the arch, vault, and dome. Structures like the Colosseum and the Pantheon combined functionality with grandeur, reflecting Rome's imperial ambitions and organizational prowess. Roman architects emphasized the practical application of geometry, creating structures that were not only visually impressive but also enduring (Hillman, 2021).

The Pantheon's domed interior, with its oculus symbolizing the heavens, represents a synthesis of engineering and spirituality. This integration of form and meaning profoundly influenced later architectural traditions, including the development of Gothic cathedrals and Renaissance domes. The Romans' ability to merge utilitarian needs with symbolic expression echoes the Masonic commitment to uniting practicality with higher ideals.

Medieval Europe: The Rise of Spiritual Architecture

With the fall of the Roman Empire, architecture in Europe took on a distinctly spiritual character. The Romanesque style, characterized by thick walls, rounded arches, and sturdy pillars, conveyed strength and permanence. These features were later refined in the Gothic style, which introduced pointed arches, ribbed vaults, and flying buttresses to achieve unprecedented verticality and light (Curl, 2002).

Gothic cathedrals such as Chartres and Notre-Dame de Paris became monumental expressions of faith, with intricate stained glass windows illustrating biblical narratives and illuminating sacred spaces. These structures embodied the medieval worldview, where architecture served as a bridge between humanity and the divine. The emphasis on light, symmetry, and upward movement in Gothic design aligns with the Masonic pursuit of enlightenment and the symbolic ascent toward higher knowledge.

The Renaissance: Rebirth of Classical Ideals

The Renaissance marked a return to classical principles, as architects rediscovered ancient texts and sought inspiration from Greek and Roman models. Figures such as Filippo Brunelleschi, Leon Battista Alberti, and Andrea Palladio brought renewed attention to symmetry, proportion, and the human scale. Brunelleschi's dome for the Florence Cathedral and Palladio's villas exemplify the harmonious balance between form and function (Matthews, 2020).

This era also saw the rise of architectural treatises, such as Palladio's I Quattro Libri dell'Architettura, which provided systematic guidance on design principles. These works influenced generations of architects, including those in the neoclassical movement, who sought to embody the timeless ideals of beauty and order. The Renaissance's intellectual rigor and emphasis on humanism resonate with Masonic teachings, which celebrate the pursuit of knowledge and the application of moral principles.

The Neoclassical Movement: A Masonic Legacy

The 18th century witnessed the emergence of neoclassicism, a movement that sought to revive the clarity and grandeur of classical architecture. Masonic architects such as Robert Adam drew heavily on Ionic and Corinthian designs, incorporating elements of proportion, symmetry, and ornamentation into their projects. Adam's works, including Osterley Park and Kedleston Hall, exemplify the integration of classical principles with contemporary needs (Watkin, 1986).

Neoclassical architecture, with its emphasis on harmony and restraint, became a symbol of enlightenment ideals. It reflected a belief in reason, order, and the potential for human progress. For Freemasonry, these principles aligned with the moral and philosophical foundations of the Craft, emphasizing the importance of balance and unity in both architecture and life.

Modern Architecture: Continuity and Innovation

The advent of modern architecture in the 19th and 20th centuries brought significant changes to the field, as new materials and technologies allowed for unprecedented forms and scales. Yet, even as modernist architects such as Frank Lloyd Wright and Le Corbusier embraced innovation, they often drew upon classical and symbolic principles. Wright's organic architecture, for instance, emphasized harmony with nature, while Le Corbusier's modular design echoed the proportional systems of classical architecture (Hillman, 2021).

Modern Freemasonry, too, has adapted its architectural expressions, using contemporary materials and designs to create spaces that reflect both tradition and innovation. The principles of balance, proportion, and symbolism remain central, ensuring continuity with the past while embracing the possibilities of the future.

Conclusion

The history of architecture is a story of humanity's enduring quest to create spaces that reflect our highest ideals. From the monumental structures of antiquity to the refined elegance of neoclassicism and the bold innovations of modernism, architecture has served as a canvas for expressing cultural values and philosophical principles. For Freemasonry, the alignment between architectural design and moral teaching underscores the Craft's commitment to harmony, order, and the pursuit of truth. By studying the evolution of architecture, we not only gain insight into the past but also find inspiration to build a future grounded in beauty, strength, and wisdom.

Reflections on the Craft: Questions for Deeper Understanding

- **Symbolism and Functionality:**
    - o In what ways does architecture, particularly within Freemasonry, balance symbolic meaning with practical utility?
- **Continuity and Change:**
    - o How have the principles of proportion and harmony persisted throughout architectural history, and how do they adapt in modern design?
- **Personal Interpretation:**
    - o How can understanding the evolution of architectural styles enhance your

appreciation of Masonic teachings and their alignment with universal truths?

Geometry: A Bridge Between the Ancient and Modern Worlds

Explore the profound legacy and modern applications of the "first science," geometry

Geometry, a mathematical discipline focusing on the properties and relations of points, lines, surfaces, and solids, has been a cornerstone of intellectual advancement for millennia. From its philosophical underpinnings in ancient Greece to its critical role in modern technology, geometry demonstrates the timeless interplay of human curiosity, logic, and creativity.

Historical Development of Geometry

The roots of geometry stretch back to ancient civilizations like Mesopotamia and Egypt, where practical needs for land measurement spurred its initial development (Katz, 2009). However, it was the Greeks who transformed geometry into a formal, deductive science. Euclid's Elements, composed around 300 BCE, remains one of the most influential mathematical works, establishing axiomatic principles and rigorous proofs (Burton, 2010).

Plato, the renowned philosopher, viewed geometry as a pathway to higher knowledge. He inscribed above his Academy's entrance: "Let no one ignorant of geometry enter here" (Plato, 1997, p. 24). Plato believed that geometric truths, immutable and universal, mirrored the forms of ideal reality. For him, geometry was not merely a tool but a means of cultivating philosophical wisdom (Livio, 2003).

During the Islamic Golden Age, scholars such as Al-Khwarizmi and Omar Khayyam preserved and expanded Greek geometry, integrating it with algebra (Stillwell, 2010).

The Renaissance period witnessed the application of geometry in art, with luminaries like Leonardo da Vinci employing geometric principles in perspective and design (Watson, 2007).

In the modern era, geometry evolved further through contributions by figures like Descartes, who introduced analytical geometry, and Gauss, whose work on non-Euclidean geometries opened new dimensions of understanding (Thurston, 1997).

Geometry as the First Science

The rigorous proofs and repeatability inherent in geometry justify its status as the "first science" (Burton, 2010). Unlike empirical disciplines that rely on observation, geometry's reliance on logic and deduction set a standard for scientific rigor. Euclid's axiomatic method, involving definitions, postulates, and propositions, became a model for scientific inquiry, influencing fields from physics to economics (Katz, 2009).

The Golden Mean and Ratio

The golden mean has captivated mathematicians, artists, and architects for centuries. This unique ratio appears in natural phenomena, from the arrangement of leaves on a stem to the spirals of galaxies (Livio, 2003). Its application in human-made structures creates a sense of balance and beauty, affirming the connection between geometry and aesthetics (Weisstein, 2023).

Geometry, with its historical depth and broad applications, stands as a testament to humanity's capacity to abstract, analyze, and innovate. From ancient philosophies to modern technologies, it bridges eras and disciplines, offering tools and insights to shape the future.

Geometry in Ancient Cathedrals

The construction of Europe's great cathedrals, such as Chartres and Notre-Dame, showcases geometry's interplay with art and spirituality. Master masons used intricate geometric designs to achieve structural stability and aesthetic appeal (Watson, 2007). The rose windows and vaulted ceilings are examples of geometric patterns that symbolize divine order and transcendence (Burton, 2010).

Applications of Geometry in the Modern Age

Technology and Telecommunications

Modern technology relies heavily on geometric principles. Satellites, for example, use orbital geometry to maintain their positions and relay data for GPS, television, and internet services (Weisstein, 2023). Cell phones depend on triangulation—a geometric technique—to determine user locations and optimize signal strength (Thurston, 1997).

Architecture and Engineering

From the Gothic cathedrals of medieval Europe to today's skyscrapers, geometry underpins structural design and integrity (Watson, 2007). The golden mean (or golden ratio, approximately 1:1.618) has been employed to create visually harmonious structures, including the Parthenon and modern concert halls (Livio, 2003).

Digital Imaging and Graphics

Computer graphics and animation use geometric algorithms to model, render, and animate three-dimensional objects. Software like Computer-Aided Design enables engineers and designers to visualize and perfect their creations geometrically (Stillwell, 2010).

Data Science and Artificial Intelligence

Geometric principles underpin algorithms in machine learning and data visualization. For instance, dimensionality reduction techniques help represent complex datasets in manageable forms, aiding insights and decision-making (Thurston, 1997).

Reflections on the Craft: Questions for Deeper Understanding

- **Philosophical Insights:**
  - Plato viewed geometry as a path to understanding universal truths. How might the study of geometry influence your approach to problem-solving and philosophical inquiry?
- **Symbolism in Structures:**
  - Cathedrals and monuments often embody geometric symbolism. What modern structures inspire you, and how do they reflect the principles of harmony and order?
- **Connecting the Past and Present:**
  - Geometry links ancient wisdom with modern innovation. How can you apply its principles to navigate challenges in today's complex world?

Exploring the Infinite: The Meaning Behind "Numberless Worlds Are Around Us"

Uncovering the layers of Masonic wisdom in the contemplation of infinity.

The phrase "numberless worlds are around us" invites awe and reflection, symbolizing humanity's quest to understand the infinite cosmos and our place within it. Frequently found in Masonic teachings, this phrase is more than a poetic expression—it serves as a bridge between science, philosophy, and spirituality. In this essay, we explore the historical roots, symbolic implications, and reflective power of this evocative idea.

The Infinite Cosmos in Historical and Philosophical Context

The notion of "numberless worlds" finds its origins in the writings of Renaissance thinkers like Giordano Bruno, who challenged geocentric views by proposing an infinite universe populated with countless worlds. This radical concept influenced both scientific inquiry and philosophical discourse, paving the way for Enlightenment-era thinkers to explore creation's boundlessness (Smith, 2018). Freemasonry embraced these ideas, seeing them as reflections of divine artistry and infinite potential.

"Freemasonry draws on such cosmological insights to emphasize that the pursuit of truth and understanding is unending, much like the universe itself" (Johnson, 2020, p. 56). This belief intertwines with the Craft's core tenets, encouraging members to explore both the macrocosm of the universe and the microcosm of the self.

The Phrase in Masonic Teachings

Within Freemasonry, the phrase "numberless worlds are around us" holds a central place in the Fellow craft degree. Here, the phrase symbolizes the interconnectedness of creation and the Mason's obligation to study the natural world. The 47th Problem of Euclid, often referenced in this degree, underscores the relationship between mathematical principles and universal harmony (Anderson, 2019).

Masonic rituals frequently utilize celestial imagery to evoke awe and remind members of their place within a vast, ordered cosmos. "By considering numberless worlds, Freemasons are inspired to remain humble and committed to the pursuit of enlightenment" (Brown, 2017, p. 112). This alignment with universal truths elevates the symbolic value of Masonic teachings, connecting them to broader philosophical and scientific principles.

Broader Interpretations: From Esoteric to Secular

The esoteric interpretations of "numberless worlds" extend beyond Masonry's rituals, resonating with spiritual philosophies that view the infinite cosmos as a reflection of the divine spark within every individual (Taylor, 2021). This perspective encourages self-discovery and emphasizes that personal growth mirrors the boundless nature of the universe.

Moreover, the phrase resonates with contemporary scientific theories, such as the multiverse hypothesis, which suggests that our universe is one among countless others. This alignment demonstrates Freemasonry's enduring relevance, as its teachings continue to harmonize with modern intellectual pursuits (Green, 2019).

The contemplation of "numberless worlds" challenges Freemasons to balance intellectual curiosity with humility. It asks members to acknowledge their limitations while striving for enlightenment. "Through this lens, the phrase becomes a tool for introspection, urging Masons to align their actions with universal principles" (Walker, 2020, p. 89).

As a call to both wonder and responsibility, the phrase inspires Masons to respect the mysteries of nature and their role in the interconnected web of existence. By doing so, it aligns with Freemasonry's foundational commitment to self-improvement and ethical engagement with the world.

Reflections on the Craft: Questions for Deeper Understanding

- **Balancing Curiosity and Humility**:
    - How can the phrase "numberless worlds are around us" inspire you to balance curiosity with humility in your personal and Masonic endeavors?
- **Cycles of Exploration and Introspection**:
    - The infinite nature of "numberless worlds" symbolizes unending discovery. How do you embrace the dual cycles of exploration and introspection in your life to maintain growth and understanding?
- **Symbolism in Daily Life:**
    - How does the concept of "numberless worlds" enhance your understanding of Masonic symbols like the Square and Compasses, helping you navigate the balance between personal discipline and your role in the universal order?

Shibboleth and the Deeper Secrets of Jephthah's Sacrifice: A Masonic Reflection

A single word, a subtle reference, and a debated passage—what deeper truths does Freemasonry's focus on "Shibboleth" reveal?

Freemasonry has long held "Shibboleth" as a symbol of identification and unity, drawn from the story in Judges 12 where Jephthah and the Gileadites use it to distinguish friend from foe among the Ephraimites. The term has transcended its biblical origins, finding a place in literature and common parlance to signify a test of belonging or a marker of cultural distinction. However, beneath its surface meaning lies a connection to a smaller, highly debated biblical passage: Jephthah's sacrifice of his daughter (Judges 11:29–40). This essay explores how "Shibboleth," so central to Masonic symbolism, subtly points to this sacrifice and reflects six complex theological ideas with profound Masonic implications.

"Shibboleth" in the Lexicon

The term "Shibboleth" has become a cultural marker, appearing in works like George Orwell's Politics and the English Language to critique superficial distinctions and groupthink. Harriet Beecher Stowe's Uncle Tom's Cabin uses the term to signify a decisive cultural division. Its continued use underscores its enduring power as a symbol of identity, but this broader adoption often overlooks its tragic biblical context and the surrounding narratives.

Freemasonry's focus on "Shibboleth" emphasizes the power of words and their ability to unify or divide. Yet the deeper Masonic secret may lie in how the word—and the story it inhabits—points to questions of moral responsibility, divine justice, and human folly, as seen in Jephthah's vow and its devastating consequences.

Theological Ideas in Jephthah's Story

The Nature and Binding Power of Vows

Jephthah's vow highlights the gravity of promises made to God. Freemasonry's emphasis on oaths mirrors this seriousness, demanding integrity from its members. Yet, Jephthah's story raises a critical question: Should vows be fulfilled when they conflict with moral law? Masonic oaths are designed to uphold virtue, never to violate divine or ethical principles, suggesting a cautionary stance toward rash commitments.

Human Sacrifice vs. God's Law

Jephthah's potential offering of his daughter directly contravenes divine prohibitions against human sacrifice (Leviticus 18:21). Freemasonry's moral teachings emphasize the sanctity of human life and the alignment of actions with divine will. The story warns against zealous actions that misinterpret God's desires, aligning with Masonic ideals of measured reflection and adherence to ethical principles.

Cultural Influence and Syncretism

Jephthah's actions may reflect the influence of surrounding pagan practices. Freemasonry, while embracing universal truths, warns against adopting practices that compromise moral integrity. This echoes the Masonic pursuit of truth and the rejection of external influences that dilute foundational principles.

Divine Responsibility vs. Human Folly

The Spirit of the Lord comes upon Jephthah before his vow, raising questions about divine involvement in his tragic decision. Freemasonry encourages the pursuit of wisdom and understanding to navigate the interplay of divine inspiration and human agency. The story serves as a reminder of the need for discernment and alignment of actions with higher principles.

Interpretation of the Sacrifice

Scholars debate whether Jephthah's sacrifice was literal or figurative (e.g., dedicating his daughter to perpetual virginity). Freemasonry values diverse interpretations, fostering dialogue and deeper understanding of symbolic narratives. This ambiguity challenges Masons to seek wisdom in the face of uncertainty and to reconcile differing perspectives within their moral framework.

Tragedy and Redemption

Jephthah's story is a tragedy born of rash zeal, yet it offers lessons in humility and the consequences of unchecked ambition. Freemasonry's focus on self-improvement and the pursuit of moral perfection resonates with this theme, urging members to temper zeal with wisdom and to prioritize reflection over impulsivity.

While "Shibboleth" signifies unity and belonging within Freemasonry, it also calls attention to the consequences of division and misjudgment. The tragic narrative of Jephthah's sacrifice serves as a backdrop, urging Masons to reflect on their commitments, seek wisdom, and uphold the sanctity of life. The intersection of "Shibboleth" and Jephthah's story challenges Freemasons to balance identity and integrity with the higher pursuit of divine truth.

Reflections on the Craft: Questions for Deeper Understanding

- **Vows and Integrity:**
    - o How does the Masonic emphasis on oaths guide your understanding of Jephthah's vow? How can Masons ensure their commitments align with moral and divine principles?
- **Cultural Influence and Ethical Action:**
    - o Freemasonry embraces universal truths but warns against compromising core values. How can Masons navigate cultural pressures while remaining true to their principles, as contrasted with Jephthah's actions?

- **Tragedy and Redemption:**
    - o Jephthah's story warns of the dangers of zeal without wisdom. How do Masonic teachings on reflection and self-improvement help prevent similar moral missteps?

Unveiling the Symbolism: The Significance of the Letter "G" to Freemasons

A Universal Symbol of Geometry, Divinity, and Moral Wisdom in Freemasonry Across Cultures

The letter "G" is one of the most recognizable and thought-provoking symbols in Freemasonry, prominently displayed in many English-speaking lodges, often as part of the square and compass emblem. However, the historical incorporation of the letter "G" into Masonic symbolism, its meanings, and its use across linguistic and cultural contexts reveal a rich and evolving narrative. This essay delves into the origins of the letter "G" in Freemasonry, its symbolism, and its adaptations in non-English-speaking lodges.

Origins of the Letter "G" in Freemasonry

The letter "G" became a formalized symbol in Masonic ritual during the development of speculative Freemasonry in the 18th century. Its first recorded use in a Masonic context appeared in English-speaking lodges around the mid-1700s, coinciding with the Enlightenment's emphasis on geometry, science, and rationality. As noted by Stevenson (2013), "The letter 'G' emerged as a bridge between Masonic geometry and the Enlightenment ideals of order and reason." Its central position in Masonic symbology reflects the Craft's commitment to unifying scientific knowledge with spiritual and moral principles.

Symbolism of the Letter "G"

The meanings attributed to the letter "G" in Freemasonry are multifaceted, encompassing geometry, divinity, and morality:

Geometry and the Divine Architect

The most prominent interpretation of the "G" is its connection to Geometry, regarded as a divine science that reveals the order and harmony of the universe. Freemasons refer to the "Great Architect of the Universe," a term that embodies both the Creator and the guiding principles of symmetry and balance in the natural world. Mackey (1909) explained, "Geometry is the foundation upon which Freemasonry's teachings are built, symbolizing the perfect order of creation."

Gnosis and Knowledge

Another interpretation associates the "G" with Gnosis, the pursuit of spiritual enlightenment and deeper understanding. Freemasonry encourages members to continually seek knowledge and truth, aligning with the "G" as a representation of this transformative journey. As de Hoyos (2018) observes, "The Masonic path is one of perpetual learning, where Gnosis bridges the mundane and the divine."

Moral and Ethical Principles

The letter "G" also reflects Masonic virtues such as goodness, gratitude, and generosity, serving as a reminder of the moral character expected of members. Turner (2004) emphasized that "the 'G' inspires Masons to integrate ethical living with their pursuit of knowledge and spirituality."

The Letter "G" in Non-English-Speaking Lodges

In non-English-speaking lodges, the use of the letter "G" varies based on linguistic and cultural differences. While the symbol is prominent in English-speaking jurisdictions, lodges in other regions often substitute equivalent symbols or terms that convey the same principles:

French-Speaking Lodges: The letter "G" often represents *"Géométrie"* (geometry) or "Génie" (genius/creative spirit), aligning with the broader Masonic focus on intellectual and spiritual development.

Spanish-Speaking Lodges: The emphasis is placed on *"Gran Arquitecto del Universo"* (Great Architect of the Universe), with less reliance on the visual representation of the letter "G."

German-Speaking Lodges: The focus shifts to "Gott" (God) or *"Geometrie,"* emphasizing divine and geometric principles through language rather than the symbol itself.

In these contexts, while the symbolic essence remains consistent, the specific letter "G" may be replaced or de-emphasized to better align with local linguistic traditions. The adaptability of Masonic symbolism ensures that its core teachings transcend language and cultural barriers.

Alternatives to the Letter "G"

In jurisdictions where the letter "G" is not prominently used, other symbols often take its place to convey the same philosophical and spiritual principles. For example:

The All-Seeing Eye:
Representing divine oversight and the search for truth.

The Square and Compasses:
These tools often suffice as a universal emblem, encapsulating geometry and moral conduct without the explicit use of the letter "G."

Sacred Books:

Depending on the dominant religion or cultural context, sacred texts like the Bible, Torah, or Quran may underscore the connection to divine principles.

Conclusion

The letter "G" serves as a powerful and multifaceted symbol in Freemasonry, representing Geometry, the Divine Creator, moral principles, and the pursuit of knowledge. Its incorporation into Masonic lodges during the 18th century reflects the fraternity's commitment to uniting rational thought with spiritual enlightenment. While the "G" is widely recognized in English-speaking lodges, its use and representation in non-English-speaking jurisdictions adapt to cultural and linguistic contexts, ensuring that its underlying meanings remain accessible and relevant.

By understanding the history and flexibility of the letter "G," Freemasons worldwide honor its profound teachings while celebrating the diversity of their traditions. This universal adaptability ensures that the symbol's essence—connecting humanity to the divine, to knowledge, and to moral excellence—continues to inspire across all languages and cultures.

Reflections on the Craft: Questions for Deeper Understanding

- **The Evolution of Symbols:**
  - How does the incorporation of the letter "G" reflect the evolving nature of Masonic traditions across different historical and cultural contexts?
- **Symbolism Without Borders:**
  - In what ways can non-English-speaking lodges reinterpret the letter "G" to preserve its meanings while embracing local customs?

- **Timeless Teachings:**
  - How do the principles embodied in the letter "G"—geometry, God, and moral virtue—guide your personal and Masonic journey?

The Charge of a Fellow Craft Mason: A Journey of Growth and Responsibility

Unveiling the Fellow Craft's Path – A Step Towards Moral and Intellectual Enlightenment

The Charge of a Fellow Craft Mason is a profound directive delivered to a Mason as they advance to the second degree of Freemasonry. This ceremonial address, rich in meaning and symbolism, guides the initiate in understanding the responsibilities, expectations, and spiritual growth associated with their new status.

What is a Masonic Charge?

In Masonic tradition, a charge is a formal instruction imparted during the conferment of degrees. It encapsulates the ethical, moral, and practical guidelines that the candidate must internalize and manifest in their life. These addresses often include historical insights, philosophical directives, and symbolic interpretations that connect the Mason's duties with the broader principles of Freemasonry (Mackey, 1924).

The charge serves as a bridge between the speculative aspects of Freemasonry and the operative application of its teachings in daily life. It emphasizes individual reflection, societal responsibility, and adherence to Masonic virtues such as integrity, fidelity, and the pursuit of knowledge (Pound, 1953).

Exploring the Fellow Craft's Charge

Congratulatory Introduction: The Fellow Craft's Charge begins with an acknowledgment of the initiate's advancement, congratulating them on their preferment. This recognition underscores the progressive nature of Masonry as a moral science, emphasizing continuous growth and self-improvement (Dudley, 2010).

The Nature of Duties: The charge subtly reiterates the duties of a Fellow Craft without explicitly listing them, trusting in the Mason's commitment to virtuous conduct. It highlights the expectation of discretion, virtue, and dignity—qualities befitting a Mason's esteemed character (Jackson, 2005).

Support of Laws and Regulations: Central to the charge is the Fellow Craft's obligation to uphold Masonic laws and assist in their enforcement. This includes exercising justice, offering admonitions with friendship, and judging transgressions with fairness and candor.

The Liberal Arts and Sciences: A significant portion of the charge directs the Fellow Craft's attention to the study of the liberal arts and sciences, with particular emphasis on geometry. This focus reflects Masonry's historical roots and its philosophical embrace of knowledge as a pathway to understanding moral and divine truths (Mackey, 1924).

Fidelity and Honor: The charge concludes by impressing upon the initiate the solemnity of their obligations, binding them by fidelity and honor. This solemn commitment ensures that the Mason adheres to the fraternity's values and sets an example for others.

Interpretation

The Charge of a Fellow Craft Mason intertwines duty with enlightenment, urging the initiate to seek personal and intellectual growth while upholding their moral and social responsibilities. The emphasis on geometry as the foundation of Masonry's teachings invites Masons to view their journey as an exploration of both the natural and spiritual worlds.

By integrating these principles, the Fellow Craft transitions from speculative understanding to practical application, embodying the Masonic ideal of improving themselves and their communities.

Reflections on the Craft: Questions for Deeper Understanding

- **Balancing Growth and Responsibility:**
  - How do you interpret the balance between personal advancement and the responsibilities outlined in the Fellow Craft's charge?
- **Geometry and Morality:**
  - What insights do you draw from the emphasis on geometry in the charge, and how can this be applied to your personal and Masonic journey?
- **Enforcing Justice with Friendship**:
  - How can the principles of candor, friendship, and justice guide your interactions with others both within and beyond the lodge?

Ethical Leadership through the Lens of the Fellow Craft Degree

Discover how the Fellow craft degree equips Freemasons to embody ethical leadership in the modern world

The Fellow craft degree within Freemasonry provides a profound framework for personal growth, intellectual development, and moral responsibility. These teachings hold significant relevance in the modern context, particularly in shaping ethical leadership. This essay explores how the lessons of the Fellow craft degree can be applied by Masons to exemplify ethical leadership in today's complex societal landscape.

The Foundations of Ethical Leadership in the Fellow craft Degree

The Fellow craft degree emphasizes intellectual growth and the pursuit of knowledge, symbolized by the Trivium and Quadrivium—the classical liberal arts and sciences. This focus fosters a well-rounded intellectual foundation, essential for leaders who must navigate nuanced ethical dilemmas and make informed decisions. By mastering the liberal arts, a Fellow craft gains the tools to reason clearly, communicate effectively, and discern moral truths.

Moreover, the degree's symbolism underscores balance and integrity. The use of tools such as the Square and Level serves as metaphors for ethical alignment and equality. Ethical leadership, as taught through the Fellow craft, demands that leaders treat all individuals with fairness and act with moral uprightness. These principles are as timeless as they are critical in modern governance, business, and community leadership.

Core Teachings of the Fellow craft Degree as Ethical Principles

The Winding Staircase: A Path of Continuous Improvement

The Winding Staircase in the Fellow craft degree symbolizes the journey of intellectual and moral ascent. For modern leaders, this represents the commitment to lifelong learning and self-reflection. Ethical leadership necessitates an ongoing effort to improve oneself, to remain informed, and to align actions with moral principles. A leader who ceases to learn stagnates, losing the ability to adapt to changing circumstances or to inspire those they lead.

Climbing the Winding Staircase also represents the ability to confront challenges and overcome obstacles. Each step is a test of resilience, determination, and vision. In modern leadership, this can be seen in the need to evaluate and adjust strategies, balancing short-term decisions with long-term goals. The Winding Staircase reminds leaders that ethical success requires diligence, patience, and a willingness to grow beyond one's initial capabilities. Leaders must also inspire others to ascend alongside them, fostering a culture of collective improvement and shared purpose.

Additionally, the Winding Staircase emphasizes the importance of ethical foresight. Leaders must anticipate the consequences of their actions and ensure they align with the principles of justice and equity. By embodying the perseverance symbolized by the Staircase, leaders demonstrate that ethical leadership is not a destination but a journey of continuous ascent.

The Plumb, Square, and Level: Tools of Ethical Calibration

These tools embody principles vital for ethical leadership:

The Plumb symbolizes uprightness and truthfulness, reminding leaders to remain morally upright. The Plumb calls for ethical alignment in both private and public life. A leader guided by the Plumb understands the importance of accountability and the necessity of aligning actions with values. It ensures that decisions are made with integrity and that leaders remain consistent in their moral stance, irrespective of external pressures. This principle fosters trust, a critical component of ethical leadership, enabling leaders to build and maintain strong relationships within their teams and communities.

The Square represents fairness, ensuring that decisions are just and equitable. More than a symbol, the Square serves as a moral compass that guides leaders to treat others with impartiality and respect. It reinforces the importance of setting ethical standards and holding oneself accountable to them. A leader who applies the Square in daily interactions demonstrates the importance of equality and inclusion, ensuring that all voices are heard and valued. This approach builds a foundation of respect and cooperation, essential for creating ethical and harmonious environments.

The Level signifies equality, advocating for a leadership style that respects the inherent value of every individual. The Level encourages leaders to recognize the humanity in everyone they encounter, regardless of status or background. It serves as a reminder that ethical leadership is rooted in humility and the recognition that all individuals deserve dignity and respect. By using the Level as a guide, leaders can foster environments where collaboration and mutual support thrive, enabling collective success. The Level also reminds leaders to remain grounded, ensuring that power and privilege do not overshadow their commitment to serve.

By applying these tools metaphorically, a Fellow craft is equipped to build a framework of ethical decision-making and equitable leadership.

The Liberal Arts and Sciences: The Pillars of Wisdom

The Trivium (grammar, rhetoric, and logic) and Quadrivium (arithmetic, geometry, music, and astronomy) provide the intellectual tools necessary for sound judgment. Ethical leaders leverage these skills to articulate visions, analyze situations, and inspire action rooted in truth and justice. In a rapidly changing world, such intellectual grounding is indispensable.

The Trivium teaches the foundational skills of effective communication and critical thinking. Grammar ensures clarity of expression, rhetoric empowers leaders to inspire and persuade, and logic sharpens reasoning abilities. These skills are crucial for leaders navigating complex ethical dilemmas, as they provide the tools to articulate solutions and build consensus. The Quadrivium expands this intellectual foundation by introducing leaders to the interconnectedness of the universe. Geometry and arithmetic teach precision and structure, music fosters harmony and creativity, and astronomy inspires a sense of wonder and purpose. Together, these disciplines encourage leaders to adopt a holistic perspective, balancing analytical rigor with imaginative insight.

In applying the Liberal Arts and Sciences, ethical leaders develop the capacity to address challenges with wisdom and creativity. They learn to view problems from multiple angles, integrating diverse perspectives to achieve balanced and innovative solutions. This intellectual framework, grounded in the Fellow craft teachings, ensures that leaders remain adaptable, visionary, and committed to the greater good.

Practical Applications for Ethical Leadership

Decision-Making with Integrity

A Fellow craft's commitment to balance, symbolized by the Level, ensures impartiality in decision-making. Leaders must weigh diverse perspectives and avoid biases, fostering trust among those they lead. This impartiality enhances credibility and ensures outcomes that prioritize collective well-being over individual gain.

Guiding with Compassion and Fairness

The Square teaches leaders to measure their actions against ethical standards. Compassionate leadership, guided by fairness, not only strengthens organizational cohesion but also fosters loyalty and respect.

Promoting Lifelong Learning

The Fellow craft's emphasis on intellectual pursuit inspires leaders to continually seek knowledge and wisdom. By embracing lifelong learning, leaders can adapt to emerging challenges and innovate responsibly.

The Fellow craft as a Model for Ethical Leadership

The teachings of the Fellow craft degree provide timeless principles that empower Masons to embody ethical leadership in the modern world. By integrating the values of intellectual growth, moral integrity, and fairness into their actions, Masons can navigate the complexities of contemporary challenges with wisdom and compassion. As ethical leaders, they illuminate the path for others, upholding the enduring tenets of Freemasonry in service to society.

Reflections on the Craft: Questions for Deeper Understanding

- **Ethical Calibration and Leadership**
    - How can you apply the tools of the Fellow craft degree—the Plumb, Square, and Level—to ensure integrity, fairness, and equality in your leadership decisions?
- **Continuous Growth**
    - The Winding Staircase symbolizes the journey of self-improvement. How do you commit to lifelong learning and apply the knowledge gained to ethical leadership in your community and profession?
- **Knowledge as a Guiding Light**
    - How do the liberal arts and sciences equip you to approach modern challenges with wisdom and uphold the ethical principles of Freemasonry in your leadership endeavors?

The Raised Master Mason: The Pinnacle of Masonic Transformation

Under the Almond Tree: A Mason's Reflection on Mortality and Renewal

Reflecting on mortality and the wisdom of life's fleeting nature, Ecclesiastes 12 offers profound insights for the spiritually inclined and the Mason alike

As the writer of Ecclesiastes approached the culmination of his reflections, Chapter 12 emerges as a deeply poetic and philosophical passage. It invites readers to contemplate life's transient nature and the inevitability of its end. The chapter, particularly in the King James Version, brims with metaphors and imagery that poignantly describe the journey from youth to old age and beyond. It begins with a call to remember the Creator in youth and transitions into a vivid description of aging, concluding with reflections on life's ultimate return to its source.

Verses 1-2: The Call to Remember the Creator

The opening verses set a tone of urgency: "Remember now thy Creator in the days of thy youth, while the evil days come not, nor the years draw nigh, when thou shalt say, I have no pleasure in them." These words encourage readers to value and honor their relationship with God before the trials of aging dim their capacity for joy and action.

The imagery of "the sun, or the light, or the moon, or the stars" being darkened evokes a cosmic metaphor for the decline of vitality and hope. As life progresses, the youthful energy symbolized by light gives way to the shadows of age. This exhortation to act while the light remains is echoed in various biblical teachings, such as Christ's words in John 9:4: "I must work the works of him that sent me, while it is day."

Verses 3-7: The Poetics of Aging

In verses 3 through 7, the writer employs a cascade of metaphors to describe the physical and emotional decline that accompanies old age.

"The keepers of the house shall tremble" likely refers to trembling hands.

"The strong men shall bow themselves" symbolizes the weakening of legs and physical strength.

"The grinders cease because they are few" poetically refers to the loss of teeth.

"Those that look out of the windows be darkened" describes the dimming of eyesight.

These lines paint an evocative picture of the gradual deterioration of the body, further emphasized by the poignant statement that "the doors shall be shut in the streets." This imagery reflects a withdrawal from the world, as the elderly often retreat into solitude.

Verse 5, which speaks of fears and the almond tree flourishing, transitions to a reflection on mortality: "Man goeth to his long home, and the mourners go about the streets." The image of an almond tree in bloom, with its striking display of white blossoms, serves as a poignant metaphor for the white hair of old age, symbolizing the fleeting beauty and fragility of life. This profound acknowledgment of life's finite nature invites readers to consider how they wish to live in light of their inevitable departure, urging them to reflect on the legacy they leave behind and the values they embody.

Verses 8-12: Vanity and the Pursuit of Wisdom

The refrain, "Vanity of vanities, saith the preacher; all is vanity," reappears in verse 8, underscoring the transient and ultimately futile nature of earthly pursuits. The writer's conclusion is not one of despair but of sober wisdom: to seek God and live righteously amidst life's fleeting pleasures and trials.

Verse 11's mention of the "words of the wise" as goads and nails affirms the enduring power of wisdom to guide and anchor the soul. A goad, traditionally a pointed stick used to prod animals to move forward, symbolizes how wise words can spur individuals into action or provoke deeper thought. The imagery highlights the way wisdom, though sometimes uncomfortable, pushes us toward growth and understanding. The "nails," securely fastened by the "masters of assemblies," represent the stability and permanence of wisdom, anchoring it firmly in the truths provided by the "one shepherd," often interpreted as God. This profound acknowledgment of wisdom's ability to inspire and stabilize is complemented by the chapter's recognition of human limitations in comprehending divine mysteries: "of making many books there is no end; and much study is a weariness of the flesh." Together, these reflections encourage a pursuit of wisdom that balances action, stability, and humility, acknowledging both its transformative power and the finite scope of human understanding.

Verse 13: The Conclusion of the Matter

The final verse encapsulates the chapter's message: "Fear God, and keep his commandments: for this is the whole duty of man." This succinct conclusion reminds readers of the ultimate purpose of life. Reverence for the Creator and adherence to divine laws form the foundation of a meaningful existence, transcending the vanities of worldly endeavors.

Masonic Reflections on Ecclesiastes 12

For Freemasons, Ecclesiastes 12 resonates deeply with the Craft's teachings on morality, wisdom, and mortality. The descriptions of aging parallel Masonic allegories that remind members of life's fleeting nature. Masonic symbols like the hourglass and the scythe emphasize the relentless passage of time, while the call to remember the Creator aligns with the spiritual journey Freemasons undertake to seek enlightenment.

The imagery of the "strong men bowing" and the "darkened windows" can be seen as metaphors for humility and introspection—virtues cultivated in Masonic practice. The almond tree's bloom, symbolizing resilience, mirrors the Craft's emphasis on renewal and self-improvement.

Moreover, the final exhortation to "fear God and keep his commandments" aligns with the Masonic commitment to live virtuously, guided by principles of brotherhood, charity, and reverence for the Grand Architect of the Universe.

Ecclesiastes 12 invites readers to confront the reality of aging and mortality with wisdom and faith. Its vivid imagery and profound insights offer guidance for living a purposeful life, even as physical vitality wanes. For Freemasons, the chapter provides a rich tapestry of symbols and teachings that affirm the values of the Craft and the universal journey toward enlightenment.

Reflections on the Craft: Questions for Deeper Understanding

- **The Passage of Time:**
  - How does Ecclesiastes 12 encourage you to reflect on the ways you prioritize your time and energy in alignment with spiritual and Masonic values?
- **The Role of Wisdom:**
  - In what ways can the "words of the wise" serve as anchors in both personal and communal Masonic endeavors?
- **Mortality and Purpose:**
  - How can the chapter's acknowledgment of life's transience inspire a deeper commitment to the Masonic ideals of self-improvement and service to others?

All the Tools of the Craft: Building Character Through Masonic Teachings

Discover how Masonic tools offer timeless guidance for harmony, morality, and self-improvement.

Freemasonry, with its rich tapestry of tools and symbols, provides profound lessons applicable to everyday life. Among its most renowned implements are the Twenty-Four Inch Gauge, Common Gavel, Plumb, Square, Level, and Trowel. These tools, originally designed for operative masonry, have been transformed into speculative symbols that guide moral behavior, foster unity, and inspire personal growth. Together, these tools imprint upon the memory wise and serious truths essential to leading a virtuous and fulfilling life. Furthermore, their sequential use mirrors how a stonemason would build a mighty edifice, reflecting the progressive journey of personal and moral development.

The Twenty-Four Inch Gauge: Balancing Time

The Twenty-Four Inch Gauge divides the day into three equal parts: service to God and others, vocation, and refreshment. This division highlights the necessity of balance in life. As Claudy (1931) notes, "The Gauge teaches us the nobility of work, the joy of service, and the necessity of rest." This tool reminds individuals to align their time with their values and responsibilities. For a stonemason, the gauge would have been used to measure and prepare materials, ensuring precision before the work began.

The Common Gavel: Refining the Self

The Common Gavel, used by operative masons to trim stones, symbolizes self-improvement in speculative Freemasonry. It encourages individuals to "chip away" vices and excesses, molding themselves into virtuous beings. Benjamin Franklin, a Freemason, encapsulated this when he said, "Without continual growth and progress, improvement and success have no meaning" (Franklin, 2024). This tool inspires daily reflection and commitment to personal excellence. Operatively, it helped shape raw stones into the perfect form required for construction.

The Plumb: Living Uprightly

The Plumb represents alignment and uprightness, both in physical construction and moral life. It reminds Masons to conduct themselves with integrity and fairness. As Amos (7:7–8) declares, "I am setting a plumb line among my people Israel; I will spare them no longer." This metaphor reflects divine justice and moral rectitude. Masonic teachings elevate the Plumb as a symbol of living an upright life, encouraging individuals to align their actions with ethical principles and truth. For the stonemason, the plumb ensured that walls were perfectly vertical, critical for structural integrity.

The Square: Aligning Actions with Virtue

The Square is a cornerstone of Masonic symbolism, representing morality and virtue. It teaches Masons to "square" their actions by the principles of honesty and fairness. Biblically, the square's significance is echoed in passages like Isaiah 28:17: "I will make justice the measuring line, and righteousness the plumb line." For the operative mason, the square ensured that stones were cut and placed at perfect right angles, laying the foundation for stability and harmony in the structure.

The Level: Embracing Equality

The Level teaches fairness and equality, reminding Masons that all meet "on the level" in the lodge, irrespective of social or economic distinctions. Its biblical resonance, as Isaiah (40:4) declares, "Every valley shall be raised up, every mountain and hill made low," underscores the importance of eliminating disparities to foster unity. Literature further captures this ethos; Shakespeare's "Measure for Measure" reflects on living uprightly and balancing power with fairness (Stevens, 2009). In construction, the level ensured that all elements aligned horizontally, maintaining balance and symmetry.

The Trowel: Spreading Unity

The Trowel's practical role in spreading mortar parallels its symbolic function in Freemasonry: to foster unity and brotherly love. As Masonic teachings emphasize, "The trowel spreads the cement of brotherly love and affection that unites us into one sacred band" (Pike, 1871). This tool encourages individuals to mend divisions and build connections within their communities. For the mason, the trowel was the final tool, uniting stones with mortar to create a cohesive and enduring structure.

Practical Applications of Masonic Teachings

A stonemason's work began with the Twenty-Four Inch Gauge, measuring and preparing the raw materials to ensure precision and readiness. Next, the Common Gavel was used to refine these materials, trimming away imperfections and shaping the stones to fit their intended purpose. The Plumb followed, ensuring that the stones were set upright, forming strong and aligned walls. The Square was then applied to guarantee perfect angles, creating a stable and harmonious foundation. With the Level, the mason verified horizontal alignment, ensuring balance and symmetry in the structure.

Finally, the Trowel united the stones with mortar, binding them into a cohesive and enduring edifice.

Similarly, a man seeking self-improvement can metaphorically employ these tools to construct his character. The Twenty-Four Inch Gauge reminds him to balance his time wisely, laying the groundwork for a disciplined life. The Common Gavel encourages the removal of personal flaws, refining his character. The Plumb inspires him to live with integrity, aligning his actions with ethical principles. The Square guides him to measure his behavior against moral virtues, ensuring fairness and honesty. The Level teaches him to treat others as equals, fostering unity and mutual respect. Finally, the Trowel calls him to spread kindness and harmony, building lasting connections and a strong community.

Reflections on the Craft: Questions for Deeper Understanding

- **Selecting Your Tool:**
    - Which of the Masonic tools resonates most with your current personal journey, and why is it the most appropriate starting point?
- **Ordering the Tools:**
    - In what sequence would you apply these tools to address a challenge in your life, and how does each step build upon the last?
- **Using the Tools:**
    - How can you actively incorporate the lessons of one or more tools into your daily actions to achieve personal growth and harmony?

Fleeting Days and Eternal Hope: Reflections on Job 14

Exploring Job 14 through the lenses of Christianity, Judaism, and Masonic wisdom, revealing insights into mortality, hope, and eternal truth.

The poetic lament of Job 14, with its vivid imagery and existential musings, grapples with the themes of human mortality, divine sovereignty, and the yearning for renewal. The passage unfolds as Job meditates on the brevity and fragility of human life, employing metaphors like a fading flower and a fleeting shadow. This analysis examines Job 14:1-12 in the contexts of Christianity, Judaism, and Freemasonry, particularly within the Third Degree ritual.

Scriptural Analysis and Its Meaning in Christianity and Judaism

In verses 1-6, Job acknowledges the ephemeral nature of human existence: "Man that is born of a woman is of few days and full of trouble. He cometh forth like a flower, and is cut down: he fleeth also as a shadow, and continueth not." The metaphor of a flower highlights the fleeting beauty of life, while the imagery of a shadow evokes life's intangibility and impermanence. For Job, this brevity is compounded by divine sovereignty—"Thou hast appointed his bounds that he cannot pass" (v. 5, KJV), which reflects a belief in God's ultimate control over life and death.

In Christian theology, Job's lament underscores humanity's fallen state and the need for redemption through Christ. Augustine interpreted this passage as a reminder of original sin, which brought mortality into the world (Gorday, 2012). The Apostle Paul echoes this sentiment in Romans 8:20-23, where he speaks of creation's bondage to decay and its hope for liberation through Christ.

Judaism approaches Job's reflections as a profound exploration of divine justice. The Talmud regards Job as a figure who wrestles with theodicy, exemplifying humanity's struggle to reconcile suffering with faith in a just God (Steinberg, 1989). Job's plea in verses 7-9, where he compares human mortality to the potential renewal of a tree, conveys an inherent tension between despair and hope: "For there is hope of a tree, if it be cut down, that it will sprout again." This imagery resonates with Jewish eschatological beliefs in resurrection and the enduring covenant between God and Israel.

The Masonic Perspective and the Third Degree

Freemasonry imbues this passage with profound symbolic meaning, particularly within the Third Degree, or Master Mason, ritual. The themes of mortality and hope are central to this degree, which teaches the inevitability of physical death and the transcendence of the spiritual journey.

The metaphor of the tree's potential renewal aligns with the Masonic concept of rebirth. In the Third Degree, the candidate symbolically undergoes a figurative death, represented by the legend of Hiram Abiff. This allegory emphasizes perseverance, moral integrity, and the hope of immortality—qualities echoed in Job's vision of a tree's regeneration. As Mackey (1927) explains, "Freemasonry's doctrines of immortality are symbolized by the evergreen, which is a reminder that the soul endures beyond the grave."

Moreover, Job's acknowledgment of human limitations ("Man's days are determined") underscores the Masonic teaching that life's brevity necessitates a commitment to virtuous living. The Square and Compasses, fundamental Masonic symbols, serve as a daily reminder to balance personal ambitions with ethical principles—an endeavor reflected in Job's quest for understanding and righteousness amidst suffering.

Reflection and Relevance Today

Job 14 invites readers to confront the fragility of life while embracing the possibility of renewal. Within Christianity, it reinforces the hope of resurrection through Christ's triumph over death. In Judaism, it celebrates enduring faith amidst adversity and the promise of divine justice. For Freemasons, the passage inspires contemplation of mortality and the pursuit of immortality through spiritual enlightenment and moral rectitude.

As modern readers, Job's reflections challenge us to balance the acceptance of life's transience with an enduring hope for renewal—a message that transcends time and tradition.

Reflections on the Craft: Questions for Deeper Understanding

- **Balancing Zeal and Wisdom:**
  - How can you integrate the Masonic lesson of life's transience, as reflected in Job 14, into your personal and Masonic endeavors?
- **Cycles of Growth and Reflection:**
  - The imagery of the tree in Job 14 symbolizes renewal. How do you embrace cycles of growth and renewal in your spiritual and ethical life?
- **Symbolism in Daily Life:**

o How do Masonic symbols, such as the evergreen, inspire hope and perseverance in your daily challenges?

The Masonic Trowel: Building Bridges between Craft and Symbolism

The trowel—from operative tool to emblematic virtue—connects ancient craftsmanship with Masonic brotherhood.

The trowel, though seemingly a humble tool, carries profound significance in both operative masonry and speculative Freemasonry. Its practical applications and symbolic interpretations intertwine, offering lessons on unity, harmony, and spiritual edification. By examining its use in operative masonry, biblical references, literary portrayals, and Masonic symbolism, we can uncover the multi-faceted dimensions of this enduring implement.

The Operative Trowel

In operative masonry, the trowel is indispensable. It is primarily used to spread mortar, which binds bricks or stones, creating durable structures. The precision and care with which a mason uses a trowel directly influence the stability and aesthetic of the construction. For example, during the building of medieval cathedrals, masons relied on the trowel to secure the intricate stonework of flying buttresses and arches, ensuring that each piece fit seamlessly into the overall design. The trowel's role in such projects exemplifies its importance in achieving architectural harmony.

Biblical References to the Trowel

Biblical texts provide indirect but relevant insights into the significance of construction tools like the trowel. In the Book of Nehemiah, the rebuilding of Jerusalem's walls highlights the collaborative spirit of the builders:

"The builders each wore his sword at his side as he worked."
(Nehemiah 4:18, NIV)

Though the trowel itself is not named, its implied presence symbolizes the labor of construction amidst adversity. Similarly, the tools of building, including the trowel, signify preparedness and dedication in achieving divine and communal goals.

The prophet Isaiah also draws metaphorical parallels:

"Behold, I lay in Zion a stone for a foundation, a tried stone, a precious cornerstone, a sure foundation..." (Isaiah 28:16, NKJV)

Here, the emphasis on a cornerstone underscores the importance of careful craftsmanship, wherein the trowel's role in spreading mortar aligns with creating enduring foundations.

The Trowel in Literature

The trowel appears in literature as a symbol of both literal and metaphorical construction. In Edgar Allan Poe's "The Cask of Amontillado," the trowel takes on a dark turn as Montresor uses it to enact his grim revenge. While this narrative underscores the tool's practicality, it also hints at the duality of creation and destruction inherent in all tools.

Conversely, in poetic and allegorical works, the trowel often symbolizes unity and effort. It serves as a reminder of human agency in building connections and communities, emphasizing collective endeavors over individual pursuits.

Masonic Symbolism of the Trowel

In speculative Freemasonry, the trowel is elevated from a mere tool to a profound symbol of fraternity and unity. Freemasons use the trowel to metaphorically spread the cement of brotherly love, uniting members of the Craft in common purpose and moral rectitude. As stated in Masonic lectures:

"The trowel teaches us to spread the cement of brotherly love and affection, which unites us into one sacred band or society of friends and brothers."

This allegorical use reinforces the virtues of harmony and mutual support. The trowel symbolizes the application of moral principles to everyday actions, encouraging Freemasons to "build" lives of integrity and compassion.

Religious Significance of the Trowel

The trowel's religious connotations stem from its role in creating sacred spaces. In constructing temples, cathedrals, and altars, the trowel becomes a mediator between the physical and the divine. It represents the human endeavor to connect with higher principles through tangible works. For Freemasons, the trowel's spiritual significance resonates in its call to apply ethical teachings in the "mortar" of daily life, uniting disparate elements into a cohesive whole.

From operative masonry to speculative Freemasonry, the trowel bridges practical craftsmanship and spiritual enlightenment. It reminds us of the importance of unity, both in the physical structures we build and in the communities we nurture. By spreading the cement of brotherly love, the trowel embodies the core tenets of Freemasonry—charity, fraternity, and integrity.

Reflections on the Craft: Questions for Deeper Understanding

- **Building with Purpose:**
    - o How does the practical use of the trowel in operative masonry inspire your approach to constructing relationships within the Masonic fraternity?
- **From Foundations to Fulfillment:**
    - o The trowel spreads mortar to bind stones, creating lasting structures. How can you apply this metaphor to strengthen the moral and spiritual foundations of your life?
- **Unity in Diversity:**
    - o The trowel unites different stones into a single structure. How can Freemasonry's teachings help you embrace diversity and foster unity in your community?

The Names Hiram and Abif: A Narrative Journey through Symbolism and Legacy

The enduring legacy of Hiram and Abif as cornerstones of moral and spiritual ideals in Freemasonry and beyond.

In the annals of history and the echoes of tradition, the names Hiram and Abif emerge as symbols of craftsmanship, collaboration, and integrity. These names, rooted in ancient narratives, transcend their origins to become emblems of ethical and spiritual ideals. This narrative journey seeks to unravel the stories of Hiram and Abif, exploring their profound impact from biblical times to modern interpretations.

The Origins of Two Names

The names Hiram (חירם) and Abif (אביף) carry meanings steeped in reverence and mastery. Hiram translates to "exalted," while Abif signifies "father" or "master" (Strong, 1890). These linguistic roots underline their association with leadership and skill, a reputation that extends through history. Across Greek and Latin adaptations, their names retained a sense of dignity and expertise (Brown, Driver, & Briggs, 1906).

A Partnership Forged in Building

In the Bible, Hiram, King of Tyre, is immortalized as a crucial ally of King Solomon in the construction of the Temple. He supplied cedar wood and skilled artisans, creating a partnership that exemplified unity and purpose (1 Kings 5:1-10). This collaboration not only fulfilled a divine mission but also set a precedent for teamwork in service of higher goals (Freedman, 1992).

Meanwhile, Hiram Abif's narrative lives predominantly in the legends surrounding the temple's construction. As a master craftsman, his role in shaping the temple reflects unparalleled dedication. Though absent from biblical texts, his story—woven into post-biblical traditions—emphasizes themes of sacrifice, loyalty, and mastery (Ridley, 2011).

The Masonic Reverence for Hiram Abif

In Freemasonry, Hiram Abif is more than a historical figure; he is a moral archetype. His tragic death, resisting betrayal, serves as an allegory for unwavering integrity and sacrifice (Mackey, 1921). Masonic rituals honor his memory, embedding his story into teachings about ethical conduct and perseverance. Hiram's steadfastness inspires Masons to uphold principles of honesty and courage.

The symbolic teachings of Hiram and Abif resonate deeply in Freemasonry. Their stories illustrate ideals of craftsmanship, leadership, and collaboration, encouraging members to pursue excellence in both personal and communal endeavors (Jackson, 1996).

Artistic and Cultural Echoes

The legacy of Hiram and Abif is perpetuated through art and literature, bridging ancient narratives with modern values. From the intricate medieval illuminations in Gothic manuscripts, such as the Bible Moralisée, to the symbolic interpretations found in Albert Pike's Morals and Dogma (1871), their stories continue to inspire creative and philosophical explorations. Medieval illuminations, which depicted the construction of Solomon's Temple, celebrated the craftsmanship and unity of figures like Hiram Abif, preserving their allegorical significance and influencing later Masonic traditions (Knoop & Jones, 1978). In modern literature, Pike's exploration of Hiram Abif's symbolic death highlights themes of sacrifice, integrity, and ethical leadership, central to Masonic teachings.

Beyond artistic and literary representations, the broader symbolism of Hiram and Abif profoundly influences leadership paradigms. Their tales of dedication, collaboration, and mastery inform ethical frameworks, emphasizing the importance of unity, shared purpose, and perseverance in achieving great works (Stevenson, 1988). These enduring narratives continue to resonate, offering timeless lessons that inspire both creativity and moral development

Modern Resonance

Today, the symbolic resonance of Hiram and Abif extends beyond their historical and Masonic roots. Their narratives inspire modern discussions on integrity, leadership, and the pursuit of mastery. In a world seeking ethical role models, their stories offer timeless lessons on collaboration and excellence (Ridley, 2011).

Reflections on Legacy

The names Hiram and Abif encapsulate values that transcend time: dedication, integrity, and the power of collaboration. Their enduring significance in Freemasonry and beyond highlights the relevance of ancient ideals in contemporary thought. As we reflect on their legacy, we are reminded of the profound impact that stories of mastery and sacrifice can have on shaping ethical and spiritual frameworks.

Reflections on the Craft: Questions for Deeper Understanding

- **Balancing Craftsmanship and Integrity:**
  - o How do the lives and legacies of Hiram and Abif inspire you to pursue excellence while maintaining steadfast integrity in your personal and Masonic journey?
- **Symbolism of Sacrifice and Unity:**
  - o The collaboration between Hiram and King Solomon symbolizes unity in purpose and sacrifice for a greater good. How can this example guide your efforts in fostering teamwork and ethical leadership?
- **Timeless Lessons for Modern Masons:**
  - o The story of Hiram Abif continues to resonate as a moral allegory. In what ways can the principles embodied by these figures be applied to navigate contemporary challenges in Freemasonry and society?

The Building of King Solomon's Temple

Discover the awe-inspiring history and sacred symbolism of King Solomon's Temple, a cornerstone of ancient Israelite identity.

The Temple built by King Solomon stands as one of the most significant architectural and spiritual achievements in human history. Rooted in the narratives of the Bible and illuminated further by the works of the Jewish historian Flavius Josephus, this monumental structure encapsulates the religious aspirations, political acumen, and architectural mastery of ancient Israel.

Historical Context and Divine Mandate

The construction of the Temple was a fulfillment of King David's vision, passed to his son Solomon, who was divinely chosen to bring it to fruition. According to 1 Kings 5:5, Solomon declared, "I intend, therefore, to build a temple for the Name of the Lord my God, as the Lord told my father David." The Temple symbolized God's covenant with Israel, serving as the spiritual heart of the nation and the dwelling place of His presence.

Flavius Josephus, in Antiquities of the Jews, reinforces the notion of divine sanction for the Temple's construction, emphasizing its central role in consolidating the religious and political unity of Israel. Josephus notes, "The Temple was designed not only to be a sanctuary for worship but also a symbol of national unity and divine favor" (Antiquities, VIII.3.8).

Architectural Grandeur

Solomon's Temple was designed with meticulous attention to detail, as described in the biblical accounts of 1 Kings 6 and 2 Chronicles 3. The Temple was constructed with dimensions of 60 cubits in length, 20 cubits in width, and 30 cubits in height. Its interior was adorned with cedar wood overlaid with gold, and its most sacred space, the Holy of Holies, housed the Ark of the Covenant.

Josephus adds a vivid description of the Temple's brilliance: "The exterior gleamed with golden plates that reflected the sun's rays, making it appear like a mountain covered with snow" (Antiquities, VIII.3.8). This account highlights the Temple's unparalleled beauty and symbolic resonance as a beacon of divine glory.

Two prominent features of the Temple were the pillars Jachin and Boaz, which flanked the entrance. These pillars symbolized strength and stability, underscoring the covenantal relationship between God and Israel.

Construction and Sacred Labor

The construction of the Temple took seven years to complete, with resources gathered through alliances, such as with King Hiram of Tyre, who provided cedar and skilled craftsmen (1 Kings 5:6). The labor force consisted of tens of thousands, working in shifts to quarry stone, prepare timber, and build the structure.

One of the most remarkable aspects of the construction process was the prohibition of using iron tools on-site, as stated in 1 Kings 6:7: "The Temple was built of stone finished at the quarry so that no hammer, chisel, or any other iron tool was heard in the Temple while it was being built." This silence reflected the sanctity of the site and the reverence for God.

Spiritual Significance and Dedication

The Temple was not merely an architectural marvel but a spiritual center for Israel. At its dedication, Solomon's prayer beseeched God to make it a place where His name would dwell, where prayers would be heard, and forgiveness granted (1 Kings 8:22-53). The divine response, with fire descending to consume the offerings and the glory of the Lord filling the Temple, affirmed its sanctification (2 Chronicles 7:1-3).

The Temple's design, from the Holy of Holies to the altar of incense, was imbued with profound symbolism, representing the cosmos, divine order, and the covenant between God and His people.

Legacy and Reflection

Solomon's Temple became the focal point of Jewish worship and identity until its destruction by the Babylonians in 586 BCE. Josephus laments its loss but acknowledges its enduring legacy as a symbol of divine presence and human aspiration. Its memory and significance persist in religious, historical, and cultural contexts, influencing countless spiritual traditions, including Freemasonry.

Reflections on the Craft: Questions for Deeper Understanding

- **Architectural Symbolism in the Craft:**
  - How can the detailed design of King Solomon's Temple inspire Masonic teachings on precision and harmony in our personal and communal endeavors?
- **Labor and Unity:**

- o In what ways can the collaborative efforts in the Temple's construction remind Masons of the importance of unity and shared purpose in building a better world?
- **Sacred Space and Silence:**
  - o How does the Temple's silent construction resonate with Masonic values of reverence and reflection in the pursuit of personal and spiritual growth?

Flavius Josephus: Chronicler of a Tumultuous Era

Discover the life and influence of Flavius Josephus: historian, priest, and pivotal chronicler of the Jewish-Roman era.

Flavius Josephus, born Yosef ben Matityahu in 37 CE, stands as one of the most significant historians of the ancient world. His works provide a detailed account of Jewish history and the complex relationship between the Jewish people and the Roman Empire. A figure of controversy and historical importance, Josephus' life and writings have sparked debates over loyalty, truth, and historical narrative.

Early Life and Context

Born in Jerusalem into a priestly family, Josephus was well-educated and became a Pharisee, aligning himself with a sect known for its rigorous interpretation of Jewish law. His early life coincided with a period of increasing tension between the Jewish population and Roman authorities. Josephus was deeply influenced by this volatile environment, which would shape his later role as a historian and mediator.

In his autobiographical work, The Life of Josephus, he describes his initial education and the influence of various Jewish sects: the Pharisees, Sadducees, and Essenes. He notes, "When I was about sixteen years old, I determined to gain personal experience of the three groups" (Josephus, 1976, p. 9). This exploration laid the groundwork for his deep understanding of Jewish society and theology.

Role in the Jewish Revolt

Josephus' life took a dramatic turn during the First Jewish-Roman War (66–70 CE). Initially serving as a commander in

Galilee, he defended Jewish cities against Roman forces. Captured by the Romans, Josephus defected to their side, a decision that has earned him the label of traitor among many of his contemporaries and later historians.

He became an advisor to the Flavian dynasty, claiming that he had prophesied Vespasian's rise to the throne. In The Jewish War, Josephus recounts this event: "I went boldly to Vespasian and said that he and his sons would be emperors" (Josephus, 1981, p. 57). While some view this as opportunism, others interpret it as a pragmatic choice to preserve his life and ensure the survival of Jewish culture through his writings.

Works and Contributions

Josephus' literary legacy includes four key works: The Jewish War, Antiquities of the Jews, Against Apion, and The Life of Josephus. Together, these writings chronicle the history of the Jewish people from their biblical origins to the destruction of the Second Temple.

In The Jewish War, Josephus provides a detailed account of the revolt, including the tragic fall of Jerusalem. His vivid description of the siege offers insights into the devastation: "The famine widened its progress, and devoured whole houses and families" (Josephus, 1981, p. 311). This work remains an indispensable source for understanding the conflict and its consequences.

Meanwhile, Antiquities of the Jews serves as a comprehensive history of the Jewish people, intended to explain Jewish customs and beliefs to a Roman audience. In it, Josephus demonstrates his ability to navigate complex cultural narratives, often balancing his Jewish heritage with his Roman patronage.

Historical Impact and Legacy

Josephus' writings have been both celebrated and scrutinized. For Jewish and Christian historians, his works serve as a vital source for understanding the period. However, his perceived biases—both toward his Roman benefactors and against certain Jewish factions—have prompted critical analysis.

Modern scholarship often wrestles with these biases. Historian Steve Mason notes, "Josephus walked a fine line, negotiating his identity as both a Jew and a Roman client" (Mason, 2003, p. 134). This duality underscores the complexity of interpreting his legacy.

Josephus' life invites reflection on themes of loyalty, survival, and the preservation of culture. His decision to collaborate with Rome ensured that future generations would have a record of Jewish history, albeit one shaped by his unique perspective. As such, Josephus remains a figure of enduring significance, both for his historical contributions and the ethical questions his life raises.

Reflections on the Craft: Questions for Deeper Understanding

- **Balancing Loyalty and Truth**:
  - How can Josephus' actions during the Jewish revolt inspire discussions about the balance between personal survival and fidelity to one's community?
- **Preservation of Knowledge:**
  - In what ways does Josephus' detailed chronicling of Jewish history reflect Masonic values of learning and enlightenment?
- **Interpreting Historical Bias:**

o How might Josephus' perceived biases serve as a reminder to critically examine all sources of knowledge?

Master Lesson on Building the Temple Within

Exploring the timeless principles from the Third Degree

Life is a grand construction project, akin to building a temple. Each individual works with their tools, striving to craft a structure that reflects their highest values and virtues. However, the challenges of temptation, shortcuts, and misguided alliances often test the strength and stability of this endeavor. By examining the metaphors of construction, the dual nature of determination, and the influence of companionship, we can uncover profound lessons on personal and spiritual growth.

The Value of Constructive Effort

Building a meaningful life requires deliberate effort and patience. Each choice and action is like a stone placed in a temple, contributing to its overall strength and beauty. When effort is substituted with shortcuts, the resulting instability threatens the integrity of the whole.

This principle mirrors the teachings of ancient builders who emphasized the importance of diligence and precision. As Jackson (1999) explains, "Every stone represents a virtue or discipline, and the labor required to shape it symbolizes the journey of self-improvement" (p. 134). Skipping essential steps in this process, whether in moral development or personal achievement, risks undermining the foundation of one's character.

Tools of Transformation

As the Master Mason learns, the tools used in life's construction hold profound symbolic meaning. Each tool, whether it measures, shapes, or builds, reflects a virtue essential to personal and spiritual growth. Yet, these same tools can be misused, transforming their purpose from creation to destruction.

- **The Rule:** A tool for measurement and order, it represents justice and fairness. Its misuse, however, symbolizes the distortion of truth and equity.
- **The Square:** A symbol of morality and upright behavior, its integrity is compromised when wielded unethically.
- **The Maul**: A representation of constructive power, it reminds us that force, when misdirected, can lead to destruction rather than progress.

"Every tool carries the potential for both instruction and harm, depending on how it is employed," observes Hammer (2013, p. 162). This duality urges us to wield our capabilities responsibly, ensuring they align with ethical principles and virtuous intentions.

The Dual Nature of Determination

Determination is a powerful force that can either build or destroy, depending on its alignment with virtue. A steadfast commitment to one's goals, when guided by ethical values, leads to extraordinary achievements. However, when determination is misdirected, it becomes a force of destruction.

A metaphor for determination can be seen in the mirror. When we look into this reflective surface, we see both our potential for greatness and the shadows of our flaws. As Wilmshurst (1922) explains, "Self-reflection reveals not only our virtues but also the traits that, if unchecked, can lead us astray" (p. 45). Through introspection, we can align our determination with positive values, ensuring that our drive contributes to the construction of a strong, harmonious life.

The Temple as a Metaphor for Life

The temple, as a symbol of life, embodies the balance between physical and spiritual growth. Each brick represents an experience, and each tool symbolizes a virtue required for its placement. The process of building this temple teaches patience, discipline, and a respect for the journey.

The pursuit of shortcuts—seeking rewards without effort—often leads to disaster. This truth resonates in both historical and contemporary contexts. As MacNulty (2006) notes, "Only a carefully constructed foundation can support the weight of a meaningful life" (p. 87). Those who attempt to bypass the necessary labor find their structures crumbling under the weight of unmet challenges.

The Influence of Companionship

Companions play a critical role in life's construction. Surrounding oneself with individuals who uphold similar values reinforces one's moral and spiritual integrity. Conversely, negative influences can erode even the strongest foundations.

"The companions we choose shape our moral and spiritual landscapes, guiding us either toward or away from the ideals we strive to embody," asserts Hodapp (2005, p. 82). Building relationships with those who support and inspire ensures a supportive framework for life's journey, while toxic alliances risk pulling us into actions and decisions that compromise our principles.

The construction of life's temple is an ongoing process, requiring diligence, self-reflection, and careful selection of companions. By understanding the value of effort, the symbolism of tools, and the dual nature of determination, we can ensure our labor contributes to a strong and harmonious structure. Choosing virtuous companions further strengthens the foundation, enabling us to weather life's challenges with integrity.

Ultimately, the metaphor of the temple serves as a timeless reminder that life's greatest achievements arise from patience, effort, and alignment with ethical values. Each brick we lay is an opportunity to create something lasting and meaningful—an enduring testament to our commitment to growth and virtue.

Reflections on the Craft: Questions for Deeper Understanding

- **The Power of Reflection:**
  - How does the metaphor of the mirror encourage you to examine both your strengths and the areas where you might risk misdirecting your determination?
- **Building Your Temple:**
  - In what ways are you carefully constructing your personal and spiritual "temple," and how do you guard against the temptation of shortcuts?
- **Choosing Companions:**
  - How do your relationships reflect and support the values and virtues you strive to uphold in your own life?

The Pot of Incense: A Symbol of Purity and Gratitude

An emblem that connects the heart's purity with divine devotion and moral excellence

The Pot of Incense, as depicted in Masonic symbolism, represents a pure heart, an offering perpetually acceptable to the Divine. It invites reflection on themes of purity, gratitude, and fervent devotion, all of which resonate across biblical narratives, philosophical thought, and Masonic teachings. This essay explores the significance of the Pot of Incense by delving into its historical, scriptural, and ethical dimensions, underscoring its role in inspiring moral and spiritual elevation.

The Historical and Scriptural Context of Incense

Incense has been a sacred element in rituals across cultures, symbolizing divine presence and human reverence. In the Bible, its role is vividly illustrated in Exodus 30:34-38, where God commands Moses to prepare a holy incense, "a perfume compounded after the art of the apothecary," for exclusive use in the Tabernacle. This incense symbolizes sanctity and the prayers of the faithful ascending to God, as emphasized in Revelation 8:4: "And the smoke of the incense, which came with the prayers of the saints, ascended up before God out of the angel's hand."

Philosophically, incense has parallels in the writings of Plato, who viewed purification as essential for attaining higher truth. The burning incense mirrors the soul's journey toward enlightenment, a concept that underscores its universal symbolism.

Purity of Heart: A Moral and Spiritual Ideal

Masonic teachings emphasize purity of heart as a cornerstone of ethical and spiritual life. This aligns with the Beatitude in Matthew 5:8: "Blessed are the pure in heart: for they shall see God." A pure heart, like incense, emits an untainted essence, free from selfishness and corruption. As Albert Mackey, a Masonic scholar, observes, "The Pot of Incense is emblematic of a pure heart, ever ascending in fervent prayer and gratitude to the Great Architect of the Universe" (Mackey, 1924).

In both Masonic and biblical traditions, purity of heart is tied to universal love and selflessness. The Apostle Paul, in 1 Corinthians 13:1-3, highlights that without love, even the most virtuous acts are hollow. This parallels the Masonic ideal of fraternity, where love for humanity is the essence of moral practice.

Gratitude and Fervent Devotion

Gratitude, as symbolized by the Pot of Incense, is central to both biblical and Masonic teachings. Psalm 141:2 encapsulates this connection: "Let my prayer be set forth before thee as incense; and the lifting up of my hands as the evening sacrifice." This verse reflects the inseparable link between gratitude and devotion, which are central to spiritual growth.

The burning incense also represents fervency, a quality urged in Romans 12:11: "Not slothful in business; fervent in spirit; serving the Lord." This fervor, as echoed in Masonic teachings, inspires a commitment to self-improvement and service to humanity. As Stevenson (2005) notes, "Incense symbolizes the warmth of devotion and the active energy of a life dedicated to higher principles" (p. 47).

Contemporary Reflections on the Symbol

In modern contexts, the Pot of Incense serves as a metaphor for ethical living and spiritual mindfulness. Its symbolism encourages individuals to cultivate moral purity and live with gratitude. Reflecting on Ecclesiastes 9:10— "Whatsoever thy hand findeth to do, do it with thy might"— we are reminded that daily actions, performed with integrity and fervor, contribute to a life of purpose and fulfillment.

This symbolism extends beyond personal ethics to community engagement. As Keller (2018) writes, "The fragrance of moral actions, like incense, impacts the wider society, creating a legacy of harmony and goodwill" (p. 102).

The Pot of Incense is more than a symbolic emblem; it is a spiritual guide that calls individuals to embody purity, gratitude, and fervent devotion. Rooted in biblical teachings and philosophical reflections, it serves as a reminder that a pure heart, glowing with sincerity and gratitude, is always an acceptable offering to the Creator. In embracing these principles, we find a pathway to both personal and collective moral excellence.

Reflections on the Craft: Questions for Deeper Understanding

- **Embodying Purity of Heart**
  - How does the Pot of Incense inspire you to examine and cultivate the purity of your own heart in daily life?
- **Living with Gratitude**
  - In what ways can you incorporate the spirit of gratitude, as symbolized by the incense, into your Masonic and personal endeavors?
- **Applying Symbolism in Modern Life**

o How can the burning incense inspire you to balance personal discipline with service to others in today's world?

The Bee-Hive: An Emblem of Industry and Higher Purpose

Explore the Bee-Hive as a timeless emblem of industriousness, interdependence, and the alignment of labor with higher purposes.

The Bee-Hive is a central symbol in Masonic philosophy, representing industriousness and communal effort. Its lessons are relevant across nature, literature, and philosophy, guiding Freemasons to view labor not only as a personal duty but also as a higher spiritual calling. From the tireless work of bees that sustain life on Earth to their metaphorical representation in human society, the Bee-Hive illustrates the importance of diligence, interdependence, and moral duty.

The Industrious Bee

Bees are archetypes of labor and harmony. Each bee, unaware of its broader impact, contributes to the hive's survival. This microcosmic industry exemplifies a universal truth: the smallest contributions can have profound consequences. Beyond producing honey, bees play an essential role in pollinating crops, ensuring agricultural sustainability and human survival (Goulson, 2015). Without bees, modern agriculture would falter, showcasing their unwitting role in a greater divine purpose.

Biblical and Philosophical Resonance

The Bible frequently references bees as examples of strength and purpose. In Judges 14:8, Samson encounters a swarm of bees in a lion's carcass, symbolizing sweetness derived from strength. Proverbs 6:6-8 exhorts individuals to emulate the ant's industriousness, a sentiment easily translatable to the bee's communal effort (King James Bible, 1987). Such scriptural insights align with the Masonic view of the Bee-Hive as a call to labor in harmony with others for mutual and spiritual benefit.

Philosophers, too, have drawn from the symbolism of bees. Marcus Aurelius, in his Meditations, reflects on the interconnectedness of humanity, emphasizing that individual actions should contribute to the greater good, much like bees serve their hive (Aurelius, 2006). Similarly, Enlightenment thinkers admired the bees' social structure, seeing it as a model for human society (Wilson, 1975).

The Metaphor of Labor in Masonic Thought

Freemasonry holds that man, as a rational and intelligent being, is bound to industriousness. Laziness, symbolized by the drone, is antithetical to the principles of the craft. In this sense, the Bee-Hive is not just an emblem of labor but also a moral guidepost, urging Masons to labor not for selfish gain but to contribute to society's collective well-being (Pike, 1871). Dependence, one of the strongest bonds of society, is reflected in the Masonic ideal of mutual aid and brotherhood. Just as bees depend on each other to sustain the hive, humans rely on one another to fulfill their social and spiritual duties. This interdependence fosters reciprocal love, friendship, and protection.

Bees and a Higher Purpose

While bees work for the hive's survival, they unknowingly contribute to the greater ecological balance. This analogy offers Masons a profound reflection: our labors, humble as they may seem, might align with a higher, divine purpose. Labor imbued with virtue transcends material concerns, enriching both the individual and the community (Wirth, 1924).

In literature, the Bee-Hive often symbolizes productive order. Virgil's Georgics celebrates the bees' disciplined society as a metaphor for human governance (Virgil, 2006). Similarly, Masonic teachings draw from such representations, encouraging members to emulate the bees' virtues of industry, cooperation, and selflessness.

The Bee-Hive inspires Freemasons to labor diligently, uphold communal harmony, and seek alignment with a higher purpose. By internalizing the lessons of the hive, individuals and societies alike can achieve balance, sustainability, and fulfillment. Freemasons, as "bees" in the "hive" of humanity, are charged with the sacred duty of adding to the "common stock of knowledge and understanding," ensuring that their work resonates beyond the temporal and into the divine.

Reflections on the Craft: Questions for Deeper Understanding

- **Balancing Individual and Collective Purpose:**
  - How can you emulate the bee's example of serving both the hive and a higher ecological purpose in your Masonic journey and daily life?
- **Interdependence and Reciprocity:**
  - Reflecting on the dependence within the hive, how do you foster mutual aid and brotherhood among your peers and community?
- **Industry and Higher Calling:**
  - How can the lessons of the Bee-Hive guide your labors toward contributing to both personal growth and the greater good of society?

The Sword and the Book: Guarding the Masonic Virtues of Silence and Circumspection

The Tiler's Sword's symbolic connection to vigilance, ethical action, and Masonic tradition

The image of the Book of Constitutions guarded by the Tiler's Sword is rich in Masonic symbolism, urging members to exercise constant vigilance and prudence in thought, word, and deed. This potent metaphor carries a historical and spiritual legacy that continues to shape the principles of Freemasonry today.

The Book of Constitutions

The Book of Constitutions, in Masonic context, refers to the written regulations and principles governing the fraternity. It includes the ancient charges, rituals, and obligations that define the framework of Masonic practice. Authored initially by James Anderson in 1723, the Constitutions establish a foundational unity across lodges while respecting local traditions and governance. According to Coil (1961), "the Constitutions are the keystone of Masonic jurisprudence, embodying the ancient landmarks and moral law of the Craft" (p. 102).

The guarding of this book represents the safeguarding of Masonic values and the preservation of the Order's integrity. It underscores a commitment to both personal discipline and collective accountability among Freemasons.

The Tiler's Sword: A Symbol of Vigilance

The Tiler's Sword is traditionally used to protect the lodge from external intrusion. However, it also serves a deeper metaphorical purpose: it reminds members to guard their actions and words, particularly in the presence of those who may misunderstand or misuse Masonic teachings. Historically, the sword symbolizes justice, strength, and vigilance, qualities essential to maintaining the harmony and purpose of the fraternity. As Mackey (1924) explains, "The Tiler's Sword is emblematic of the internal and external vigilance that every Mason must practice" (p. 234).

In broader philosophical traditions, the sword has often symbolized protection and discernment—cutting away falsehoods to reveal truth. For example, in Christian iconography, it is associated with Saint Michael, the protector, and in classical mythology, with the justice of figures such as Nemesis (Waite, 1913, p. 312).

Metaphorical Interpretations of the Sword

In a Masonic context, the sword's protective function can be interpreted as an internal reminder to uphold silence and circumspection. These virtues are central to Freemasonry, where members are encouraged to practice self-restraint and measured communication. Silence, as a Masonic virtue, entails not only the literal keeping of secrets but also the discipline of thoughtful speech. Circumspection, on the other hand, involves acting with careful consideration of consequences, embodying the wisdom of the Two Saints John, often associated with the solstices—symbolizing balance and reflection. "Circumspection is not merely a guide to Masonic conduct; it is a pathway to universal ethical principles," asserts Waite (1913, p. 187).

Guarding the Book: Practical and Ethical Implications

The guarding of the Book of Constitutions with the Tiler's Sword is more than a ritualistic image; it serves as a call to action for Freemasons. Practically, it reminds members to protect the sanctity of their gatherings. Ethically, it emphasizes the need to safeguard the principles of equality, fraternity, and truth that form the bedrock of Freemasonry. As Anderson (1723) writes, "The duties of vigilance are not confined to the lodge alone but extend to every interaction, where integrity must be our sword and shield" (p. 45).

In today's world, this vigilance extends beyond the lodge room. Freemasons are encouraged to apply these virtues in their daily lives, guarding their moral integrity and engaging with society in a way that reflects the values of the Craft. The Tiler's Sword thus becomes a symbol not only of defense but also of proactive ethical engagement.

The enduring image of the Book of Constitutions guarded by the Tiler's Sword captures the essence of Masonic vigilance. It is a vivid reminder of the responsibilities Freemasons bear in protecting the integrity of their Order and embodying its values in their personal lives. Through the interplay of silence and circumspection, members are guided to live with purpose, wisdom, and ethical fortitude.

Reflections on the Craft: Questions for Deeper Understanding

- **Balancing Vigilance and Discretion**
    - How can you incorporate the virtues of silence and circumspection into your daily interactions, ensuring your actions align with Masonic principles?
- **Symbolism and Personal Growth**
    - The sword has historically symbolized protection and justice. How can you embody these attributes while safeguarding the Masonic values in your own life?
- **Guarding Ethical Integrity**

o How does the image of the Tiler's Sword guarding the Book of Constitutions inspire you to uphold and protect ethical conduct in your personal and professional endeavors?

The Sword Pointing to a Naked Heart: A Reflection on Justice and Masonic Symbolism

The Sword Pointing to a Naked Heart: A Symbol of Justice, Vulnerability, and Moral Reckoning.

The allegorical image of the sword pointing to a naked heart is deeply evocative, resonating with themes of justice, transparency, and moral accountability. Within the Masonic tradition, this symbol emphasizes that justice will inevitably prevail and that no thoughts, words, or deeds can remain hidden indefinitely. To fully understand this emblem's implications, it is essential to explore the historical and cultural significance of the sword and heart as individual metaphors and then synthesize their meanings within the Masonic context.

Historical and Cultural Symbolism of the Sword

Throughout history, the sword has been a symbol of power, authority, and justice. In medieval Europe, it represented the knightly virtues of courage and chivalry, as well as the divine right of kings. As Jacobus de Voragine noted in The Golden Legend, the sword was an instrument of divine justice, wielded by saints and martyrs to defend faith and virtue. Similarly, in Eastern traditions such as Japanese Bushido, the sword embodied the samurai's honor and discipline, often viewed as an extension of the soul.

Biblical references also highlight the sword's connection to justice. In the King James Bible, Hebrews 4:12 states, "For the word of God is quick, and powerful, and sharper than any two-edged sword." This verse underscores the sword's ability to discern truth and execute judgment, cutting through deceit to reveal moral clarity.

Historical and Cultural Symbolism of the Heart

The heart, conversely, has been universally recognized as the seat of emotion, morality, and the human spirit. In ancient Egyptian theology, the heart was weighed against the feather of Ma'at to determine a soul's righteousness. Similarly, in Christian theology, the heart signifies divine love and human devotion, epitomized in the Sacred Heart of Jesus as a representation of compassion and sacrifice.

Literature often portrays the heart as a locus of vulnerability and sincerity. Shakespeare's The Merchant of Venice poignantly illustrates this through Shylock's demand for a "pound of flesh closest to the heart," symbolizing ultimate accountability and the peril of unbridled justice.

Synthesizing the Sword and Heart

When the sword and heart are combined, the resulting image speaks to the dual nature of justice and compassion. The sword's precision ensures accountability, while the heart's vulnerability reminds us of humanity's emotional and ethical dimensions. This juxtaposition reflects the delicate balance between enforcing justice and exercising mercy, a theme prevalent in legal and moral philosophy.

For Freemasons, the sword pointing to a naked heart represents the inevitability of moral accountability. It is a reminder that one's inner thoughts and outward actions must align with the principles of truth, justice, and integrity. Masonic teachings emphasize that while human judgment is limited, divine justice is all-seeing and infallible.

Masonic Reflection on the Symbol

Within Freemasonry, the sword and heart function as powerful tools for introspection. They challenge members to evaluate their own conduct and motives. The naked heart, unshielded and exposed, symbolizes sincerity and openness, while the sword's pointed presence serves as a deterrent against vice and hypocrisy.

The ritualistic use of these symbols in Masonic practices underscores the commitment to moral uprightness. As Freemasons, individuals are reminded that their actions— even those concealed from human observation—are subject to the unerring justice of the Great Architect of the Universe.

The sword pointing to a naked heart is a profound metaphor for justice's inexorable nature and the necessity for ethical congruence in all facets of life. By examining the historical and cultural symbolism of the sword and heart, and their integration within Masonic teachings, we uncover a powerful reminder of our moral obligations. In embracing this dual symbolism, Freemasons and individuals alike are encouraged to pursue justice tempered with compassion and transparency.

Reflections on the Craft: Questions for Deeper Understanding

- **Balancing Justice and Compassion:**
  - How can you integrate the precision of justice symbolized by the sword with the vulnerability and sincerity represented by the heart in your daily decisions and interactions?
- **The Visibility of Truth:**
  - Reflecting on the inevitability of divine justice, how do you ensure that your private

thoughts, words, and deeds align with the ethical principles you outwardly profess?

- **The Sword and Heart in Masonic Practice:**
    - In what ways do the sword and heart as Masonic symbols challenge you to cultivate accountability and transparency within your Masonic and personal endeavors?

The All-Seeing Eye: A Universal Symbol of Watchfulness and Justice

The All-Seeing Eye reminds us that in the grand design, no action escapes divine observation.

The All-Seeing Eye, often depicted within a radiating triangle or surrounded by celestial bodies such as the sun, moon, and stars, holds profound significance across historical, religious, and cultural contexts. Its meaning spans millennia, encompassing divine watchfulness, human accountability, and cosmic order. This essay explores the historical and cultural roots of the symbol, its religious interpretations, and its Masonic significance, ultimately weaving together these perspectives to uncover its universal message.

Historical and Cultural Roots

The All-Seeing Eye has ancient origins, appearing in the art and architecture of diverse cultures. In ancient Egypt, the Eye of Horus symbolized protection and restoration, embodying divine insight and order. According to Assmann (2001), "The Eye of Horus was a critical symbol for the balance of cosmic order, representing healing and divine vigilance." Similarly, in Greco-Roman traditions, the eye served as a metaphor for the omnipresence of divine forces, often associated with Zeus or Jupiter.

During the Renaissance, the All-Seeing Eye became integrated into Christian iconography, often depicted within a triangle symbolizing the Holy Trinity. As Campbell (1988) notes, "Renaissance artists utilized the All-Seeing Eye to reinforce the omnipotence and omniscience of God, an idea central to Christian theology." This symbolic evolution highlights the adaptation of ancient imagery to fit evolving religious paradigms.

The symbol also gained prominence in political contexts. The inclusion of the All-Seeing Eye on the Great Seal of the United States reflects its adoption as a symbol of divine providence and societal ideals. Turner (1978) explains, "The placement of the All-Seeing Eye above the unfinished pyramid signifies a nation under divine guidance, aspiring toward completion and perfection." This cultural adaptation underscores the symbol's enduring relevance as a marker of moral and collective responsibility.

Additionally, indigenous cultures worldwide have employed similar motifs. For instance, Native American traditions often use the eye within geometric patterns to signify spiritual guardianship and interconnectedness. These variations emphasize the universality of the eye as a symbol of divine oversight and protection.

Religious Interpretations

In religious contexts, the All-Seeing Eye is often tied to the divine's omnipresence and omniscience. In the Judeo-Christian tradition, it symbolizes God's eternal vigilance over humanity. Proverbs 15:3 of the King James Bible states, "The eyes of the Lord are in every place, beholding the evil and the good," reinforcing the idea that nothing escapes divine awareness.

The symbol also appears in Hinduism and Buddhism. The concept of the "Third Eye" in these traditions signifies spiritual awakening and insight, reflecting the capacity to perceive deeper truths beyond the material realm. In this sense, the All-Seeing Eye becomes a bridge between human consciousness and divine wisdom.

Masonic Significance

In Freemasonry, the All-Seeing Eye represents the Great Architect of the Universe, underscoring the principle of universal surveillance and accountability. It is a symbol of moral and ethical awareness, reminding Masons of their duty to uphold the tenets of brotherly love, relief, and truth. Positioned within the Masonic lodge, the eye serves as a constant reminder of the Creator's omnipresence and the Mason's obligation to lead a life of integrity.

The inclusion of the sun, moon, and stars within the Masonic context further amplifies the symbol's meaning. These celestial bodies signify the balance and harmony of creation, emphasizing the interconnectedness of all things under divine care. The watchful care of comets performing their "stupendous revolutions" reflects a cosmic order governed by the Creator's wisdom.

As Mackey (1869) asserts, "Freemasonry's All-Seeing Eye unites the ancient with the modern, linking universal truths to the moral compass of each Mason." This connection highlights the symbol's role as a guide for ethical behavior and spiritual reflection within the Craft.

Combining Perspectives

When combining the historical, religious, and Masonic interpretations, the All-Seeing Eye emerges as a multifaceted symbol of vigilance, morality, and universal interconnectedness. It bridges human aspirations with divine governance, offering a lens through which individuals can reflect on their actions and responsibilities. Across cultures and eras, it has remained a poignant reminder that no deed, whether noble or ignoble, escapes observation.

Ultimately, the All-Seeing Eye challenges humanity to align their lives with ethical and spiritual principles. As Turner (1978) remarks, "The symbol's persistence across civilizations demonstrates its capacity to encapsulate humanity's deepest yearnings for order, justice, and purpose." Its enduring presence in art, architecture, and philosophy underscores its universal appeal as a symbol of higher accountability and cosmic justice.

Reflections on the Craft: Questions for Deeper Understanding

- **Divine Surveillance and Accountability:**
    - How does the concept of the All-Seeing Eye inspire you to maintain integrity in your personal and professional life?
- **Symbolism of Cosmic Order:**
    - How do the sun, moon, and stars as part of the All-Seeing Eye motif encourage you to seek balance and harmony in your daily endeavors?

- **Interpreting the Masonic Eye:**
    - How can the Masonic interpretation of the All-Seeing Eye deepen your understanding of your obligations to the Craft and society?

The Anchor and Ark: Emblems of Hope and Shelter in Masonic Philosophy

Discover how the Anchor and Ark encapsulate timeless wisdom on navigating life's trials and seeking rest in unwavering values

Throughout history, symbols have been a means of expressing complex ideas through simple imagery, and Freemasonry excels in this practice. The Anchor and Ark are two profound emblems within Masonic philosophy that symbolize hope, stability, preparation, and resilience. This essay explores these symbols through historical, philosophical, religious, and cultural perspectives, blending their meanings into a unified understanding. Additionally, their metaphorical significance will be examined, particularly the Anchor's role as a hidden stabilizer and the Ark's representation of a constructed haven, culminating in their synthesis as a guide for navigating life's challenges.

The Anchor

The Anchor has long represented stability and hope. In ancient Greece and Rome, it symbolized safety amidst uncertainty, a meaning that persisted into early Christianity when it became a covert symbol of faith. As stated in Hebrews 6:19, "Which hope we have as an anchor of the soul, both sure and steadfast," the Anchor embodies faith's power to hold us firm amidst life's tempests. Philosophically, it reflects the Stoic emphasis on inner stability, where an individual's virtues anchor them against external chaos. Culturally, the Anchor resonates across societies, particularly in maritime traditions, as a talisman of perseverance and safe passage. For Freemasons, the Anchor reminds members to cultivate unseen yet powerful values—

faith, steadfastness, and moral integrity—that act as stabilizing forces during adversity.

The Ark

The Ark, on the other hand, symbolizes preparation and sanctuary. Its roots lie in the biblical account of Noah's Ark, where foresight and obedience preserved life during destruction. Genesis 6–9 demonstrates how faith and action combined to create a vessel of salvation. The Ark also represents humanity's ongoing endeavor to build shelters against chaos, whether physical, emotional, or spiritual. In cultural contexts, the Ark often reflects collective resilience, as seen in narratives emphasizing cooperation and faith. Masonically, it symbolizes the temple of one's character—a haven constructed through moral diligence and adherence to higher principles. Albert Mackey states in his Encyclopedia of Freemasonry, "The Ark is an emblem of that refuge which the righteous man finds in a life well-spent."

Together, the Anchor and Ark offer a harmonious lesson. The Anchor emphasizes unseen values that stabilize us, while the Ark represents tangible actions that safeguard our futures. Their combination underscores the balance of introspection and outward preparation essential for a well-rounded life. As a metaphor, the Anchor's unseen presence mirrors the quiet strength of values like faith and integrity, while the Ark's visible construction represents deliberate efforts to create security and purpose. In Freemasonry, these symbols inspire members to lead lives of hope and preparation, exemplifying the ideals of a well-grounded hope and a well-spent life.

The synthesis of these symbols—one grounding and the other sheltering—reminds us of the dual necessity of stability and action. Masons are called to anchor themselves in enduring principles while also building arks of moral and spiritual fortitude. As Albert Pike notes in Morals and Dogma, "The wise man anchors his soul in truth and builds his life's Ark upon the solid foundation of integrity."

Reflections on the Craft: Questions for Deeper Understanding

- **Anchored in Values:**
    - How does the anchor, as a symbol of unseen stability, inspire you to strengthen your value system in challenging times?
- **Building Your Ark**:
    - What steps can you take to create a personal or communal Ark that safeguards against the "tempestuous sea" of life?
- **Harmony of Action and Introspection:**
    - How can the balance between the Anchor's inward stability and the Ark's outward preparation guide you in your Masonic journey?

The Forty-Seventh Problem of Euclid

Unveiling the Masonic bridge between ancient mathematics and philosophical symbolism.

The Forty-Seventh Problem of Euclid, often referred to as the Pythagorean Theorem, embodies the profound relationship between mathematics, philosophy, and Freemasonry. Attributed to Pythagoras, an ancient Greek mathematician and philosopher, and later formalized by Euclid, this theorem reflects both mathematical innovation and universal truths. Euclid, known as the "Father of Geometry," was a Greek mathematician active in Alexandria, Egypt, during the reign of Ptolemy I (323–283 BCE). He founded a mathematical school in Alexandria, where he compiled and systematized the geometrical knowledge of his predecessors into Elements, a work that profoundly influenced mathematics for over two millennia. According to Proclus, when asked if geometry could be simplified, Euclid famously remarked, "There is no royal road to geometry," emphasizing the need for disciplined study (Proclus, 1873).

Pythagoras

Pythagoras of Samos (circa 570–495 BCE) was a mathematician and philosopher who profoundly influenced the fields of mathematics, astronomy, and ethics. Aristotle described him as a pioneer who "sought to explain the natural world in terms of numerical harmony" (Ranganathan, 1993). Pythagoras founded a philosophical community in Croton, southern Italy, emphasizing the study of numbers and harmony as key to understanding the universe. His belief in *kosmos*, a universal order governed by proportion, and the interconnectedness of life reflects his teachings' profound ethical and mathematical dimensions.

Music played a vital role in his philosophy, illustrating how numerical relationships create harmony, both in sound and the cosmos.

Although the proposition is found in Euclid's Elements, it is traditionally credited to Pythagoras. Historical evidence suggests the theorem was known to Babylonian mathematicians around 1800 BCE, but Pythagoras is celebrated for proving its universal applicability. Euclid later formalized it as Proposition 47 in Book I of Elements, preserving its legacy for future generations. Known as both "The Forty-Seventh Problem of Euclid" and "The Pythagorean Theorem," the dual naming honors both figures' contributions to its development.

Geometry

A proposition in geometry is a statement, either a theorem (proven) or a problem (requiring proof or solution), structured logically and supported by definitions and axioms. Euclid's Elements organizes these propositions meticulously, showcasing a logical progression of geometric principles. The Forty-Seventh Problem states that in a right triangle, the square of the hypotenuse is equal to the sum of the squares of the other two sides. This principle has had profound implications in fields ranging from architecture to astronomy.

The theorem's practical utility is evident in construction and engineering. For example, a builder ensuring a wall is perpendicular to the ground can measure 3 feet along the base, 4 feet up the wall, and confirm the diagonal measures exactly 5 feet, validating the right angle with . This simple yet precise method demonstrates the theorem's enduring relevance.

Legend holds that Pythagoras, upon discovering the theorem, exclaimed "Eureka!" — a Greek term meaning "I have found it!" — and offered a hecatomb, or sacrifice of 100 oxen, to the gods. While this story is debated, given Pythagoras's vegetarian ethics, it illustrates the theorem's monumental significance in ancient times. The theorem bridges finite and infinite realms by linking concrete, measurable lengths to an abstract formula universally true. This duality mirrors the Masonic pursuit of uniting material and spiritual knowledge, embodying universal order in tangible applications.

The 47th Problem and Freemasonry

Freemasonry venerates the Forty-Seventh Problem as a symbol of knowledge, order, and truth. Albert G. Mackey explains that "The Forty-Seventh Problem of Euclid... teaches the operative Mason the art of accurately squaring his work, and instructs the speculative Mason to square his conduct by the precepts of virtue" (Mackey, 1874). The theorem's dual utility in practical craftsmanship and moral philosophy underscores its importance in Masonic tradition. Pythagoras's cry of "Eureka" resonates with the joy of discovery celebrated by Freemasons in their quest for enlightenment.

Reflections on the Craft: Questions for Deeper Understanding

- **Balancing Knowledge and Symbolism:**
  - How does the Forty-Seventh Problem inspire balance between technical skill and philosophical reflection in your Masonic journey?
- **Cycles of Discovery and Application:**

- o How do its lessons influence personal challenges in both your professional and Masonic endeavors?
- **Symbolism in Practice:**
  - o How might this mathematical principle serve as a metaphor for equilibrium in moral, spiritual, and professional endeavors?

The Hourglass: A Timeless Emblem of Life's Passage

The hourglass stands not just as a marker of fleeting time but as a profound reminder of renewal and the cyclical journey of the soul, encapsulating the wisdom of ages for those who choose to reflect upon its message

The hourglass, a ubiquitous symbol across cultures and traditions, epitomizes the transitory nature of human existence. Its design, with sand slipping steadily through the narrow neck, offers profound lessons about time, life, and renewal. This essay delves into the hourglass as an emblem, exploring its metaphorical meanings and connections to the Bible, philosophy, literature, and Freemasonry, providing insights into how this ancient symbol encourages reflection on the cyclical nature of life.

The Passage of Time: A Universal Metaphor

The hourglass serves as a poignant metaphor for time's passage. Initially, the grains of sand appear to move slowly, much like time in youth, but as the sands dwindle, they seem to accelerate—a sensation akin to time's swift march as one ages. The Bible captures this sentiment in verses such as James 4:14 (King James Version), which states, "Whereas ye know not what shall be on the morrow. For what is your life? It is even a vapour, that appeareth for a little time, and then vanisheth away." The hourglass, like this verse, underscores life's fleeting nature.

Philosophers, too, have contemplated this metaphor. Martin Heidegger, in his exploration of being, emphasized the urgency of existence. His concept of "being-towards-death" aligns with the hourglass's symbolism, reminding us of the finite nature of life and the importance of living with purpose.

Renewal and Continuity: Turning the Hourglass Over

Unlike a clock, the hourglass has a transformative quality—it can be turned over, allowing the cycle to begin anew. This ability symbolizes renewal and the perpetual cycles of life, death, and rebirth. In literature, this theme finds resonance in T.S. Eliot's "Four Quartets," where he writes, "In my end is my beginning," highlighting the interconnectedness of endings and new beginnings.

Freemasonry embraces this symbolism as well. The hourglass reminds Masons of mortality while encouraging them to live virtuously and contemplate the eternal. This duality reflects the Masonic pursuit of spiritual enlightenment through cycles of introspection and action.

The Hourglass in Masonic Thought

Freemasonry imbues the hourglass with profound significance. It is prominently featured as a symbol of mortality in Masonic rituals, urging members to reflect on the brevity of life and the inevitability of death. Yet, it also signifies the endless opportunities for spiritual growth and the enduring nature of the human spirit.

Famed Masonic philosopher Albert Pike noted, "Time, that destroys and renews all things," in his work Morals and Dogma. The hourglass thus aligns with the Masonic ideal of perpetual self-improvement, as the renewal of the sands mirrors the renewal of the soul in its journey toward greater enlightenment.

The Hourglass as a Tool for Reflection

The steady flow of sand through the hourglass is a call to mindfulness. Its quiet and deliberate action reminds us to focus on the present moment while recognizing the continuity of time. Writers like Johann Wolfgang von Goethe, himself a Freemason, explored similar themes in his works. In Faust, he expresses a deep awareness of time's passage, mirroring the hourglass's lessons of urgency and renewal.

Reflections on the Craft: Questions for Deeper Understanding

- **Cycles of Renewal:**
    - How can the hourglass inspire you to embrace the cyclical nature of challenges and opportunities in your personal and spiritual life?
- **Mindfulness in Action:**
    - The hourglass encourages present-moment awareness. How can you apply this lesson to your daily endeavors and Masonic practice?
- **Mortality and Purpose:**
    - How does reflecting on the finite nature of time help you prioritize actions that align with Masonic virtues and your broader life goals?

The Scythe: Emblem of Time and Eternity

Harvesting the fruits of life's endeavors, the scythe unites mortality with the eternal

The scythe, an enduring symbol etched deeply into human consciousness, holds profound significance across biblical, Masonic, philosophical, and literary contexts. As an instrument of reaping, it carries dual connotations: the inevitability of mortality and the reward of a life well-sown. This essay explores the origins, symbolism, and the multifaceted meaning of the scythe, drawing from ancient texts, Freemasonry, philosophy, and literature.

Biblical References: The Harvester of Souls

In the Bible, the scythe often appears as a metaphor for divine judgment and the gathering of souls. Revelation 14:14-16 (KJV) vividly describes an angel wielding a sharp sickle[8] to reap the earth's harvest, symbolizing the righteous judgment of God. This imagery reinforces the notion that life's actions yield an eternal harvest, aligning with the spiritual law of sowing and reaping (Galatians 6:7). The scythe, wielded in these passages, not only represents the end of earthly toil but also the commencement of eternal reward.

Masonic Symbolism: Time and Perfection

---

[8] Although the terms "sickle" and "scythe" are used somewhat interchangeably in this essay, they refer to distinct tools. A sickle is a smaller, handheld implement with a short handle and a curved blade, used for close-range harvesting of crops or grasses. In contrast, a scythe features a long handle and a larger, curved blade, allowing for efficient cutting of larger areas of vegetation from a standing position.

In Freemasonry, the scythe underscores the transient nature of life. It serves as a somber reminder that time, like the scythe, cuts down all—regardless of station or achievement. Yet, its presence is not merely a *memento mori*[9]; it is also an emblem of perfection. The matured harvest signifies a life lived in pursuit of Masonic virtues: truth, charity, and temperance. A Mason is called to embrace this duality, living with the awareness of mortality while striving for moral and spiritual completion.

Philosophical Perspectives: Time as the Great Equalizer

Philosophers have long revered the scythe as an allegory for time's impartiality. The ancient Greeks associated it with Cronos, the god of time, who was often depicted with a sickle. Martin Heidegger, in Being and Time, similarly reflects on human finitude, arguing that confronting mortality enables authentic living. The scythe, in this view, encourages the cultivation of a life imbued with meaning, as it continually reminds us of the temporality of existence.

Literary Insights: From Despair to Renewal

The scythe also holds a potent place in literature. In Nathaniel Hawthorne's The Scarlet Letter, the grim reaper's scythe evokes the inevitability of death as a moral reckoner. Conversely, in pastoral poetry, such as Robert Burns' "To a

---

[9] Memento mori, meaning "remember that you must die," serves as a reminder of life's fleeting nature, encouraging virtue, mindfulness, and reflection on what truly matters. Historically, it was used in Ancient Rome, medieval Christianity, and the Renaissance to prompt repentance and preparation for mortality. Symbolic representations, such as skulls and hourglasses, convey the inevitability of death, inspiring both artistic expression and personal introspection in modern times

Mouse," the scythe is a tool of renewal, clearing the old to make way for the new. This dual symbolism reflects humanity's ongoing tension between despair over mortality and hope in renewal.

Etymology and Cultural Roots

The word "scythe" derives from the Old English siðe, meaning "to cut." Its agricultural roots emphasize its role as an instrument of harvesting. This etymology bridges its symbolic and practical uses, reinforcing its association with preparation, maturity, and reward.

The Positive Aspect: Harvesting Readiness

While the scythe's association with death may seem foreboding, its deeper implication lies in readiness. A ripe harvest reflects a life well-prepared for transition, emphasizing maturity and fulfillment. This notion resonates with Freemasonry's goal of building a spiritual edifice ready to endure the test of eternity.

The scythe, as an emblem of time, captures humanity's shared journey from mortality to eternity. It urges reflection on the quality of our sowing and the maturity of our harvest. Across biblical, Masonic, philosophical, and literary traditions, it serves as both a reminder and a guide, shaping how we live with the inevitability of time.

Reflections on the Craft: Questions for Deeper Understanding

- **Embracing Mortality as Inspiration:**
  - How does the scythe's symbolism in Freemasonry inspire you to lead a life of integrity and purpose?

- **Balancing Harvest and Renewal**:
  - o How can the dual role of the scythe—as a symbol of both ending and renewal—help you navigate transitions in life?
- **Sowing for Eternity:**
  - o What "seeds" are you planting in your personal and Masonic life to ensure a bountiful and meaningful harvest?

Masonic Ode: Pleyel's Hymn (Dirge)

Explore the solemnity and symbolism of Freemasonry through the timeless verses of Pleyel's Hymn

Pleyel's Hymn, often referred to as the "Dirge," occupies a significant place in Masonic rituals, particularly during funerary and memorial ceremonies. Composed by Joseph Pleyel, a prominent composer of the 18th century, the hymn encapsulates themes of mortality, spiritual aspiration, and the profound journey of life and death. This essay explores the historical, ritualistic, and symbolic dimensions of Pleyel's Hymn within Freemasonry, highlighting its enduring resonance and reflective power for the Craft.

Historical and Ritualistic Context

Joseph Pleyel, a contemporary of Haydn and Mozart, was renowned for his ability to evoke deep emotions through his compositions. His hymn was adopted by Freemasons as a means of solemn reflection and communal unity during rites of passage. According to Mackey (1924), "Freemasonry's adoption of music like Pleyel's reflects its commitment to the elevation of moral and spiritual values" (p. 214). The hymn became particularly associated with Masonic funerals, where its contemplative melody underscored the universal themes of life's transience and the hope for immortality.

Music has always played a central role in Masonic ceremonies, serving as a bridge between the temporal and the divine. Pleyel's Hymn is emblematic of this tradition, offering members an opportunity to meditate on their Masonic obligations and spiritual aspirations.

Analysis of the Lyrics

The opening line, "Solemn strikes the funeral chime," immediately establishes a reflective tone, inviting participants to contemplate the inevitability of death. This chime symbolizes the universal passage of time and its eventual cessation. As Horne (1958) notes, "The funeral chime in Masonic rites is not merely an instrument of sound but a profound metaphor for the cyclical nature of existence" (p. 67).

The stanza, "As we journey here below, through a pilgrimage of woe," evokes the idea of life as a sacred journey filled with challenges and growth. This aligns with Masonic teachings that view life's trials as opportunities for moral and spiritual development. The reference to a "pilgrimage" resonates with the allegorical journeys depicted in Masonic rituals, such as the candidate's progression through degrees.

In "Mortality is here," the hymn confronts the reality of death head-on, a theme central to the Craft's teachings. This acknowledgment serves as a reminder of the Masonic charge to "act upon the square" and live a virtuous life. According to Coil (1961), "Masonic rituals consistently emphasize mortality to instill humility and purpose among brethren" (p. 89).

Finally, the concluding lines, "Take us to Thy Lodge on high," express the ultimate hope for reunion in the celestial lodge. This aspiration reflects the Craft's spiritual dimension, wherein earthly labors culminate in divine recognition and eternal harmony.

Pleyel's Hymn is imbued with rich symbolism that transcends its Masonic context. The "funeral chime" symbolizes the passage of time, while the "pilgrimage" metaphor captures the essence of life's journey. These elements resonate with the universal human experience, making the hymn a powerful medium for reflection.

The reference to the "Lodge on high" underscores Freemasonry's spiritual aspirations. As Jones (1996) explains, "The celestial lodge symbolizes the ultimate attainment of truth and unity, mirroring the fraternity's goal of universal brotherhood" (p. 112).

Contemporary Relevance

Despite being composed centuries ago, Pleyel's Hymn continues to hold relevance in modern Masonic practice. Its themes of mortality, virtue, and spiritual aspiration remain central to the Craft's teachings. The hymn serves as a reminder for Masons to live with integrity, embrace their mortality, and strive for a higher purpose.

Pleyel's Hymn stands as a testament to the enduring power of music and symbolism in Freemasonry. Its solemn tones and profound lyrics invite members to reflect on life's transience, embrace their spiritual aspirations, and live in accordance with Masonic principles. As a cornerstone of Masonic funerary rituals, the hymn continues to inspire and unify brethren, bridging the gap between the temporal and the eternal.

Reflections on the Craft: Questions for Deeper Understanding

- **Mortality and the Journey of the Soul**
    - How does Pleyel's Hymn inspire reflection on the impermanence of life?
- **Symbolism of the Lodge Above**

- How does the concept of a "Lodge on High" influence your perspective on spiritual progression?
- **Music as a Masonic Tool**
  - How does the inclusion of hymns enhance the ritual experience and Masonic teachings

The Master Mason's Charge: Values and Duties

Exploring the enduring principles guiding Master Masons in ethical leadership and personal growth.

The principles and responsibilities of Freemasonry serve as a moral compass for its members, offering guidance in personal development and ethical leadership. The Charge, addressed to a Master Mason, underscores the philosophical foundations of Freemasonry while outlining the practical implications of its teachings. Analyzing the text reveals a commitment to zeal, fidelity, mentorship, and the preservation of traditions, which collectively shape the role of a Master Mason both within the fraternity and in society at large.

Zeal and Progress in Masonry

Zeal, as highlighted in the Charge, is essential for personal and communal advancement in Freemasonry. A Master Mason is celebrated for their enthusiasm and commitment to the craft's principles. This zeal must be tempered by wisdom, ensuring that passion does not overshadow reason. As noted by Hamill and Gilbert (2004), "Freemasonry requires a balance between enthusiasm for its teachings and a disciplined adherence to its tenets, fostering an environment of reflective growth." Such balance ensures that zeal serves as a catalyst for progress rather than disruption.

Faithfulness and Responsibility

The charge to "be faithful to every trust" emphasizes the importance of integrity and responsibility in a Master Mason's character. This fidelity is not only to the institution but also to the broader ideals of truth and justice. As Coil

(1996) observes, "The moral obligations of Freemasonry demand unwavering commitment to ethical principles, reinforcing the trust placed in its members." The Master Mason's role as a steward of these values extends to their personal and professional lives, reflecting the broader societal expectations of the fraternity.

Exemplary Conduct and Leadership

Leadership in Freemasonry is grounded in exemplary behavior. The Charge emphasizes that "exemplary conduct...will convince the world that merit is the just title to our privileges." This aligns with the fraternity's meritocratic ethos, where recognition is based on virtue and contributions rather than status. Hodapp (2005) explains, "Freemasonry's emphasis on character development ensures that its leaders inspire trust and respect through their actions." By modeling ethical behavior, a Master Mason fulfills their duty to the fraternity and enhances its reputation.

Universal Benevolence

The principle of universal benevolence underscores Freemasonry's commitment to charity and goodwill. The Charge's call to "zealously inculcate" this value reflects its centrality to Masonic practice. The emphasis on benevolence aligns with Anderson's Constitutions (1723), which state that Masons should "relieve the distressed and contribute to the welfare of society." This principle transcends ritual and becomes a practical guide for everyday interactions.

Preservation of Traditions

The charge to preserve the "Ancient Landmarks" reinforces the importance of continuity and respect for tradition in

Freemasonry. As Harland-Jacobs (2007) notes, "Freemasonry's adherence to its landmarks ensures a connection to its historical roots while providing a framework for navigating modern challenges." This fidelity to tradition safeguards the fraternity's identity and ensures its teachings remain relevant across generations.

Broader Implications

The responsibilities of a Master Mason extend beyond the fraternity. By embodying Masonic values, they contribute to a society that values integrity, service, and ethical leadership. This dual focus on personal growth and societal contribution reflects the fraternity's holistic approach to character development. As Hodapp (2005) succinctly states, "Freemasonry shapes individuals who, in turn, shape the world around them."

The principles outlined in the Charge provide a roadmap for a Master Mason's journey, emphasizing zeal, fidelity, and mentorship while advocating for the preservation of tradition. By adhering to these values, a Master Mason not only fulfills their obligations to the fraternity but also contributes positively to society. Freemasonry's teachings continue to inspire ethical leadership and personal growth, ensuring its enduring relevance in a changing world.

Reflections on the Craft: Questions for Deeper Understanding

- **Balancing Zeal and Wisdom**
    - How can you integrate the qualities of zeal and wisdom, as exemplified in Masonic teachings, into your personal and Masonic endeavors?
- **Leadership Through Example**

- In what ways can exemplary conduct as a Master Mason influence both the fraternity and broader societal perceptions of Freemasonry?

- **Preserving and Adapting Traditions**
  - How can a Master Mason balance the preservation of ancient traditions with the need for adaptability in modern times?

The Master Mason's Guide to Ethical Leadership

Applying the tools of Freemasonry to lead with integrity in a complex world.

Freemasonry is not merely a set of rituals or traditions; it is a living philosophy that provides tools for personal refinement and societal betterment. Each degree—Entered Apprentice, Fellow craft, and Master Mason—offers symbolic implements and lessons designed to shape moral character and ethical leadership. A Master Mason receives all the tools and instruction he needs to succeed—not just in his role within the Lodge but also as a brother, community member, leader, and mentor.

At the Master Mason level, he is entrusted with profound symbolic tools and the "light" of Masonic knowledge. These tools are more than mere objects; they represent skills and principles to be understood deeply. To fulfill his potential, a Master Mason must learn to use these tools instinctively, understanding their strengths, weaknesses, proper uses, and potential misuses. This mastery reflects the essence of Freemasonry: an ongoing commitment to self-improvement, ethical behavior, and service to others.

This essay explores how the tools of the Master Mason degree extend the teachings of the first two degrees, offering a framework for leading with integrity, wisdom, and service in the modern world

Recap of Entered Apprentice and Fellow craft Tools

Entered Apprentice: Foundations of Virtue

The Entered Apprentice degree introduces the foundational tools of Freemasonry:

- **The Twenty-Four Inch Gauge**: A symbol of time management, reminding Masons to divide their day among work, service, and rest.

- **The Common Gavel**: Emphasizing the need to chip away personal vices and cultivate moral character.

These tools teach the importance of discipline, self-refinement, and the judicious use of time—qualities essential for ethical leadership.

Fellow craft: Building Upon Knowledge

The Fellow craft degree expands on these lessons with tools that symbolize growth and mastery:

- **The Plumb**: Encourages uprightness and integrity in all dealings.

- **The Square**: Represents fairness and morality, ensuring actions align with ethical principles.

- **The Level**: Reminds Masons of equality and the shared dignity of all people.

Through these tools, the Fellow craft degree emphasizes wisdom, justice, and the pursuit of knowledge as critical components of ethical leadership.

Master Mason Tools: Ethical Leadership in Action

The Master Mason degree culminates the journey of moral and ethical development, equipping Masons with tools and principles to navigate the complexities of leadership. Drawing from the symbolic teachings of the degree, ethical leadership for the Master Mason involves integrating the virtues of previous degrees with new insights:

The Trowel: Building Unity

The Trowel is unique to the Master Mason degree and represents the spreading of brotherly love and affection. Leaders wield the Trowel to foster unity and collaboration, bridging divides and creating environments of mutual respect. In ethical leadership, the Trowel symbolizes the importance of inclusivity and the deliberate cultivation of harmony within teams and communities. By spreading the "cement of brotherly love," the Trowel teaches leaders the value of connection and the bonds that unify individuals toward a common purpose.

In practice, this tool also challenges leaders to prioritize empathy and understanding. A leader who uses the Trowel effectively builds not just functional teams but communities rooted in shared values and mutual trust. This tool reminds leaders that true success is measured not only by individual achievement but by the strength and unity of the group they lead. It is a call to actively weave together diverse perspectives and talents into a cohesive and purpose-driven whole.

The Working Tools in Retrospect

While not explicitly new, the lessons of the Square, Level, and Plumb take on enhanced significance in the Master Mason degree. The Square, for instance, transitions from a tool of fairness to one of justice in action, urging leaders to apply their moral convictions to real-world challenges. Similarly, the Plumb's call for uprightness evolves into a mandate for unwavering accountability.

The Sprig of Acacia: Symbol of Resilience

The Sprig of Acacia, prominent in the Master Mason degree, serves as a reminder of the immortality of the soul and the enduring nature of truth. Ethical leaders draw inspiration from this symbol to act with resilience and faith, even in the face of adversity. It underscores the importance of maintaining moral clarity and vision amid challenges.

Ethical Leadership Explored

Drawing from the teachings of the Master Mason degree, ethical leadership involves embodying the virtues of Brotherly Love, Relief, and Truth. By examining key essays and articles, we can further elucidate the practical application of these principles:

Balancing Zeal and Wisdom

The lessons of the Two Saints John in balancing zeal with wisdom emphasize the importance of thoughtful action. Ethical leaders must temper passion with prudence, ensuring their decisions are driven by long-term benefits rather than short-term gains. This balance fosters trust and credibility, hallmarks of effective leadership.

Cycles of Growth and Reflection

The solstices, tied to Masonic symbolism, represent cycles of action and reflection. Ethical leaders embrace this duality, dedicating time to both active engagement and introspection. By reflecting on past actions and their outcomes, leaders refine their strategies and align them with overarching principles of justice and equity.

Truth and Integrity

The All-Seeing Eye, another prominent Masonic symbol, serves as a reminder of accountability and the omnipresence of truth. Ethical leaders operate with transparency, ensuring their actions withstand scrutiny. Truth forms the cornerstone of trust, enabling leaders to inspire confidence and loyalty.

Service and Charity

The Trowel's call to spread brotherly love aligns with the principle of Relief. Ethical leadership demands a commitment to service, prioritizing the welfare of others. Whether through mentorship, advocacy, or community engagement, leaders who embody this principle elevate not only themselves but also those they serve.

The Pot of Incense and the Bee Hive

The Pot of Incense symbolizes purity and gratitude. Leaders who embody this principle act with sincerity and foster an atmosphere of genuine appreciation. The Bee Hive, a symbol of industry and cooperation, teaches leaders the importance of hard work and collaborative effort. Together, these tools underscore the value of selfless service and the collective power of teamwork.

The Sword and Book of Constitutions, and the Sword Pointing to a Naked Heart

The Sword and Book of Constitutions symbolize justice, law, and the ethical frameworks that guide leadership. The Sword pointing to a Naked Heart reminds leaders of their moral accountability and the responsibility to act with integrity. These tools emphasize the balance between authority and moral duty.

The 47th Problem of Euclid

The 47th Problem of Euclid represents knowledge, logic, and the pursuit of intellectual excellence. Ethical leaders apply these principles to solve problems and build systems grounded in reason and equity, ensuring sustainable and fair outcomes.

The Hourglass and Scythe

The Hourglass symbolizes the fleeting nature of time and the urgency of purposeful action, while the Scythe represents the inevitability of mortality. Together, they remind leaders to act with both immediacy and foresight, leaving a legacy of positive impact.

The Master Mason degree encapsulates the journey of personal transformation and societal contribution. By integrating the tools and lessons of all three degrees, a Master Mason is equipped to lead with integrity, wisdom, and compassion. Ethical leadership, as envisioned by Freemasonry, is a commitment to building a better world— one guided by the timeless principles of Brotherly Love, Relief, and Truth.

Reflections on the Craft: Questions for Deeper Understanding

- **Tools for Personal Growth:**
  - How can the Common Gavel and Trowel guide you in fostering unity and moral clarity within your sphere of influence?
- **Balancing Action and Reflection:**
  - The solstices symbolize cycles of growth and introspection. How can you integrate these cycles into your leadership approach to ensure balanced decision-making?

- **Legacy of Service:**
    - o How does the Sprig of Acacia inspire you to leave a legacy of ethical leadership and unwavering commitment to truth?

Living the Masonic Philosophy: Incorporating the Teachings into Daily Life

The Master of a Masonic Lodge: Guiding Light and Guardian of Tradition

Discover the Master's pivotal role in shaping the Lodge's tradition, leadership, and personal growth

At the heart of every Masonic Lodge stands a dedicated leader known as the Master. This esteemed position carries significant responsibilities and plays a vital role in upholding the principles and traditions of Freemasonry. As the highest-ranking officer in the Lodge, the Master embodies the guiding light and guardian of the Lodge's principles. This essay explores the Master's duties, qualifications, and the profound impact they have on the Lodge and its members.

The Master's Duties

As the presiding officer, the Master is responsible for maintaining the harmony and integrity of the Lodge. Key duties include conducting meetings, presiding over rituals, and leading discussions on Masonic principles. The Master's wisdom and guidance shape the Lodge's atmosphere, fostering fraternity, personal growth, and moral improvement (McLeod, 2006).

Guardian of Tradition

One of the Master's most significant roles is to preserve and perpetuate Masonic traditions. By ensuring that rituals and ceremonies adhere to established practices, the Master connects the Lodge to its historical roots. This preservation of custom ensures the continuity of the Craft and its values across generations (Coil, 1996).

Mentor and Teacher

The Master serves as a mentor and teacher, imparting knowledge of Masonic symbolism, philosophy, and ethics. Through educational efforts, the Master encourages members to deepen their understanding of the teachings and apply them in daily life. This commitment to mentoring fosters personal development and inspires members to embody Masonic values (Henderson, 2012).

Exemplifying Leadership

As the Lodge's highest authority, the Master must lead by example. Demonstrating integrity, compassion, and dedication, the Master's actions inspire trust and respect among the members. This leadership fosters unity and camaraderie within the Lodge, contributing to a sense of shared purpose (Jones, 2010).

Presiding Over Degrees

Among the Master's most significant duties is presiding over the conferral of Masonic degrees. These symbolic initiations convey essential lessons and values to candidates. The solemnity and depth of the Master's role in these rituals enhance the candidates' understanding of their Masonic journey (Haggard, 2013).

Qualifications and Preparation

To become a Master, a Freemason must demonstrate dedication to the Craft, deep understanding of its principles, and leadership qualities. The journey often involves progressing through various officer roles, providing practical experience and knowledge. These preparatory steps ensure readiness to assume the responsibilities of Mastership (Macoy, 2000).

The position of Master of a Masonic Lodge is an honorable and sacred role. With wisdom, guidance, and dedication to preserving traditions, the Master serves as a guiding light for members. By embodying the values of the Craft, the Master fosters an environment of fraternity, personal growth, and moral improvement. This role ensures that Freemasonry's timeless principles endure, inspiring future generations.

Reflections on the Craft: Questions for Deeper Understanding

- **The Role of Tradition:**
  - How do you perceive the balance between upholding Masonic traditions and adapting to contemporary challenges?
- **Leadership in Action:**
  - In what ways can the Master's example of leadership inspire both personal and collective growth within the Lodge?
- **Mentorship and Learning:**
  - How does the Master's role as a mentor influence your understanding and application of Masonic teachings?

The Lodge and Temple: Metaphors for the Human Condition

Explore the profound symbolism of King Solomon's Temple as a metaphor for Masonic virtue and the human condition

In Freemasonry, the Lodge is more than just a physical place of gathering; it is a symbolic space that mirrors both the ancient wisdom of King Solomon's Temple and the human condition itself. As Masons enter the Lodge, they are not merely stepping into a room; they are entering a sacred and transformative space that reflects the ideals of wisdom, strength, and beauty. These elements, which are metaphorically represented by the three great pillars of the Lodge—Wisdom, Strength, and Beauty—are essential to the success of any great and important undertaking. Just as King Solomon's Temple was supported by pillars of great strength and significance, so too is the Masonic Lodge supported by these same symbolic virtues. These parallels highlight the enduring influence of the Temple's principles, which serve as both a moral compass and a spiritual foundation for Freemasonry (Leoni, 2013).

The Orientation of the Lodge: East to West

The Masonic Lodge is traditionally oriented from east to west, a design deeply rooted in symbolism and ancient traditions. This orientation reflects the path of the sun, which rises in the east and sets in the west, symbolizing enlightenment, progress, and the cycle of life. The east is associated with the dawn of knowledge and the source of light, while the west represents the completion of life's journey and the quest for wisdom.

In King Solomon's Temple, the Holy of Holies faced west, while the entrance was positioned in the east, symbolizing the progression from the temporal world to the spiritual. Similarly, in Freemasonry, the Worshipful Master presides in the east, symbolizing their role as a source of light and guidance for the Lodge. The west, where the Senior Warden is seated, symbolizes the culmination of efforts and preparation for the spiritual ascent. This alignment emphasizes the importance of striving toward enlightenment and moving from darkness to light, a central tenet of Masonic philosophy (Hamill & Gilbert, 1995; MacNulty, 2006).

The east-west orientation also represents the connection between the material and spiritual realms, echoing the Masonic pursuit of harmony between earthly duties and spiritual growth. This symbolic path serves as a reminder of the cyclical nature of existence and the perpetual journey toward moral and intellectual perfection (Coil, 1996).

The Three Pillars: Wisdom, Strength, and Beauty

The three great pillars of Freemasonry—Wisdom, Strength, and Beauty—serve as foundational elements within the Lodge, each reflecting a crucial aspect of both the Temple and the human condition. In King Solomon's Temple, the pillars were not just architectural structures; they symbolized the principles upon which the Temple—and by extension, the world—was built. These same principles guide the Masonic Lodge and its members (Hamill & Gilbert, 1995).

Wisdom represents the ability to think, plan, and act with clarity and understanding. It is through wisdom that Masons are able to understand the mysteries of life and the teachings of the Craft. The Master of the Lodge, representing Wisdom, holds the responsibility of guiding the Lodge and its members toward truth and knowledge. This reflects the ancient wisdom imparted to Solomon, who was known for his divine understanding and judgment (Hamill & Gilbert, 1995).

Strength embodies the fortitude and resolve needed to support the Lodge's mission and to maintain the principles of Freemasonry in the face of adversity. The Senior Warden, as the embodiment of Strength, plays a critical role in supporting the Lodge's work and ensuring its stability. Much like the physical support provided by the pillars of Solomon's Temple, the strength of the Lodge is rooted in its members' commitment to uphold the principles of the Craft and to support one another in their moral journey (Jones, 2008).

Beauty, the final pillar, represents the harmony and perfection achieved when wisdom and strength are applied in balance. It is the Junior Warden who embodies Beauty, ensuring that the Lodge maintains harmony and order in all its undertakings. Just as the Temple was adorned with intricate designs and beautiful symbolism, the Lodge too is a place where beauty is reflected not just in the physical space, but in the relationships and interactions between its members. This beauty is not mere ornamentation; it is the expression of harmony and virtue, where all members work together toward a common goal (MacNulty, 2006).

The Covering of the Lodge: A Metaphor for Spiritual Aspiration

The covering of the Lodge, often described as a "clouded canopy or star-decked heaven," is symbolic of the celestial realm that Masons hope to reach through their spiritual and moral journey. This concept draws directly from the Biblical vision of Jacob's ladder, where the ladder reaches from earth to heaven, with three principal rounds: Faith, Hope, and Charity. These three virtues are essential to Masonic teachings and are integral to a Mason's progress within the Lodge (Coil, 1996).

Faith represents the belief in a higher power and the guiding force of the universe. It is through faith that Masons trust in the principles of Freemasonry and the wisdom they seek to uncover. The faith in the teachings of the Craft serves as the first step on the ladder, grounding the individual in a belief that transcends the material world.

Hope symbolizes the belief in a better future, the promise of spiritual progress, and the aspiration for enlightenment and personal growth. Hope is what drives a Mason to continue their journey, even in the face of adversity or doubt. It is the hope for immortality, for a better world, and for the fulfillment of their own moral and spiritual development (Morris, 2015).

Charity, the greatest of the three, extends beyond earthly life. Charity is the foundation of Masonic values—it embodies love, compassion, and selflessness toward all humanity. In Freemasonry, Charity is not just about giving material help, but also about demonstrating kindness, understanding, and empathy toward others. It is the virtue that connects Masons to one another and to the greater world, making it the highest aspiration in the journey toward becoming a more perfect man.

The Lodge as a Reflection of the Human Condition

The symbolism of the Masonic Lodge—its pillars, its covering, and its teachings—mirrors the journey of self-improvement that each Mason must undertake. The journey is a microcosm of the greater human condition, reflecting the need for balance between wisdom, strength, and beauty, and the ongoing aspiration to live a life based on the virtues of Faith, Hope, and Charity (Leoni, 2013). In the same way that Solomon's Temple was a place of divine purpose and spiritual significance, the Lodge is a space where Masons strive to build their own moral and spiritual temple (MacNulty, 2006).

As the candidate enters the Lodge, they are embarking on a path that will test their ability to balance these virtues. Just as the ancient Temple was built with precision and care, so too must the Mason build their own character, guided by the principles embodied in the pillars of Wisdom, Strength, and Beauty, and the virtues of Faith, Hope, and Charity. The Lodge provides the space for this transformation, offering both the tools and the support needed to grow in virtue and wisdom (Hamill & Gilbert, 1995).

In conclusion, the Masonic Lodge, like King Solomon's Temple, is a symbol of moral and spiritual aspiration. Its pillars and covering reflect the ideals that Masons strive toward—strength, wisdom, beauty, faith, hope, and charity—qualities that are central to the human condition. Through Freemasonry, Masons are not only encouraged to build a temple of virtue within themselves but also to work together as a community to uplift one another toward the greater good. The Lodge, as a reflection of the Temple, remains a sacred space where Masons are guided toward enlightenment and the fulfillment of their highest potential.

Reflections on the Craft: Questions for Deeper Understanding

- **Balancing Wisdom and Action:**
    - How can the three pillars guide your personal and Masonic life toward achieving moral and spiritual harmony?

- **The Interplay of Virtues:**
  - o In what ways do Wisdom, Strength, and Beauty interconnect in your daily life to create a harmonious balance between personal discipline and community engagement?
- **Symbolism of Orientation:**
  - o How does the Lodge's east-to-west alignment inspire your understanding of the journey from enlightenment to spiritual completion?

Immovable Jewels

Harmonize the earthly and the divine through the timeless wisdom of the Square, Level, and Plumb—the immovable jewels of Freemasonry

In Freemasonry, the immovable jewels—the Square, the Level, and the Plumb—are powerful symbols representing the core principles guiding Masons' conduct both inside and outside the Lodge. These jewels are symbolic tools for measuring the conduct of individuals and represent the foundation upon which Masons build their moral and spiritual lives. The Square symbolizes morality, the Level stands for equality, and the Plumb represents rectitude of life. Beyond their symbolic significance, these jewels hold a special place in Masonic ritual as the symbols of the Pedestal Officers, highlighting their integral role in the Lodge's governance and moral instruction.

Why Freemasons Consider Them Immovable Jewels

Freemasons regard these tools as "immovable jewels" because they symbolize unchanging principles that form the ethical foundation of the Craft. Albert G. Mackey referred to them as "tools of governance, unyielding and steadfast, representing the eternal nature of Masonic values" (Mackey, 1909). These jewels are immovable because they do not leave the Lodge—they remain ever-present, symbolizing their perpetual guidance. They are jewels because they are of inestimable worth, representing the moral treasure that Masons strive to cultivate.

The Pedestal Officers and Their Jewels

The Square, Level, and Plumb are assigned as the jewels of specific Pedestal Officers within the Lodge: the Worshipful

Master, the Senior Warden, and the Junior Warden, respectively. These officers are the principal leaders of the Lodge, and their roles are intimately connected to the principles these jewels symbolize.

The Worshipful Master and the Square

The Worshipful Master, as the presiding officer of the Lodge, holds the Square as his jewel. The Square symbolizes morality, serving as a reminder that the Worshipful Master is charged with maintaining the moral integrity of the Lodge and ensuring that all proceedings are conducted "on the square." As Mackey explains, "The Worshipful Master's use of the Square signifies his role as a moral arbiter, ensuring that justice and ethical conduct prevail" (Mackey, 1909). The Square also underscores the Master's duty to lead by example, embodying virtue in his words and actions.

The Senior Warden and the Level

The Senior Warden, second in authority within the Lodge, bears the Level as his jewel. The Level symbolizes equality and justice, reflecting the Senior Warden's responsibility to maintain harmony among the brethren. As Hegel emphasized, "Equality is the basis of freedom and recognition" (Hegel, 1821). The Senior Warden's use of the Level reminds all members that, within the Lodge, distinctions of wealth, rank, and social status are set aside, and all Masons meet as equals.

The Junior Warden and the Plumb

The Junior Warden, who oversees the Lodge during periods of refreshment and ensures proper conduct, holds the Plumb as his jewel. The Plumb represents uprightness and integrity, symbolizing the Junior Warden's duty to ensure that every

Mason remains true to the principles of the Craft. Johann Wolfgang von Goethe noted, "To act according to our highest values is the greatest challenge" (Goethe, 1810). The Junior Warden's role mirrors this philosophy, encouraging members to align their actions with their ideals.

The Level as Horizontal: Symbolizing the Physical Plane

The Level, as a horizontal object, symbolically represents the physical plane of existence. In many traditions, horizontal lines or objects denote the material and earthly realms, grounding the individual in the tangible aspects of life. According to Wilkinson (2003), "Horizontal forms in art and architecture often evoke the stability and permanence of the earth, symbolizing the physical plane of human existence." The Level's horizontal nature emphasizes balance, fairness, and the grounding of Masonic principles in everyday actions.

The Plumb as Perpendicular: A Symbol of the Divine

The Plumb, with its perpendicular orientation, symbolizes the connection between the earthly and the divine. Perpendicular objects, such as obelisks, have historically been viewed as sacred representations of divine aspirations. Eliade (1958) writes, "The vertical axis in sacred architecture often symbolizes the connection between heaven and earth, a channel through which divine energy flows." The Plumb's perpendicular nature thus underscores the Mason's moral responsibility to align with higher spiritual principles.

The Plumb's significance is further highlighted in the Book of Amos, where it is used as a divine instrument of judgment:

> "Behold, I am setting a plumb line in the midst of my people Israel; I will not again pass by them any more" (Amos 7:8, KJV).

In this context, the plumb line serves as a tool for measuring uprightness and adherence to divine laws, paralleling its Masonic interpretation as a symbol of moral rectitude.

The Level and Plumb Together: Forming the Master's Square

When the Level and Plumb are combined, they form a right angle—symbolic of the Master's Square. The Master's Square, a cornerstone of Masonic symbolism, represents perfection, balance, and the harmonious relationship between the material and spiritual realms. As the horizontal Level intersects with the perpendicular Plumb, their union signifies the Mason's journey to balance physical actions with spiritual ideals.

Albert Mackey explains, "The right angle, or Master's Square, serves as a reminder that Masons must harmonize their earthly duties with their spiritual aspirations" (Mackey, 1909). Together, the Level and Plumb encapsulate the dual responsibilities of a Mason: to live justly among men while striving for moral and spiritual alignment.

The Immovable Jewels as Ethical and Spiritual Guides

The Square, Level, and Plumb transcend their practical origins to embody profound ethical and spiritual principles. As the jewels of the Pedestal Officers, they serve as guiding symbols for the governance of the Lodge, emphasizing morality, equality, and integrity. Their geometric orientation further deepens their symbolism, with the Level grounding

Masons in the physical realm and the Plumb connecting them to the divine.

When united to form the Master's Square, these tools symbolize the Mason's ultimate aspiration: achieving harmony between the earthly and the spiritual, the tangible and the transcendent. By contemplating these immovable jewels, Freemasons not only honor their ancient traditions but also find timeless guidance for their moral and spiritual journeys.

Reflections on the Craft: Questions for Deeper Understanding

- **Balancing the Physical and the Spiritual:**
    - The Level symbolizes the physical plane, while the Plumb represents the divine connection. How can you use these symbols to achieve balance in your daily life, aligning material responsibilities with spiritual aspirations?
- **Unity in Principles:**
    - The Master's Square is formed by the union of the Level and Plumb. How does this union inspire you to integrate fairness, morality, and integrity into your personal and Masonic journey?
- **Ethical Leadership:**
    - As the jewels of the Pedestal Officers, the Square, Level, and Plumb guide the governance of the Lodge. How can these tools help you embody principles of ethical leadership in your interactions within the Craft and beyond?

Navigating Knowledge in Freemasonry: Participatory and Perspectival Knowing

Discover how Freemasonry intertwines action and insight to illuminate the path to moral and intellectual growth.

In Freemasonry, the pursuit of knowledge transcends the intellectual realm, intertwining with experiential and moral dimensions. The Craft's profound teachings are deeply rooted in a philosophy of how we come to know—not merely by observing but by participating. This essay explores two fundamental modes of knowledge—participatory and perspectival knowing—and examines how they are integral to the Masonic journey. By reflecting on the moral science of Freemasonry, it becomes evident that true understanding arises through active engagement within the lodge and the changing perspectives offered by progression through its degrees and offices.

The Philosophy of Knowing

Philosophers have long deliberated on the nature of knowledge. Participatory knowing involves direct engagement—learning by doing, embodying, and experiencing. It is knowledge rooted in the active interplay between the individual and the world (Polanyi, 1966). In contrast, perspectival knowing relates to understanding shaped by one's position or viewpoint. It highlights the significance of observing from various perspectives to grasp the broader meaning of any subject or phenomenon (Varela et al., 1991).

Freemasonry exemplifies the integration of these epistemological approaches. The lodge is not merely a space for abstract reflection but a living arena where lessons are enacted, roles are performed, and truths are realized through experience. The participatory dimension engages members in rituals, while the perspectival aspect is cultivated as Masons progress through degrees and offices, each offering a distinct vantage point on the Craft.

Participation in the Lodge: The Core of Masonic Learning

Freemasonry teaches its moral science most effectively through active participation. The initiation rituals, degree work, and regular lodge meetings immerse members in symbolic actions that convey profound lessons. For example, the candidate's blindfolded journey during initiation is not merely a metaphor; it is an embodied experience of moving from darkness to light, symbolizing the pursuit of knowledge and moral enlightenment (Hamill, 2004).

As officers move through the line—progressing from roles like Junior Steward to Worshipful Master—they gain participatory knowledge by performing specific duties. Each station and role offers unique responsibilities and challenges, deepening their connection to the Craft's teachings. For instance:

- **Junior Officers**: Learn humility and service through practical duties such as arranging the lodge (Jackson, 2016).

- **Senior Officers**: Develop leadership and responsibility, gaining a broader perspective on the lodge's functioning and its members.

The shift from one station to another not only enhances participatory engagement but also changes the officer's perspective, enriching their understanding of the lodge as a cohesive unit.

Degrees and Rituals: Evolving Perspectives

Each degree in Freemasonry serves as a lens through which the initiate views the principles of the Craft. The Entered Apprentice degree introduces foundational concepts and symbolism, focusing on the building blocks of moral character. As the Mason advances to the Fellow craft and Master Mason degrees, their perspective shifts, revealing deeper layers of meaning and interconnection (Stevenson, 1996).

The dual nature of knowing is evident in these degrees. Participation in the degrees—standing in the center of the lodge, enacting symbolic journeys, and reciting obligations—embeds the teachings experientially. Observing others perform these rituals in subsequent meetings adds a perspectival dimension, allowing members to see their earlier experiences from a new vantage point. This dynamic interplay between participation and perspective fosters a comprehensive understanding of Freemasonry's moral science.

Social Activities and Charity: Extending Knowledge Beyond the Lodge

Freemasonry's emphasis on participatory and perspectival knowing extends to its social and charitable activities. Lodge events, such as dinners, community outreach programs, and charity drives, serve as platforms for Masons to practice the principles they learn within the lodge. These activities exemplify participatory knowing, as members engage directly in acts of fellowship, compassion, and service (Hodapp, 2005).

Charity events, in particular, offer transformative experiences. Organizing and participating in a fundraiser for a local cause enables Masons to witness the practical application of Masonic principles like relief and brotherly love. Observing the impact of their efforts provides a perspectival understanding of how their collective actions align with the broader mission of the Craft.

Social gatherings, too, enrich the Masonic journey. Through shared meals, informal discussions, and communal celebrations, members forge bonds that transcend ritual. These moments of connection offer insights into the human condition, teaching lessons of empathy, patience, and humility that reinforce the lodge's moral teachings (Turner, 2010).

The Integration of Knowing in Freemasonry

Freemasonry's approach to knowledge is holistic, blending participatory and perspectival knowing into a unified experience. The lodge provides a sacred space where members actively engage in rituals and take on evolving roles, while also stepping back to observe and reflect. This dual process transforms mere instruction into wisdom.

As Masons progress through the degrees and participate in the lodge's social and charitable endeavors, they gain a deeper appreciation of the Craft's principles. Through participation, they embody the teachings; through perspective, they understand their significance. Together, these modes of knowing form the cornerstone of true Masonic enlightenment.

Freemasonry invites its members to embark on a journey of moral and intellectual growth through active engagement and evolving perspectives. By participating in rituals, fulfilling roles within the lodge, and engaging in charitable and social activities, Masons gain a profound understanding of the Craft's teachings. The balance of participatory and perspectival knowing not only enriches individual members but also strengthens the collective fabric of the fraternity, ensuring that its light continues to shine brightly for generations to come.

Reflections on the Craft: Questions for Deeper Understanding

- **Balancing Action and Reflection:**
  - How do the participatory and perspectival aspects of Freemasonry enhance your understanding of its teachings?
- **Personal Growth Through Participation**:
  - What lessons have you learned by actively engaging in lodge rituals and roles?
- **Extending Knowledge Beyond the Lodge:**
  - How do social and charitable activities deepen your connection to the principles of Freemasonry?

The Significance of the Number Three in Patterns, Rhetoric, Religion, and Freemasonry

Discover the timeless power of the number three across diverse disciplines and traditions.

The number three has long been regarded as the first number to form a recognizable pattern, serving as a foundation in geometry, cultural narratives, religious systems, and even Freemasonry. Its prominence can be traced to its ability to create structure, evoke meaning, and symbolize completeness. This essay explores the cognitive, mathematical, and cultural underpinnings of the number three, its role in rhetorical frameworks, its theological significance across major world religions, and its centrality in Masonic symbolism and rituals.

Cognitive and Mathematical Basis of Three

Cognitively, humans are naturally attuned to recognizing patterns, and the number three often serves as a threshold for this recognition. A single item stands alone, two form a pair, but three items create a shape or pattern—a triangle, for instance—that conveys structure and stability (Dehaene, 1997). Geometrically, three points are the minimum required to define a plane or form a triangle, the simplest polygon and a cornerstone of pattern recognition (Livio, 2002).

Culturally, the "rule of three" dominates storytelling and art, appearing in fairy tales, mythology, and writing. For example, stories often feature three trials or wishes, reflecting a universal human preference for triadic structures to enhance memorability and impact (McKee, 1997).

The Role of Three in Rhetoric

Aristotle's rhetorical theory underscores the importance of the number three through the triad of ethos, pathos, and logos. These components form the bedrock of effective persuasion:

- **Ethos (Character):** Establishing credibility and authority as a speaker is foundational to gaining trust. Aristotle noted that a speaker's moral character often determines their ability to persuade (Aristotle, trans. 1991).

- **Pathos (Emotion):** Emotionally engaging the audience strengthens the persuasive impact of a message. This is achieved through storytelling and evocative language.

- **Logos (Logic):** Logical arguments, supported by evidence and reason, provide the intellectual basis for persuasion.

This triadic approach continues to influence modern communication strategies, demonstrating the enduring power of three in rhetoric.

Theological and Spiritual Significance of Three

Across religious systems, the number three symbolizes divine completeness, harmony, and balance.

- **Christianity**:
    - The Holy Trinity—Father, Son, and Holy Spirit—is central to Christian theology, representing one God in three persons (Matthews, 2000).

- Jesus' resurrection on the third day reinforces the number's association with renewal and hope (1 Corinthians 15:4).
- **Hinduism**:
  - The Trimurti—Brahma (creator), Vishnu (preserver), and Shiva (destroyer)—symbolizes the cyclical nature of existence.
  - The three Gunas (Sattva, Rajas, and Tamas) represent the essential qualities of the universe (Radhakrishnan, 1957).
- **Buddhism**:
  - The Three Jewels—the Buddha, the Dharma (teaching), and the Sangha (community)—are foundational to Buddhist practice (Gethin, 1998).
- **Judaism**:
  - The three Patriarchs—Abraham, Isaac, and Jacob—establish the lineage and covenant of the Jewish faith.

The symbolic role of three extends to Islam, Taoism, Zoroastrianism, and indigenous traditions, emphasizing its universal resonance.

The Number Three in Freemasonry

Freemasonry elevates the number three to a central position within its rituals, symbols, and teachings. The triadic nature of Masonic principles reflects the number's symbolic depth and philosophical significance.

Symbols and Emblems

- **The Three Great Lights:** The Holy Bible (or sacred text), the Square, and the Compasses serve as the principal guides of Masonic practice (Hamill & Gilbert, 1991).

- **The Three Lesser Lights:** Representing the Sun, Moon, and Worshipful Master, these lights symbolize guidance and enlightenment.

- **The Three Pillars**: Wisdom, Strength, and Beauty are seen as the foundational supports of a lodge and its members' moral and spiritual development.

Rituals

- **Three Degrees:** Freemasonry is organized into three degrees—Entered Apprentice, Fellow Craft, and Master Mason—symbolizing the stages of personal and spiritual growth.

- **Three Principal Officers**: The Worshipful Master, Senior Warden, and Junior Warden govern the lodge, reflecting different aspects of leadership and cooperation.

- **Three Knocks and Movements**: Ceremonial knocks and gestures often occur in threes, emphasizing unity and reverence.

Allegorical Significance

- **Three Ruffians**: In the Master Mason degree, the allegory of three ruffians represents challenges and the ultimate triumph of integrity and perseverance.

- **Faith, Hope, and Charity**: These graces are core to Masonic teaching and are often depicted in symbolic triads.

- **Brotherly Love, Relief and Truth**: The three principal tenents of Freemasonry.

Freemasonry's reverence for the number three underscores its alignment with harmony, balance, and enlightenment. The ubiquity of the number three in patterns, rhetoric, religion, and Freemasonry reflects its profound role as a symbol of structure, completeness, and connection. From the ancient world to modern times, this triadic concept continues to shape human thought and creativity.

Reflections on the Craft: Questions for Deeper Understanding

- **Recognizing Patterns:**
  - How does the recognition of patterns in groups of three influence your understanding of structure and balance in daily life?
- **Masonic Triads:**
  - How do the Masonic principles of Wisdom, Strength, and Beauty apply to personal and communal endeavors?
- **Universal Triads:**
  - Why do you think the number three resonates so strongly across cultures, religions, and disciplines?

Harmony's Hidden Flaw: How Deceit Thrives in the Absence of Truth

Unmasking the Fragile Peace: Exploring how harmony, when divorced from truth, becomes a breeding ground for deceit and ethical compromise

Harmony, as a concept, is deeply ingrained in the fabric of human society. It represents balance, unity, and the pursuit of a shared goal, making it a cornerstone of successful relationships, organizations, and communities. Within the Masonic tradition, harmony is considered the "strength and support of all societies," reflecting its pivotal role in fostering a spirit of fraternity and mutual respect. However, harmony—when pursued at all costs—can be corrupted, becoming the fertile ground for deceit. This insidious connection between harmony and deceit, the latter thriving in the absence of truth, reveals the darker consequences of prioritizing superficial peace over honesty and integrity.

The Masonic View on Harmony and Its Vulnerabilities

Freemasonry, with its emphasis on moral and ethical principles, views harmony as essential to its ethos. The charge to "pay the craft their wages if any be due, that none may go away dissatisfied" underscores the importance of fairness, transparency, and equitable treatment. Yet, even within this noble framework, the overzealous pursuit of harmony can lead to the suppression of dissent, marginalization of minority voices, and the avoidance of necessary conflict—all of which create an environment where deceit can flourish.

When harmony is misunderstood as the mere absence of conflict, it risks becoming a superficial veneer. In such cases, members of a group might hide their true feelings or observations to maintain a semblance of peace, allowing dishonesty to infiltrate the very structure that harmony seeks to uphold. This is particularly harmful within organizations like Masonic lodges, where integrity and moral uprightness are foundational.

Deceit Thrives in the Absence of Truth

Deceit flourishes when truth is suppressed, often under the guise of maintaining harmony. Unlike harmony, which seeks genuine unity and mutual understanding, deceit manipulates perceptions and obscures reality. The two are linked by the human tendency to avoid discomfort; when the goal of maintaining harmony becomes more important than addressing underlying issues, deceit finds its opportunity to grow.

One prominent example of this dynamic is groupthink, where the desire for consensus overrides the critical evaluation of ideas. In such scenarios, individuals may suppress their own thoughts or observations to avoid creating discord. This leads to a collective deception, where the group's apparent harmony masks unresolved tensions and potentially disastrous decisions.

The Ethical Pitfalls of Superficial Harmony

Superficial harmony, characterized by the suppression of dissent and the avoidance of difficult conversations, can have profound ethical implications. It undermines the integrity of relationships and organizations, as individuals are forced to prioritize a false sense of peace over honesty. This dynamic is particularly troubling in leadership, where the refusal to address uncomfortable truths—whether due to fear of conflict or a misplaced commitment to harmony— can lead to poor decision-making and systemic failures.

For example, a leader who avoids confronting unethical behavior to "maintain harmony" within a team is complicit in perpetuating that behavior. In such cases, harmony becomes a shield for deceit, eroding trust and moral accountability within the group. The Masonic emphasis on justice and equitable treatment serves as a reminder that harmony without truth is not true harmony at all, but rather a deceptive imitation.

The Role of Conflict in Achieving True Harmony

True harmony is not the absence of conflict but the resolution of it. Healthy conflict—rooted in respect and a shared commitment to truth—is essential for growth, innovation, and the maintenance of integrity within any group. The Masonic principles of brotherly love and truth emphasize this balance, encouraging members to address disagreements openly and constructively.

By embracing conflict as a necessary part of achieving harmony, individuals and organizations can guard against the infiltration of deceit. This requires courage, transparency, and a commitment to fairness, ensuring that harmony is not achieved at the expense of truth. In this way, harmony becomes a dynamic and resilient force, capable of withstanding the challenges posed by deceit.

Conclusion

Harmony—when divorced from truth—becomes a fragile and deceptive ideal. The Masonic emphasis on harmony as the "strength and support of all societies" serves as a guiding principle, reminding us that true harmony is not about avoiding conflict but addressing it with honesty and fairness. By recognizing the dangers of false harmony and embracing the role of conflict in fostering genuine unity, we can ensure that harmony remains a force for good, untainted by the corrosive influence of deceit.

Reflections on the Craft: Questions for Deeper Understanding

- **Harmony and Integrity:**
  - How can you ensure that your pursuit of harmony within a group or organization remains rooted in truth, rather than becoming a superficial avoidance of conflict?
- **The Balance Between Harmony and Truth:**
  - Freemasonry teaches the importance of brotherly love and truth. How do you balance the desire for harmony with the need to address uncomfortable truths in your personal and Masonic relationships?
- **The Role of Conflict in Growth:**
  - How can you embrace healthy conflict as an essential tool for fostering genuine unity and avoiding the pitfalls of superficial harmony?

Building on the Pillars: How Wisdom, Strength, and Beauty Create a Thriving Lodge

Discover how the timeless principles of Wisdom, Strength, and Beauty can transform your lodge into a center of growth, engagement, and community impact

The three pillars of Wisdom, Strength, and Beauty are among the most enduring symbols of Freemasonry, representing foundational principles that guide the Craft's moral and spiritual framework. While these pillars hold profound symbolic meaning, they also serve as practical tools for fostering healthy, vibrant lodges that reflect the ideals of Freemasonry in their operations and in their service to the broader community. By embracing these pillars as actionable principles, a lodge can become a thriving center for Masonic education, participation, and community engagement.

The Traditional Significance of the Pillars

In Masonic tradition, Wisdom, Strength, and Beauty are the supports of a well-governed lodge. Each pillar carries its own distinct significance:

- **Wisdom**: Associated with the Worshipful Master, Wisdom represents prudence, knowledge, and sound judgment—qualities necessary for guiding the lodge and ensuring its harmony.
- **Strength**: Represented by the Senior Warden, Strength signifies stability, determination, and perseverance, providing the lodge with the resilience needed to uphold its principles.
- **Beauty**: Symbolized by the Junior Warden, Beauty embodies harmony, balance, and inspiration,

adorning the lodge and its workings with the pursuit of perfection and moral refinement.

These pillars are more than structural supports—they are the essence of a lodge's moral integrity and operational success.

Insights from Masonic Scholars

Albert G. Mackey described the pillars as virtues essential to the moral and spiritual growth of Freemasons. In his *Encyclopedia of Freemasonry*, Mackey emphasized that Wisdom guides ethical decision-making, Strength sustains resolve, and Beauty inspires the pursuit of harmony and excellence (Mackey, 1921).

Manly P. Hall, in *The Lost Keys of Freemasonry*, viewed the pillars as complementary forces that balance intellect, will, and creativity. Hall asserted that Wisdom illuminates the path to truth, Strength provides the fortitude to act on that truth, and Beauty ensures that truth is expressed in a way that inspires and uplifts (Hall, 1923).

These perspectives highlight the interconnectedness of the pillars and their role in creating a balanced and principled lodge.

Applying the Pillars to Build a Healthy Lodge

To foster a thriving lodge, the principles of Wisdom, Strength, and Beauty can be reinterpreted as practical strategies for Masonic education, participation, and community engagement:

- **Wisdom as Masonic Education**: A healthy lodge prioritizes education that explores the deeper meanings of Masonic ritual and applies these teachings to daily life. By offering lectures, discussions, and study groups, the lodge can inspire intellectual curiosity and ethical reflection. This commitment to education ensures that members not only understand the Craft but also embody its principles in their actions.

- **Strength as Participation**: Strength within a lodge means creating pathways for all members to engage meaningfully. While leadership roles are important, a thriving lodge provides opportunities for every member to contribute, whether through mentoring, organizing events, or participating in charitable initiatives. Inclusivity fosters a sense of belonging and ensures that the lodge remains dynamic and resilient.

- **Beauty as Community Engagement**: Beauty extends beyond the lodge walls to the community it serves. A lodge that embodies Beauty inspires its members to reflect Masonic values in their daily lives and to engage in collective acts of service. By hosting charitable events, supporting local causes, and maintaining a visible presence in the community, the lodge becomes a beacon of Freemasonry's principles.

A Lodge as a Center for Masonic and Civic Life

When a lodge fully integrates the principles of Wisdom, Strength, and Beauty, it transcends its role as a meeting place for Masons and becomes a cornerstone of the community. Educational programs rooted in Wisdom can extend to public lectures or workshops, sharing Masonic insights with a broader audience. Strength can be demonstrated through mentorship and collaboration, ensuring that all members feel valued and included. Beauty shines outward through visible contributions to the community, from organizing charity drives to supporting local initiatives.

By embracing these principles, a lodge can fulfill its mission of personal and collective growth while embodying the spirit of Freemasonry in a way that inspires both its members and the world around it.

Reflections on the Craft: Questions for Deeper Understanding

- **Wisdom and Education**:
    - How can your lodge enhance its educational programs to inspire members and deepen their understanding of Masonic principles?
- **Strength and Engagement**:
    - What strategies can your lodge implement to ensure that all members, regardless of their roles, feel valued and included in its activities?
- **Beauty and Community Impact**:
    - In what ways can your lodge extend the beauty of Freemasonry into the broader community through acts of service and engagement?

Masonic History, Custom and Etiquette

Why a Brother Should Not Cross Between the Master and the Altar During Open Lodge

Preserving tradition and symbolism: Understanding the sacred connection between the Worshipful Master and the altar.

In Freemasonry, it is customary for members to avoid crossing between the Worshipful Master and the altar during an open lodge session. This practice, rooted in Masonic symbolism and etiquette, emphasizes respect for the sacredness of the lodge's rituals and the authority of the Master. The prohibition is based on symbolic, traditional, and practical reasons, all of which are integral to the proper functioning of a Masonic lodge.

Symbolic Connection Between the Master and the Altar

The altar, positioned at the center of the lodge, represents the heart of Freemasonry and serves as the resting place for the Great Lights: the Bible or Volume of the Sacred Law, the square, and the compasses. These are central to Masonic teachings and symbolize wisdom, moral guidance, and spiritual enlightenment. The Worshipful Master, seated in the East, embodies wisdom and the light of understanding.

Crossing between the Master and the altar is considered disruptive to the symbolic connection between these two focal points. As Roberts (2008) explains, "The unbroken line between the Master and the altar symbolizes the flow of wisdom and divine guidance that governs the lodge." To pass through this line is to interrupt this connection and cast a shadow over the sacred space.

Respect for Masonic Rituals and Traditions

Freemasonry is steeped in tradition, and the avoidance of crossing between the Master and the altar is a long-standing custom. This practice demonstrates respect for the sacredness of Masonic rituals and ceremonies. Hamill (2010) notes, "The solemnity of ritual work requires that the altar, as the symbolic center of the lodge, remain undisturbed during meetings." Crossing this line can be perceived as a breach of decorum and a distraction from the lodge's proceedings.

The altar and its surrounding space are treated with great reverence, and maintaining their sanctity is a matter of Masonic etiquette. This practice serves as a reminder of the discipline and focus required to engage meaningfully with the teachings of Freemasonry.

Maintaining Order and Decorum

The physical layout of the lodge room is designed to facilitate orderly conduct and maintain a focus on the rituals being performed. Allowing members to cross between the Master and the altar could create unnecessary disruptions or confusion. As Mackey (1921) states, "The architectural arrangement of the lodge room is intentional, ensuring that movement within the lodge supports the dignity and solemnity of its activities."

By observing this custom, Masons contribute to an atmosphere of respect and attentiveness that is essential for meaningful engagement with the Craft's principles.

Educational Significance

The prohibition against crossing between the Master and the altar is not only practical but also symbolic of broader Masonic teachings. It reinforces lessons of humility, discipline, and reverence for the sacred. As the Grand Lodge of Iowa (2013) explains, "This practice reminds members of the importance of discipline and respect within the lodge, teaching Masons to honor the symbolic framework that underpins the Craft."

By adhering to this tradition, Masons internalize the values of order and respect that are central to their personal and communal growth within the fraternity.

The practice of avoiding the space between the Worshipful Master and the altar during an open lodge session is an important aspect of Masonic etiquette. Rooted in the symbolic relationship between the Master and the altar, it underscores the sanctity of Masonic rituals and the discipline required to maintain the lodge's order. By upholding this custom, Freemasons demonstrate their commitment to the principles of respect, reverence, and symbolic understanding that are integral to the Craft.

Reflections on the Craft: Questions for Deeper Understanding

- **Symbolic Alignment and Respect:**
  - How does the act of refraining from crossing between the Master and the altar reflect the Masonic values of discipline, respect, and harmony within the lodge?
- **Ritual Significance and Awareness:**
  - Considering the altar's central role in representing wisdom and enlightenment, how can Masons cultivate greater awareness of the symbolic connections in their daily lives?
- **Tradition and Unity:**
  - What steps can you take to ensure that traditions like this one continue to unify and

inspire members, reinforcing the solemnity and purpose of Masonic rituals?

The Ancient Landmarks of Freemasonry: Preserving a Legacy of Integrity

Exploring the timeless principles that define Freemasonry and safeguard its ethical and spiritual legacy

The term "landmarks" historically refers to fixed boundaries or markers that define property or territory. In a broader, metaphorical sense, landmarks signify the essential and unchanging principles or traditions that guide a community or institution. Within Freemasonry, the Ancient Landmarks embody the foundational principles and practices that delineate its identity and perpetuate its philosophical and ethical framework. These landmarks are viewed as inviolable, preserving the integrity and universality of the Craft.

Biblical Foundations: Landmarks in Scripture

The importance of landmarks as immutable guides is a theme richly addressed in biblical literature. Proverbs 22:28 exhorts, "Remove not the ancient landmark, which thy fathers have set" (King James Version), emphasizing respect for established boundaries and traditions. Similarly, Deuteronomy 19:14 warns, "Thou shalt not remove thy neighbor's landmark, which they of old time have set in thine inheritance." These verses underscore the societal and moral significance of respecting inherited traditions, equating the removal of landmarks with dishonesty and corruption. The biblical consequences of disregarding such boundaries are severe, often associated with divine retribution and societal disorder, reflecting a universal principle of safeguarding ethical and spiritual continuity.

Historical Emergence of Masonic Landmarks

The concept of Ancient Landmarks within Freemasonry emerged as a means of identifying the essential elements of the Craft that must remain unchanged to preserve its character and legitimacy. While the idea of landmarks was referenced informally in early Masonic writings, it was Mackey[10] who, in 1858, systematically cataloged and articulated them. Mackey's
"Twenty-Five Ancient Landmarks" were presented in his seminal work, A Textbook of Masonic Jurisprudence, which remains a cornerstone of Masonic scholarship. Mackey's landmarks outline the core principles, practices, and governance structures of Freemasonry, distinguishing it

---

[10] Albert Gallatin Mackey (1807–1881) was an American physician, educator, and one of the most influential Masonic scholars of the 19th century. Born in Charleston, South Carolina, Mackey graduated from the Medical College of South Carolina in 1832 and initially pursued a career in medicine. However, his passion for Freemasonry soon became his life's work. Mackey joined the fraternity in 1841 and quickly rose to prominence as a prolific author and historian, focusing on the rituals, symbols, and philosophy of Freemasonry.

Mackey's most notable works include The Encyclopedia of Freemasonry (1874), Lexicon of Freemasonry (1845), and The Symbolism of Freemasonry (1869), which are considered foundational texts for Masonic study. Through these works, he sought to codify the history and esoteric principles of the Craft, emphasizing its moral and spiritual significance. Mackey's writings continue to influence Masonic thought and education worldwide.

In addition to his literary contributions, Mackey served as the Grand Secretary of the Grand Lodge of South Carolina from 1842 to 1867 and was a founding member of the Supreme Council of the Ancient and Accepted Scottish Rite in the Southern Jurisdiction of the United States. His dedication to Freemasonry earned him widespread recognition as a central figure in the development of Masonic scholarship

from other fraternal organizations and ensuring its adherence to its historical and philosophical roots.

Mackey's Twenty-Five Ancient Landmarks

1. Modes of Recognition: Specific methods of identifying Masons.

2. Division of Symbolic Degrees: The Craft is composed of three degrees: Entered Apprentice, Fellow craft, and Master Mason.

3. Legend of the Third Degree: The central legend of Hiram Abiff.

4. Government by a Grand Master: The fraternity is governed by a Grand Master.

5. Prerogative of the Grand Master to Preside: He can preside over any Masonic assembly.

6. Prerogative of the Grand Master to Grant Dispensations: Authority to grant dispensations for forming lodges.

7. Prerogative of the Grand Master to Make Masons at Sight: Ability to create a Mason without the usual process.

8. Necessity of Masons to Congregate in Lodges: Lodges are the central units of Freemasonry.

9. Government of Lodges by a Master and Wardens: A lodge is ruled by these officers.

10. Necessity of a Volume of Sacred Law: Every lodge must have a holy book.

11. Legend of the Temple: The central allegory concerning Solomon's Temple.

12. Symbolism of Operative Masonry: Masonry retains its symbolic connection to stonemasonry.

13. Secrecy: The obligation of maintaining Masonic secrets.

14. Foundation on Speculative Science: Masonry is speculative and philosophical.

15. Equality of Members: All Masons are equal within the lodge.

16. Right of Masons to Appeal: Members can appeal lodge decisions.

17. Right of Visiting: Masons have the right to visit other lodges.

18. Prerogative of the Grand Lodge to Regulate Freemasonry: Grand Lodges govern Masonic affairs.

19. Universality of Freemasonry: The fraternity is universal in its principles.

20. Belief in a Supreme Being: Masons must believe in a higher power.

21. Belief in the Immortality of the Soul: Central to Masonic teachings.

22. Exclusion of Women: Only men are admitted.

23. Landmarks Cannot Be Changed: They are inviolable and unalterable.

24. Election of the Master by the Lodge: The Master of a lodge is chosen by its members.

25. Qualification of Candidates: Candidates must meet specific moral, ethical, and legal qualifications.

Conclusion

The Ancient Landmarks of Freemasonry serve as the bedrock of its traditions, symbolizing continuity, integrity, and universality. From their metaphorical roots in biblical scripture to their formalization by Mackey in 1858, these landmarks provide Freemasonry with a resilient framework that transcends time and geography. By adhering to these principles, Freemasonry not only preserves its identity but also fulfills its mission of moral and ethical upliftment.

Reflections on the Craft: Questions for Deeper Understanding

- **Respecting Tradition**:
    - o How does the preservation of Masonic landmarks reflect the values of continuity and integrity within the Craft, and how can these values be applied in your personal life?
- **Biblical Parallels:**
    - o Biblical scriptures emphasize the importance of landmarks as moral boundaries. How do these teachings enhance your understanding of the Masonic commitment to unchanging principles?

- **Evolving Practices vs. Immutable Principles:**
  - In a world of constant change, how can Freemasons balance adherence to the Ancient Landmarks with the need to address contemporary challenges?

Ancient Mystery Schools: Guardians of Esoteric Wisdom

A journey through the sacred teachings of antiquity and their echoes in modern Freemasonry.

Throughout history, humanity has sought to understand the mysteries of existence. Ancient mystery schools, deeply rooted in spiritual and philosophical traditions, served as centers of esoteric learning and transformation. These schools not only shaped the cultural and intellectual fabric of their respective societies but also laid the groundwork for modern esoteric traditions, including Freemasonry. This essay explores the history, beliefs, and practices of these ancient schools and examines their relationship to contemporary Masonic thought.

Ancient Mystery Schools: A Historical Overview

The ancient mystery schools of Egypt, Greece, and Rome were highly secretive organizations that offered spiritual and philosophical teachings to initiates. These schools sought to guide individuals on a journey of self-discovery, universal understanding, and moral transformation.

Egyptian Mysteries

The Egyptian mysteries, dating back to 3000 BCE, centered on the teachings of Thoth, Osiris, and Isis. They emphasized the soul's journey beyond death and the principles of universal balance, or Ma'at. Initiates engaged in rituals and studied sacred texts to prepare for the afterlife (Assmann, 2001). These schools were deeply entwined with Egyptian religion and governance, as temples like those at Karnak served as centers of learning and spiritual practice.

Eleusinian Mysteries

The Eleusinian mysteries flourished in ancient Greece from around 1500 BCE to the 4th century CE. Centered on the myth of Demeter and Persephone, they symbolized the cycle of life, death, and rebirth. Initiates participated in secret rituals, including fasting, symbolic reenactments, and sacred feasts (Mylonas, 1961). This initiation granted them a sense of renewal and divine protection, highlighting the transformative power of sacred rites.

Orphic Mysteries

The Orphic mysteries, rooted in the mythical figure Orpheus, emerged in Greece around the 6th century BCE. They emphasized purification, the soul's immortality, and reunification with the divine. Practices included the recitation of hymns, rituals involving music, and strict dietary rules to cleanse and elevate the soul (Witt, 1997).

Pythagorean School

Founded by Pythagoras around 570 BCE, this school combined philosophy, mathematics, and mysticism. The Pythagoreans believed in the harmony of the cosmos, expressed through numerical principles, and the immortality of the soul (Kahn, 2001). Members practiced ethical discipline, communal living, and the study of music and astronomy, emphasizing intellectual and spiritual growth.

Mithraic Mysteries

Originating in Persia and adopted by Roman society, the Mithraic mysteries celebrated Mithras, the god of light and truth. They emphasized moral integrity and the cosmic struggle between good and evil (Cumont, 1903). Initiates underwent complex rituals in underground temples, reenacting Mithras' mythos through symbolic meals and ceremonies.

Dionysian Mysteries

The Dionysian mysteries revolved around the worship of Dionysus, the god of wine, ecstasy, and nature's cycles. These mysteries emphasized the liberation of the individual through ecstatic rituals, music, and dramatic performances. Participants sought spiritual transcendence by engaging in symbolic acts of death and renewal (Ridley, 2011).

Hermetic Mysteries

Rooted in the Hermetic texts attributed to Hermes Trismegistus, these mysteries flourished in Hellenistic Egypt between the 1st and 3rd centuries CE. They focused on the unity of the divine and human and employed alchemy[11] as a metaphor for spiritual transformation. Meditation on Hermetic writings and symbolic rituals played a central role in their practices (Yates, 1964).

Ancient Mysteries with Modern Freemasonry

---

[11] Alchemy, often regarded as both a proto-science and a mystical tradition, is rooted in the ancient quest to transform base materials into noble substances, such as turning lead into gold. Beyond its literal interpretation, alchemy served as a rich metaphor for spiritual refinement, symbolizing the transmutation of the soul from a base, imperfect state to a higher, enlightened one. Emerging in Hellenistic Egypt and heavily influenced by Hermetic, Greek, and Egyptian thought, alchemy combined esoteric philosophy with practical experimentation. Its practitioners, known as alchemists, sought not only material perfection but also the "Philosopher's Stone," a symbol of ultimate wisdom and eternal life (Principe, 2013).

Ancient mystery schools and modern Freemasonry share foundational principles, such as initiation processes and the use of symbols. Both traditions emphasize personal transformation and moral refinement. For example, the Pythagorean emphasis on harmony is echoed in Freemasonry's focus on the moral geometry of life.

Symbolic and Ritualistic Parallels

Several symbols and rituals connect ancient mystery schools and Freemasonry:

- **Light**: Light is used as a metaphor for knowledge and enlightenment.

- **Geometry**: The Pythagorean focus on harmony through numbers resonates with the Masonic emphasis on the square and compass.

- **Pillars**: Inspired by the Hermetic and Eleusinian schools, Masonic rituals feature twin pillars symbolizing strength and wisdom.

- **Allegorical Journeys**: Freemasonry's degrees mirror the initiatory journeys of ancient schools.

- **Sacred Geometry**: The significance of the number three and triangular symbols appears in both traditions.

- **Death and Rebirth**: Reflecting the Mithraic and Dionysian rituals, Masonic degrees often symbolize a metaphorical death and rebirth.

- **Cosmic Harmony**: The emphasis on balance in Egyptian and Pythagorean teachings is mirrored in Masonic concepts of justice and morality.

- **Circle and Square**: Representing eternity and material existence, these geometric shapes are central in both.

- **Ritual Silence:** Periods of silence used for reflection and spiritual preparation are integral to both practices.

- **Architectural Symbols**: The Temple of Solomon in Freemasonry reflects architectural and symbolic elements from Egyptian and Hermetic traditions.

Evolutionary Influence

The primary divergence lies in accessibility and cultural context. Mystery schools were highly exclusive and deeply integrated into their religious frameworks. Freemasonry, while selective, operates within a secular and fraternal context, emphasizing ethical development over mystical experience (Steinmetz, 2016).

Freemasonry inherits symbolic practices and initiation models from ancient traditions. However, it adapts these elements to modern philosophical ideals, reflecting Enlightenment values of reason and equality (Ridley, 2011). The Masonic emphasis on universal brotherhood transforms the exclusivity of ancient mystery schools into a system accessible to individuals across different cultural and religious backgrounds.

While ancient mysteries often integrated worship of deities and cosmological exploration, Freemasonry reinterprets these practices into moral allegories and lessons. For instance, the Hermetic focus on unity between the divine and human becomes the Masonic pursuit of spiritual and ethical balance within society. Additionally, while the Eleusinian and Mithraic mysteries included intense personal rituals that aimed for divine connection, Freemasonry emphasizes intellectual growth and community engagement through structured rituals that are open to scrutiny and adaptation.

Modern Freemasonry's symbols and rituals also reflect the Enlightenment's influence, focusing on reason, science, and progress. This shift makes Freemasonry less about achieving mystical experiences and more about fostering a philosophical approach to morality and human connection. Its evolution highlights the adaptation of ancient wisdom to the intellectual and societal needs of contemporary times.

Reflections on the Craft: Questions for Deeper Understanding

- **Continuity of Symbols:**
  - o How do symbols shared by ancient mystery schools and Freemasonry, such as light and geometry, help us explore universal truths?
- **Transformation through Ritual:**
  - o What role does ritual play in fostering personal growth and moral integrity in both ancient and modern contexts?
- **Adapting the Ancient to the Modern:**
  - o In what ways can the ethical teachings of Freemasonry be seen as an evolution of ancient esoteric wisdom?

Early Speculative Masons

How the inclusion of non-operative members and formalization of the Craft shaped the evolution of Freemasonry

The early 17th century marked a pivotal transformation in Freemasonry, as the operative traditions of medieval stonemasons began to evolve into speculative practices emphasizing moral, intellectual, and philosophical pursuits. Central to this transition was the inclusion of non-operative members—men who were not stonemasons by trade but brought fresh perspectives, resources, and social influence to the Craft. The evolution of Freemasonry during this period was also shaped by critical legal frameworks, such as the Schaw Statutes, which formalized the governance of operative stonemason guilds and laid the groundwork for their eventual transition into speculative lodges. Together, these developments ensured the survival of Freemasonry and established its modern identity as a universal fraternity.

In the late 16th century, the stonemason guilds of Scotland began to adopt written regulations to ensure the integrity and operation of their craft. A significant milestone came with the issuance of the Schaw Statutes in 1598 and 1599. Drafted by William Schaw, Master of Works to King James VI of Scotland, these statutes sought to formalize the practices of stonemasons, regulate their lodges, and codify their ancient customs. Schaw's intent was clear: to strengthen the operative guilds and ensure their ethical conduct and technical excellence. As Stevenson (1988) observes, "The Schaw Statutes transformed the informal practices of Scottish stonemasons into a formalized structure, elevating their lodges to institutions governed by rules and traditions" (p. 23).

The First Statute of 1598 introduced the hierarchical structure that would later influence speculative Freemasonry, mandating that all masons obey their elected warden or deacon. It stated:

> *"That all maisters and fellowis of craft within this realme be obedient to thair wardane deacon and maisteris in all thingis concerning the said craft."*

This emphasis on governance created a framework of accountability and structure that speculative lodges would later adopt, ensuring orderly administration and discipline among members.

The Schaw Statutes also emphasized the education and moral conduct of masons, requiring apprentices and journeymen to adhere to strict guidelines. The Fourth Statute of 1598 stressed the importance of proper training, prohibiting masters from taking on more apprentices than they could adequately teach:

> *"That na maister or fellow of craft tak upoun handis to sett any wark to any persone or personis except he be ane qualifeit and wail tryit workman, worthie of the same, and*
> *of guid conscience."*

This focus on discipline and morality resonated deeply with the philosophical aspirations of later speculative Freemasonry.

The Eighth Statute of 1599 required regular lodge meetings, which not only maintained order but also fostered a sense of community among masons:

> *"That the wardane of everie lodge sail convene the haill maisteris within thair boundis quarterlie for reuling and ordering of all thingis amangis thame concerning thair craft."*

The act of meeting regularly to discuss matters of craft and conduct mirrors the later speculative practice of convening lodges for philosophical and moral discourse.

Perhaps most significantly, the Schaw Statutes recognized Kilwinning Lodge as the "Mother Lodge" of Scotland, granting it authority over other lodges and establishing a sense of hierarchy.

The Fifth Statute of 1599 stated:

> *"The warden of the lodge of Kilwinning sall be principal overseer and judge over all the maisters of work."*

This recognition reinforced Kilwinning's importance and provided a model of precedence that speculative lodges would later follow.

While the Schaw Statutes were designed to strengthen operative lodges, they inadvertently laid the groundwork for the inclusion of non-operative members. Operative lodges historically admitted other craftsmen who contributed to major construction projects, such as carpenters, blacksmiths, and glaziers. This practice of inclusion created a precedent for welcoming men outside the craft entirely. As Stevenson (1988) notes, "The lodges of Scotland, while still dominated by stonemasons, began admitting non-masons by the late 16th century, a practice that would pave the way for speculative Masonry" (p. 10).

As the demand for grand architectural projects diminished in the late 16th and early 17th centuries, operative lodges faced financial challenges. To sustain their activities, they began admitting non-operative members who could afford to pay higher dues. These men, often from the upper classes, brought much-needed financial resources while simultaneously elevating the social status of the lodges. Harrison (2009) explains, "The inclusion of wealthy patrons in lodges not only secured their economic stability but also allowed Freemasonry to transition from a declining trade guild into a thriving philosophical society" (p. 54).

The early 18th century saw a growing cultural trend toward the formation of clubs and societies, which provided spaces for intellectual discourse and social engagement. Freemasonry, with its rich symbolism and structured rituals, became a natural fit for this movement. As Hamill (2007) observes, "The early 18th century saw the rise of gentlemen's clubs across Europe, and Freemasonry emerged as one of the most structured and enduring of these societies" (p. 28).

Patronage also played a crucial role in the expansion of speculative Freemasonry. Wealthy and influential individuals were not only valued for their financial contributions but also for the prestige they brought to the Craft. Their involvement provided lodges with access to broader social networks and opportunities for growth. This patronage was mutually beneficial, as it gave influential figures a platform for social engagement and moral expression. As Stevenson (1988) describes, "Patrons brought legitimacy and visibility to the lodges, transforming them into spaces of social and intellectual prominence" (p. 12).

Amid this evolution, some of the earliest speculative masons began to emerge. Sir Robert Moray, a Scottish soldier and scientist, was among the first recorded non-operative members. His initiation in 1641 at Newcastle-upon-Tyne, conducted by an operative lodge, symbolized the blending of practical and philosophical traditions. Moray's intellectual pursuits, including his founding role in the Royal Society, reflected the aspirations of speculative Freemasonry to cultivate knowledge and moral improvement.

Another significant figure was Elias Ashmole, an English antiquarian and scholar. Ashmole's initiation in 1646 at Warrington marked a milestone in the transition to speculative Masonry. His detailed diary entry documenting the event provides a rare glimpse into early speculative practices. As Knoop, Jones, and Hamer (1943) note, "Ashmole's initiation highlights the appeal of Freemasonry to intellectuals and gentlemen during a period of growing interest in morality and philosophy" (p. 42).

The participation of these early speculative masons transformed Freemasonry into a space where moral teachings, symbolic lessons, and intellectual inquiry coexisted. Their involvement also influenced the development of the Entered Apprentice Degree, the foundational step in speculative Masonry. Rooted in the tools and traditions of operative stonemasonry, this degree symbolized the transition from ignorance to knowledge and introduced initiates to Freemasonry's core moral principles.

By the early 18th century, with the formation of the Grand Lodge of England in 1717, speculative Freemasonry had fully emerged. Rituals were standardized, and the Entered Apprentice Degree became the formal entry point into the Craft, emphasizing humility, discipline, and self-refinement. As Hamill (2007) explains, "The standardization of Masonic degrees, beginning in 1717, helped solidify speculative Freemasonry as a philosophical and moral institution, rooted in centuries of tradition yet forward-looking in its ideals" (p. 34).

The early speculative masons were more than just participants in a fraternity; they were architects of a new vision for Freemasonry. By bringing intellectual curiosity, social influence, and financial support to the Craft, they ensured its survival and evolution. Their legacy endures in the rituals, teachings, and values that continue to inspire Freemasons worldwide.

Reflections on the Craft: Questions for Deeper Understanding

- **The Role of Regulation and Tradition:**
  o How did the Schaw Statutes influence the formalization of Freemasonry and the inclusion of speculative members?
- **Contributions Beyond the Craft:**
  o In what ways did the financial and social contributions of non-operative members shape the evolution of the Craft?
- **Inspiration from the Past:**
  o How can the intellectual curiosity and moral aspirations of early speculative masons inspire modern Freemasons to uphold the fraternity's principles?

Lodge Zero: The Mother Lodge of Kilwinning, Scotland

Discover the origins and enduring legacy of the world's oldest Masonic Lodge

Kilwinning, Scotland, holds a special place in the history of Freemasonry as the home of Lodge Zero, also known as the "Mother Lodge of Kilwinning." Widely regarded as one of the oldest Masonic Lodges, its origins intertwine legend and historical fact. This essay explores the origins, historical significance, and global influence of Lodge Zero, shedding light on its role in shaping Freemasonry as we know it today.

Origins of Lodge Zero

The origins of Lodge Zero are believed to trace back to the 12th century, during the construction of Kilwinning Abbey. The Abbey, established by monks of the Tirón order in France around 1140, is thought to have provided a gathering place for stonemasons working on its intricate Romanesque design. These craftsmen, united by their trade, formed a guild that laid the foundation for what would later become Lodge Zero (Stevenson, 1988).

Though evidence directly connecting Lodge Zero to this period is limited, its prominence in the Schaw Statutes of 1598 and 1599 highlights its historic importance. These statutes, issued by William Schaw, Master of Works to King James VI, recognized Kilwinning as the principal lodge of Scotland, granting it a supervisory role over other lodges. This designation established Lodge Zero's legacy as the "Mother Lodge" (Mackey, 1924).

Kilwinning Abbey and Its Symbolism

Kilwinning Abbey's association with Lodge Zero is both historical and symbolic. Its ruins evoke human imperfection, while its construction represents the Masonic ideal of transforming the "rough ashlar" into the "perfect ashlar" through labor and self-improvement (Stevenson, 1988). The Abbey's architectural grandeur not only testifies to the skill of the stonemasons but also serves as a metaphor for moral and spiritual refinement.

The Abbey's connection to Lodge Zero underscores the transition from operative masonry, focused on building physical structures, to speculative Freemasonry, where moral and philosophical teachings became central (Ussishkin, 1996). This evolution marked a significant moment in the history of the Craft, setting the stage for its modern practices.

Transition to Speculative Freemasonry

By the late 16th and early 17th centuries, Lodge Zero began admitting non-operative members, including scholars and gentlemen, thus paving the way for speculative Freemasonry. This transition is documented in the Haddington Manuscript of 1693, one of the earliest records of Masonic catechisms. The inclusion of non-operative members introduced intellectual and philosophical dimensions to Freemasonry, transforming it into a fraternity centered on self-improvement and moral discourse (Stevenson, 1988).

The establishment of the Grand Lodge of Scotland in 1736 further solidified Freemasonry's speculative nature. Although Lodge Zero initially resisted joining the Grand Lodge, it later accepted a charter as "Lodge Mother Kilwinning Number 0," preserving its historical identity while contributing to the unification of Scottish Freemasonry (Mackey, 1924).

The Modern Legacy of Lodge Zero

Today, Lodge Zero remains active in Kilwinning, attracting Masons from around the globe who seek to connect with its rich history. The Lodge serves as a living testament to the Craft's origins, preserving its traditions while remaining a vital part of contemporary Freemasonry. The Kilwinning Heritage Centre further enhances this legacy by housing artifacts, historical records, and exhibits that document the Lodge's pivotal role in Masonic history (Ussishkin, 1996).

Kilwinning Abbey, though in ruins, continues to inspire Masons with its symbolism. It represents the enduring principles of labor, knowledge, and self-improvement, reminding Freemasons of their responsibility to uphold these values in their own lives.
Conclusion

Lodge Zero stands as a beacon of Freemasonry's journey from its operative roots in medieval Scotland to its speculative practices today. Its association with Kilwinning Abbey underscores the timeless values of craftsmanship, knowledge, and self-improvement. As the "Mother Lodge," it continues to inspire Freemasons worldwide to uphold the principles of Brotherly Love, Relief, and Truth. In its ruins and rituals, Kilwinning offers a window into the origins of Freemasonry and its enduring relevance.

Reflections on the Craft: Questions for Deeper Understanding

- **Historical Roots:**

- How does the history of Lodge Zero enhance your understanding of the connection between operative and speculative Freemasonry?
- **Symbolism and Inspiration:**
  - What lessons can you draw from Kilwinning Abbey's transformation from a physical structure to a symbol of moral refinement?
- **Tradition and Innovation:**
  - How can Lodge Zero's preservation of ancient practices guide modern Freemasons in balancing tradition with contemporary challenges?

The Founding of the Grand Lodge of London and Its Evolution

From Operative Craft to Speculative Society: The Formation of the Grand Lodge of London and Freemasonry's Enduring Legacy

The Grand Lodge of London, established in 1717, represents a foundational moment in the history of Freemasonry. Four London lodges convened at the Goose and Gridiron Ale House in St. Paul's Churchyard to form what is now regarded as the first Grand Lodge in the world. This marked a pivotal transition from operative to speculative Freemasonry, cementing the organization as a force for philosophical and moral development.

Transition from Operative to Speculative Freemasonry

Originally, Freemasonry was an operative craft, composed of skilled stonemasons who built cathedrals, castles, and other significant structures during the medieval period. Membership in these operative lodges was strictly limited to those actively engaged in the trade. Over time, however, as the demand for large stone structures declined, the lodges began admitting non-operatives, or "gentlemen masons." This shift allowed Freemasonry to evolve from a trade organization into a philosophical society focused on moral development, intellectual exploration, and camaraderie.

Several factors influenced this transition:

- **Decline in Cathedral Building**: By the 16th and 17th centuries, the need for large-scale stone construction diminished, leading to fewer operative masons. Lodges sought to sustain their existence by admitting members who were not part of the building trade but were interested in the symbolism and teachings of Freemasonry.

- **Rise of Enlightenment Thought**: The philosophical climate of the Enlightenment emphasized reason, scientific inquiry, and individual liberty. Speculative Freemasonry resonated with these ideals, attracting thinkers, writers, and professionals who found value in its allegories and moral lessons (Stevenson, 1988).

- **Expansion of Networks**: Including speculative members, often from influential social classes, provided lodges with opportunities to broaden their networks and enhance their standing within society (Hamill & Gilbert, 1991).

Reasons for Establishing a Grand Lodge

In 1717, the four founding lodges recognized the need for greater organization and unity within the fraternity. Several motivations prompted their historic meeting at the Goose and Gridiron Ale House:

- **Standardization of Practices:** Without centralized oversight, rituals, symbols, and traditions varied widely between lodges. A Grand Lodge offered the potential for standardizing practices, ensuring uniformity while preserving the integrity of Freemasonry (Anderson, 1738).

- **Preservation of Tradition:** The transition from operative to speculative Freemasonry risked losing some of the craft's original character. A Grand Lodge could safeguard and codify these traditions for future generations (Stevenson, 1988).

- **Enhancing Legitimacy**: By forming a Grand Lodge, the fraternity could establish a clear structure and hierarchy, lending credibility to Freemasonry in the eyes of society and protecting it from accusations of disorganization or subversion (Hamill & Gilbert, 1991).

- **Social and Philosophical Unity**: The lodges sought to create a forum where members could exchange ideas, collaborate on philanthropic efforts, and foster mutual understanding across social and intellectual divides (Jackson, 2006).

The Four Original Lodges

The four lodges that laid the foundation for the Grand Lodge of London in 1717 were deeply tied to the social and cultural fabric of their time, meeting in some of the era's most well-known taverns. These meeting places were more than just casual venues; they were integral to the fellowship and unity that defined early Masonic gatherings:

- **The Goose and Gridiron Ale House** (Lodge of Antiquity, No. 2) - This lodge retains its identity today as the Lodge of Antiquity, now numbered 2 under the United Grand Lodge of England.

- **The Crown Ale House** (No longer extant) - Unfortunately, this lodge did not survive into the modern era.

- **The Apple Tree Tavern** (Fortitude and Old Cumberland Lodge, No. 12) - This lodge later merged with others and exists today as No. 12.

- **The Rummer and Grapes Tavern** (Royal Somerset House and Inverness Lodge, No. 4) - Still active, this lodge continues as Royal Somerset House and Inverness Lodge, No. 4.

The First Grand Master

Anthony Sayer was elected as the first Grand Master. Sayer's selection reflected the egalitarian principles of Freemasonry at the time, where merit and character outweighed social rank. Though his later years were marked by financial hardship, his role remains a seminal moment in Masonic history.

Transition to the Grand Lodge of England

In 1721, the Grand Lodge began referring to itself as the "Grand Lodge of England," symbolizing its growing influence and ambition. This transition mirrored Freemasonry's expansion beyond London and its adaptation to include speculative members from varied professions and social standings. By adopting this broader identity, the Grand Lodge reinforced its role as a unifying force for the fraternity across England (Hamill & Gilbert, 1991).

Key Historical Milestones

- **Last Operative Grand Officer:** The last known Grand Officer with operative stonemason origins was George Payne, who served as Grand Master in 1718 and again in 1720.

- **Modern First Degree:** The first recorded conferral of a modern First Degree as part of the restructured three-degree system occurred in 1730, as documented in Samuel Prichard's Masonry

Dissected. This marked a formalization of Masonic ritual into its recognizable contemporary form.

Reflection on the Grand Lodge's Legacy

The establishment and evolution of the Grand Lodge of London underscore the adaptability and enduring appeal of Freemasonry. Its foundational ethos of moral improvement, intellectual engagement, and community service continues to inspire. Freemasonry's transition from an operative craft to a speculative organization represents a profound shift in purpose and influence, allowing the fraternity to engage with broader societal changes. The adaptability of the Grand Lodge has enabled it to remain relevant across centuries, responding to the needs of its members while upholding its core values.

The Grand Lodge's ability to integrate members from diverse social and professional backgrounds has been one of its greatest strengths. By emphasizing equality, moral development, and shared purpose, Freemasonry became a model of unity in an increasingly stratified society. This inclusivity not only enriched the organization but also expanded its influence, fostering intellectual and cultural advancements through the contributions of its members.

Furthermore, the philanthropic initiatives spearheaded by Freemasonry have had a lasting impact on communities worldwide. These efforts, rooted in the values of charity and brotherhood, exemplify the practical application of Masonic principles. The Grand Lodge's legacy serves as a testament to the enduring power of collective effort guided by a commitment to ethical and intellectual growth.

Reflections on the Craft: Questions for Deeper Understanding

- **Unity through Diversity:**
  - How can the collaboration among the four original lodges inform modern approaches to fostering unity within diverse Masonic communities?
- **Preserving Heritage:**
  - What lessons can be drawn from the survival and transformation of the Lodge of Antiquity and others to ensure the continuity of Masonic traditions?

- **Balancing Tradition and Innovation:**
  - How does the formalization of Masonic degrees in 1730 illustrate the balance between maintaining tradition and embracing progress?

The Anderson Constitutions in Freemasonry

Unveiling the blueprint of modern Freemasonry through Anderson's foundational Constitutions.

The Anderson Constitutions stand as a cornerstone in the history of Freemasonry, encapsulating its principles, governance, and cultural ethos. Compiled by Reverend James Anderson in 1723 under the commission of the Grand Lodge of England, these documents sought to unify Masonic practices and lay the foundation for its global expansion. Their impact resonates to this day, shaping Masonic traditions and values worldwide.

The Historical Background

The early 18th century witnessed the formalization of speculative Freemasonry, transitioning from operative guilds to a fraternity emphasizing moral philosophy and enlightenment ideals. In 1717, the Grand Lodge of England emerged to standardize practices and foster unity among Lodges. Amid this backdrop, Anderson's Constitutions provided a much-needed codification of Masonic principles, delineating its philosophy and operational framework (Hamill, 1986).

James Anderson: The Man Behind the Constitutions

Rev. James Anderson, a Scottish Presbyterian minister, played a pivotal role in shaping Freemasonry's identity. As a member of the Lodge in London, Anderson's scholarly background and dedication to the Craft positioned him as the ideal candidate for this monumental task. Commissioned by the Grand Lodge of England, his work reflected a blend of historical mythos and contemporary ideals, bridging

Freemasonry's operative past with its speculative future (Stevenson, 1990).

Content of the Anderson Constitutions

The 1723 Constitutions comprised two main sections: "The Charges of a Free-Mason" and "The General Regulations." The Charges outlined the ethical and philosophical guidelines for Masons, emphasizing loyalty to civil authorities, religious tolerance, and the pursuit of moral excellence. Meanwhile, the General Regulations offered practical rules for Lodge governance, including the election of officers and procedural conduct.

Anderson's historical narrative, though romanticized, sought to trace Freemasonry's origins to biblical and ancient times, reinforcing its universalist aspirations (Knoop, Jones, & Hamer, 1949). The revised 1738 edition included significant updates, reflecting the evolving priorities and challenges of the fraternity, such as broader inclusivity in religious beliefs and stricter organizational structures (Coil, 1961).

Significance of the Anderson Constitutions

The Anderson Constitutions transformed Freemasonry by providing a unified identity and operational framework. They were instrumental in establishing Freemasonry as a global fraternity, adaptable to various cultural and political contexts. Their emphasis on enlightenment values such as reason, tolerance, and fraternity resonated with the intellectual currents of the time and attracted diverse membership (Hamill, 1986).

Criticism and Controversy

Despite their significance, the Anderson Constitutions have not been without criticism. Scholars have debated the historical accuracy of Anderson's narrative, arguing that it prioritized allegory over factuality (Stevenson, 1990). Anderson's work often blended myth with history, creating a narrative that some critics claim lacks credibility as a true historical account. For instance, the assertion of Freemasonry's origins in biblical times and its connections to ancient civilizations have been challenged for their lack of concrete evidence.

Furthermore, the Constitutions' emphasis on Christianity in its early iterations faced scrutiny as Freemasonry evolved into a more inclusive institution. This initial religious exclusivity was seen by some as contradictory to the fraternity's later universalist values. As Freemasonry expanded internationally, cultural and religious diversity within Lodges highlighted the limitations of Anderson's original framework, necessitating revisions and regional adaptations to accommodate broader inclusivity.

Critics have also noted the Constitutions' lack of clarity in defining certain Masonic principles and practices, leaving room for varying interpretations that occasionally led to discord among Lodges. Additionally, the hierarchical structure outlined in the General Regulations has been criticized for potentially stifling democratic governance within individual Lodges.

These criticisms underscore the challenges of creating a unifying document for a dynamic and evolving fraternity. While the Anderson Constitutions provided a foundational framework, they also highlighted the need for continuous adaptation to meet the changing needs of Freemasonry and its diverse membership.

Legacy

The Anderson Constitutions remain a foundational text in Freemasonry, influencing its rituals, governance, and philosophical outlook. Their legacy endures not only in Masonic lodges but also in the broader cultural and intellectual history of the Enlightenment. As a testament to their enduring relevance, modern Masonic scholars and practitioners continue to revisit these documents for guidance and inspiration (Coil, 1961).

The Anderson Constitutions symbolize the synthesis of tradition and innovation, bridging Freemasonry's operative origins with its speculative aspirations. By codifying its principles and practices, Anderson provided a roadmap for a global fraternity rooted in enlightenment ideals and universal values. As Freemasonry continues to evolve, the Constitutions serve as both a historical anchor and a source of inspiration.

Reflections on the Craft: Questions for Deeper Understanding

- **Balancing Historical Integrity and Modern Relevance:**
  o How can Freemasons honor the historical roots of the Anderson Constitutions while adapting their principles to contemporary societal challenges?
- **Philosophical Foundations and Universal Values:**
  o How do the ethical and philosophical guidelines outlined in the Anderson Constitutions resonate with your personal and Masonic journey?

- **Continuity and Change in Freemasonry:**
    - How has the evolution of the Anderson Constitutions influenced the way modern Lodges operate and engage with diverse communities?

The Controversy Between the Grand Lodges of London and York

A Historical Clash of Ideals That Shaped Modern Freemasonry

Freemasonry, with its blend of tradition and fraternity, has long been a beacon for those seeking enlightenment and brotherhood. However, its rich history is not without internal divisions. One of the most pivotal moments in Masonic history was the controversy between the Grand Lodge of England—known as the "Moderns"—and the Grand Lodge of York, or the "Ancients." This schism not only defined English Freemasonry but also left an enduring impact on its global structure.

Historical Background

The Grand Lodge of London[12], established in 1717, is often celebrated as the first organized Grand Lodge in Masonic history. This body sought to unify lodges under a centralized authority, emphasizing a modernized approach to rituals. On the other hand, the Grand Lodge of York, which claimed lineage to ancient Masonic traditions, emerged as a competing authority, advocating for what it perceived as the "original" practices of Freemasonry (Hamill, 2004).

The ideological differences between the two lodges were stark. The Moderns introduced innovations in ritual and governance, which they believed made Freemasonry more

---

[12] The Grand Lodge of London, formed in 1717, became the Grand Lodge of England in 1738 to reflect its expanded jurisdiction beyond London and Westminster, asserting itself as the central governing body for Freemasonry in England and formalizing its authority during a period of institutional growth and unification.

adaptable to contemporary society. Conversely, the Ancients accused the Moderns of deviating from time-honored traditions. As historian John Hamill notes, "The York Masons saw themselves as custodians of ancient Masonic customs, resisting what they viewed as unnecessary alterations" (Hamill, 2004, p. 53).

Ritualistic Divergences

Central to the conflict were disagreements over Masonic rituals. The Moderns were accused of omitting certain symbolic elements, including references to the Royal Arch Degree[13], which the Ancients considered integral to the Craft. Margaret C. Jacob (2007) argues, "This omission not only fueled animosity but also symbolized a deeper philosophical rift over the purpose of Freemasonry" (p. 125).

Territorial and Jurisdictional Disputes

The territorial disputes were another flashpoint. The Grand Lodge of York exerted influence over northern England and claimed jurisdiction over many lodges that resisted affiliating with the Moderns. This rivalry extended to international territories, as both bodies sought to establish lodges abroad.

Authenticity and Recognition

---

[13] The Royal Arch Degree is a key component of the York Rite of Freemasonry, often considered the culmination of a Master Mason's journey through the Craft. It is regarded as essential by some Masonic traditions, particularly the Ancients, as it reveals the "lost word" and completes the symbolic story of the Third Degree. The degree explores themes of restoration, enlightenment, and the search for hidden truths, connecting members to the allegorical rebuilding of King Solomon's Temple.

The Ancients accused the Moderns of straying from the true essence of Freemasonry. They often referred to themselves as the legitimate heirs to the fraternity's ancient traditions. "Authenticity became a powerful tool for legitimizing claims, often used to discredit the opposing faction," writes Andrew Prescott (2005, p. 89).

The Union of 1813

Efforts to reconcile the two factions culminated in the creation of the United Grand Lodge of England in 1813. This monumental event merged the Moderns and Ancients into a unified body, resolving key ritualistic differences and establishing a standardized framework for Freemasonry.

The path to union was not without challenges. The Ancients, or "Ancient and Accepted Masons," were deeply committed to preserving their interpretation of the Craft's traditions. Meanwhile, the Moderns, now more commonly referred to as "Free and Accepted Masons," were equally determined to retain the innovations they believed necessary for Freemasonry's progress. Negotiations required both sides to make significant compromises, particularly in ritual practices, governance structures, and recognition protocols.

One key point of resolution was the inclusion of the Royal Arch Degree as a central component of Freemasonry. This concession by the Moderns was instrumental in bridging the ideological divide. Additionally, the union established a uniform administrative structure, ensuring equal representation for both traditions within the United Grand Lodge.

Today, the terms "Free and Accepted Masons" and "Ancient and Accepted Masons" reflect this historical division and its resolution. This dual heritage continues to influence

Masonic practices and identities worldwide, serving as a reminder of the organization's capacity for reconciliation and growth.

The Union of 1813 not only resolved an era of conflict but also laid the groundwork for modern Freemasonry's unified approach. By harmonizing divergent traditions, it strengthened the fraternity and positioned it as a model of unity within diversity.

Aftermath and Legacy

The Union had profound effects on Freemasonry. Rituals were standardized, and the administrative structure was streamlined, creating a cohesive identity for English Freemasonry. The influence of this unification extended beyond England, shaping the practices of lodges worldwide.

Reflections on the Craft: Questions for Deeper Understanding

- **Balancing Tradition and Progress:**
  - How can modern Freemasons reconcile the tension between preserving historical traditions and adapting to contemporary needs?
- **Learning from Conflict:**
  - What lessons can today's Masonic leaders draw from the resolution of this historic controversy?
- **Unity Through Diversity:**
  - How does the integration of differing rituals and practices enhance the fraternity's core mission?

The Art of Harmony: Ensuring Decorum in Masonic Meetings

Elevate the Craft by mastering the blend of Masonic etiquette and structured order.

Freemasonry, one of the world's oldest and most enduring fraternal organizations, thrives on principles of mutual respect, equality, and disciplined conduct. At the heart of Masonic practice lies the lodge meeting, a structured environment where brethren convene to conduct the business of the Craft and reflect on its timeless teachings. Harmony in these meetings is not an incidental byproduct but a deliberate outcome achieved through adherence to Masonic etiquette and Robert's Rules of Order. Together, these frameworks establish a balance of tradition, respect, and procedural rigor that enables the Craft to operate effectively while preserving its sacred values.

The Foundations of Masonic Etiquette

Masonic etiquette is a cornerstone of lodge harmony, emphasizing the respect and decorum that underpin all interactions among brethren. Central to this ethos is the supreme authority of the Worshipful Master, whose decisions during meetings are final. As articulated in Coil's Masonic Encyclopedia, "The Worshipful Master's role is paramount, embodying the trust and respect of the brethren who elected him to guide the lodge" (Coil, 1996, p. 537). His authority is symbolized by the gavel, whose sound calls the lodge to order and resolves disputes with finality. Failing to heed the gavel's call is considered a severe breach of Masonic conduct, reflecting the Craft's emphasis on discipline.

Another essential aspect of Masonic etiquette is the manner in which members address the lodge. When rising to speak, a brother must stand, salute the Master, and address him directly, regardless of the topic or the intended recipient of the comment. This practice not only maintains order but reinforces the Master's role as the meeting's guiding authority. Furthermore, members are expected to salute the Master upon entering or leaving the lodge, a gesture of respect deeply rooted in Masonic tradition. These customs, though formal, imbue lodge meetings with an atmosphere of solemnity and reverence.

Punctuality and confidentiality further underscore the ethos of Masonic etiquette. Arriving late to a meeting disrupts proceedings, while discussing lodge business outside its walls compromises the integrity of the Craft. In his seminal work, Freemasonry Through Six Centuries, Bernard Jones observes, "The secrecy of Masonic discussions is not an exclusionary device but a means to ensure that trust and fraternity flourish without external interference" (Jones, 1956, p. 203).

The Role of Robert's Rules of Order

While Masonic etiquette establishes the tone and respectfulness of interactions, Robert's Rules of Order provides the procedural structure necessary for orderly decision-making. Developed by Brigadier General Henry Martyn Robert in the late 19th century, these rules are widely recognized as the standard for parliamentary procedure. Within a Masonic context, they ensure that lodge meetings are conducted efficiently and fairly, allowing every brother the opportunity to voice his thoughts.

Key to Robert's Rules is the principle of recognition by the chair. Members may only speak when acknowledged by the

Worshipful Master, ensuring orderly discussion. As Robert himself noted, "The fundamental right of deliberative assemblies requires that all members have an equal opportunity to express their views" (Robert, 1915, p. 12). This approach aligns seamlessly with Freemasonry's democratic principles.

Another foundational element is the handling of motions. Only one main motion can be discussed at a time, with secondary motions (e.g., amendments or postponements) required to directly pertain to the primary motion. This system maintains focus and prevents the confusion of simultaneous debates. Additionally, most motions require a second to proceed, reflecting the collective nature of decision-making within the lodge.

The voting process, typically by simple majority, embodies the equality of all members, with each vote carrying equal weight. However, certain motions, such as closing debates, necessitate a two-thirds majority, ensuring that significant actions reflect a broader consensus. These procedural safeguards reinforce the fraternity's commitment to unity and fairness.

Harmonizing Tradition and Modernity

The integration of Masonic etiquette and Robert's Rules of Order highlights the enduring relevance of Freemasonry's ancient traditions in a contemporary framework. Etiquette, with its emphasis on respect and decorum, preserves the sacredness of the Craft's rituals and teachings. In contrast, Robert's Rules provide the adaptability and procedural clarity necessary for navigating modern organizational challenges.

For example, the confidentiality of lodge discussions—a hallmark of Masonic etiquette—ensures that sensitive topics are addressed in a secure and trusting environment. Simultaneously, the procedural rigor of Robert's Rules allows the lodge to address these topics systematically, ensuring that all voices are heard and decisions are reached democratically. As Christopher Hodapp notes in Freemasons for Dummies, "Freemasonry's strength lies in its ability to blend ancient customs with modern governance, creating a unique and enduring framework for personal and collective growth" (Hodapp, 2005, p. 189).

By adhering to these dual frameworks, Masons uphold the integrity of their meetings and the unity of their fraternity. The result is a lodge environment where tradition and progress coexist harmoniously, fostering both reverence for the Craft's history and responsiveness to contemporary needs.

Simply, among the etiquette and rules are:

Masonic Etiquette

1. The Worshipful Master's authority is supreme during meetings.

2. Members must immediately obey the sound of the Master's gavel.

3. Members must stand, salute, and address the Master before speaking.

4. Salute the Master upon entering or leaving the lodge.

5. Confidentiality of lodge proceedings must be maintained.

6. Members should arrive punctually to avoid disrupting proceedings.

7. Use respectful and appropriate language at all times.

8. Avoid leaving the lodge during balloting procedures.

9. Disputes must cease immediately upon the Master's command.

10. Visiting brethren must be properly vouched for and introduced.

Robert's Rules of Order

1. Only one main motion may be considered at a time.

2. Members must be recognized by the chair before speaking.

3. Motions must be seconded to proceed.

4. Debate is limited to the pending motion.

5. Members may only speak again after all others have had the opportunity.

6. A simple majority vote decides most motions.

7. Amendments to motions must follow proper debate and voting procedures.

8. A quorum is required to conduct business.

9. A two-thirds vote is required to close debate or suspend rules.

10. Minutes must be recorded and approved as the official record of proceedings.

Reflections on the Craft: Questions for Deeper Understanding

- **Leadership and Authority:**
  - o How does the role of the Worshipful Master exemplify the balance between leadership and service within a Masonic lodge?
- **Respectful Communication:**
  - o In what ways can the practices of standing to speak and addressing the Master enhance mutual respect and effective communication in your personal and professional interactions?
- **Balancing Structure and Flexibility:**
  - o How can the structured approach of Robert's Rules of Order help you manage discussions and decision-making in other aspects of your life?

The Harmony of the Craft: Music in Freemasonry

Discover how music weaves through the rituals and culture of Freemasonry, resonating with its timeless values

Music holds a prominent place in the traditions and culture of Freemasonry. Beyond its aesthetic appeal, music serves symbolic, ritualistic, and social functions within the Craft. From the orchestral compositions of Wolfgang Amadeus Mozart to the simple melodies of Masonic hymns, the role of music in Freemasonry is multifaceted. This essay explores the historical context of music in Freemasonry, its symbolic and ritualistic applications, and its broader cultural significance, with a detailed analysis of Mozart's The Magic Flute and commentary on other Masonic themes in music.

Historical Context

Music has been integral to Freemasonry since its formalization in the 18th century. Early speculative lodges incorporated hymns and songs to accompany rituals, fostering unity and reflection among members. Wolfgang Amadeus Mozart, himself a Freemason, is among the most celebrated contributors to this tradition. His opera The Magic Flute is an exemplar of Masonic ideals in music. As Masonic historian Paul Nettl notes, "Mozart's The Magic Flute is permeated with Masonic symbolism, from its structure to its thematic content" (Nettl, 1957).

Symbolism and Rituals

Music serves as a symbolic language in Freemasonry, embodying ideals such as harmony, unity, and balance. Specific melodies and instruments are chosen to resonate with Masonic allegories. For example, the opening overture of The Magic Flute employs three chords in succession, symbolizing the three principal officers of a Masonic lodge—the Master, Senior Warden, and Junior Warden. These triadic elements emphasize unity and order, aligning with the Masonic principle of harmony.

Ritualistic use of music amplifies the emotional and psychological impact of Masonic ceremonies. Albert Mackey writes, "Music in the lodge is not merely ornamental but essential, creating an atmosphere of reverence and solemnity" (Mackey, 1873). Specific musical pieces, such as hymns during initiations, underscore the transformative journey of candidates, helping them internalize the moral and spiritual lessons of the Craft.

Social and Cultural Functions

Music also fosters unity and fellowship among Freemasons outside formal rituals. During festive boards, members sing Masonic songs that celebrate brotherhood and charity. These communal experiences reinforce the bonds among brethren. As Margaret C. Jacob observes, "Masonic music serves as a cultural bridge, connecting members across diverse backgrounds" (Jacob, 1991).

Moreover, music often serves an educational purpose, conveying moral and philosophical lessons. In lectures and public events, musical compositions help illustrate Masonic principles such as equality, brotherly love, and truth. These pieces act as accessible mediums to share Masonic teachings with a broader audience.

Analysis of The Magic Flute

Mozart's The Magic Flute is a masterpiece laden with Masonic symbolism. The opera tells the story of Prince Tamino and his quest to rescue Pamina, culminating in their initiation into a brotherhood that embodies Masonic virtues. The work mirrors the structure of Masonic rituals, including trials of wisdom, courage, and virtue.

The number three—a significant symbol in Freemasonry—pervades the opera. From the three chords in the overture to the three temples Tamino must visit, this motif underscores the triadic structure central to Masonic thought. As Steven C. Bullock explains, "The triadic symbolism in The Magic Flute reflects Masonic teachings on the interplay of wisdom, strength, and beauty" (Bullock, 1996).

Another notable feature is the character Sarastro, who represents the Master of a Masonic lodge. His role emphasizes enlightenment and the triumph of reason over ignorance, aligning with Freemasonry's philosophical mission. The aria "O Isis und Osiris" highlights themes of divine guidance and moral duty, encapsulating Masonic ideals of reverence and virtue.

The female character Pamina, who undergoes her own series of trials, symbolizes the balance of the feminine and masculine within the pursuit of enlightenment. Her role affirms the inclusive spiritual journey central to Masonic teachings, even as historical lodges were predominantly male. The Queen of the Night, in contrast, represents chaos and irrationality, standing in opposition to the Masonic ideals of harmony and wisdom.

Musical contrasts in The Magic Flute further underscore its Masonic ethos. The solemn choruses of Sarastro's temple contrast with the frenetic arias of the Queen of the Night, reflecting the opposition between light and darkness. As Leonard Stein notes, "Mozart's deliberate use of musical texture amplifies the symbolic journey from ignorance to enlightenment" (Stein, 2005). The opera's concluding scenes celebrate unity and harmony, encapsulating the moral victory of light over darkness—a central tenet of Freemasonry.

Other Masonic Themes in Music

Beyond The Magic Flute, many composers and musicians have infused Masonic themes into their works. For instance, Franz Joseph Haydn's "Harmoniemesse" incorporates Masonic ideals of harmony and spiritual transcendence. Louis Armstrong, a Prince Hall Mason, celebrated Masonic values through his improvisational jazz, which exemplifies freedom and creativity within a structured framework.

Music also plays a role in modern Freemasonry. Contemporary composers create new Masonic pieces that honor tradition while engaging with current musical trends. These adaptations demonstrate the Craft's ability to integrate timeless values into contemporary contexts.

Challenges and Modern Adaptations

Preserving traditional Masonic music faces challenges in an era dominated by digital media and changing cultural tastes. However, digital platforms offer opportunities to archive and share Masonic compositions globally. Modern adaptations, such as orchestral performances of Masonic works or jazz interpretations of Masonic hymns, ensure the continued relevance of music within the Craft.

Music in Freemasonry is far more than an art form; it is a vital medium for expressing the Craft's values and fostering unity among its members. From the symbolic richness of Mozart's The Magic Flute to the communal songs sung at festive boards, music resonates deeply with Masonic ideals. By embracing both tradition and innovation, Freemasonry ensures that its musical heritage continues to inspire and enlighten future generations.

Reflections on the Craft: Questions for Deeper Understanding

- **Symbolism in The Magic Flute (after listening to the piece):**
    - In what ways do the characters of Sarastro and the Queen of the Night represent opposing Masonic ideals?
- **Music and Ritual:**
    - In what ways can music deepen the emotional and spiritual impact of Masonic rituals?
- **Adapting Tradition:**
    - How can contemporary Freemasonry balance the preservation of its musical heritage with the incorporation of modern musical forms?

Beyond the Blue Lodge

Exploring the Layers of Fellowship, Leadership, and Rituals that Extend Freemasonry's Impact.

Freemasonry, one of the world's most enduring and influential fraternal organizations, is steeped in ritual, symbolism, and community service. At its foundation lies the "Blue Lodge," a term traditionally used to describe the basic and essential Masonic organization where the three primary degrees of Freemasonry are conferred: Entered Apprentice, Fellow craft, and Master Mason. The term "Blue Lodge" is believed to originate from the significance of the color blue in Freemasonry, symbolizing fidelity, the heavens, and universality (Mackey, 1909). Beyond the Blue Lodge, Freemasonry's structure expands into various appendant bodies and youth organizations, which offer additional degrees, teachings, and opportunities for service.

Appendant bodies of Freemasonry provide members with avenues for further exploration of Masonic philosophy, history, and service. Each body introduces unique degrees and rituals that expand upon the foundational lessons of the Blue Lodge.

The York Rite

The York Rite, one of the most prominent appendant bodies, comprises three key organizations: the Royal Arch Masons, the Cryptic Masons, and the Knights Templar. Each division has its own unique degrees and focuses.

- **Royal Arch Masons**: Considered the continuation of the Master Mason degree, the Royal Arch seeks to "complete" the story of the Blue Lodge with four degrees: Mark Master, Past Master, Most Excellent

Master, and Royal Arch Mason. These degrees emphasize themes of duty, discovery, and divine guidance (Roberts, 1996).

- **Cryptic Masons**: Often referred to as the "Council," this group confers three degrees: Royal Master, Select Master, and Super Excellent Master. These degrees explore themes of secrecy, preservation, and the construction of King Solomon's Temple.
- **Knights Templar**: Unique in its Christian orientation, the Knights Templar consists of three chivalric orders: the Order of the Red Cross, the Order of Malta, and the Order of the Temple. These ceremonies draw heavily on medieval Christian history and emphasize faith, chivalry, and charity (Hackett, 2014).

The Scottish Rite

The Scottish Rite offers a rich tapestry of degrees, extending from the 4th to the 33rd degree. Often referred to as the "University of Freemasonry," its rituals delve deeply into philosophy, morality, and spiritual symbolism.

- **Structure**: The degrees are divided into four bodies: the Lodge of Perfection, Council of Princes of Jerusalem, Chapter of Rose Croix, and the Consistory.
- **Key Themes**: Degrees explore themes of light and darkness, personal transformation, and universal truths. For example, the 14th degree, "Perfect Elu," focuses on fidelity and justice, while the 32nd degree, "Master of the Royal Secret," synthesizes the lessons of all preceding degrees (Pike, 1871).
- **Ceremonial Significance**: The initiation rituals often involve symbolic trials that emphasize moral and ethical growth.

Shriners International

Shriners International, often known for its philanthropy, particularly Shriners Hospitals for Children, emphasizes fellowship and fun alongside service.

- **Membership**: To join, a Mason must first complete the Blue Lodgedegrees.
- **Rituals**: Initiations focus on the themes of camaraderie and charity. Shriners often use Arabic motifs, reflecting their "mystic" heritage (Smith, 2007).

The Order of the Eastern Star

The Order of the Eastern Star, one of the largest Masonic organizations open to both men and women, emphasizes moral teachings drawn from biblical heroines.

- **Degrees**: Each degree is associated with a biblical figure: Adah, Ruth, Esther, Martha, and Electa, symbolizing virtues like fidelity, loyalty, and faith.
- **Rituals**: Initiation ceremonies are highly symbolic, involving scripts, tableaux, and lectures that teach moral and ethical lessons (Brown, 2010).

Freemasonry's Youth Groups

Youth organizations within Freemasonry serve to instill leadership, service, and Masonic values in younger generations.

Order of DeMolay

Named after Jacques de Molay, the last Grand Master of the Knights Templar, this organization for young men emphasizes leadership and character development.

- **Structure**: Members progress through ceremonies such as the Initiatory Degree and the DeMolay Degree, which highlight virtues like filial love and patriotism.
- **Activities**: DeMolay fosters personal growth through public speaking competitions, community service, and leadership training (Morris, 2012).

International Order of the Rainbow for Girls

This organization focuses on empowering young women through service, education, and character-building activities.

- **Degrees**: Members advance through a series of color-themed degrees representing virtues such as hope, charity, and faith.
- **Ceremonial Elements**: Rituals often involve symbolic props and colorful ceremonies that inspire moral reflection.

Job's Daughters International

Open to daughters and relatives of Master Masons, Job's Daughters encourages confidence, public speaking, and service.

- **Ceremonies**: The organization's initiations involve reenactments of the story of Job, emphasizing perseverance and faith.
- **Leadership Opportunities**: Members are encouraged to participate in leadership roles, preparing them for future endeavors.

Community and Philanthropy

Appendant bodies and youth organizations are deeply engaged in philanthropic efforts. Shriners Hospitals for Children, scholarships offered by the Scottish Rite, and countless local charity initiatives showcase Freemasonry's commitment to improving lives.

Reflections on the Craft: Questions for Deeper Understanding

1. **Balancing Tradition and Innovation**:
   o How can Freemasonry's appendant bodies balance the preservation of ancient traditions with the need for modernization and inclusivity?
2. **Masonic Education Beyond the Blue Lodge**:
   o How do the lessons of the Scottish Rite or York Rite enhance your understanding of Masonic principles?
3. **Youth and the Future of Freemasonry**:
   o In what ways can youth organizations like DeMolay and Rainbow Girls prepare the next generation of leaders?

Bibliography

1. Abernethy, T. (1980). A congressman's legacy: Freedom and duty. Washington, DC: Government Printing Office.
2. About, E. F. V. (1851). La question de l'Algérie. Paris: Garnier Frères.
3. Abrahams, H. (1924). The joy of achievement. London: British Library.
4. Abrahams, H. (1924). The quest for excellence: Reflections of an Olympian. London: Allen & Unwin.
5. Abrams, B. (1951). American Business Journal.
6. Abt, F. (1864). Reflections on music and life.
7. Adams, J. P. (2009). The Roman Concept of Fides. Department of Modern and Classical Languages and Literatures, California State University Northridge.
8. Alberta Masonic Library. (n.d.). Obligation in Freemasonry. Retrieved from https://albertamasoniclibrary.ca
9. Allen, R. H. (1899). *Star Names: Their Lore and Meaning*. Dover Publications.
10. Anderson, J. (1723). Constitutions of the Free-Masons. London: Benjamin Franklin Press.
11. Anderson, J. (1723). The Constitutions of the Free-Masons. London: W. Hunter.
12. Anderson, J. (1738). The Constitutions of the Free-Masons. London: Benjamin Franklin.
13. Anderson, J. (1738). The Constitutions of the Free-Masons. London: Printed by William Hunter.
14. Anderson, P. (2019). The Fellow craft's Guide to Symbols and Meaning. London: Masonic Publications.
15. Aristotle. (1991). Rhetoric (W. Rhys Roberts, Trans.). Dover Publications.

16. Aristotle. (2009). Nicomachean ethics (M. Ostwald, Trans.). Prentice Hall.
17. Arnold, H. H. (1949). "Global mission". Harper & Brothers.
18. Assmann, J. (2001). The search for God in ancient Egypt. Cornell University Press.
19. Aurelius, M. (2006). Meditations (G. Long, Trans.). Dover Publications. (Original work published ca. 180)
20. Baigent, M., & Leigh, R. (1989). The temple and the lodge. Jonathan Cape.
21. Beard, M., North, J., & Price, S. (1998). Religions of Rome: Volume 1: A History. Cambridge University Press.
22. Beecher Stowe, H. (1852). Uncle Tom's Cabin; or, Life Among the Lowly. Boston: John P. Jewett and Company.
23. Biddle, M. (1990). The Making of Medieval Rome: A New Profile of the City. Oxford University Press.
24. Blum, C., et al. (2018). The Liberal Arts Tradition: A Philosophy of Christian Classical Education. Classical Academic Press.
25. Bright, J. (2000). A History of Israel (4th ed.). Westminster John Knox Press.
26. Brown, F., Driver, S. R., & Briggs, C. A. (1906). "A Hebrew and English lexicon of the Old Testament". Oxford University Press.
27. Brown, J. (2010). The Eastern Star: An In-Depth Look at Its Rituals and Teachings. Lexington Press.
28. Brown, J. T. (2017). Cosmic Insights in Freemasonry. New York: Philosophical Library.
29. Brown, R. (2002). Freemasonry and the Art of Symbolism. HarperCollins.
30. Brunelleschi, F. (n.d.). Dome of Florence Cathedral. Retrieved from [museum or archival source].

31. Bullock, S. C. (1996). Revolutionary Brotherhood: Freemasonry and the Transformation of the American Social Order, 1730-1840. University of North Carolina Press.
32. Bunyan, J. (1678). The Pilgrim's Progress.
33. Burns, R. (1785). "To a Mouse."
34. Burton, D. M. (2010). The History of Mathematics: An Introduction (7th ed.). McGraw-Hill.
35. Campbell, J. (1949). The Hero with a Thousand Faces. Princeton University Press.
36. Campbell, J. (1988). The Power of Myth. Doubleday.
37. Carter, J. (2009). Rites of enlightenment: Oil and sacred traditions. Cambridge University Press.
38. Charleston, SC: Supreme Council.
39. Churchill, W. (1941). Speech at the Conservative Party conference, 1941. In The collected speeches of Winston Churchill (pp. 200-201). London: Hutchinson & Co.
40. Clark, R. (2007). Sirius: Brightest diamond in the night sky. Harvard University Press.
41. Clarke, A. (1831). Clarke's Commentary on the Bible.
42. Claudy, C. H. (1931). "Introduction to Freemasonry". Masonic Publishing Company.
43. Claudy, C. H. (1931). Introduction to Freemasonry. Masonic Publishing Company.
44. Cleary, T. (2020). The Craft: How Freemasonry Made the Modern World. New York: Pegasus Books.
45. Coil, H. W. (1961). Coil's Masonic Encyclopedia. Macoy Publishing & Masonic Supply Co.
46. Coil, H. W. (1961). Coil's Masonic Encyclopedia. Richmond, VA: Macoy Publishing and Masonic Supply Co.
47. Coil, H. W. (1996). Coil's Masonic Encyclopedia. Macoy Publishing.

48. Commentary on the Charge after Initiation. Retrieved from The Square Magazine. (2022).
49. Cumont, F. (1903). The mysteries of Mithra. Open Court Publishing.
50. Curl, J. S. (2002). The Art and Architecture of Freemasonry: An Introductory Study. Bury St. Edmunds: St. Edmundsbury Press.
51. Curl, J. S. (2006). A dictionary of architecture and landscape architecture (2nd ed.). Oxford University Press.
52. Curl, J. S. (2013). The Classical Tradition in Architecture. Routledge.
53. De Hoyos, A. (2010). The Scottish Rite Ritual Monitor and Guide. Washington, D.C.: Supreme Council, Southern Jurisdiction.
54. De Hoyos, A. (2018). The Scottish Rite Ritual Monitor and Guide. Supreme Council, Southern Jurisdiction.
55. De Voragine, J. (1993). The Golden Legend. Princeton University Press.
56. Dehaene, S. (1997). The Number Sense: How the Mind Creates Mathematics. Oxford University Press.
57. DeLashmutt, G. (2019). Symbols of Freemasonry: The Craft and Its Meaning.
58. Deuteronomy 19:14, King James Version.
59. DeVries, S. J. (1975). 1 Kings. Word Biblical Commentary. Thomas Nelson.
60. Dickens, C. (1859). A tale of two cities. Chapman & Hall.
61. Dudley, L. (2010). The Craft and Its Symbols: Opening the Door to Masonic Symbolism. St. Paul: Minnesota Masonic Heritage Center
62. Duncan, M. C. (1866). Duncan's Masonic ritual and monitor: Entered apprentice, or first degrees. Retrieved from https://sacred-texts.com

63. Durant, W. (2010). Our Oriental heritage. Simon and Schuster.
64. Edgar Allan Poe. (1846). The Cask of Amontillado. Retrieved from Project Gutenberg.
65. Eliade, M. (1958). The Sacred and the Profane: The Nature of Religion. Harcourt Brace.
66. Eliot, T. S. (1943). Four Quartets. New York: Harcourt, Brace, and Company.
67. Emerson, R. W. (1841). Essays: First series. James Munroe and Company.
68. Emerson, R. W. (2024). Quote on self-determination. In Grand Lodge of Massachusetts (Ed.), Masonic reflections. Boston, MA: Grand Lodge of Massachusetts.
69. Euclid. (1956). *The Elements*. (T. L. Heath, Trans.). Dover Publications.
70. Feldman, L. H. (1998). Josephus and Modern Scholarship. Walter de Gruyter.
71. Fleming, D., & Honour, H. (2005). A world history of art. Laurence King Publishing.
72. Fletcher, B. (1996). A History of Architecture on the Comparative Method. London: B.T. Batsford.
73. Franklin, B. (1750). Poor Richard's Almanack.
74. Franklin, B. (1771). The autobiography of Benjamin Franklin. New York, NY: Macmillan.
75. Franklin, B. (1791). Autobiography of Benjamin Franklin.
76. Franklin, B. (2024). Quote on continual growth. In Grand Lodge of Pennsylvania (Ed.), Principles of Freemasonry. Philadelphia, PA: Grand Lodge of Pennsylvania.
77. Freedman, D. N. (1992). "The Anchor Yale Bible Dictionary". Yale University Press.
78. Gethin, R. (1998). The Foundations of Buddhism. Oxford University Press.
79. Gill, J. (1809). Gill's Exposition of the Entire Bible.

80. Goethe, J. W. (1806). Faust: A tragedy.
81. Goethe, J. W. (1810). Theory of Colours. T. T. Boardman.
82. Goethe, J. W. (1825). Goethe's autobiography.
83. Goethe, J. W. (1832). Conversations with Eckermann. Da Capo Press.
84. Goethe, J. W. (2024). Faust: A Tragedy. (Original work published 1806).
85. Goethe, J. W. (n.d.). Selected writings.
86. Goethe, J. W. von. (1808). Faust. (Bayard Taylor, Trans.). Modern Library.
87. Gorday, P. (2012). Commentary on Job: Ancient Christian Texts. IVP Academic.
88. Gould, R. F. (1882). The History of Freemasonry.
89. Goulson, D. (2015). The importance of bees to agriculture. Science Progress, 98(4), 418–435.
90. Grand Lodge of Alberta. (2020). Masonic Obligations: A Covenant of Integrity
91. Grand Lodge of Iowa. (2013). Masonic Etiquette and Protocols. Retrieved from https://grandlodgeofiowa.org
92. Green, H. (2019). "The Multiverse Hypothesis and Its Symbolic Resonance." Journal of Philosophical Cosmology, 14(3), 45–62.
93. Hackett, D. G. (2014). *That Religion in Which All Men Agree: Freemasonry in American Culture.* University of California Press.
94. Haggard, F. (2013). The Masonic Degree: A Guide to Symbolism and Ritual. Cornerstone Publishing.
95. Hall, M. P. (1923). *The Lost Keys of Freemasonry.* Macoy Publishing.
96. Hall, M. P. (1928). The Secret Teachings of All Ages. H. S. Crocker Company.
97. Hamill, J. (1994). The Craft: A History of English Freemasonry. Crucible.

98. Hamill, J. (2004). *The Craft: A History of English Freemasonry*. Cornerstone Press.

99. Hamill, J. (2007). "The Craft: A History of English Freemasonry". London: Crucible Press.

100. Hamill, J. M. (1986). The Craft: A History of English Freemasonry. London: Crucible.

101. Hamill, J. M. (2010). The craft: A history of English Freemasonry. London, UK: Cornerstone.

102. Hamill, J. M., & Gilbert, R. (1991). Freemasonry: A Celebration of the Craft. London: Angus & Robertson.

103. Hamill, J., & Gilbert, R. (1994). *Freemasonry: A Celebration of the Craft*. Angus & Robertson.

104. Hamill, J., & Gilbert, R. (1995). The Freemasons: A History of the World's Most Powerful Secret Society. Cornerstone.

105. Hamill, J., & Gilbert, R. (2004). Freemasonry: A Celebration of the Craft. Angus & Robertson.

106. Hamill, J., & Gilbert, R. (2010). "Freemasonry: A Celebration of the Craft". London: Lewis Masonic.

107. Hammer, D. (2013). The Masonic Paradigm: Symbols and Their Meaning. Cornerstone Press.

108. Hancock, J. (1776). Letter to Joseph Warren. American Revolution Letters, p. 154.

109. Harland-Jacobs, J. L. (2007). Builders of Empire: Freemasonry and British Imperialism, 1717-1927. University of North Carolina Press.

110. Harris, J. (1881). The Freemason's Guide and Compendium. London: George G. Harrap & Co.

111. Harrison, D. (2009). The Genesis of Freemasonry. Lewis Masonic.

112.   Harrison, R. (2016). The Symbolic Journey: Freemasonry and the Path to Enlightenment. Cambridge University Press.

113.   Hawthorne, N. (1850). The Scarlet Letter.

114.   Hawthorne, N. (1851). The house of the seven gables. Ticknor and Fields.

115.   Hegel, G. W. F. (1821). Philosophy of Right. Cambridge University Press.

116.   Heidegger, M. (1927). Being and Time. (J. Macquarrie & E. Robinson, Trans.). Harper & Row.

117.   Henderson, A. (2015). Masonic cornerstones: Rituals and their meanings. Grand Lodge Publications.

118.   Henderson, W. (2012). The Craft's Mentor: Guiding Light in Freemasonry. Anchor Press.

119.   Henry, M. (1706). Commentary on the Whole Bible.

120.   Hesiod. (c. 700 BCE). Works and Days.

121.   Hillman, E. (2021). Architectural symbolism through the ages. Cambridge Press.

122.   Hillman, J. (2021). The Soul's Code: In Search of Character and Calling. Harper Perennial Modern Classics.

123.   Hodapp, C. (2005). Freemasons for Dummies. Indianapolis, IN: Wiley Publishing.

124.   Holy Bible, 1 Kings 7:21; 2 Chronicles 3:15-17.

125.   Holy Bible, King James Version

126.   Holy Bible, New International Version

127.   Holy Bible, New International Version. (1984). Biblica, Inc.

128.   Holy Bible, New International Version. (1984). Zondervan.

129.   Holy Bible, New International Version. (2011). Biblica, Inc.

130.	Holy Bible, New International Version. (2011). Grand Rapids, MI: Zondervan.

131.	Horne, A. (1958). Masonic Music and Ritual: An Exploration. Cambridge University Press.

132.	Hubbard, R. L. (1988). The Book of Ruth. Grand Rapids, MI: William B. Eerdmans Publishing.

133.	Isaiah 28:16, New King James Version. (1982). Thomas Nelson, Inc.

134.	Isaiah 28:17, Ezekiel 40–47, 1 Kings 6:7. (n.d.). In The Holy Bible.

135.	Isaiah 40:4. (1984). Holy Bible, New International Version. Biblica, Inc.

136.	Jackson, A. (1996). "Freemasonry: A Celebration of the Craft". Macmillan.

137.	Jackson, J. (1999). Builders of the Kingdom: A Masonic Guide. Lewis Masonic.

138.	Jackson, K. (2006). Builders of the Temple: The History of Freemasonry. New York: Masonic Books Press.

139.	Jackson, K. (2016). Masonic Leadership: Principles and Practices for Lodge Officers. Square Publishing.

140.	Jackson, K. B. (2005). Builders of the Spiritual Temple: A Comprehensive Guide to Freemasonry. London: Routledge.

141.	Jacob, M. C. (1991). Living the Enlightenment: Freemasonry and Politics in Eighteenth-Century Europe. Oxford University Press.

142.	Jacob, M. C. (2007). *Living the Enlightenment: Freemasonry and Politics in Eighteenth-Century Europe*. Oxford University Press.

143.	James, W. (1890). The Principles of Psychology. Henry Holt and Company.

144.   Johnson, R. (2020). "Infinite Creation: A Masonic Perspective on the Universe." Freemason Quarterly, 12(2), 54–58.

145.   Jones, B. (2005). *Pythagorean Symbolism in Ancient Traditions*. Cambridge University Press.

146.   Jones, B. (2008). Freemasonry and its Symbolism. Masonic Publications.

147.   Jones, B. E. (1950). *Freemasons' Guide and Compendium.* London: Harrap.

148.   Jones, B. E. (1956). Freemasonry Through Six Centuries. Lewis Masonic.

149.   Jones, B. E. (1996). The Masonic Lodge: A Study in Symbolism and Tradition. Oxford University Press.

150.   Jones, M. (2010). Leadership in Freemasonry: Principles and Practices. Masonic Books.

151.   Jones, T. (2013). Freemasonry: Principles, Practices, and Beliefs. Oxford University Press.

152.   Josephus, F. (1976). The Life of Josephus. Translated by H. St. J. Thackeray. Harvard University Press.

153.   Josephus, F. (1981). The Jewish War. Translated by G. A. Williamson. Penguin Classics.

154.   Josephus, F. (1987). Antiquities of the Jews. (W. Whiston, Trans.). Hendrickson Publishers.

155.   Kahn, C. H. (2001). Pythagoras and the Pythagoreans: A brief history. Hackett Publishing.

156.   Katz, V. J. (2009). A History of Mathematics: An Introduction (3rd ed.). Addison-Wesley.

157.   Keller, T. (2018). The Fragrance of Moral Actions: Ethical Symbolism in Modern Contexts. Oxford University Press.

158.   Kenner, H. (1989). The Symbolism of the Heart in Religious and Cultural Traditions. Oxford University Press.

159.   King James Bible. (1611/2023). Proverbs 15:3.
160.   Knoop, D., & Jones, G. P. (1947). The Genesis of Freemasonry. Manchester University Press.
161.   Knoop, D., & Jones, G. P. (1978). "The Genesis of Freemasonry". Manchester University Press.
162.   Knoop, D., Jones, G. P., & Hamer, D. (1943). The Early Masonic Catechisms. Manchester University Press.
163.   Knoop, D., Jones, G. P., & Hamer, D. (1949). The Early Masonic Catechisms. Manchester: Manchester University Press.
164.   Kooten, G. H. (2006). The Architecture of Solomon's Temple: A Study in Biblical Cosmology. Brill Academic Publishers.
165.   Kubba, S. (2016). Architectural Forensics. Oxford: Butterworth-Heinemann.
166.   Leach, N. (2005). Cambridge Companion to Modern Architecture. Cambridge: Cambridge University Press.
167.   Lear, J. (1988). Aristotle: The desire to understand. Cambridge University Press.
168.   Lee, H. (1960). To kill a mockingbird. J.B. Lippincott & Co.
169.   Leoni, F. (2013). King Solomon's Temple in the Masonic Tradition. Cambridge University Press.
170.   Levine, R. (1995). "Theodore Roosevelt: An American Mind". Carbondale: Southern Illinois University Press.
171.   Levine, R. (1995). "Theodore Roosevelt: An American Mind". Carbondale: Southern Illinois University Press.

172.   Livio, M. (2002). The Golden Ratio: The Story of Phi, the World's Most Astonishing Number. Broadway Books.

173.   Livio, M. (2003). The Golden Ratio: The Story of Phi, the World's Most Astonishing Number. Broadway Books.

174.   Locke, J. (1706/2024). Essays Concerning Human Understanding

175.   Lodge, G. (2015). Ritual and Reflection: Freemasonry's Moral Teachings. Masonic Publishing House.

176.   Lomas, R. (1999). The Secret Teachings of the Masonic Lodge. HarperOne.

177.   MacArthur, D. (1945). Address to West Point Graduates.

178.   Mackey, A. G. (1858). A textbook of Masonic jurisprudence. New York: Clark & Maynard.

179.   Mackey, A. G. (1865). The Symbolism of Freemasonry. New York: Clark & Maynard.

180.   Mackey, A. G. (1869). An Encyclopedia of Freemasonry and Its Kindred Sciences.

181.   Mackey, A. G. (1869/2024). A Manual of the Lodge.

182.   Mackey, A. G. (1873). The Symbolism of Freemasonry. New York: Clark & Maynard.

183.   Mackey, A. G. (1874). *Encyclopedia of Freemasonry*. New York: Masonic History Co. Pythagoras. (2010). *Philosophical Fragments*. Dover Publications.

184.   Mackey, A. G. (1909). Encyclopedia of Freemasonry and Its Kindred Sciences. Masonic History Company.

185.   Mackey, A. G. (1909). *The History of Freemasonry*. Masonic History Company.

186.   Mackey, A. G. (1909). The Symbolism of Freemasonry. Masonic Publishing.

187. Mackey, A. G. (1912). An Encyclopaedia of Freemasonry and Its Kindred Sciences. The Masonic History Company.

188. Mackey, A. G. (1912). *The Symbolism of Freemasonry.* New York: Gramercy Books.

189. Mackey, A. G. (1917). The Symbolism of Freemasonry. New York: Clark & Maynard.

190. Mackey, A. G. (1921). "The History of Freemasonry". Masonic History Company.

191. Mackey, A. G. (1921). Encyclopedia of Freemasonry. New York, NY: Masonic Publishing Co.

192. Mackey, A. G. (1924). A Manual of the Lodge. Macoy Publishing & Masonic Supply Co.

193. Mackey, A. G. (1924). Encyclopedia of Freemasonry. Masonic History Company.

194. Mackey, A. G. (1924). The History of Freemasonry. New York: Masonic Publishing Company.

195. Mackey, A. G. (1924). The Symbolism of Freemasonry: An Interpretation of the Symbols of the Order. Masonic Publishing.

196. Mackey, A. G. (n.d.). "Encyclopedia of Freemasonry". Masonic History Company.

197. MacNulty, W. K. (2006). Freemasonry: Symbols, Secrets, Significance. Thames & Hudson.

198. MacNulty, W. K. (2006). The Way of the Craftsman. Central Press.

199. Macoy, R. (2000). Freemasonry and Leadership Roles. Macoy Publishing.

200. Mason, S. (2003). Josephus and the New Testament. Hendrickson Publishers.

201. Mastermind Content. (n.d.). The esoteric meaning of the circle.

202. Matthews, K. (2000). The Holy Trinity: Insights into Christian Theology. Cambridge University Press.

203. Matthews, K. (2020). The Renaissance and architectural rebirth. Oxford University Press.

204. Matthews, R. (2020). Freemasonry and its symbolism. Cambridge University Press.

205. McKee, R. (1997). Story: Substance, Structure, Style and the Principles of Screenwriting. ReganBooks.

206. McLeod, W. (2006). Freemasonry: An Introduction to Its Traditions and Practices. Oxford University Press.

207. Meyers, C. L., & Rogerson, J. W. (2001). The Temple: Its Symbolism and History. Cambridge University Press.

208. Morris, B. (2006). The Complete Idiot's Guide to Freemasonry. New York, NY: Alpha Books.

209. Morris, B. (2015). The Complete Idiot's Guide to Freemasonry. New York, NY: Alpha Books.

210. Morris, E. (2010). "Colonel Roosevelt". New York: Random House.

211. Morris, R. (2012). *The Young Craftsman: DeMolay and Its Role in Shaping Leaders.* Beacon Hill Publications.

212. Morris, R. (2015). Freemasonry: Its Hidden Meaning. Macoy Publishing.

213. Morris, R. W. (1868). Freemasonry in the Holy Land. Chicago: Masonic Publishing.

214. Mylonas, G. E. (1961). Eleusis and the Eleusinian mysteries. Princeton University Press.

215. Nehemiah 4:18, New International Version. (1978). Biblica, Inc.

216. Nettl, P. (1957). Mozart and Masonry. Philosophical Library.

217.   New International Version. (2011). The Holy Bible. Biblica, Inc.

218.   Newton, J. F. (1922). The builders: A story and study of Masonry.

219.   NIV Bible. (1984). The Holy Bible: New International Version. Grand Rapids, MI: Zondervan.

220.   Oliver, G. (1823). "The Antiquities of Freemasonry". J. W. Leonard & Co

221.   Orwell, G. (1945). Animal farm: A fairy story. Secker & Warburg.

222.   Orwell, G. (1946). Politics and the English Language. Horizon.

223.   Perley, S. (n.d.). Fides Romana: Aspects of Fides in Roman Diplomatic Relations during the Conquest of Iberia.

224.   Pfingsten, M. (n.d.). Roman Virtues and Stoicism.

225.   Pike, A. (1871). *Morals and Dogma of the Ancient and Accepted Scottish Rite of Freemasonry.* Charleston: Supreme Council, Southern Jurisdiction.

226.   Pike, A. (1871). Morals and Dogma of the Ancient and Accepted Scottish Rite of Freemasonry. Charleston: Supreme Council.

227.   Pike, A. (1872). Morals and Dogma of the Ancient and Accepted Scottish Rite of Freemasonry.

228.   Pike, A. (1899). Ex Corde Locutiones...: Words from the Heart Spoken of His Dead Brethren....

229.   Plato. (1997). The Republic (G. M. A. Grube, Trans.). Hackett Publishing.

230.   Plato. (2007). The Republic (B. Jowett, Trans.). Dover Publications. (Original work published ca. 380 BCE)

231.   Plato. (trans. 2008). Symposium (R. Waterfield, Trans.). Oxford University Press. (Original work ca. 385–370 BCE)

232.   Pleyel, J. (1791). Pleyel's Hymn. Original Composition.
233.   Polanyi, M. (1966). The Tacit Dimension. University of Chicago Press.
234.   Pollitt, J. J. (1972). Art and Experience in Classical Greece. Cambridge University Press.
235.   Pollitt, J. J. (1990). The Art of Ancient Greece: Sources and Documents. Cambridge University Press.
236.   Pound, R. E. (1953). Masonic Addresses and Writings. Macoy Publishing & Masonic Supply Co.
237.   Prescott, A. (2004). "The Transformation of Freemasonry." Journal for Research into Freemasonry and Fraternalism, 1(1), 45-60.
238.   Prescott, A. (2005). "The York Mysteries and Freemasonry: Tracing the Historical Links." *Journal of Masonic Studies*, 12(1), 87-99.
239.   Proclus. (1873). *Commentary on Euclid's Elements*. Cambridge University Press.
240.   Proverbs 22:28, King James Version.
241.   Pythagoras.   (2010).   Philosophical Fragments. Dover Publications.
242.   Radhakrishnan, S. (1957). The Principal Upanishads. Harper & Row.
243.   Rajak, T. (2002). Josephus: The Historian and His Society. Duckworth.
244.   Ranganathan, S. (1993). *The Theory of Numbers: Its Role in Geometry and Masonry*. Routledge.
245.   Ridley, J. (2011). "The Freemasons: A History of the World's Most Powerful Secret Society". Arcade Publishing.
246.   Rituals of the Craft. (n.d.). Published by the Grand Lodge of [your jurisdiction].
247.   Robert, H. M. (1915). Robert's Rules of Order Newly Revised. Perseus Publishing.

248.   Roberts, A. (1996). *The York Rite Unveiled.* Keystone Publishers.

249.   Roberts, A. (2008). Music in Freemasonry: Tradition and Transformation. Routledge.

250.   Roberts, M. (2008). Masonic Symbolism: Interpreting the Craft. Cambridge, UK: Cambridge University Press.

251.   Rosenman, S. (1941). "Public Papers and Addresses of Franklin D. Roosevelt". New York: Random House.

252.   Rykwert, J. (1981). The Idea of a Town: The Anthropology of Urban Form in Rome, Italy, and the Ancient World. MIT Press.

253.   Rykwert, J. (1981). The necessity of artifice: Ideas in architecture. Rizzoli International Publications.

254.   Schaw, W. (1599). The Schaw Statutes.

255.   Scherman, N., Zlotowitz, M., & Goldstein, M. (2002). The Stone Edition of the Chumash. Mesorah Publications, Ltd.

256.   Schwartz, S. (1990). Josephus and Judaean Politics. Brill Academic Publishers.

257.   Scully, V. (1979). The Earth, the Temple, and the Gods: Greek Sacred Architecture. Yale University Press.

258.   Shakespeare, W. (1600). The Merchant of Venice. Public Domain.

259.   Shakespeare, W. (1603). Hamlet. In H. Furness (Ed.), The tragedy of Hamlet, Prince of Denmark. Clarendon Press.

260.   Shakespeare, W. (1608). King Lear.

261.   Shakes peare, W. (1623). Measure for Measure.

262.   Smith, D. E. (2006). Architectural Symbolism in Ancient Greece and Freemasonry. Journal of Masonic Studies, 12(3), 45-56.

263.   Smith, E. A. (2007). *The Shriners: Charity and Fraternity.* Crescent Publishing.

264.   Smith, H. (2007). Freemasonry and Its Ancient Landmarks. London: Masonic Heritage Press.

265.   Smith, L. (2018). Giordano Bruno and the Infinite Universe. Cambridge: Academic Press.

266.   Smith, M. (1984). The Rituals of Freemasonry: Their Significance and Importance. Cambridge University Press.

267.   Smith, R. (2012). Wine and spirituality: A cultural history. Oxford University Press.

268.   Stein, L. (2005). Mozart's The Magic Flute. Oxford University Press.

269.   Steinberg, M. (1989). The Talmud: A Reference Guide. Random House.

270.   Steinmetz, D. (2016). Freemasonry and its ancient foundations. Esoteric Studies Press.

271.   Steinmetz, G. (2007). Understanding the Masonic Lexicon: History and Symbolism in the Craft. Routledge.

272.   Stevens, A. (2011). Rituals and Symbols in Freemasonry. Lewis Masonic.

273.   Stevens, A. M. (2009). The Mason's Tools: An Illustrated Guide to Masonic Symbols. New York, NY: Masonic Press.

274.   Stevens, A. T. (2007). The Craft and Its Symbols. Macoy Publishing.

275.   Stevens, W. (2002). The Symbolism of the Square in Freemasonry. Freemason Press.

276.   Stevens, W. (2009). The Mason's Tools: An Illustrated Guide to Masonic Symbols. New York, NY: Masonic Press.

277.   Stevenson, D. (1988). *The Origins of Freemasonry: Scotland's Century, 1590–1710*. Cambridge University Press.

278.   Stevenson, D. (1990). The Origins of Freemasonry: Scotland's Century, 1590-1710. Cambridge: Cambridge University Press.

279.   Stevenson, D. (1996). The Origins of Freemasonry: Scotland's Century, 1590-1710. Cambridge University Press.

280.   Stevenson, D. (2005). The Origins of Freemasonry: Scotland's Century, 1590–1710. Cambridge University Press.

281.   Stevenson, D. (2012). The Origins of Freemasonry: Scotland's Century, 1590–1710. Cambridge, UK: Cambridge University Press.

282.   Stevenson, D. (2013). The Origins of Freemasonry: Scotland's Century, 1590–1710. Cambridge University Press.

283.   Stewart, D. (2011). *Symbolism in Freemasonry*. Lewis Masonic.

284.   Stillwell, J. (2010). Mathematics and Its History (3rd ed.). Springer.

285.   Strong, J. (1890). "The Exhaustive Concordance of the Bible". Abingdon Press.

286.   Summerson, J. (1980). The Classical Language of Architecture. Thames & Hudson.

287.   Sutton, I. (2013). Western architecture: From ancient Greece to the present. Thames & Hudson.

288.   Talmud Bavli. (c. 3rd-5th centuries). Various editions.

289.   Taylor, D. (2016). Medieval Education and Modern Masonic Teachings. Routledge.

290.   Taylor, K. (2021). Esotericism and the Boundless Cosmos. Oxford: Mystical Studies Press.

291.   The Charges in Each Degree. Retrieved from Durham Freemasons. (n.d.). The Initiate's Guide.

292.   The Holy Bible, King James Version

293.   The Holy Bible, King James Version (1611).

294.   The Holy Bible: King James Version. (1611/1987). Thomas Nelson.

295.   The Square Magazine. (2021).

296.   Thoth Adan. (n.d.). Symbols based on circles.

297.   Thurston, W. P. (1997). Three-Dimensional Geometry and Topology (S. Levy, Ed.). Princeton University Press.

298.   Tinniswood, A. (2018). The History of Architecture: Great Buildings and Structures from 1000 BCE to the Present. London: Thames & Hudson.

299.   Truman, H. S. (1948). Address to Congress on Civil Rights.

300.   Turner, H. (1978). The Eye of Providence: Symbol and Significance. Journal of Religious Iconography, 12(3), 45-60.

301.   Turner, H. (2010). Tools of the Craft: A Historical Perspective. Grand Lodge Publications.

302.   Turner, J. (2010). Ritual and Social Dynamics in Freemasonry. Masonic Studies Journal.

303.   Turner, R. (2000). *Freemasonry in England and its Influence Abroad*. HarperCollins.

304.   Turner, R. (2004). Masonic Symbolism and the Quest for Knowledge. Philosophical Lodge Publications.

305.   United Grand Lodge of England. (2013). *A Celebration of the Craft: 300 Years of Freemasonry*. UGLE Publications.

306.   Upton, C. (2013). Gothic Cathedrals: A New History. New York: Yale University Press.

307.   Ussishkin, D. (1996). "The Architectural Context of Solomon's Temple." Biblical Archaeology Review, 22(4), 20–31.

308.   Van Deventer, L. (2005). *The Universal Language of Mathematics in Masonic Traditions.* Cambridge University Press.

309.   Varela, F. J., Thompson, E., & Rosch, E. (1991). The Embodied Mind: Cognitive Science and Human Experience. MIT Press.

310.   Vaughan, T. (2010). *Rituals and Rivalries: The Struggle for Authentic Freemasonry.* Blackstone Academic Press.

311.   Virgil. (2006). The Georgics (D. Ferry, Trans.). Farrar, Straus, and Giroux.

312.   Vitruvius Pollio, M. (1914). *The Ten Books on Architecture* (M. H. Morgan, Trans.). Harvard University Press.

313.   Vitruvius. (1914). De Architectura. (M.H. Morgan, Trans.). Harvard University Press.

314.   Vitruvius. (1960). The Ten Books on Architecture (M. H. Morgan, Trans.). Dover Publications.

315.   Voltaire. (1764/2024). Philosophical Dictionary

316.   Waite, A. E. (1913). A New Encyclopedia of Freemasonry. London: William Rider and Son.

317.   Waite, A. E. (1922). A New Encyclopaedia of Freemasonry. London: William Rider & Son.

318.   Walker, D. (2020). "Reflecting on the Infinite: Masonic Rituals and Celestial Symbolism." Studies in Freemasonry and the Humanities, 22(4), 83–92.

319.   Wallace, R. D. (2017). "Biology and Metaphor in Freemasonry: Insights from Cellular Renewal." *Freemasonry Today,* 46(4), 33-39.

320.   Ward, J. S. M. (1925). An Interpretation of Our Masonic Symbols. George Kenning.

321.   Washington, B. T. (1901/2024). Up from Slavery. Dover Publications.

322.   Washington, G. (1787). Address at the Constitutional Convention. In *Collected Speeches of George Washington* (Vol. 1).

323.   Watkin, D. (1986). A History of Western Architecture. Barrie & Jenkins.

324.   Watkin, D. (2005). A History of Western Architecture. London: Laurence King Publishing.

325.   Watson, J. (2007). Design and Structure: A History of Architectural Geometry. Routledge.

326.   Weil, A. (2007). *Number Theory: An Approach Through History from Hammurapi to Legendre.* Spring

327.   Weisstein, E. W. (2023). Golden Ratio. MathWorld.

328.   West, T. (2007). "The Musical Traditions of Freemasonry." Journal of Masonic Research, 12(3), 45–60.

329.   Wilde, O. (1891/2024). The Importance of Being Earnest

330.   Wilkinson, R. (2003). The Complete Gods and Goddesses of Ancient Egypt. Thames & Hudson.

331.   Williams, A. (2016). Ritual and Symbol: An Exploration of Masonic Practice. Edinburgh: Scottish Masonic Library.

332.   Wilmshurst, W. L. (1922). *The Meaning of Masonry.* London: Rider & Co.

333.   Wilson, E. O. (1975). Sociobiology: The New Synthesis. Harvard University Press.

334.   Wilson, N. G. (1984). Encyclopedia of Ancient Greece. Routledge.

335.   Wilson, R. (2008). Four Colors Suffice: How the Map Problem Was Solved. Princeton University Press.shington, B. T. (1901/2024). Up from slavery. Dover Publications.

336.   Winter, F. E. (1993). Studies in Hellenistic Architecture. University of Toronto Press.

337.   Wirth, O. (1924). The Symbols of Freemasonry. Archibald Constable & Co.

338.   Witt, R. E. (1997). Isis in the ancient world. Johns Hopkins University Press.

339.   Wright, C. J. H. (2001). The message of Amos: The day of the lion. InterVarsity Press.

340.   Wright, C. J. H. (2009). The Mission of God: Unlocking the Bible's Grand Narrative. InterVarsity Press.

341.   Wright, L. (2016). Sacred Spaces and Their Meanings. Harvard Divinity Press.

342.   Wright, N. T. (2004). Paul for Everyone: 1 Corinthians. London: SPCK.

343.   Yates, F. A. (1964). Giordano Bruno and the Hermetic tradition. University of Chicago Press.

344.   Younger, K. L. (2002). Judges and Ruth. Grand Rapids, MI: Zondervan.